Kaye Dobbie

Colours of Gold

HARLEQUIN® MIRA®

First Published 2014
First Australian Paperback Edition 2014
ISBN 978 174356531 5

COLOURS OF GOLD
© 2014 by Kaye Dobbie

Except for use in any review, the reproduction or utilisation of this work in whole or in part in any form by any electronic, mechanical or other means, now known or hereafter invented, including xerography, photocopying and recording, or in any information storage or retrieval system, is forbidden without the written permission of the publisher.

This book is sold subject to the condition that shall not, by way of trade or otherwise, be lent, resold, hired out or otherwise circulated without the prior consent of the publisher in any form of binding or cover other than that in which it is published and without a similar condition including this condition being imposed on the subsequent purchaser.

All rights reserved including the right of reproduction in whole or in part in any form.

This is a work of fiction. Names, characters, places, and incidents are either the product of the author's imagination or are used fictitiously, and any resemblance to actual persons, living or dead, business establishments, events, or locales is entirely coincidental.

Published by
Harlequin Mira
An imprint of Harlequin Enterprises (Aust) Pty Ltd.
Level 4, 132 Arthur Street
NORTH SYDNEY NSW 2060
AUSTRALIA

® and TM are trademarks of Harlequin Enterprises Limited or its corporate affiliates. Trademarks indicated with ® are registered in Australia, New Zealand and in other countries.

Printed and bound in Australia by Griffin Press.

MIX
Paper from responsible sources
FSC FSC® C009448
www.fsc.org

ACKNOWLEDGEMENTS

I dreamed about writing this book for so long and I want to thank my agent, Selwa Anthony, for keeping my dream alive. Without her confidence in me and her support I doubt I would have finished it. I also want to thank Sue Brockhoff at Harlequin for loving the story enough to take me on. And it goes without saying that I couldn't have done it without my family, they are so important to my continuing to write.

There were also people who helped me with the practical details. In Echuca, Mesh Thomson, the Port of Echuca Exhibits Manager, explained all about riverboats and their history on the Murray River. In particular he told me about the boats that pulled the timber barges, like the *Ariadne*. He also picked the brains of Kevin Hutchinson, the resident Shipwright, who took me through the steps of restoring a paddle-steamer. Heather Rendle and the Echuca Historical Society Research Team were very helpful with details I would never have otherwise have been able to put into the story. I also visited the historic port of Echuca and spent a wonderful day there, learning about the past. One of the many books I used in my research was 'River Boat Days' by Peter Phillips. The details of the train journey between Echuca and Bendigo was greatly helped along by a visit to a railway exhibition at the old Post Office building in Bendigo, where a helpful volunteer explained just how the carriages would have looked in the 1860s. I found 'Bendigo: A History' by Frank Cusack, and 'Dunolly: Story of an old gold diggings' by James Flett very useful. A website that was very helpful when I came to write about The Goldminer Hotel was Melbourne's Lost Hotels, which has some amazing photos of the heritage already lost to us.

As for Annie's job as a conservator/restorer of paintings, I was assisted by Gary Lancaster of Lancaster Painters Australia. Gary helped with some of the tricky details. I also used a book called 'The Restoration of Paintings' by Knut Nicolaus, which told me more than I would ever need to know.

Having said all this, of course any errors or deviations from the truth, for the sake of the story, are mine.

To my Gaelic speaking ancestors who came to Australia from the west coast of Scotland by way of the timber forests of Nova Scotia, thank you for inspiring this story.

And for Florence.

CHAPTER ONE

Annie's Story, Present Day

'It's down here.'

Once this had been one of the grandest hotels in Melbourne. The Goldminer Hotel was hugely popular when it was built during the boom times of the 1880s. But it had long since fallen into ruin, and now the site was destined for a new office block. It was the story of the times, and although I didn't like it or always agree with it I'd learned not to get too obviously angry at the waste and the fact that we were losing our history far too quickly, and no one seemed to have the will to stop it.

Behind me Clive knocked against a piece of broken wall and cursed. 'Are you sure this is safe?' he asked, glancing up at the sagging ceiling. 'I have a wife and six children, you know.'

'It's perfectly safe and no you don't,' I retorted.

We descended some rickety stairs shored up with new wood and now the basement was right in front of us. The door had been taken off its hinges and through the opening the basement stretched before us in a murky labyrinth. I half expected the Minotaur to come galloping towards us.

Then Clive turned on his flashlight and I saw it, just an old basement. Dust motes and mould spores did a dance in the shaft of light. Debris littered the floor and there was a pronounced smell of damp. Crates and boxes were pushed to the walls and I could see rotting carpets and fabrics, the various detritus of decades. I followed our guide past all of it to the far wall, and stood staring spellbound at what was before me.

The painting had been freed of its wrappings and propped against some of the crates. Sagging in its ornate gilt frame, damaged by time, neglect and incorrect storage, it was about two metres wide and a metre and a half high, and it was a sad mess. On one level I noticed all of that, wondered if even my skills could save it, but on another, deeper level I was already humming with excitement.

Yes, it was indeed a painting, but it was also a *Trompe L'oeil*. What was known as a trick of the eye. A painting that seemed to draw one into it, just as if you were watching a 3D movie. The *Trompe L'oeil* was my speciality, which was why I'd been called onto the site by Clive Cummings from History Victoria. To assess. To decide whether it was worth saving. Whether it was possible for me to save it.

The painting was filthy and badly damaged in places, but when Clive shone his flashlight across the surface I could pick out myriad small scenes. Vignettes. A river with a paddle-steamer and a vast bare field with gold miners beavering away. A building with a piece of red cloth dangling from a window and a man in a checked coat standing in front of a music hall. There were so many of them.

But what instantly drew my eye were the figures. They stood in the immediate foreground. Two girls hand-in-hand, and one of them was young, hardly more than a child, while the other was a woman with curly golden hair. They stood in front of a small replica of The Goldminer Hotel in its heyday, and they were staring at me.

Look at us, they seemed to be saying. *Look what we've done. This is who we are.*

In that instant I knew I was going to save this *Trompe L'oeil* and restore it. And I was going to find out who the two girls were and why they were so important to this building.

'Well?' Behind me Clive was impatiently awaiting my decision.

I turned and smiled at him and he groaned softly.

'Are you sure?' he muttered, scratching his thinning hair. 'It won't be easy carrying it up the stairs without it falling to bits, Annie.'

'Nothing that matters is easy.'

'And this matters?'

I turned back to the painting. 'Yes. I think this is going to matter very much.'

CHAPTER TWO

The Girl's Story, 1867

She tried to open her eyes but she was tired. So tired. In the cramped, hot space in which she was trapped there wasn't much room for air. The curving wooden planks supported her folded body, but a hands-breadth of water swished about, murky brown river water, soaking her pinafore and her blouse and stockings. And the water was getting deeper.

The girl was sinking.

That was how she thought of herself: the girl. That was what they had always called her. The girl this and the girl that. She felt as if she'd always been nameless.

Now, memories came and went, but they were like moths fluttering through the darkness, reaching the candlelight before vanishing again. Brief flashes of illumination. She knew she was meant to die. Surely, whoever had tumbled her into this barrel and thrown her into the river planned for her to sink without a trace? He did not want the girl to live.

Strange, then, that she was still alive.

Her arm was aching. She'd been able to push her fingers up through a gap between the barrel's lid and its rim, but now they were stuck so fast she no longer had any feeling left in them, and the awkward stretch of her arm was threatening to tear muscles and tendons.

Another memory flickered into the light. A man, his long dark coat flapping about him as the wind blew across the small patch of garden, making the dried stalks dance and jig, causing the chickens to run in fright. A man forcing her down, his hot breath in her face as his hands took the air from her lungs and the light from her eyes. A man carrying her limp body, placing her with a strange gentleness into the barrel, then using his fist to hammer on the broken lid. A section was smashed and that allowed her to breathe, but it would also let the water inside so that she would sink. But as soon as he'd thrown her into the river, she'd come to her senses long enough to thrust her hand into the gap, and for a time that had reduced the water to a trickle.

She could see a face. White with eyes as dark as coals and a faint smell of peppermint. Confusingly, another image flashed into her mind, of the same man offering her the sweets he carried in his pockets, and she giggling at some joke or other.

He's a good man. It's not his fault things haven't turned out well for him. A woman's voice whispered in her head, a voice she should recognise but didn't. *He's a good man, but his luck has turned him bad.*

But the colours had showed her what sort of 'good' man he really was. Dark and swirling. The colours had been with her for as long as she could remember. She'd believed she was the only one who could see them, but as she grew she learned that the man with the peppermint sweets could see them, too. He could get inside her head just as she could see inside his. Was it his colours that swirled so blackly? Was he the one who had lost his luck?

She cried out, semi-conscious, and felt the barrel roll in the river. There was more water sloshing about in the bottom now. When the barrel turned her trapped arm ensured she turned, and sometimes her face was dangerously close to being beneath the water. Soon she would drown.

She considered it without fear, without much emotion at all. She was beyond worldly concerns. The longing for her family was fading and she was more than ready to move on to where there was no pain. She had been told once that death was nothing more than a peaceful sleep and she so desired peace.

Sounds. Voices. The distant hum of a riverboat. Long ago she had travelled on a riverboat with many people and there was much sorrow. But the memory was gone before she could grasp hold of it, back into the darkness, hidden behind the man with the dark coat and the peppermint sweets.

But now the voices were louder and the boat engine nearer.

Her heart began to pound. Perhaps she wasn't ready for the hereafter after all, because suddenly she wanted, more than anything, to see the light again and feel the cool air on her face. She wanted to live.

She tried to wriggle her fingers, but without any feeling in them she didn't know whether or not they were moving. She tried to call out, but her throat was swollen and aching where the man had squeezed his hands and she could only make a whimper.

'Help me. Please.'

Not loud enough. Her prison was being pushed along by the river and away from the voices and the engine, for both were fading now. The barrel rolled again and the water crept up her cheek, lapped at her nose and inched towards her mouth.

* * *

Captain Arnold Potter had been watching the barrel bobbing on the surface of the river and wondering whether it once could have been a beer barrel or perhaps held flour, salt, fish or meat. Was it jettisoned when a riverboat became stuck on a sandbank and needed to lighten its load? The boats only took to the rivers when there was plenty of water flowing, but even so there was always the lurking danger of reefs and sandbars. Even the best captains ran aground.

Arnold's riverboat, *Ariadne*, was a paddle-steamer, seventy-six feet long with a draft of two feet and three inches, her boiler wood-fired. She may be small but she was strong and he used her to pull the timber barges back from the forests and properties along the Murray River and into the inland port of Echuca, tying up at the sawmill to unload the logs so that they could be cut down into various lengths. It was a good living but meant long weeks away from home and he was looking forward to getting back to his wife.

He found himself watching the barrel again.

It rolled over, spinning in the water, and when it settled this time it was much lower. Maybe it had sprung a leak? While he supervised the men and their bullock teams loading the logs onto the barge, he watched that barrel. Something about it puzzled him, but he wasn't sure what that something was.

The logs came from the property of Mr Charles Webster. The timber was mostly Murray pine, which suited the insider barge they were using. If they'd been loading red gum they would have needed an outsider or outrigger barge, because red gum was heavier than pine and didn't float.

Mr Webster was one of the squatters with vast acres along the Murray River. Mostly, he ran mobs of sheep, but he earned some extra cash in between shearing times by supplying Arnold with timber. The gold rush had begun sixteen years ago, and by now parts of the country were stripped completely bare of forest while there was an ever-increasing need for building materials. Arnold enjoyed a steady income by fulfilling that need.

He wiped the dust from his face with his sleeve and squinted up at the grey-leafed gum trees that clung to the riverbank. Brightly coloured parrots were cavorting among the creamy blossoms. Their screeching couldn't be called musical, but their way of turning somersaults as they clambered on the twigs and branches, each one trying to get to the sweetest nectar, made him chuckle. They didn't need hands, their beaks and clawed feet were more than nimble enough to . . .

'Sweet Jesus!'

Arnold didn't normally take the Lord's name in vain, but he'd just realised what it was about the floating barrel that was bothering him. Shouting for one of his men to grab the boat-pole, he took off along the deck of the barge, scrambling over the logs, until he reached the stern.

The barrel was moving swiftly with the flow of the river—there'd been heavy rain in the upper reaches and it was still coming down— but he thought he had a chance of nudging it closer. It was the only chance he did have. If he didn't get hold of it now, well, he didn't believe he'd catch up to it, even if he could get the *Ariadne* free of the barge and moving.

'Captain?'

Bluey, his second-in-command, handed him the boat-pole with the hook on the end. Just in time. Arnold lunged.

First try it grazed the barrel before it fell away. Second try it caught the top lip, held on a moment, only to send the barrel bobbing away again. Arnold noticed that it was definitely lower in the water. Realistically, he only had one more go left.

Third try he got lucky. The hook gripped and held. He began to tug the barrel closer, careful not to drag it under the surface of the swollen river.

'What's so import'nt about that old barrel?' Bluey asked. 'Think it might be full o' rum, Captain?' He sniggered at his own joke, but Arnold didn't laugh.

'Use your eyes, you bloody idiot,' he snarled. 'What's that hanging out the end there . . . where the lip sits up around the lid?'

Bluey squinted, his bright-red hair standing on end with sweat and grime. 'Looks like a piece of cloth. White. Funny shape. Oh bloody hell . . .'

Yes, Arnold thought grimly. He pulled the barrel right in, snug to the side of the barge, and the two men hurriedly reached down to steady it. Bending over to lock their arms around its curved sides, they took the weight of it and heaved it aboard.

The child's fingers were protruding like starfish from a narrow gap at the top of the barrel, between the lid and the lip. They were jammed fast and seemed very still. Arnold said a silent prayer as he reached out tentatively to touch flesh that was water-wrinkled and icy cold.

His heart sank.

Dead then, poor little soul. He was too late.

He began to walk away, needing a moment alone, and it was only then he noticed they'd gathered a crowd. The men had stopped working to come and watch. Well, he'd soon let them know what he felt about that—

'Captain!'

The excitement in Bluey's hoarse voice forced Arnold back and then he was stooping over the barrel and seeing what his second-in-command had seen. The fingers were moving, only a flutter, but they were moving.

* * *

She was bumped and bruised from being tossed about inside her prison, and a bang to her head had turned everything black for a moment. She'd come to with her face in the water and pulled back, spluttering and choking, eyes streaming.

A moment later something crashed against the planks, making the barrel shake and shiver. And then again. There was a wrenching, screeching sound as the planks were tugged apart and broken open. Light seeped through the first jagged hole and a face peered in at her.

Grey eyes, creased and lined at the corners. 'Sweet Jesus,' the man hissed through his teeth. 'It's a girl. A little girl. How old is she, Bluey?'

Bluey's face appeared, red hair standing on end, blue eyes as wide as her own. 'Seven or eight, I'd say, Captain.'

'Pinafore, dress, stockings but no shoes,' the grey-eyed man said, as if the detail was important to him.

Her shoes had been left behind when she was placed into the barrel. She could have told them that they were actually brown button-up boots with a hole in the left heel that had been patched. She hadn't had time to pull them on when the man had begun to chase her; she'd seen in the madness in his eyes there wasn't time for anything but running for her life.

'Let's get her out,' he said, and reaching in took hold of her pinafore and used it to lift her up and out of what was left of her prison.

Her legs were all wobbly, like a newborn kitten, but the man called Bluey held her carefully and sat her down on a cleared space on the deck, all hemmed about by logs. Above her were men with grimy, sweaty faces, agog with amazement.

Grey-eyes was wearing a double-breasted jacket and a soft flat-top peaked cap and she knew he was a riverboat captain because she'd seen men dressed like that before. He was handsome, although he looked tired and had a short and untidy beard. He stared back at her and then glanced at Bluey and said, 'Why isn't she crying?'

Bluey shrugged. 'Shock, I reckon, Captain.' He leaned in closer to her, his face kind, and she knew he must have children of his own. 'What's your name, sweetheart? Where d'you come from?'

She wanted to answer him. She wanted to tell him her name and where she came from and why the man in the dark coat had put her in the barrel. But she couldn't. That memory, along with all the others, had been painfully mixed and muddled up in her head. It just seemed easier not to try to sort them out.

* * *

Arnold Potter ran through the facts in his head as the girl stared back at him. According to Bluey she was only seven or eight. Her dark hair was plastered to her head with river water and the steamy airlessness of the barrel. Her stockings were grubby and he found himself focusing on her lack of shoes. He didn't know why that bothered him but it did.

Something else that bothered him were the blotches of blood on her skirt and pinafore, but once he'd satisfied himself that she wasn't badly injured, not outwardly anyway, he didn't look any further. He wasn't used to children, and this being a girl he thought she'd be better in a woman's care.

'Has anyone heard about a child going missing along the river?' he shouted over the excited voices of their audience.

The little girl was gazing about with wide eyes. Blue eyes. Frightened yet strangely blank eyes. As if she was taking part in a dream rather than the living nightmare it actually was. He couldn't blame her for not wanting to remember what had happened to her, but he wished someone knew who she was so he could hand over responsibility and get back to work.

'No one's put the word out about a missing child,' one of Webster's men assured him. 'We'd have heard. One wandered off into the bush last month, but we found him.'

No one else had heard anything about a missing child either.

'Perhaps the Websters can take her in? Look after her until her parents turn up? Or someone else is willing to have her?' Bluey had dropped his voice so the child couldn't hear him.

Arnold pondered.

'Do you want me to take her, Captain?'

'No. I'll do it. You stay here and get back to work. I want the rest of those logs loaded by tonight. We leave in the morning.'

The child stood up and took his hand, and Arnold knew then she had understood everything they'd said. Her wits weren't lacking even if her tongue was.

'Can you walk, sweetheart, or do you want the captain to carry you?' Bluey said loudly.

The little girl glanced at him sideways and shook her head.

In the end Arnold had to carry her some of the way, lifting her over the piles of logs and other obstacles strewn on the riverbank and along the track that led towards the Webster homestead. The bullocks pulling the logs watched them pass and the drivers tempered their language when they saw the young girl.

The homestead was on a rise, surrounded by stock enclosures, all hewn out of the bush. Smoke came from the chimneys and there were frilly curtains on the windows, a woman's faint touch in a male world.

Arnold strode up to the verandah. 'Do you know this house?' he asked, glancing down at the child.

But she stared up at him in mute silence.

Word had already spread that a child had been fished out of the river and the Webster children met them at the door, their mother close behind. Mrs Webster was a pretty woman, but the hard work of a station owner's wife, as well as constant childbearing, had given her a thin, exhausted appearance.

'The poor little poppet.' She sighed, gazing at the child. 'Does anyone know where she's from?'

'Not so far, Mrs Webster. I was hoping you might . . . ?'

'Goodness, no. I haven't heard a whisper. I fear,' she glanced at the girl and lowered her voice, 'I fear anyone who would do such a thing to a child would not make her disappearance common knowledge.' She sighed again. 'Bring her in then, Captain Potter. And wipe your boots.'

Arnold did as he was told, amused that the squatter's wife had the effect of making him feel like a child himself. He tried to remove his hand from his charge, thinking she would be safe here, but to his surprise she refused to let go. Other than shaking her off, he could do nothing but remain attached to her.

The Webster children were milling around, staring at the girl with big eyes, giggling, touching her as if she were a savage from another land. He found their behaviour disturbing, but then he wasn't a father himself—a state Molly, his wife, longed to remedy—so perhaps he was being ignorant. However, if these were his children, he thought, he would have been inclined to call them into line.

'I'll have Joan find some old clothes that will fit her,' Mrs Webster was saying. 'She cannot continue to wear those. And she could do with a bath,' she added, wrinkling her nose.

Joan was a buxom girl with knowing eyes and gave Arnold the benefit of her toothy smile as she tried to take the child from him. Except that she wouldn't let go, clinging to him with a desperation that made him wonder what had happened to her in the past.

'Come here,' Joan muttered, finally wrenching the girl free. She was pulled away, dragging her feet, staring back at him with those bright-blue eyes.

'I'll wait here for you,' he called after her, and then wondered why he'd said it. His intention hadn't been to wait but having seen the girl secure to return to his boat.

Mrs Webster was looking at him curiously. 'She'll be quite safe here, you know,' she assured him. 'Joan will look after her and I'll keep an eye on her. If we hear anything about a child missing we'll follow up on it.'

'I know you will, ma'am. It's just that . . .'

Mrs Webster blinked at him, her tired eyes confused. She wouldn't understand his doubts, she didn't have time. Mrs Webster had enough on her plate without worrying about the feelings of stray children.

'Thank you, ma'am.'

His capitulation made her smile with relief. 'She'll be safe with us,' she repeated, seeing him to the door.

Arnold quickened his step as he made his way back to the *Ariadne*. He had work to do and it was better if he put the memory of the girl behind him, despite the fact that her little hand had been gripping his so tightly he could still feel the shape of it.

* * *

The girl didn't like the way the children stared at her. She wished she could be back with Captain Potter and tried to say so, but Joan was only interested in stripping her out of her dirty clothing as quickly as possible. In fact, she had stripped her down to her stockings before she realised the Webster children had fallen silent. Surprised, Joan looked up and couldn't stop a choking gasp.

The girl's gaze followed Joan's and widened in astonishment. Her white skin was covered in bruises. They blossomed on her like strange and exotic tattoos. But worse were the markings around her throat, previously hidden by the collar of her dress, where the man who'd chased her had tried to strangle her. Tried very hard indeed. It was miraculous that she was still alive.

Joan put a hand to her mouth, clearly shocked by the evidence of such cruelty. Hurriedly, she shooed the children from the room and called in Mrs Webster. The two women stared, murmuring words in low voices that she could only half make out—'Hurt . . . someone . . . Should we tell . . . No, no, best not . . .'—before Joan fetched some water to sponge her down, gently dabbing her tender skin, and found some clean clothes that fitted her, more or less.

Now they'd seen the bruises the children kept their distance from her, as if she had a catching disease. Joan was kind but she, too, had that wary glint in her eyes. Mrs Webster simply ignored her. They were too polite to say so, but she knew they didn't want her. She could see it in their colours, the swirling light that surrounded them, just as it surrounded every person the girl had ever encountered.

She half-heartedly ate some of the supper brought to her on a tray before she pretended to sleep in the room crowded with Webster children. But she'd already decided she wasn't going to stay. She lay and waited until the house was quiet and then she rose and dressed in her new clothes and slipped outside. The moon was a tiny smile, but she could see the track.

Soon she was running through the bush towards the river.

* * *

'There's something I think you should see, Captain.'

Bluey had found her, huddled in a corner near the boiler, half hidden behind the tool box.

Captain Potter took a step closer.

'Take her back to the homestead,' he ordered.

But before Bluey could reach for her she darted away and started crying out in a hoarse little voice, 'Please, take me with you. Please.'

The shock of hearing her speak froze them in place. Long enough for her to reach for Arnold's hand and hold it tightly, gazing up at him with her bright-blue eyes.

'I don't want to stay with them. I don't like it there. Please.'

Bluey murmured out of the corner of his mouth. 'You can't mean to look after a young girl all the way to Echuca, Captain?'

Arnold sighed. 'She doesn't want to be left.'

'Children should do as they're told.'

But Arnold was remembering the way the Webster children had circled her, stared at her as they would a wild animal. Perhaps she was simply acting on instinct? She had survived thus far, so probably she knew what she was about when she said she didn't want something.

'Send one of the men down to the homestead to tell Mrs Webster we're taking the girl to Echuca with us.'

Bluey shrugged. 'Yes, sir,' he said without expression, but Arnold gathered his second-in-command didn't entirely approve.

'Molly'll look after her.'

Bluey's eyes slid from his and Arnold could guess what he was thinking. How would his wife feel when Arnold arrived home with a stray child? But Arnold had no doubts about Molly's reaction. Her kindness was one of the reasons he'd fallen in love with her.

Arnold had made up his mind. The girl had been hurt and then bundled into the barrel and tossed into the river to drown. And she *would* have drowned if he hadn't seen her little fingers, stuck in the top. No, it was best if he got her well away from here and into Molly's warm arms.

Where she'd be safe.

CHAPTER THREE

Present Day: Annie's Story

I was running late. Courtney hadn't wanted to go to child care today. I had won in the end, I was the mother after all and Courtney was only four years old, but not before I'd had to make promises I wasn't sure I could keep. A visit to the aquarium to see the penguins and a day at the zoo to see the gorilla enclosure. My child always seemed to sense when I was at my most vulnerable; sometimes I felt like putty in her hands.

Still, it could have been worse. Once she'd asked for a Kardashian handbag and I'd had to Google the name to see what it was. Thank God I'd said no! Where did my daughter get this stuff from? Her father's girlfriends probably, I thought darkly. No, on reflection I'd probably got off lightly with the penguins.

So I was running late when I got to work at Reuben and Reuben, and was feeling distinctly underdone. Had I even put a brush through my hair? At least I was dressed and wearing shoes, because there had been days when Courtney was a baby . . . Well, thankfully today I was dressed. Jeans and a brightly coloured blouse, a black jacket and my red boots, which were Courtney's favourite.

Greta on the desk tried to flag me down as I hurried up the stairs, but I waved at her and kept going.

'I'm late.'

'So what? You're the boss's daughter.'

It was because I was the boss's daughter that I couldn't afford to be late and I couldn't let myself be seen to be treated differently.

'There's a surprise waiting for you,' Greta called after me.

Surprise? What surprise?

I opened the door to my studio and stopped, all my troubles instantly forgotten. Because there it was, waiting for me. I actually smiled as if greeting an old friend.

I hadn't forgotten about the *Trompe L'oeil*, but I'd been busy with other projects. Reuben and Reuben may be small but we were the best in in Australia, specialising in conserving, restoring and renovating the interiors of heritage buildings, not to mention the artefacts to be found within them. We always had work—people who dealt in the dying crafts of marbling, wood graining and gilding, just to name a few, weren't easy to find. I had an enviable CV, with qualifications from my time spent studying and working in Europe. Before Courtney came along I'd still travelled, but these days I preferred to stay home.

The *Trompe L'oeil* was positioned against the opposite wall. The canvas had been relined in one of History Victoria's workshops—such jobs were too big for my small studio. At least now it wasn't sagging, but it was still dirty, damaged and desperately in need of my loving attention.

I switched on the lights, dropped my work bag on a table and went to stand before it.

Here, in my well-lit studio, I could see much more clearly what would need to be done. Flaking paint, missing paint, water damage, varnish that was discoloured, and what looked to be mould of some kind. I'd certainly be kept busy, I knew that, but I was also feeling excited in a way I hadn't felt for a long time. This was the sort of job I loved, a real challenge. I wasn't entirely confident

I could bring this piece of the past back to something like its glorious heyday, but I'd certainly try.

Although that was just one part of my role. I would be researching the piece, trying to discover who painted it and who it was painted for, and then there were the two girls. They were clearly important and I needed to know who they were, too.

I had already made a start. The Goldminer Hotel had opened to large crowds in 1879, and for over a decade it was enormously popular. These were the 1880s, Melbourne's boom time, with gold swelling the coffers and many of the most magnificent public and private buildings being constructed.

And then came the bust of the 1890s.

Gradually, the hotel began to lose money and customers until in the 1930s it was more of a lodging house for down-and-outs. Come the 1980s there was some talk of it being resurrected to its former grandeur, but the cost was too high and the project was abandoned. Lucky really, I thought. It could have been pulled down like so many other Melbourne icons and the *Trompe L'oeil* would have been lost. Instead it had languished, unloved and derelict. Demolition was still hanging over it, getting closer, but while there was life there was hope.

Whatever happened now I was glad that I had been responsible for saving a part of this grand old hotel. Perhaps even the heart and soul of it.

Now that heart and soul gazed back at me, wide-eyed, their faces so real and full of life. The girl had blue eyes, the woman green eyes. They didn't appear particularly well dressed or illustrious, just ordinary people. Yet if the scenes behind them were anything to go by their lives had been far from ordinary.

I found a pad and pencil and began to make a list of the tasks I would need to perform to restore the painting. It was frighteningly long, but I wasn't daunted. This was my job and I loved it. In fact, it was a calling. I couldn't imagine waking up one morning and thinking I was sick of it and maybe it was time to do something else. No, this was in my blood.

'Annie?'

I turned and smiled at my father, who'd come in and was standing in the doorway. My excitement faltered when I saw the sallow colour of his face, the circles under his eyes. As usual, my father was working too hard. How many times had I told him to slow down? How many times had he ignored me?

'I'm as strong as an ox,' he'd insisted.

I wanted to believe him, but I was having difficulty. Every day he seemed to be thinner and more frail. I'd tried to discuss it with him, but he just said he didn't want me to fuss, and Reuben wasn't a man who followed anyone's advice but his own. Stubborn, that was the word for him. Pig-headed was another.

'This is from The Goldminer?' he asked now, coming forward to inspect the painting, his normally eager step somehow hesitant. 'They've relined the canvas?'

'Yes. History Victoria thought it best. It'd already been relined once and there were some tears they needed to repair. The glue from the lining has also helped with the flaking paint.'

'There's much damage, Annie.' Even after all these years in Australia he still had a trace of a German accent.

'I can bring it back,' I replied with certainty, and saw his smile. He admired my confidence in myself when it came to my work. It was my messy personal life of which he disapproved, although he loved his granddaughter unconditionally.

When I'd met Ben I hadn't considered how different we were in our careers and our desires for the future. If I'd had any niggling doubts then I'd believed our love would smooth the way. Now, looking back, I could see that our relationship was doomed to failure. How could an advertising executive, who was a high-flyer with a huge salary and an exciting lifestyle, and a conservator with a low profile and a small salary and a requirement for endless patience and peace and quiet, live happily ever after?

When Ben had left me, taking his personal assistant with him, I hadn't known I was pregnant, but it wouldn't have made any difference to our breakup. I just wished he could have been less clichéd, but it was typical of Ben to go for the blonde. And he was still going for blondes, if his latest—Miss Kardashian handbag—was anything to go by.

'I want to find out more about the hotel,' I said, as my father gazed intently at the painting. 'I'd love to know who these two are . . . were. They must've meant something to the owner, or the artist, don't you think? To feature so prominently?'

Reuben shrugged. He was more interested in the piece than the people who made it. He was currently engaged in marbling fireplaces in a historic mansion in South Melbourne, carefully reproducing the effect as it would have been a hundred and fifty years ago. The job was an important one, and he was an artist. I knew that he would have worked for nothing if the money wasn't available to pay him.

I hoped I never became quite that obsessed. After all, one had to eat and keep a roof over one's head.

'I've spoken to the solicitor about my will,' he said abruptly.

For a moment I didn't understand him, and then I did and something stilled inside me.

'I've been thinking that perhaps it's time you began to take on more of the running of Reuben and Reuben,' he went on.

For a long while now I had been suggesting he let me shoulder some of the weight of running the business, but he'd always found some excuse. This seemed a rather drastic change of heart. Suddenly, I was afraid.

'I have made my will,' he went on, still gazing at the painting. 'It's all yours, Annie. It always was.'

'Papa, please, I—Are you ill? I think you should see a doctor.'

He patted my arm. 'You're upset now. Don't be. I'm not ill, I'm just being prudent. When I die I want to make certain all is as I would wish it to be. Not just yet, of course. I cannot possibly die until I'm finished marbling the fireplaces.'

I felt tears sting my eyes but I blinked them away. He would hate that. He was not an emotional man.

'Papa, I'm grateful, but why now?'

He shrugged. 'Before you were busy with your own life. Courtney was a baby. Now you have time and I can step back. Now it's your turn.'

I didn't know what to say so I didn't say anything. Instead, I waited a beat and then pointed out a detail I'd just noticed, on the far side of the painting.

'That looks like a sailing ship.'

'Sailing ship? There's a paddleboat . . .'

'No, not the boat. Look, see the sails? And there are passengers disembarking. Immigrants, Papa. This is the story of someone's life. Two lives!'

He smiled into my eyes, which were warm brown like his. 'I'll leave you to begin,' he said. 'Keep me informed of your progress, Annie.'

'Papa . . . I hope you'll be around for a long time to come. I don't know if I'm able to run Reuben and Reuben on my own. I'm not ready.'

The truth was I'd imagined sharing the running with him, not taking complete control.

He made a rude noise, and waved a hand at me as he turned to go. 'You'll never be ready but you'll do a fine job. And Courtney will follow you. I'm sixty-five years old, Annie, and I have my heir and the one after that. Our business will carry on into the future whether I'm here or not.'

I let him go and stood staring at the painted scene before me. The thought of being alone, heading Reuben and Reuben, was too much and I couldn't think about it. Why had Reuben made his will? What was he not telling me?

My father was a secretive man. He kept his own counsel and I found it difficult to pierce the armour he used to protect his thoughts. He'd always been like this, and although we'd grown close through our joy in our work and in the day-to-day challenges of our business, in other ways we were miles apart.

Guiltily, I knew I should try harder.

But not right now. The *Trompe L'oeil* was calling me, and sometimes it was simpler just to devote yourself to your work.

CHAPTER FOUR

The Girl's Story

The little *Ariadne* chugged through the swollen river, paddles churning within their paddle-boxes, smoke pouring from her stack as she dragged the laden timber barges low in the water behind her. They were three days out from Echuca. The girl spent most of her time watching the river go by. Sometimes there were other boats, bigger and smaller, and people along the banks who waved and called out.

Captain Potter was looking after her. He was a good man, she knew it in her own heart, but her being here on board his boat worried him. Sometimes she could see the colours around him darken and ripple, like rain clouds about to burst. Had she always been able to see the colours? She thought so. She couldn't remember a time when she hadn't.

Bluey whistling brought her head up and she watched him approaching, a big grin on his face. 'What's your name, sweetheart?' was his usual question as soon as he saw her. And then he would begin to make outlandish guesses about what it might be. 'I bet it's Anastasia,' he'd say with a smile. 'Or is it Boudicca?' That made her laugh.

Bluey's colours were dark, especially around his left shoulder. Crimson and black. They worried her. She wanted to tell him, to warn him, but she didn't know how to. Besides, she had a feeling that if she told him then his feelings towards her would change. He'd look at her with suspicion and no longer joke and smile—this had happened before, she thought, although the details were jumbled up in her head.

Should she speak and risk the consequences?

The decision was a difficult one.

'Come and help me steer, Constance!' he called now, with a teasing wink.

She followed him past the smelly, huffy engine and up the wooden gangway and into the wheelhouse. Captain Potter had made her a bed in the corner here and she slept as quietly as a mouse. Sometimes she found him looking at her with his grey eyes, and she worried that he'd see into her heart and he wouldn't like what he saw. He'd already told her that once they reached Echuca he was going to take her home to his wife, a kind lady who would look after her. Instead of reassuring her, the thought of that kind lady gave her an anxious feeling in her stomach.

She'd rather stay here on board the paddle-steamer, but when she'd tentatively suggested it, he'd said, 'Little girls don't live on riverboats,' with a note in his voice that meant his decision was final.

Bluey dragged a crate over for her to stand on so that she could reach the wheel, and then he helped her to hold it steady. 'We'll make a riverboat captain out of you yet,' he told her, just as he did every day.

She smiled fleetingly at him because she was frightened to let go of the wheel. But it was long enough for her to see that the colours around him were darker and near his left shoulder they were very black. That was a bad sign and he had to be told, because what if telling him meant she could prevent whatever bad thing that was going to happen from happening? How could she remain silent? Yet what if by telling, the bad thing turned on her? Something awful had already happened to her when she'd told.

There had been a boat . . . a ship . . . with so many people. The memory was fuzzy and fading, but the emotions remained. Angry and fearful faces, and an aching grief.

'Captain,' Bluey said, with a nod, as Captain Potter came and stood behind them. 'We have a new crew member,' he added, with one of his winks. 'A bit small but keen to learn.'

'So I see,' Captain Potter said. He straightened his cap and then rubbed a hand over his jaw, making his whiskers rasp.

The girl smiled at the smear of grease he'd left on his chin. He'd had some problems with the engine and he'd been fixing it, so his hands were covered in grease. Bluey began to ask him about the engine and she noticed the black colour was spreading from his shoulder around his whole body. Her own shoulder was beginning to throb and tingle, as though in sympathy. Instinctively, she reached up to touch it and then Bluey's, her palm flat against his shirt, which was stiff with sweat.

Bluey stopped talking and stared down at her in surprise. Captain Potter reached to take over the wheel, muttering beneath his breath.

'Hurt,' she said quietly but with absolute clarity. 'Bluey hurt bad.'

Bluey looked perplexed. 'I'm not hurt, sweetheart,' he assured her. 'Not me. Not ol' Bluey.'

But she nodded vigorously. How could she explain? How could she make him understand about the colours and what they meant? Tears stung her eyes as she realised she couldn't, not in a way Bluey would accept.

Her hand dropped to her side and she climbed off the crate. Outside the cool air from the river dried the tears on her cheeks. Back down on the deck she sat on the oakum-filled planks and observed the brown water surging by. Perhaps, she thought, the bad thing she dreaded wouldn't happen. Perhaps this time she was mistaken and Bluey would be all right.

But in her heart she knew the wish was a forlorn one. The colours did not lie and she was never mistaken.

* * *

Arnold noticed the logs had settled lower on one side of the furthest barge from the *Ariadne*. He brought the paddle-steamer to a stop, so that Bluey could clamber across and check they weren't about to lose the lot. He'd done it before and neither man thought anything of it. How were they to know that this time the logs would shift and roll?

By the time Arnold realised what had happened his mate was screaming in agony, thrashing about beneath the weight of the logs. Arnold managed to heave them off him, but Bluey's arm had been torn away almost completely at the shoulder and blood was spurting from the horrendous wound.

Arnold tried to stop it, tried to help, but he knew with a terrible certainty that there was nothing he could do but hold his friend in his arms and give him what comfort he could while he bled to death.

It wasn't until afterwards, Bluey's body wrapped in a tarpaulin awaiting their arrival at Echuca, that he remembered the words spoken by the girl that morning, her small hand resting on Bluey's shoulder.

Had she really known he was going to die?

Arnold knew he should dismiss it but he found he couldn't. Despite his practical nature he was as superstitious as any riverboat captain and he began to wonder if she'd caused Bluey's death in some mysterious way.

She's bad luck. The grim thought wouldn't leave him alone.

She'd been very upset over Bluey, sobbing and clinging to him, and he'd held her and comforted her in his awkward way. But all the time he was wondering about her, worrying that his bringing her aboard had caused his old friend's death.

* * *

The girl lay in a narrow cot in the room at the end of the corridor in Captain Potter's house in Echuca. There was a cat yowling outside, but it wasn't that keeping her awake, nor was it the sounds of industry from the wharf or the puffing of a steam train making its journey south. She didn't sleep. She was afraid to sleep in case someone came to take her away, despite the fact that she didn't know who that someone was or why they might hurt her. It didn't matter if the questions remained unanswered because the fear stayed the same. It hovered over her like a long dark coat, swooping down to cover her up so that she couldn't see, or hear, or breathe. The sensation was so horrible she wanted to scream, but how could she scream when Captain Potter and his wife had been so kind to her? So she tried to put it from her mind.

Hadn't someone said that to her?

Put the bad thoughts from your mind, dearie. It's the only way.

Yes, that was what she must do.

A tear rolled down her cheek. She missed Bluey with his toothless smile and silly jokes. Captain Potter believed it was her fault that Bluey had died. He blamed her. She could see it in the way he looked at her out of the corners of his eyes and the way he'd stopped patting her head and saying she was a good girl.

She shouldn't have warned them about the colours, and yet what else could she have done? Wanting to help had been instinctive. Perhaps if she had spoken earlier . . . ? Or was a person's fate already set, unchanging? The questions crowded into her mind and she had no answers. They were too difficult for her. She was just a little girl.

Another tear rolled down her cheek.

Captain Potter was different towards her. He didn't like what had happened to Bluey and he thought it was her fault. It was his wife who was kind and sympathetic, although she was thin and pale and . . .

The colours again. Dark, swirling colours. They meant only one thing, and knowing that Captain Potter's wife was unwell was a bleak fact the girl could not begin to face. If Captain Potter blamed her for Bluey's death then what would he do if she told him about his wife?

She turned towards the wall and squeezed her eyes shut. 'Put the bad thoughts from your mind, put the bad thoughts from your mind,' she whispered to herself over and over. The words comforted her and soon she fell asleep. But it wasn't a pleasant sleep. She lay twitching and moaning softly to herself, her hands pushing blindly at the darkness that threatened to smother her.

* * *

'She's hardly more than a baby!' insisted Molly, when Arnold told her of his doubts. 'And she's been mistreated, too. Someone has hurt her and then tried to hide their evil-doing by drowning the little mite. No, Arnold, you're wrong. I'm surprised at you for thinking it. If anyone in this world is bad luck then it's whoever hurt this child, not the child herself.'

Arnold knew he couldn't argue with Molly—she always believed the best of people—so he gave in with good grace. 'Has she told you her name yet? We tried to get it out of her on the way here. Poor Bluey kept calling her different names in the hope one of them would strike a chord, but she'd just stare at him with those strange eyes.' He clamped his mouth shut. He sorely missed Bluey. They'd been mates and companions for going on ten years; as a young captain, Arnold had found Bluey's experience very welcome. A man didn't recover easily from such a loss.

Molly was thoughtful, her fair hair spread about her pale face on the lacy pillowcase. 'I'm thinking she might have forgotten her name, Arnold. Or perhaps she thinks it's safer to keep it a secret? No,' she answered her own question, 'she's too young to be so sly. She has forgotten for certain.'

'Then what will we call her?' he asked, and yawned, stretching in the soft bed. Luxury, that's what it was to be back with his wife, sheer luxury.

Molly had been the widow of a paddle-steamer captain when he married her, and although some people said he married her for her boat, it wasn't true. She needed someone to captain the *Ariadne* and he'd been fit for the job, and things had developed from there. Early on she'd told him she was eight years older than him, although he knew for sure it was ten. It made no difference to the way he felt about her. They hadn't been blessed with a child and that was a grief to them both, but Arnold secretly thought it was just as well. Molly wasn't strong and he didn't want to lose her.

Molly was thinking over his question. The golden flame of the wax candle made her appear ethereal. A white ribbon was woven through the strands of her hair and he began to draw it out. She didn't notice the distraction, busy as she was deciding on a name for the girl.

His doubts about bringing her here were fading. Molly had taken to her, and Molly was lonely when he was away. The girl would be a diversion, a chance for her to be a mother.

'What about Alice?' she said.

'Alice?' He blinked, confused.

'The girl, Arnold. We could call her Alice. I always hoped that . . . if I'd been blessed with a daughter I would've named her Alice.'

He chuckled. 'Alice it is, then. Until she remembers her real name, of course.'

'I can't believe someone isn't missing her.'

Arnold repeated what he'd said already. 'We asked at Squatter Webster's place, but no one had heard anything about a missing child. Bluey wanted to stop at every station along the river, but we couldn't do that. And she could've come from anywhere—the Lord knows how far that barrel floated before we found it.'

'She has a precise way of speaking, did you notice? Almost as if English isn't her first language. She has an accent but it's soft. Musical. She might be Scottish, though she sounds nothing like Mr Douglas, the butcher. You can cut his burr with a knife.'

'She barely speaks at all, Molly.'

She nudged him with her elbow. 'You must have an opinion, Arnold!'

He struggled to please her. 'Once on the boat she was talking in her sleep. Bluey said it sounded like German.'

'Someone might come for her one day, Arnold, and then we'll have to give her back.'

Arnold shifted uncomfortably before her downcast expression, rubbing a rough palm over the dark stubble on his chin. 'I don't know, love. I think if someone was going to claim her then it would happen sooner rather than later. Perhaps you shouldn't let yourself grow too fond of her, just in case,' he added.

Molly managed a smile and shook her head at him. 'Arnold, you don't understand women very well, do you? How can you ask a woman not to love a child? I'll keep her here and treat her as our own, and if I have to give her back then I'll try to be glad for her that she has found her family.'

He kissed her lips gently, as if she was made of fine china. 'You're a wonderful woman, Molly.'

Pink colour flushed her pale skin. 'Doctor Suckling doesn't think so. He tells me I try to do far too much and that I must take my medicine three times a day.' She pulled a face. 'It's vile, Arnold, and it makes me feel sicker.'

He stroked a strand of hair from her cheek. 'The doctor wouldn't give you something that made you sicker, Molly. He's trying to make you better.' He tucked her hair behind her ear. 'Do you want me to talk to him?'

She shook her head, impatient with herself. 'I'm being silly. I know Doctor Suckling is a good man and a good physician.'

Arnold took her hand in his, holding it lightly, wondering when her skin had become so translucent that he could see the blue veins beneath it. 'You'll be well soon,' he said. 'By the time I come back from my next trip you'll be running about like a girl.'

Molly giggled and didn't resist when he took her into his arms again.

CHAPTER FIVE

Annie's Story

Courtney was chattering as we drove home. I'd picked her up from the childcare centre, and although it only took fifteen minutes from there to home, Courtney had rolled off the names of a large number of friends. Surely that was a good thing? My child made friends easily. I couldn't remember a single friend from when I was four years old, although I still had a few from later school years. Not that I saw them very often these days.

For a moment the old Kew Asylum buildings rose above us— they had been redeveloped into desirable residences in the 1980s— and then I was turning into Suckling Street and pulling into our driveway.

The two-storey Victorian-era house had been Reuben's, bought in the 1970s. Later he'd turned it into two apartments and he still owned the one at the top, but the lower one he'd gifted to me. I'd been talking about buying a place, after the breakup with Ben and before I knew I was pregnant. I'd happened to mention I was interested in somewhere on the north side of the Yarra and Reuben had turned up his nose. He came from a time when which side of the river you lived on was socially important. The south side was for those with wealth and standing in the community, the north was tougher, more avant-garde. I thought that would have suited Reuben, but it seemed he was at heart a very conventional man.

'You'll live with me,' he'd told me. 'I have plenty of room. What do I need all this room for? You're my daughter and one day this house will be yours anyway.'

I hadn't argued. Kew was an older, established suburb close to the city, and it was relatively safe. Shortly after the offer was made, I discovered I was pregnant, and safe and conventional suddenly seemed far more desirable than avant-garde. Besides, Reuben was the only living relative I had. Both he and my mother had been only children, and my mother had been the only grandchild in her family. We didn't need to book a big table for Christmas dinners.

I slipped my key into the door and once inside turned on the light, Courtney running in front of me. Immediately, Nephetiti leapt for safety on the table, giving me a resentful look. Before Courtney came along, Nephetiti had been my only child and the cat still held a grudge.

'Can I watch The Wiggles, Mummy?' Courtney was heading for the DVD player.

'Yes, all right. Just for a little while.' I set down my bags and scooped up the cat, carrying it into the kitchen.

Nephetiti was a regal name for what was a stray white tabby, abandoned by some neighbours, who found her way to my sympathetic door. Nephetiti was enough her own cat to be able to cope firstly with my long work days and irregular absences, and then Courtney's appearance. Most of the time the three of us rubbed along okay together, and if it wasn't perfect then what family was?

While Nephetiti happily lapped up her fishy food, I collected one of my bags and emptied the contents out onto the table. I'd taken digital photos of the *Trompe L'oeil* and printed them out and I wanted to look at them at my leisure. I also hoped to put them onto my computer and enhance them, because I was curious about the numerous scenes I'd noticed in the painting. Each one a small, intimate story of its own.

For my father the task itself was enough, but I wasn't like that. I craved to know the story behind the object I was working on. I needed to personalise my work to make it relevant, and this *Trompe L'oeil* felt very personal.

It was tempting to sit down and get straight to work, and once upon a time that was exactly what I would have done, but Courtney had changed all that. My daughter needed a proper meal, a bath and a bedtime story. And, if I was lucky, she would sleep through the night and allow her mother some time of her own.

So I left my work where it was and went into the bedroom to change into comfortable sweatpants, my favourite long-sleeved top and my warmest socks, all to the tune of Dorothy the Dinosaur, before returning to the lounge. The autumn weather had turned chilly, a reminder that winter was just around the corner, and Melbourne winters could be bleak, soggy affairs.

Our house was on a rising slope and the large lounge/sitting room had a view from the front of the house as well as part of the side. Outside the front windows I could see the river and beyond it the city rising up in the distance, the bright lights winking, the traffic noise muted. Outside the side windows I could look down to where the slope had been dug out to form a sunken yard and garden. The houses beside and behind us had high fences and tall trees, so it was a shadowy, damp place at the best of times, although very private. I rarely went out there and I made the excuse that it was Nephetiti's garden, and the tabby Queen of Egypt preferred I kept my interference to a minimum. One day soon, I promised myself, Courtney and I would plant some plants and maybe even some vegetables, just so my daughter understood that not all food came packaged from the supermarket.

When I'd first moved in I'd still felt as if it was Reuben's house and it had taken a while before I began to change my surroundings. A colourful rug here, a bright splash of a painting there, cushions like jewels on the immaculate white sofa. And of course Courtney had made her mark, too, with her basket of toys and little-girl clothes and vivid paintings and drawings stuck on the walls. There was a crayon portrait of Nephetiti on the fridge which I was rather proud of.

I've made my will.

My father's words from today echoed back, sobering me. Papa loved me, I knew that, but he'd had an austere upbringing. He'd never been the sort of father to give me a kiss and hug, not spontaneously anyway. Although, I had to concede, with Courtney he was far more indulgent and liberal with his hugs and kisses.

My mother, Geneva, had been a buxom, busy woman with wild, dark hair and laughing eyes. She was the extrovert, the party-giver, the exact opposite of Reuben, and yet they matched together so perfectly that no one really noticed.

Geneva died young, when I was two, so it always seemed tragically romantic to me. Perhaps they might have divorced, too, eventually, but as it was there was no chance of their happiness turning sour. It would always shine bright.

I had reached to draw the curtains over the view of the garden when something caught my eye. The yard was darker now, full of shadows, but I was certain I saw a man standing against the side fence. Stepping closer, I cupped my hand to the glass to block out the reflection of the room, and peered down.

It was just for a second, but in that second the image was imprinted on my retina. Dark coat, white face, staring up at my window. And then he was gone.

I blinked, searching the yard, my heart thumping. Where was he? How could he have vanished like that? He must be hiding. But I couldn't see any hiding places that made sense. If I didn't know better I might have thought he was a ghost.

No—I shook my head—I still wouldn't believe it. I was tired, it had been a long day, and the lights from the room behind me could have played tricks on my mind. With a determined swish I drew the curtains just as Courtney trotted into the kitchen to join me.

'What are we cooking, Mummy?' she demanded, and now the only terrifying thing I had to deal with was my daughter wielding a knife over mushrooms and stirring the cubes of beef into the marinade without upsetting the lot. Thankfully, she was yet to insist on the actual cooking part, so I did that, and then we sat down to eat our meal.

After a bath and a story Courtney's eyes were closing, and I kissed her goodnight and crept out. I stood outside the door a moment, holding my breath, but tonight wasn't going to be one of those nights when my daughter called out for another story or a drink of water.

Back in the kitchen I poured myself a glass of red wine, tidied up the dishes, and at last got to what I'd been wanting to do all along.

Nephetiti had curled up on the most comfortable chair in the room, and barely acknowledged my pat as I went by. The photos were waiting, the scenes in the painting tantalising in their incompleteness. I examined each print intently, using a magnifying glass, making notes and quick sketches. When I felt I'd done all I could, I took the memory card from the camera to the computer and downloaded it.

This was better, and I realised I'd been holding off, keeping the best till last.

There *was* a paddle-steamer. I zoomed in and I could see the captain at the wheel—tiny, for this was one of the early scenes, far back in the past, and far back in the *Trompe L'oeil*—and beside him a crewman with red hair. There was a name on the bow in almost invisible letters. I zoomed again, trying to read what it said, but it was impossible to get more than the first letter. An A.

I was about to give up when I remembered a software program a friend in photographics had thought I might find useful. He'd presented me with a copy and I had found it invaluable in situations where lettering or small details were beyond the capacity of the human eye. The program clarified the words and pictures, and, if not a perfect solution, I found I could usually make a wild guess.

I hadn't needed to use it for a while, but after a few false starts I got it up and running, and set it to work on the paddle-steamer.

It was amazing how much clearer the little boat and its crew became. I could see that the captain was smiling and he had grey eyes, and the mate had a toothless grin, and there was actually a woman seated to one side, a wide-brimmed hat shading her face, while she leaned on the raised side of the boat with a languid arm.

And most important of all the name on the boat was more decipherable. There were still two letters missing, but there was enough for me to be fairly certain about what it spelt.

Ariadne.

Leaning back in my chair I smiled, hardly noticing the ache in my back and the sting of my eyes. I had a clue. Well, two clues. The Goldminer Hotel and the *Ariadne* paddle-steamer.

It would be too much to hope, wouldn't it . . . ?

Nevertheless I brought up the search engine and put in the name and the words 'riverboat paddle-steamer' after it. The list came up. There was a classic Thames riverboat called *Ariadne*, but I skimmed over that and the next entry about cruises on the Great Barrier Reef. At the very bottom of the page I found something more hopeful, and quickly clicked onto the link.

The website came up in sepia, like an old photograph. The *Ariadne*, paddle-steamer, Echuca. Restored . . . for hire . . . revisit the past . . . And then the paragraph that told me that the *Ariadne* had been a working riverboat from the 1860s to the 1890s when she'd run aground and been left to her fate. Luckily, she'd languished undisturbed by the bank of the Murray River until she was rediscovered, raised and restored.

I felt ridiculously proud of myself. I'd made an important discovery. It may not help me to find out the identities of the two girls in the painting, but at least I knew one of the places they'd been and maybe even the people they'd met along the way. I dashed off an email to the address on the website, asking for any information and briefly explaining my reasons.

I was about to close the computer down when I decided to take one last look at the scene. That was when I noticed that the ribbon around the woman's hat was actually another word, written in deceptively flowing script.

'Molly. Her name is Molly.'

'Mummy? Are you talking to yourself?'

Courtney leaned against me, her body warm and smelling of little-girl shampoo. She blinked at the enlarged picture of the woman on the boat and smiled. 'Is that Molly?' I gave her a hug, loving her so much I was dizzy.

'Yes. Mummy is talking to herself,' I said, 'and she'd better get some sleep. How about we both get some sleep?'

'Okay.'

After I'd tucked my daughter in again I considered what I needed to do tomorrow. Back in the lounge, I turned off my computer and by the time I'd carried a mug of camomile tea into the bedroom I was yawning. There was a novel beside the bed, but as usual I never got to read more than a page of it before I had to close my eyes.

Tonight as I lay in that world between dreams and reality, I found myself remembering the faces of the two girls and their determined expressions. I still had the sense that in a way they were speaking to me, but now I was beginning to be able to hear what they were saying.

I'd already forgotten about the white-faced man in the garden.

* * *

The following morning when I arrived at work, Clive from History Victoria was there, waiting for me with another man. I felt my stomach tighten at the sight of them. I had a pretty good idea what this meant. Reading my expression, Clive gave a little grimace before turning it into a smile for the benefit of his companion.

'Annie, you remember Sebastian Rawlins?'

'Of course I do.'

We clasped hands briefly and I was subjected to Sebastian's hawklike stare before he turned again to the painting. He was in his thirties, young for a man in his position, although he had the manner of someone much older. History Victoria had its hierarchy the same as any other organisation, but because it was partially funded by the government, every decision had a political significance that needed to be taken into account. Sebastian Rawlins's job was to scrutinise those decisions for any possible fallout. Though quite why he was here now, examining my painting, I had no idea. Were they going to give the job to someone else? I felt a sliver of regret that I'd become so personally involved with the *Trompe L'oeil* so quickly. It made it almost impossible to turn my back and walk away.

'Is this a significant piece?' he said.

'An interesting piece,' I replied. 'Whether or not it's significant . . . well that will take time to determine.'

Sebastian said nothing. He seemed to be lost in the wonder of the painting, and then he reached out and touched one of the figures. I winced and it was only Clive's grip on my arm that stopped me from slapping away his finger.

'We have a problem.'

I turned to face him. 'What problem?'

'This man here.' Again he touched the surface of the painting, resting his fingertip on one particular figure. 'He is the problem.'

Curiosity momentarily overcame my agitation, and I peered closely at the man in question. His face was a blur, his features indefinable. He appeared to be wearing a checked tweed type coat and a top hat, and he was standing before a gaudy-looking building with 'Dunolly Music Hall' written on it.

'Do you know who he is?' Sebastian Rawlins demanded, and he turned to look at me. He was so close that I could feel his breath on my cheek. Against all my instincts I turned my head to look back. His eyes were hazel, but there was a ruthlessness to them, a quality that made me want to back away. Despite the warning bells ringing, or perhaps because of them, I kept eye contact. I was as stubborn as my father.

His mouth twitched, amused by my stance.

'This is Gervais Whistler, goldfields' entrepreneur, respectable businessman,' he finally answered my question. 'What isn't widely known is that much of his wealth came from music halls and brothels, and some travelling entertainers he signed up and then exploited. At one stage he was a business partner of George Coppin of Melbourne theatre fame, and he also owned or ran The Goldminer Hotel.'

I frowned, too interested now to play games. 'How do you know all this? I've only just started my research.'

'Ah, but I have friends in high places, and some of those friends aren't keen for Mr Whistler's colourful past to become common knowledge. He's been sanitised over the years and now you're threatening all that careful work.'

The penny dropped. 'He's somebody's grandfather. The skeleton in the cupboard. Is that it?'

That little smile again.

'Well I can't help family history. This is too important a piece to be shut up in a warehouse and forgotten. I won't let that happen.'

'I told you,' Clive muttered with a glance in my direction. 'Annie doesn't do compromise.'

Sebastian's lips tightened. 'She just might have to.' He took one more look at the painting, and this time his gaze swept across it, only to rest on a scene towards the left-hand side, where the paintwork was the most badly damaged. It lingered longer than I would have thought necessary before he turned away, making for the door with the stride of a man with a full day ahead.

'Keep me informed,' he barked over his shoulder.

Clive paused long enough to pat me supportively on the shoulder before scuttling after him.

When they were gone I took a moment to gather my wits. Sebastian was worried about some person portrayed in the painting because of the connection to his masters. I didn't pretend to be naive enough to believe that person couldn't have the painting taken from me if they were fearful enough for their reputation. The spin, the way things looked, seemed to mean everything in politics these days. It only took one misstep for the media, or the other side of the house, to tear down a politician's carefully constructed reputation, and I could see that a dodgy ancestor might be awkward if one were Minister of Finance or in some other monetarily responsible position.

But I couldn't be worried about that, I had my own job to do. If they tried to stop me then I'd fight them. Whoever this Gervais Whistler once was he was now only a small part of the lives spread out before me. Still, if he had once owned The Goldminer Hotel it would be interesting to find out more about him. Discreetly, of course. Under the radar.

I moved to the left, trying to decide where Sebastian had been staring just before he left. This part of the *Trompe L'oeil* was quite seriously damaged, but there were patches that had survived. I could see the thick trunk of a gum tree, and a building . . . a house or a hut? There wasn't enough of it to tell. Part of a long skirt and perhaps a woman's shoulder covered in a shawl? A dark patch with a section of white, almost like a face staring out at me . . .

My heart gave a little jump.

No, my eyes were forming pictures that weren't there. This wasn't a man in dark clothes with a white face—the man in my garden. There *was* no man in my garden. Certainly, when I looked closer I could see nothing to persuade me this was a person at all. The paint was damaged, too badly damaged for the miracles of my photographic friend's software, and although I could clean it up, I would need to find a contemporary copy of the painting to be able to understand the story it was telling.

Had History Victoria found one? Was that how Sebastian knew so much? Well, if he wasn't going to share with me . . . I smiled—I had my own sources.

According to Sebastian, the painting was a threat to someone important, but if he'd thought by telling me that he was putting me off then he was making a huge mistake.

My smile grew; I'd always enjoyed untangling secrets.

CHAPTER SIX

The Girl's Story

Alice sat blinking in the sunshine, her new rag doll clasped in her arms. Molly sat in a cane chair enfolded among the cushions, a wide-brimmed hat shading her pale face and shadowed eyes, exhausted by the simple act of getting out of bed and going into the garden.

'Are you warm, Alice?' she said, wrapping her shawl more securely about her own thin shoulders. 'The breeze is chilly.'

'Yes, Molly,' Alice assured her.

Mrs Potter had asked the girl to call her Molly—Mrs Potter seemed far too formal. The alternative was Mama, but she was not Alice's mother and there may come a day when her real mother arrived to claim her.

Alice was happy here with Molly. She had trouble remembering her new name sometimes, but it was getting easier and Molly did not seem to mind. Despite the kindness and the comfort of her new life, Alice couldn't relax and settle in as Molly wanted her to.

It was the fault of the colours.

They swirled around Molly in a never-ending maelstrom that made Alice's head hurt. Usually, it was after the medicine when they were at their darkest and most violent. The medicine that Doctor Suckling insisted Molly take three times a day and which she said made her feel sicker.

'Nonsense, Mrs Potter! I really don't know where you get these foolish notions from.' The doctor had glanced at Alice as he said it, as if he blamed the girl for his patient's complaints. He had examined Alice at Molly's request, taking note of her bruises—almost gone now—and the marks on her throat. He'd pronounced her in good health physically, although he thought she was perhaps lacking in the mind.

'Does she speak much? Does she understand what you're saying to her?' the doctor had asked, lowering his voice, although Alice could still hear him perfectly well. He'd brought his son with him and the boy, who was twelve, had seemed bored.

He cast her a scornful glance. His hair was the colour of hay and his eyes were the same sharp hazel as Doctor Suckling's. He was also dressed as a miniature version of his father, although his coat had a rounded collar.

'She's as bright as a button,' Molly said. 'There's nothing wrong with her mind, Doctor.'

Doctor Suckling looked unconvinced. 'I heard what happened to your husband's second-in-command, Mrs Potter. The gossip seems to suggest that the child foretold the awful event.'

'Surely you're not superstitious, Doctor?'

'Not at all, but you should not discount the reactions of those who are. Perhaps Alice would be better off in an orphanage, for her own sake as well as yours.'

Molly's breath was ragged and Alice saw her hold it a moment, to control her temper, before she replied. 'Alice will remain with me, Doctor, thank you very much.'

Doctor Suckling was none too pleased to have his advice disregarded and he gave Alice another narrow look. 'As you wish, Mrs Potter. I sincerely hope you'll not regret your decision.'

His son smirked in Alice's direction, enjoying the clash of wills. He crossed his eyes, as if inferring she was mentally deficient, and

Alice kicked his shin. Hard. He yelped, but his father was already out the door and not inclined to return, so the boy had to limp hurriedly after him.

'Hateful man,' Molly murmured, barely noticing Alice's retaliation. 'I wish I didn't have to listen to him, Alice, but unfortunately he's the best doctor in Echuca. In fact, he's the *only* doctor, although there are several quacks who call themselves by the title.'

She laughed softly, her smiling eyes inviting Alice to smile back.

'What is the name of his son?' Alice said.

'I'm not sure. Vincent? Something like that. Was he horrid to you? I wouldn't be surprised. His mother spoils him dreadfully—when she's sober.'

Alice knew she was meant to be scornful of the spoilt boy, but she was wistful instead. How wonderful to be loved so much people considered you spoilt.

Now, remembering the moment, remembering the dark shadow that had fallen over Molly after the doctor's visit, Alice knew she must speak. She did so before she could stop herself, before she could remind herself of the pitfalls that speaking always caused her.

'The medicine is bad, Molly.'

Molly's brown eyes widened. For a moment she did not reply, staring at Alice. Alice was still, afraid to move. Molly leaned forward and took Alice's hands in her cold ones. 'Do you mean it's making me sicker? Have I been right all along?'

Alice nodded.

But Molly was not cross or angry. She spoke with a sort of suppressed excitement. 'I knew it. Thank you, Alice. I will not take it again.'

Alice waited for more. Recriminations, perhaps, or disbelief. Instead, Molly leaned her head back and closed her eyes, lifting her face towards the spring sun. A smile curved her lips and there was a faint flush on her pale cheeks. Alice could see her colours and they were still dark, but now there was yellow, like the sunshine in the garden, peeping through the rain clouds.

Could she save Molly? And if she did, would it make up for Bluey's death? More than anything Alice hoped so.

* * *

'Do you know, Alice, I feel well enough to walk down to the shops!'

Molly's eyes were shining as she took Alice's hand. They set off, making their way along the main street, with the bustling red gum wharf fronting the river on one side and a variety of taverns and hotels and other businesses on the other. During the four months they had been together Molly had been teaching Alice to read—there was talk of sending her to school in the new year—and she was able to repeat the signs in her head or aloud if Molly was testing her.

There was Shackell's Star Hotel where Elliot's Prize Ale could be bought and drunk in the coolness of the underground bar. Very popular, Molly said, in the stifling heat of summer, although it was not a place fit for ladies. There was also the Cumberland Hotel and the Garter Hotel and the Steam Packet Hotel and . . . but Molly walked too quickly past them for Alice to name them all. There were Aborigines in the shade of the verandahs, with little to do but sit and stare out at the changing world. Sometimes Molly bought possum skin rugs from them, but today she just tutted and shook her head, and Alice wasn't sure whether that was because she disapproved or was sorry for them.

Apart from the hotels there were stables and blacksmiths and shipwrights. The wharf was always busy, with boats coming and going, unloading their cargoes or loading up again. The screech of the sawmill hurt her ears, and the stench of the boiling-down works made her hold her nose and make silly noises to amuse Molly. Wherever she looked the town seemed to be full of men. There were men riding in with mobs of sheep or cattle, men working on the wharves or the riverboats, men drinking at the hotels or fighting in the streets, men fitting themselves up for the journey to the goldfields to make their fortunes. Men from all over the world.

'Echuca is a frontier town,' Molly said when Alice asked why there were so many men and so few women, 'although we ladies are trying our very best to civilise it.'

Alice enjoyed being out and about, seeing all there was to see, but at the same time she liked to keep her hand firmly clasped in Molly's, and she never left Molly's side.

At night her dreams were still full of the man with the long dark coat. He seemed to be all that was left of her memories of her past and she was always on the lookout for him. She knew in her heart that one day he would come to find her. That even now he was searching for her. She knew it in the same way she'd known Bluey was going to die.

Now they were passing by the Bridge Hotel, with its delicious smells, and into the next street. They were almost at Mr Fortescue's Drapers, a business Molly favoured with her custom. They'd been discussing buttons and braid for Alice's new dress, and Alice skipped with excitement. But just as they were passing by the front of a narrow, two-storey building, a young woman wandered into their path. Alice thought she did it on purpose—there was a forwardness in her manner, as if she wanted to be looked at and noticed.

'Oops, pardon me, ladies,' she said. Her hair was golden with wild ringlet curls and her eyes were as green as a cat's, but there was a glint in them, a smile, that Alice liked.

Not so Molly.

'How dare you!' she declared, eyeing the girl up and down as if she were covered in dirt. 'Echuca may be short of women, but we don't need your sort here. Go back to Dublin where you belong!'

The girl looked surprised rather than shocked, and then she struck a pose with a hand on her hip and tossed her head. She was wearing a pink dress with lace sewn on the front and on the elbow-length sleeves. It was old and faded, but the girl wore it like a queen.

'Oh lah de dah!' she mocked. 'And it's Cork, I'll have you know, not Dublin.' Then she curtseyed, gave a loud laugh and went on her way, slipping in through the doorway of what Alice saw was yet another tavern. She looked up at the sign above the door and squinted to read it in the glare of the sun.

The Red Petticoat.

Molly took a deep breath to recover herself, pressing her hand to her throat. 'A disgrace,' she whispered. A moment later they entered the draper's shop and spent a pleasant hour examining new rolls of cloth and braiding, buttons, beads and thread. Molly wanted Alice to have more than one new dress for the warmer weather—her clothes were all hand-me-downs from Molly's friends and neighbours. They chose a length of pretty blue and a length of pale green, although Alice would have preferred pink for a dress like the one worn by the girl with the green eyes and curly hair.

Not that she would have dared to say so.

When they reached home Molly was very weary and would have gone to her bedroom to rest, except she had a visitor. The visitor was seated in the parlour, gloved hands clasped in her lap, her beaky nose red from the sun. Alice knew she shouldn't be eavesdropping but she couldn't help it. She was worried. Molly was getting better, but only she could see it because only she could see the colours. Everyone else believed in the doctor and his medicine.

'Really, Molly, how can you listen to a simple child rather than your own doctor? You know what they're saying about her, don't you? She's cursed. She brings bad luck. Look what happened to Bluey. Please, Molly. You must take the medicine or you'll never get better.'

'Oh tosh,' Molly said mildly, but there was an angry flush in her cheeks.

'Did you know Miss Richards is failing? Well she is, Molly, and Doctor Suckling is certain it's due to her stopping her treatment. Do you want to end up like Miss Richards?'

'I feel much better, thank you,' Molly said, but now Alice could see her hands shaking as she poured tea into her flowery cups. 'You're worrying too much—'

'I'm concerned for you. As a friend.'

When beaky-nose had gone Alice heard Molly sigh. They were wearing her down. Why should she believe a child from nowhere over her friends and the physician? Molly was strong, but she was the sort of woman who liked to please those she loved.

Alice crept into the parlour and knelt by Molly's chair, reaching up to take her hand. Molly's eyes opened abruptly and at first she seemed not to know who Alice was, and then she grew intense.

'Are you sure, Alice? Is the medicine making me ill?'

Alice nodded vigorously. 'The colours,' she whispered. 'I can see. Please, Molly, do not take it anymore. I'm afraid that if you do you'll die.'

Molly nodded her head. 'You mean well, Alice. I can see that. I can see it in your eyes.'

The room was very warm and after a time Molly dozed, but Alice didn't leave her side, watching, worrying and hoping.

* * *

'What on earth are you talking about?' Arnold shouted. He was distraught and he forgot to be gentle with the woman he loved. 'Doctor Suckling met me at the wharf. You've stopped taking his medicine and he fears you'll grow worse because of it. Molly, please, what are you thinking to disobey the man?'

'I told you, I feel better without taking the medicine—'

'But he explained that that is a false belief. You've convinced yourself that it's the medicine making you ill when it's no such thing. Molly, please, I'm begging you. Do as he says. If you keep refusing to take your medicine then you'll never get well!'

There were tears running down Molly's face and he wanted to comfort her, to give in to her, anything to please her. But Arnold knew he could not. This was a matter of life or death and he must prevail.

The fear had been with him when the doctor accosted him and only grew stronger as he strode down the busy streets of Echuca, head bowed, heart thudding. 'Dr Suckling told me Alice has convinced you to stop. How can a child know what's wrong with you, Molly?'

'She does know, Arnold. She has some power that allows her to see what's wrong.'

Arnold strode to the window and turned. He felt like tearing out his hair, but he made his voice quieter, firmer. If he was to convince her, if he was to save her life, then he must not frighten her or put her back up. All the same he knew now he should never have brought Alice home to his wife.

'Bluey died from an accident, Molly. The child didn't save him, did she? And it was a coincidence she said those things, I'm convinced of it now. To imagine she can save lives is ridiculous.'

'You didn't believe that before,' she whispered, her face stark.

'I was a fool. You must do as Doctor Suckling tells you, Molly, I beg you. For your own sake. For mine.'

She stared at him a moment longer, trying to hold firm, but her gaze was full of doubt and finally she capitulated. Relieved, Arnold wrapped her in his arms and held her fast.

'You must get well, Molly,' he said against her damp cheek. 'Please, take your medicine and get well.'

* * *

Alice tried to tell him but he wouldn't listen. She tried again, but his face got hard and angry and he sent her to her room. Even when Molly began to fail, her colours darkening, thickening, he refused to believe she was not getting better.

Within a fortnight she was dead.

Doctor Suckling found reasons for her sudden decline. Her refusal to take the medicine for those crucial weeks, he thought, had contributed to her death. If Alice was in the vicinity he glanced at her with dislike and she took to avoiding him. Captain Potter was in mourning and did not speak to her at all, or seem to notice her. Perhaps that was just as well because Alice sensed his anger with her.

He blamed her.

No one understood.

One morning Alice was sitting at the window of the parlour, wishing she could go outside and run in the garden but knowing Captain Potter would not like it, when a man came walking towards the house.

At first she wasn't sure, and yet her limbs grew heavy and she felt as if she was choking. He was tall and thin and he wore a long dark coat. As she sat, staring, too afraid to move or make a sound, the man reached the door and rapped on it.

She thought if he came into the parlour she would not be able to move, she was so frightened. Was it him? Had he come for her at last?

But it wasn't him. This man wasn't so thin, he was fuller in the face, his skin was sallow rather than pale, and he walked without that graceful swinging movement she remembered, as if nothing in the world worried him.

She heard Captain Potter at the door and their voices, and then the man was walking away. In her mind she saw the stranger in a room with lots of jars and bottles, and a machine that made pills. The smell of the place was strong, and even the vision made her eyes water. When Alice was able to move and speak again she asked Eliza the kitchen maid who the man was.

'Him? He's Mr Kent from the pharmacy,' Eliza said. 'Where they make up the doctor's medicine. Come to offer his condolences I expect.'

'It was the medicine that killed Molly.' The words tumbled out, shocking them both. Eliza bent close to her, eyes wide.

'Don't you go saying that,' she breathed. 'Captain already thinks you're bad luck. Or mad. He'll send you away, mark my words. Keep whatever you're thinking to yourself, Alice.' She gave Alice a rough shake. 'Are you listening? Sometimes I think you're queer in the head. But the mistress was fond of you, Alice, and with her dying breath she asked me to look out for you, so that's what I'm doing.'

Alice spun away, running down the hallway and into her room where she slammed the door. She stayed there, silent, trying to disappear into the wallpaper. As much as she hated this house without Molly in it she didn't want to leave its safe and familiar walls.

Eventually, Captain Potter returned to the *Ariadne* and the river, and he sent Alice to live with the beaky-nosed lady, whose name was Mrs Turner. And the day after he chugged away, Mrs Turner rid herself of the girl.

CHAPTER SEVEN

Annie's Story

In Melbourne the sky was cloudy and there'd been rain, but as I drove further north the weather began to clear and the sun shone out. Self-righteously, I tried not to enjoy it, reminding myself this was a side trip I could do without. This was Saturday and I'd planned to take Courtney to the zoo, but now Ben and his latest blonde had that pleasure, because when I'd arrived home on Friday night there was an email waiting for me.

If you want to know about the **Ariadne** *come and see for yourself.*

And there'd been a printable ticket attached, for the one o'clock sail aboard the *Ariadne* on Saturday afternoon. An hour up the river and back, with a glass of champagne thrown in.

At first I'd shaken my head, reminding myself of all the things I should be doing, of the promises I'd made, but at the back of my mind treacherous thoughts were stirring.

I needed to see the boat, to take photos and compare them to the scene in the painting. And then there was Molly. What if by going I was able to find out who Molly was?

I also knew that now the idea was in my head if I didn't go today then I'd end up going eventually, and in the meantime it would drive me to distraction. Of course if Ben had been unavailable to take Courtney then that would have been that, but he'd agreed with so much good humour that I was relieved of much of my guilt. Courtney seemed happy, too, and I remembered yet again how much she enjoyed her father's company. Ben was fun, if you were four years old.

Once my daughter was safely delivered, I set off out of the city and northwards, towards the Murray River.

Yesterday I'd worked solidly on the *Trompe L'oeil*, but Gervais Whistler was playing on my mind and I'd rung a friend at the State Library and left a message. A discreet message. I wasn't worried that Maren would discuss it with anyone, and I didn't want her to get into trouble, but I needed to know as much as possible about this character who could turn up from the past and ruin my chances of restoring the painting. Knowledge was definitely power in this instance.

Part of my journey was through old goldmining country and the old gold rush centre of Bendigo. The city had once been called Sandhurst and the wealth from the mines had left its mark in a glorious fountain and grand boom-era buildings. Once through Bendigo it wasn't much further to the river and the Port of Echuca, and I arrived just after noon. By the time I'd found somewhere to park and made my way to the historic precinct, which included the huge old wharf and the restored buildings around it, the time was getting close to one o'clock.

I found the *Ariadne* tied up along the giant red gum wharf, a sign set up with an arrow pointing to stairs. During flood times the river could rise well up the wharf, but today it was low and that made it necessary for me to climb down lots of stairs, through a maze of wooden struts and beams, before I could reach the waterline. And here at last was the boat, her paintwork new and shiny, smoke pouring from her chimney and her engine grumbling loudly. The *Ariadne* let out a piercing warning whistle and the man standing by the boarding ramp reached out to help the last passengers aboard.

As I waited my turn to cross the ramp onto the deck, I glanced up and saw that there was another man in the upstairs wheelhouse, visible through a glassed-in window. I wondered who had sent me the ticket and decided that whoever it was I was grateful, because now I was here I was glad I'd come. Was this the *Ariadne* from the *Trompe L'oeil*? I thought I recognised it, and I wanted to clamber all over the paddle-steamer and take photos of her and learn about her past.

'Welcome aboard,' said the man on the ramp. His grin was friendly and he looked to be in his early twenties. His overalls were smeared in grease and his skin was browned by long days in the sun. He was obviously busy and I let him get on with his work, telling myself I'd seek him out later and introduce myself.

Meanwhile, I made my way to the covered stern and found a seat among the other passengers. There were about twenty of them scattered around the deck, family groups mainly, but there were a few couples and lone travellers like myself. Courtney would have loved it, I thought, but if I'd brought my daughter I'd never have been able to do my research. Besides, I reminded myself, Courtney was no doubt having a wonderful time with her father at the zoo.

The ropes were cast off and we began to edge away from the wharf and out into the river. Then the shrill whistle sounded again and we were on our way.

Being on the river was relaxing, a cooling breeze ensured it was not too hot, and the passing scenery slipped by at such a leisurely pace that I began to feel sleepy. I made myself take out my camera to snap some photos, mostly of the *Ariadne* herself. To my inexperienced eye it did look like the boat in the painting. I got up from my seat and walked along the side of the deck, looking for the place where I thought Molly was leaning against the bulwark. Although the scene had been painted in miniature and necessarily foreshortened, making it difficult to say for sure, I felt confident that I'd found it.

Molly, who are you? Why were you so important that you were immortalised in paint?

I was about to take another photo when a voice called down to me.

'Hey! Annie, is it?'

Startled, I looked up. The captain had come to the door of his wheelhouse and was leaning out. The sun was in my eyes and I squinted, holding up my hand to shield them, and in that moment I could have sworn I was looking at the figure in the painting, the captain with grey eyes wearing a double-breasted jacket and flat cap. The next moment I blinked and found myself, instead, staring up at an unshaven man, about thirty, my own age, with a baseball cap over messy hair wearing a checked shirt and jeans. Oh, and he was handsome. Despite his unkempt appearance he had no trouble capturing my full attention.

'Come up!' he called again.

I looked uneasily at the narrow vertical gangway.

'We can talk up here, it's quieter.'

The engine was very noisy. I approached the wooden steps with trepidation, but once at the top I found his hand waiting for me, either to steady me or to give a friendly shake, I wasn't sure. He had the same grin as the younger man who'd welcomed me aboard and I thought they must be brothers.

'Thank you for the ticket, but there was no need . . .'

'You seemed interested.' He brushed it off.

He led me into the wheelhouse which had windows on two sides and openings on the other two. I stepped back out of his way and turned to gaze out over the stern. The view was wonderful, and here I was somewhat sheltered from the smell of the hot engine and the puffing smoke. He'd taken up his place at the wheel again, narrowing his eyes against the glare from the water, and I saw that we had reached a bridge over the river and were about to go underneath.

'We'll be serving the champagne soon,' he said. 'I'll have Kenny bring one up for you, if you like.'

'Thank you.'

He pulled the cord that blew the whistle. I jumped—it sounded louder up here. I caught his smile and thought that maybe he'd done it on purpose. But then again we were passing under the bridge and it could be the law of the river or something.

'Did you restore the *Ariadne*?' I said, positioning my camera and clicking off a photo of him at the wheel.

His turn to look startled. 'Ah, my father. Worked on it all his life. Never got to see it finished. I think of him every day I'm aboard her.'

'Can I show you something?'

He glanced at me as I removed the enlarged photographs from my bag, and then took the one I offered. He looked closely at it for a moment, then smiled in amazement. His whole face seemed to light up.

'Looks like the *Ariadne*,' he said. 'Is this the whatsit you're restoring? You said something about it in the email.'

'The *Trompe L'oeil*.'

'Trump Loy,' he echoed my pronunciation.

'Yes. It's a three-dimensional painting, or at least it tricks the eye into thinking it is. This particular painting gives you the sense that you're gazing into someone's life, with all the little moments that went into making it. Some of the scenes are tiny—like this one—but it stood out. It took me a while to make out the name of the paddle-steamer, but when I did I Googled it and you came up.'

'You think it's the same boat?'

'It has to be, surely? One of the other scenes shows miners digging. I'm assuming that's the gold rush and we can date the story back to the 1850s or 60s. I'd be more inclined to say the 1860s, because there are mines with poppet heads, and they were later than the alluvial diggings so . . .' I smiled at his bemused expression. 'I'm losing you.'

'No, no, I'm just a bit flabbergasted. So this painting . . .'

'*Trompe L'oeil*.'

He gave me a look. 'So this *Trompe L'oeil* has all of the detail of someone's life in it, and that includes the *Ariadne*?'

'Yes. I'm sure it's not just scenery for the sake of it. It tells a story. A life story. And I want to find out all I can about it because knowing helps me with the restoration. I want to do justice to those people who commissioned it as well as those who painted it or appear in it.'

His eyes crinkled around the edges as he smiled again in a way that made me feel embarrassed about my enthusiasm. Not everyone understood the intensity of it.

'I'm sorry, I don't know your name,' I said, suddenly awkward.

'Max Taylor,' he replied with that smile. 'And my brother down there is Kenny.' He began to turn the wheel. 'Hang on a moment, we're heading back.' When we'd made the turn he paused, the little boat marking time in the swirling water, then he leaned out of the door of the wheelhouse and called down to his brother. 'Kenny, champagne up here!'

I didn't believe anyone could carry a glass of champagne up the narrow gangway, but the next moment Kenny appeared, not a drop spilled, and handed it over with a grin.

'Better get the food out, too,' Max called after him. 'And remember to take the money this time. We're not a charity.'

'Yes, sir!' Kenny shouted back just before his head vanished.

'Kenny's the mate, the engineer, waiter and sometimes the cook,' Max explained. 'I have the easy part. I just steer the boat.'

I was sure there was more to it than that and he was just being modest, but I let it pass. 'Tell me about restoring the *Ariadne*. Is she all new now or are there some parts from the original boat?'

'There are still some original parts. We managed to save some of the original timbers. It took Dad years to rebuild the hull—he was working his day job at the same time—then he had to replace the deck and cabin, and of course the boiler, but the engine is the original. The *Ariadne* was the love of his life, kept him going after Mum died.'

'On your website you say she was lying in the mud and you lifted her up?'

Max smiled. 'Dad had planned to exhume her for years before he could finally afford to do it. She'd been down in the river since 1891, around a hundred years. We had to dig the mud and silt from under the hull then we used water jets . . . well, it was a mammoth job. Eventually, we were able to lift her and then she was pumped out and floated. All the way up the river we thought something would go wrong, her back would break or she'd just disintegrate and sink back to the bottom. But she's made of strong stuff, our girl.' He said it proudly and I realised Max loved this boat as much as his father did.

'And you work her yourself?'

'Yes, she's owned entirely by us. The Port Authority owns quite a few of the old paddle-steamers, but there are also a few private operators. I wouldn't say we were rich, but we make a living.'

I wondered what it would be like to live in this place, to spend your days chugging up and down the river, to know every ripple of the water and every curve of the riverbank. The thought was unexpectedly enticing.

'You were telling me about your *Trompe L'oeil*.' Max interrupted my reverie.

He seemed interested so I began to describe more of the scenes and the two girls. 'We managed to save the painting from The Goldminer Hotel in Melbourne, which is being demolished very soon. Actually, I wouldn't mind taking another look inside the building. I think it's important. Photos are useful, but when it comes to getting the sense of a place's history, its heart and soul if you like, then you need to stand there and look with your own eyes.'

He nodded as if he understood, or maybe he just thought I was crazy and he was humouring me. Though I hoped not—I liked him. 'Can I have another look at that photo?' he said, holding out his hand.

I passed it over, and added the other two I'd brought. One of them was a close-up of Molly, showing each stroke and daub of paint, as well as the chinks and flakes and discolouration of the many years of neglect. The other was a shot of the entire painting in all its intricate detail. He gave each photograph his full attention before handing them back.

'Looks to me as if your girls knew the owner of the *Ariadne* in their day. You should get on to the Echuca Historical Society. They have a museum and you can look up the names of all the riverboats from way back, along with their captains and crew. Maybe one of the owners of the *Ariadne* had a wife called Molly.'

'Thank you. I'll do that after we get back to the wharf.'

He turned and gave me a long look. 'Of course you will,' he said. 'You seem like a pretty meticulous sort of person.' He wasn't being sarcastic, in fact he sounded quite admiring. And I had the strangest feeling when he was looking at me, as if we knew each other much better than was possible for two people who'd just met.

It was disconcerting. I felt my skin prickle. It was a long time since I'd felt an attraction as strong as this, and I was relieved when Max turned away and got busy steering his boat again. My champagne was nearly finished and I took a final sip and set the plastic flute down on the floor, out of the way.

'Thank you for talking with me, and thank you for the ticket. I've enjoyed it.' I almost said I didn't get out much, but that sounded pathetic and wasn't strictly true. I got out, just not on my own.

He looked at me again, and hesitated as if he was about to ask me something, but then he simply said, 'Let me know how you get on with Molly.'

We were approaching the wharf again and I was certain he'd need all his concentration to bring the boat in to the mooring. I made to slip past him, back to the door, but he stopped me.

'The picture you have of the painting, the bit with the *Ariadne* in it, do you think I could have a copy? I might be able to ask around. There are people still alive who remember the old days. Stories are passed down.'

'Umm. I don't know . . .'

'It's okay. I understand if there's some reason you don't want me—'

'No, it's not that. At the moment I'm not sure what's going to happen with the painting, things are a bit sensitive at head office.' He wouldn't understand, but head office was my name for History Victoria. 'Look, I'm sure you won't put them up on your website. Not yet anyway. Maybe later, when I've finished, you could . . .'

I was rambling. I cut myself short and handed him the enlargements.

'I'd appreciate any help you can give me,' I added in a more professional tone.

'Sure,' he said. 'Good luck, Annie.'

'Bye, Max. And thanks again.'

The gangway was best approached by going down backwards, and I was relieved to get to the bottom. I took a deep breath and paused to lean against the wooden bulwark and gaze over the river. The scene relaxed me. There probably wasn't that much difference between this view and what it must have been like a hundred and fifty years before, if one discounted the obvious modernisations like powerlines and jet skis. Water birds were floating past and populating the gum trees along the shore, while a gentleman with a long beard was fishing from a fallen log. A white cloud of cockatoos flew screeching through the blue sky.

My imagination conjured up the captain with the grey eyes and his red-headed mate, and there was Molly with her broad-brimmed hat. I was sure that these three people had meant something important to one or both of the girls in the painting, and now, standing here on the deck of the *Ariadne*, I was more determined than ever to find out what it was.

CHAPTER EIGHT

The Girl's Story

The room felt warm and musty. And unfriendly. Mrs Turner was speaking to the other woman in a very fast voice, her cheeks flushed, her gloved hands clasped tightly at her waist. She seemed nervous, or perhaps just desperate to have her way.

Alice wasn't really listening. She'd already been told what her future was to be. Mrs Turner believed it was better for an orphan to work for a living rather than to be coddled, and in Alice's case that meant working in a position where she could do no more damage to decent people. Miss Oliver, who owned the Red Petticoat, had a need for a kitchen maid and Mrs Turner had heard about it.

But Alice knew the real reason she was here. Mrs Turner blamed her for Molly's death and wanted to see her punished.

The door to the musty room wasn't properly closed. There was a gap, and if Alice tilted her head slightly she could see through it. There was a girl staring back at her from the other side, a girl with a pale face framed by curling fair hair, and Alice recognised her.

It was the same girl she and Molly had met in the street the day they went to buy materials for Alice's dresses that Molly had never had made. The girl with the pink dress that Alice had coveted, who'd said *lah de dah* in that mocking tone.

Miss Oliver seemed to know the girl was there, or perhaps Alice gave her away with her movement, for suddenly she barked out a name that sounded like, 'Rosey!' making everybody jump.

Rosey grimaced and then straightened her face into a remarkably innocent mask just before she pushed open the door and stepped into the room. 'Yes, Miss Oliver?' she said, meek as a lamb.

'This is our new kitchen maid. Show her where to go. And see she cleans the place up before the new cook comes. I've secured the Chinese cook from the Bridge Hotel,' she added to Mrs Turner with obvious pride.

Rosey looked doubtfully at Alice, opened her mouth and shut it again. She held out her hand and Alice warmed to her as she clasped her fingers.

'Goodbye, Alice, I shall pray for you,' Mrs Turner said, but Alice didn't thank her and she didn't look back.

'Old cow,' Rosey said, as soon as they were out of earshot. 'I believe the girl should work for a living,' she said in such perfect mimicry of Mrs Turner that Alice gasped. Sensing she had an appreciative audience, Rosey continued. 'Of course the true reason I want her gone is that she's much prettier than me.'

Alice giggled, and soon she was laughing. She hadn't laughed since Molly had died and it felt good and sad at the same time.

'Your kingdom awaits you, m'lady.' Rosey curtseyed at the kitchen door, her wicked green eyes dancing.

Alice took a step inside and stopped.

Her lip wobbled, her eyes glistened. All the laughter of a moment ago drained out of her. The kitchen was dark and cramped and smelt of old food. There were sticky splotches on the slate floor and streaks on the walls, and the table was covered in unwashed pots, plates and utensils, while the scullery was a dark hole in the wall. It was as unfriendly as Miss Oliver and Alice wanted to go home to her bright little room, she wanted her rag doll, and most of all she wanted Molly.

Alice flopped down onto the floor and wrapped her arms about herself, wishing she could disappear.

After a moment she felt a tentative hand on her head, and then Rosey knelt down beside her, saying, 'Hush, little one. Shoosh now. If Miss Oliver hears you making such a noise she'll send you off to the orphanage after all, and you really don't want that. We've had some orphan girls here and you should hear the mucky tales they tell.'

Alice didn't care what happened to her, not now that Molly was dead, but Rosey seemed to, so she gulped and uncurled herself. If Molly had been here she would have taken Alice in her arms and held her tight and comforted her. She would have saved her. But Rosey wasn't Molly—Alice could tell she wasn't the cuddling type. And anyway, no one could save her now.

'You'll be fine,' Rosey said in confident tones, but her eyes were watchful.

'Why are you here?' Alice said. 'Are you a maid, too?'

Rosey smiled. 'You're an innocent little thing, aren't you? No, I'm here to entertain the gentlemen, that is until I make my fortune and leave for Melbourne. I can tell you now I won't be coming back.'

Alice heard her, but she wasn't really listening. She was looking at Rosey's colours. They were so bright and cheerful compared to all the others she'd seen today. Colours that made her want to smile. She wanted to tell Rosey what she was seeing but wisely said nothing. She'd already suffered enough because of her need to help and she wasn't going to risk losing Rosey.

Rosey had been watching her, too. 'How old are you?' she asked curiously.

Alice shrugged one shoulder. 'Don't you know?' she said with a grimace of sympathy.

'I'm eighteen. I was born on the same day as the patron saint of Cork, the twenty-fifth of September, so I never forget.'

'What was his name?'

'Finbarr, and I should rightly have been named after him, but I'm very glad I was not.' Rosey planted her hands on her hips and looked around the kitchen. 'What an awful place,' she said. 'The new cook will never stay if he sees this and then it's certain we'll starve to death. Come on, Alice, I'll help you to clean up.'

* * *

The wharf was as busy as an ants' nest. Rosey picked her way through boxes and bales, making for the hydraulic crane that was in the process of hauling logs up the sloping bank from the river to the sawmill. She could see Captain Potter standing with one of the managers, their heads together as they strove to make themselves heard over the noise.

Rosey had learned from one of her 'gentlemen' that the captain had just arrived back from a trip gathering red gum in the Barmah Forest, probably his last until the rains came again. Now he and the other riverboat captains would spend the drier months tied up, waiting for the river to rise. Word was Captain Potter was leaving Echuca for other parts, so this was probably Rosey's only chance to try to persuade him to take Alice away from the Red Petticoat.

As she approached the two men looked up. She knew the manager better than she'd like and his smirk made her want to slap his face, but she was trying to be amiable so she smiled sweetly. Her gaze slid to Captain Potter and she considered him.

He was a handsome man, but he had hollows under his eyes and his mouth was drawn into a tight line. She almost turned around and walked away. She knew she was probably wasting her time, but if she didn't try then who would?

It was fortuitous that at that moment the manager was called away by one of his workers and she was alone with Captain Potter.

'You left Alice with Miss Turner,' she said abruptly, all attempts at smiling done. She felt her heart bumping but Rosey had never been one to shirk a fight.

'Yes, I did, if it's any of your business. Who are you?'

'I'm Rosey, probably the only friend Alice has. Miss Turner sold her to Miss Oliver as a kitchen skivvy at the Red Petticoat. Did you know that, Captain?'

His grey eyes narrowed. She could see his hands clenching and unclenching at his sides and wondered if he'd ever hit his wife, if he was one of *those* men.

'I did know that. Miss Turner explained to me that the girl is well looked after and—'

Rosey gave a choking laugh. 'She's living and working in a brothel, Captain. Doesn't that concern you?'

'Miss Turner didn't want her to go to the orphanage and I concurred with her.'

'Miss Turner has a house, couldn't she care for Alice herself?' Rosey asked, trying to reason with him, but she knew her eyes were blazing.

'This is none of your business. Kindly leave it be.'

'Alice is a child. She didn't do anything wrong. You're punishing her, aren't you?'

The truth was there in his face as he turned away.

Rosey punched him, hard, on the shoulder. He spun to face her and just for a moment she thought he really would hit her, and she wanted him to, so that she could let herself loose on him. But he pulled in his anger, sucked it down into his cold heart.

'You don't understand,' he gritted between his teeth. 'Alice isn't like other girls. She has this . . . she's unlucky.'

Rosey gave a hoot of laughter. 'Unlucky? Well, she was unlucky when it came to you.'

'She's responsible for the death of my wife.'

'How could she be?' But Rosey could see it was a losing battle, he wasn't listening, too caught up in his own grief and self-pity. She wanted to shout into his face, *make* him listen, and yet there was such pain in his grey eyes . . .

'I can't even look at her at the moment,' he muttered in a low voice. 'I can't have her near me. I need to . . . Miss Turner has assured me the girl is safe where she is. When I'm able to I'll fetch her out of there. Just not now. Not yet.'

He was staring back at her and she hoped he might see sense. Then he barked, 'Leave me alone,' and walked away.

This time she let him.

* * *

'Next!'

Doctor Suckling's expression spoke of his disapproval, the lines either side of his mouth deep and forbidding, but Rosey noticed he didn't refuse to do the job or to take Miss Oliver's money. Every month he came to inspect the health of the girls who worked at the Red Petticoat under Miss Oliver's watchful eye. Rosey waited her turn, kicking up her skirts with her pointy-toed boots, poking out her tongue at the doctor when he gave her a frown, although she was clever enough to wait until he'd turned his back.

The air was sweltering inside and out, but that was summer in Echuca. The river was down too low for travelling on and the boats were tied up along the wharf, and in the meantime the men spent a lot of time drinking in places like the Red Petticoat.

The brothel was set one street back from the port, but those who knew it would have travelled much further to reach its smoky, alcohol-infused rooms. During the day there were plenty of customers enjoying the tavern's comforts, and at night the roaring crowd stayed well past midnight. As well as the crews from the riverboats, there were gold seekers on their way north, over the border to the goldfields in the state of New South Wales, or south to the Victorian ones at Bendigo or Ballarat. Employees from the sheep stations along the Murray dropped in to spend their hard-earned pay, but the trouble with them was, once they caught a whiff of gold fever, they usually didn't go back to work.

According to Miss Oliver, the Red Petticoat was more than a pub and better than a brothel—it was a refined mixture of both and specialised in the best of everything, from the quality and quantity of liquor it sold, to the women who carried the drinks to the tables. Rosey was one of those women, and although she made certain to smile and simper as much as the next girl, underneath her fancy gown and her face powder and rouge she wasn't happy. She'd never intended to live the life of a whore, but somehow she'd fallen into it. Now she planned to escape as soon as she had saved up enough money for the coach fare to Melbourne.

That was where a girl could really live. Bloated with gold, it was said no one slept in Melbourne. They danced and celebrated day and night, and when a miner struck it rich he married the first girl he saw and made her rich, too. Rosey told everyone she wanted to be one of those girls.

But she didn't tell them about Sean.

Well, anyway, she knew it was pointless dreaming because she simply couldn't manage the journey. Money was the thing. There were always unforeseen expenses and just when she thought she was getting ahead something would crop up—a new dress needing to be bought to bring her more customers or a rise in board for the upstairs room she shared with two others. The meals weren't free, either, and no matter how she tried Rosey couldn't seem to rein in her hearty appetite.

How could she walk out of this life and set off to Melbourne when she only had enough to last her a day when she got there? Rosey knew her nature well enough to recognise she'd soon fall back into whoring. And what Sean would do if he ever found out didn't bear thinking about.

Now to make matters worse there was Alice. How could she leave Alice here, alone?

Rosey remembered seeing the poor little mite with Captain Potter's wife one day in the street, and making fun of their lah-de-dah ways. Alice remembered it, too, and they'd giggled over it many times since, although usually Alice ended up in tears because she missed Molly Potter. And Rosey would burn inside, remembering her confrontation with the captain at the sawmill. He'd said he was going to fetch Alice out of the Red Petticoat, but it seemed to be taking an awfully long time for him to get over his grief and blame.

At the moment Alice was working her fingers to the bone in the kitchen, washing plates and scraping the muck off pots and pans. Sometimes the cook let Alice help prepare the meals, and the girl was quick to learn. It was usually so hot in there that Rosey wondered how Alice could draw breath, and she was definitely getting skinnier. There was typhoid about, too, and although she and Alice had so far avoided that, they'd both had a bout of eye-itch—conjunctivitis, according to Doctor Suckling—to go with the constant whine of mosquitoes.

Shortly after Alice arrived, there'd been a question of food poisoning, and Miss Oliver had soon discovered why the Bridge Hotel wasn't too worried about losing its Chinese cook. He spent most of his time lying in the opium palace in Chinatown, and Miss Oliver had sacked him quick smart and found an Englishwoman, the wife of one of the workers at the sawmill, to take his place. Her name was Lena and her meals were filling and wholesome and so everyone was happy.

Except Alice.

For her things got worse, because as well as helping the cook, she was still left with piles of dishes and pots to get through every day and every night. Rosey was indignant on her behalf. But anything was better than the orphanage, and that's where Alice would have ended up because no one had come to claim the little mite. Not one person in the whole country was missing her enough to come looking for her.

Made her furious, it did. Rosey knew she had a strong sense of justice and she made sure to help Alice with her chores, or sneak down to the cupboard where Alice had her bed and bring her a treat. Alice liked to read the newspapers along with any other reading matter left by the guests, and the poor little soul saved them under her pillow for later. Once one of Miss Oliver's books went missing and she claimed Alice had taken it. She searched the cupboard that was Alice's room, but it wasn't there.

'I know you took it,' the sour-faced creature had declared.

Rosey still boiled inside when she remembered it. But Alice had stood up straight and taken the reprimand. Later on, when Rosey crept in to see her between customers, she'd said in her solemn way, 'I did take it, Rosey. I couldn't help it. You see, I'm educating myself.'

How could such a young girl be so grown up? Sometimes Rosey thought her blue eyes looked quite ancient. There were rumours about what had happened with Bluey on the *Ariadne*, and there were times when the others looked twice at Alice. But even if she was bad luck Rosey didn't care. Alice was like the little sister she'd left behind in Cork, and she loved her just as much.

'I hope one day you'll remember who you are and where you come from,' she'd said, pinning Alice's fine brown hair back from her face. Alice said nothing to that, but then she never did; she was probably afraid to express such a wish. Three months went past and then it was March and no one came, and it seemed more and more as if Alice's future was to be here in the Red Petticoat.

That troubled Rosey. She could see herself in the child, could see Alice ending up in her own unhappy position just because there was no one with either the willpower or the determination to change things.

'Next!'

Doctor Suckling was ready for another girl. The doctor had his son with him; he usually did. Rosey wondered what the boy thought of kicking his heels in a place like this, although at least he was downstairs in the kitchen, with Alice. What sort of mother would allow her young son to come here? But from what Rosey had heard, the genteel Mrs Suckling was a drunk. A very genteel drunk.

Perhaps that was the reason the good doctor had a permanently pinched and miserable expression on his face.

* * *

Alice had been ignoring the doctor's boy, pretending he wasn't sitting at the scrubbed table and watching her through the scullery door. Lena always spoilt him with her biscuits and cakes, but she wasn't here just now so he had nothing to do but bother Alice.

His name was Gilbert Suckling. Molly had thought it was Vincent, but then, Alice recalled with a wistful smile, Molly was always muddling things up.

'Why aren't you in the orphanage?' Gilbert asked, banging the heels of his boots against the leg of his chair. 'My father says that's the place for you, not here with a lot of nasty whores.'

Alice ignored him. She didn't like the way he belittled her friends. She didn't like the way he stared at her so fiercely.

'You killed Captain Potter's mate. On the timber barge. And you killed Molly Potter, too. You should be locked up.'

Alice felt a tremor growing inside her. She swallowed and kept scrubbing. Ignore him, she told herself, what he said and thought weren't important. The trouble was Alice was fairly sure it was what everyone else was thinking when they looked at her, only unlike Gilbert they didn't say it aloud.

'You're bad luck. That was why Captain Potter threw you out. That's what my father says. Pity he didn't throw you in the river in a sack.'

It was too much. With a crash Alice dropped the pot she'd been scrubbing and marched out of the scullery, the dripping dishrag dangling from her hand. She raised her arm and water sprayed about her and splattered the boy's clothing. He tried to jump backwards and he fell to the floor, still in his chair. She stood over him, her thin chest heaving, and he stared up at her with wide hazel eyes, each of his freckles standing out separately on his pale face.

He was afraid of her.

Alice recognised it, shocked, but instead of being triumphant she felt ill. Her lip trembled and a tear trickled down her cheek. She didn't want him to see her weakness, so she turned and hurried back to the scullery.

It wasn't fair, it wasn't fair. She hadn't done anything wrong. She'd just tried to help and now they blamed her. Why did she see the colours? She'd never asked for this curse. She'd never wanted it. She didn't want it now.

After a moment she felt Gilbert standing behind her. He came closer, edging into the space beside the sink, and peered into her face.

'You're crying,' he said in surprise.

'No I'm not.'

'Yes you are. I didn't mean to make you cry.'

Alice flicked a sideways glance at him. 'Yes you did.'

He considered that, then nodded with a wry smile. 'Maybe I did. I'm sorry. You're just so . . . strong. As if nothing bothers you.'

Alice stared at him in amazement. 'Nothing bothers me!' she burst out. 'Is that why you've been so nasty to me?'

He shrugged. 'Sometimes, at home I wish I was here, like you, with no father and no mother.'

Gilbert was just as unhappy and lonely as she was. Unexpectedly, she felt sorry for him. 'At least you have a home,' she muttered.

He bowed his head, ashamed.

Alice glanced at him again and then handed him the dishcloth. 'If you're sorry you can help,' she said. 'You made me cry and now I'm behind. Lena will tell me off.'

He thought about that, and she waited for him to refuse, but to her surprise he took the cloth and began to mop ineffectually at some plates. 'Do you go to school?' he said. 'I'm going to school in Melbourne soon. Boarding school. The best school in Victoria, my father says.'

Alice only partially listened to him. He went on about becoming a doctor like his father and the grand future he expected to have one day. Her dislike of him faded. He really was lonely and bored and that was why he was so horrid to her. He was just a boy, not much older than she was.

'Rosey says I should go to school,' she said when he'd wound down to silence.

'Who's Rosey?'

'My friend,' Alice said proudly. She saw the poor job he'd made of his plates and with a sigh took them off him to do them herself. Lena would inspect her work and if it was wanting then she'd tell Miss Oliver, who would reduce Alice's meagre wage. Life was very different here from the one she had led as Molly's little pet, but it was better not to think too hard about that when Alice knew there was nothing she could do about it.

'Rosey's going to find gold and then she'll be rich,' she went on, talking quickly to hold back a fresh wave of sadness. 'We're off to the goldfields soon.'

Gilbert looked inclined to sneer but remembered himself in time. 'My father tried to find gold once. He got sick instead. He makes more money being a doctor than a digger.'

'Maybe he didn't dig in the right places.'

Gilbert considered. 'Maybe he didn't.'

'When Rosey and I are rich we'll need a doctor. The best doctor in Melbourne.'

'Oh?'

'You!' Alice reminded him impatiently.

Gilbert went pink. Alice wondered if all his talk had been nothing more than that. Or wishful thinking. Everyone had their dreams, she thought, and sometimes it was the only thing that kept him or her from giving up.

Alice had made an unexpected friend. Today had been a good day after all.

* * *

The weather stayed hot, got hotter, then one particular day, with the sun making the sky too painfully blue to look at, Rosey was in the yellow salon, sitting with a gentleman from up river who'd come into town to negotiate selling his wool. He wasn't really a gentleman, but Miss Oliver insisted the girls call them all 'gentlemen'.

This gentleman had bought her several drinks, not knowing Rosey was being served water to keep her sober and to save the tavern money. The gentleman was tipsy and starting to touch her in places that suggested he was ready and willing to go upstairs to one of the bedrooms. She just wished he'd get on with it.

That was when she saw Alice standing in the doorway.

Rosey jumped up, knowing how angry Miss Oliver would be with the girl for wandering about, but at the same time she was worried by the expression on Alice's face. The girl was terrified, her blue eyes so big you could see the whites all around them.

'The man in the coat,' she said in a breathless voice, as soon as Rosey had pulled her away, out of sight. 'I saw him. Outside.'

'What man in the coat?' Rosey repeated, with a glance over her shoulder, because the fear in Alice's face was catching. 'It's too hot for a coat, isn't it?'

'I saw him and he saw me.' And she shuddered from deep inside her little being. Rosey thought she was going to be sick and hurriedly found a corner without the rich rugs Miss Oliver so prized, but Alice just retched and sagged down onto the bare boards.

'Is he your father, Alice?' Rosey tried, even knowing this was all wrong. There was no prospect of a happy reunion in the child's eyes.

Alice's gaze slid to the side and she pressed herself against the wall, as if she wanted to squeeze behind the wallpaper. 'He tried to kill me once,' she whispered. 'I thought he'd believe I was dead already, but he must have found out I'm alive. He must have found out where I live.'

Making up her mind, Rosey grasped hold of Alice's hand and pulled her to her feet. 'Come on,' she said with grim intent. 'You're going to show me this man in the coat and then I'm going to give him a piece of my mind.'

Alice fought and struggled, but Rosey was filled with a reckless and righteous anger, and she dragged the young girl down the hallway from the salon, through the bar which was full of amused and staring patrons, and out into the hot sun.

The street was busy despite the relentless heat. There were some wagons and carts, emptied of their produce, the horses patiently waiting in their harnesses, their tails flicking at the flies, while their owners spent the proceeds of their sales at the tavern. Someone was riding slowly by, hat pulled down low, and there was a man smoking a pipe and eyeing Rosey up and down with interest.

But no man in a coat.

'Where is he, then?' she said impatiently. It was hot and steamy out here, the weather building up to a storm. 'Point him out to me.'

Alice took one brief look at the street and then dropped her head again, as if she was trying to burrow into her own chest. 'He's gone,' she breathed. 'You scared him away.'

Rosey hoped it was true but suspected the man in the coat had only ever been in Alice's head. Although if he was real, she didn't particularly want to meet the man who had put Alice in a barrel and thrown her into the river to drown.

'Come on,' she said with rough gentleness, the nearest she could ever come to tenderness. 'Let's get back inside before someone comes lookin' for us.'

But it was too late.

Miss Oliver was standing behind them, her pinched face even more pinched, her eyes like ice. She was petite and plain, and she looked and spoke like a governess, but there was something about her that frightened the life out of Rosey, and, feeling Alice's hand tighten its grip on hers, she knew she wasn't alone in that.

'What are you doing out there?' said Miss Oliver, her quiet voice venomous. 'Who said you were to go out into the street like a common trollop?'

Rosey wanted to shout at her, to tell her what she really thought, but she couldn't. She needed to save more money. 'The child was feeling poorly and I thought some fresh air—' She rushed through the words, but Miss Oliver still managed to cut into them, her tongue like a knife.

'The child is not yours. If she's feeling unwell then she should come to me.'

That was so unlikely to happen that Rosey stared at her, mouth agape, until she remembered to close it.

'You've left your gentleman alone in the salon,' Miss Oliver said. 'He's complaining. Go back to him. Now.'

Rebellion was on the tip of Rosey's tongue, but she bit it back, nodded, gave Alice one heartfelt look, and left them together. She looked back when she reached the door into the bar, but she couldn't see more than their silhouettes, dark against the bright glare.

'I'm not leaving without her,' she muttered to herself, striding in a most unladylike manner towards the salon. 'I'm not going without Alice.' It felt good to be unladylike—something Miss Oliver was always ramming down their throats.

The gentleman was annoyed with her, but Rosey soon brought him around. Upstairs, two minutes of huffing and puffing on top of her and he was done. She made him pay her extra and slipped the coins into the pouch sown on the inside of her petticoat. There was enough money in there to give a pleasant jingle if she cared to shake it.

All the slights and taunts, all the 'gentlemen' who made her skin crawl, all the nights where she'd lain awake and wondered what in God's name she was doing here and why she still missed Sean, once the love of her life. Oh, but it would all be worth it when Rosey walked out of the door. And one thing was certain, she was never coming back.

* * *

Alice didn't sleep. She lay staring at the darkness, rigid with terror as she waited for the man in the coat. He was coming, she was certain of it. When she'd seen him outside the tavern he'd seen her, in fact he'd been waiting for her. She hadn't told Rosey—she hadn't had the time or the ability in that moment before Miss Oliver found them—but there'd been a message brought to her by Lena.

'Someone out the front there waiting to see you,' she'd said, with a disinterested glance. 'Better be quick, don't let Miss Oliver see you.'

'Someone? Is it Captain Potter?'

'I don't know. Just be quick, all right?'

She'd immediately thought of Captain Potter with his handsome face and grey eyes. She'd been waiting for him for so long. No matter what he thought of her, she still liked him. It didn't occur to her to wonder why he was back in Echuca when everyone knew he'd gone off somewhere, or to ask herself why he wouldn't just come inside to see her.

Sometimes her 'sight' allowed her to see the captain. She had visions of him alone, his colours dark, far away from his home on the river. She saw him walking on unfamiliar streets, his hands in his pockets, fighting his overwhelming anger and grief. She smelled the sour beer as he lifted it to his lips.

Gratefully, Alice left behind her kitchen chores and slipped out into the tavern. She was small and insignificant and didn't have any trouble making her way around the customers. She'd grown good at fading into the scenery where it was necessary. Even Miss Oliver, deep in conversation with the barman, didn't see her go by. When she reached the door she stepped out, blinking in the light like a possum woken from its hollow tree. Even for one used to the heat in the kitchen, the air was so hot she felt like a beef steak on a griddle.

At first she didn't see anyone she recognised. People were moving about, intent on doing their daily tasks. Across the road a general store had taken delivery of a cart full of fruit and vegetables from the Chinese market garden, and customers were gathering around, eager to sample anything fresh. A woman in a green bonnet with a feather in it hurried past the door of the Red Petticoat, purposely not looking in case she got dirty from being so close.

That made Alice smile, remembering Molly, but then the smile froze like frost on her lips because she saw *him*.

He was standing on the other side of the road, half hidden by the grocer's cart, and he was so still. Tall and thin in his black coat, he stood straight-backed, his hair slicked back beneath his top hat, his face white and hollow in the cheeks and she could see his lips moving, while his eyes . . . they were fixed on hers.

Her head felt as if it was bursting with horrible things, half memories of running and being caught and the sound of her voice screaming, although in truth she could not make a sound. And he was remembering, too, she knew it. His colours were angry and inky, swirling like an octopus's tentacles. He was thinking of her dead and drowned in the river. There was something about him that was pulling at her, drawing her like an ebbing tide, so strong that Alice couldn't seem to take her eyes off him, couldn't move, although she knew she should, she told herself that she must.

He had come for her and in a moment he would lope across the road and spring upon her.

With a sobbing gasp she'd flung herself around and back into the tavern. All she wanted to do was hide, make herself very small and disappear from the world. But as she ran towards her cupboard she heard Rosey's voice. Rosey was her friend and she knew she would help. With all her heart she wanted Rosey to hold her tight and never let her go.

But Rosey hadn't held her, she'd just got angry. Alice had been forced to go with her and look again for the man in the coat. He was gone, but she knew he'd be back. Oh yes, now he knew where she was he would be back to get her. She sensed the awful need in him to have her in his hands. And this time there would be no Captain Potter to save her because Captain Potter had gone away and no one knew where.

'I took you on out of a sense of charity,' Miss Oliver had said when she'd caught her and Rosey outside. 'You know you're not to leave the kitchen and move among the customers. I've told you this before. Do you want me to send you away? Back to Mrs Turner perhaps, I'm sure she'd be pleased to have you knocking on her door.'

Miss Oliver had laughed, a snuffling sound that wasn't a real laugh at all. She took out her posh lady's handkerchief, as Rosey called it, and dabbed at her face.

'Please no, miss,' Alice had said, dully, knowing it was expected she should grovel, but not having the heart for it.

'Children who are disobedient are more trouble than they're worth, Alice. You're a hard worker, I grant you, but you disturb the other staff. They don't like the way you look at them. They tell me you have the evil eye.'

The story about Bluey was common knowledge, and once or twice, forgetting herself, Alice had used her sight to try to help the other staff. Alice would hear them whispering about her behind her back, but at least they never spoke the rumours to her face. So far they were too afraid of her to do that, but she expected that soon someone would become brave. They'd begin to tease her and say hurtful words to her, and then her life at the Red Petticoat wouldn't be worth living.

'I see things, that's all,' she'd said, her voice shaking with distress. 'Rosey calls it the "sight". It means I *know* things. But I don't say anything. I know better than to say anything, miss.'

Miss Oliver had looked taken aback. She'd frowned and her mouth had twitched, but this time she wasn't laughing. '*See* things? What on earth do you *see*?'

Alice had wondered if Miss Oliver really wanted to know, but that feeling of pressure was building in her head and with it, rising up inside her throat, was the terrible urge to speak.

And once she'd started she couldn't stop.

When her voice did finally trickle to a close a dreadful silence fell and she knew Miss Oliver would never forgive her. The woman's face was a yellowy colour, like the congealed mutton fat Alice scraped off the pans, and she was breathing heavily, her hand pressed so hard to her stomach that it was white about the knuckles.

'You'll be sorry, my God you'll be sorry . . .'

'I didn't mean—'

'Go,' she'd hissed. 'Get out. Go!'

Alice had run. She'd crawled into her bed and closed the cupboard door so that not even a crack of light found its way inside, and that's where she'd been ever since.

Lying in the darkness and waiting.

It was airless in here, and every now and then Alice had to take a deep breath, to ease the sensation of suffocation. Outside a storm was building over the river. Something was about to happen, something was about to happen, something . . .

When the door creaked open she was certain it was the man in the coat, and she was ready for him. She slipped her hand under her pillow and felt the book she'd taken from Miss Oliver, and then the wooden handle of the peeling knife. It wasn't much, but it was sharp and perhaps if he saw it he would go away and leave her alone.

'Alice? What are you doing in here? Oh, you poor little thing!'

Rosey, it was Rosey, and she was holding her tight, just as she'd longed for her to do. Alice wrapped her arms about her friend and hung on. But soon Rosey was back to her normal self, asking questions, demanding answers, and slowly, reluctantly, Alice told her what had happened with Miss Oliver.

For a long time after that Rosey was quiet, which was unusual, because Rosey was never quiet. Then, when she spoke, it was in such a serious voice Alice was frightened she'd become like Captain Potter and no longer wanted to be her friend. She looked up at Rosey, trying to read the emotions behind her green eyes. Rosey was so pretty, so kind, surely she would not abandon Alice like the others?

'Are you listening to me, Alice?' she was saying. 'We're leaving the Red Petticoat and Miss Oliver and never ever coming back.'

'Can we go now?'

'Not yet but soon.'

'Can we go and look for gold?'

Rosey smiled. 'Why not?'

'But . . .' Alice was confused. 'What I said to Miss Oliver . . .' Usually, people were afraid of her when she spoke of impending death. They turned their backs on her and made the sign of the evil eye.

'Yes, I heard,' Rosey said, narrowing her eyes as she always did when she was angry.

'Do you hate me now? Captain Potter hates me.'

'Well, I'm not Captain Potter, am I? Besides, I had a cousin had the sight. Not quite like you, but . . . I had no reason to hate her, either.'

Alice thought about that. 'I did see it,' she assured her friend. 'Death. Dark colours around her middle. They're growing. It's been there ever since I came. I see it all the time. There're times it's been so *hard* not to say anything.'

'I'm sure it has, Alice.' Rosey gave her a penetrating look. 'How long do you think she's got, then? Before she's dead?'

'Not long. It's strange because just now there was a darkness all around her head. That's new. And there's blood. I think,' she hesitated but it had to be told. 'I think my sight is getting stronger, Rosey. I know things now without the colours. I just *know*. But then there're things I should know that I don't, no matter how hard I try. It doesn't make sense. When I saw him, the man in the dark coat, I wanted to go to him. I felt like I needed to be with him. Even though another part of me was remembering what he'd done.'

Rosey nodded, but she wasn't really listening. When she spoke again her voice was pragmatic. 'I should be sorry for her, but I can't pretend something I don't feel. She's sacked the barman, did you know? Told him that after tonight he's to leave. Accused him of all sorts of things. I wouldn't be surprised if we're next. So save up your pennies, Alice. We'll need every one of them.'

She reached down and gave Alice another hug. Outside thunder rumbled; the storm had arrived. When Rosey was gone Alice lay back and wondered at her good luck. She had a friend who wasn't going to abandon her, who was going gold hunting with her, and they would have so many adventures.

As long as the man in the long dark coat didn't catch her first.

CHAPTER NINE

Annie's Story

After I got back from Echuca, I went to pick up Courtney from Ben's house and stayed for a quick meal from a new takeaway franchise. Ben was doing advertisements for them and thought that sampling their product would help inspire him. I wanted to protest, to point out how much fat and salt were in each serving, and how little nutrition, but I didn't feel I could take the moral high ground when Courtney had had such a wonderful time. Despite her drooping eyelids, she chatted all the way home, clutching a large, stuffed gorilla in her arms.

'His name is Tarzan,' she said sleepily.

When we got home there was a red light flashing on my answering machine and I played the message while hurriedly undressing my exhausted daughter and putting her into her pyjamas.

Maren was calling back about Gervais Whistler.

'Sorry, I lost my phone and couldn't find your mobile number,' she said, with her distinctive Danish accent. 'You know me. I have a kangaroo loose in my top paddock.' She laughed, as she always did at the old saying. I had taught it to her as part of a crash course in

Australian idiomatic expressions one night in a Lygon Street cafe, shortly after Maren arrived in Melbourne, and it was still an ongoing joke between us.

'Now you wanted to know about our friend, Mr Whistler. Gervais was a bit of a character, a larger-than-life sort. We don't hear much about him these days, but I think there was a book written a couple of years ago. It was all boxed up and ready to go out to the shops and then somebody pulled the pin on it. Bought up all the rights. It never appeared on the shelves. I doubt it exists anymore, but I'll hunt around. Talk to you on Monday.'

Once Courtney was in bed I had a shower, and, as I often did once I was standing under the running water, a good think.

I'd brought home a list of riverboat captains from the Echuca Historical Society, two of whom had captained the *Ariadne*. It was up to me to search out marriage and death records from the relevant government department if I wanted to find the connection with Molly. There were also other bits and pieces the museum curator had thought I might find interesting, but by the time I'd had a bite to eat after the cruise and found my way to the museum, it had only been an hour until closing. Still, I was pleased with the result and the curator had promised to check out other possibilities as they occurred to her and email me.

It felt like a good day's work.

I closed my eyes and lifted my face to the sting of the hot water. I'd met a very attractive man called Max, a man I'd never have met if it wasn't for the *Trompe L'oeil*. Not that I expected to meet him again, and if I did then I probably wouldn't like him nearly as much.

Would I have been quite as struck with a refined Max Taylor in a suit in the city as I was with the rugged captain at the wheel of a paddle-steamer? Probably not. But the memory of his smile still gave me a little frisson of uncomplicated desire, something I hadn't felt in a long time.

With a sigh I turned off the water.

Tomorrow was Sunday but on Monday I would take a look at the recorded lives of the two riverboat captains I'd found and get back in touch with Maren, as well as continuing my work on the painting. It felt like I had plenty to do and the excitement was like a low electric current, buzzing through me.

I always felt some sort of vibe when I started a big job, an important job, but this was different. More intense. And there was a sense of anxiety, too, the worry that Sebastian Rawlings might decide to put a stop to it. Oh I'd fight, but I didn't want to waste time and energy on fighting when I could be working on the *Trompe L'oeil.*

Nephetiti was waiting for me when I came out of the bathroom, but instead of winding around my ankles as I would have expected after another day home alone, the cat ran to the curtained side window and stared up intently.

It was a little strange, but I followed her over and bent to pat her. Nephetiti stretched up her paws towards the sill, letting out one of her more siren-like meows. I drew back the curtain and looked out.

My heart gave an incredible jump.

He was there!

Not by the fence this time but closer to the house, in the middle of the yard, looking up. White-faced, his black clothes hanging on his spare frame, his hands by his sides as he gazed towards me with a fixed intensity that struck me with ice-cold fear.

I stumbled back—it was as if the man's stare was able to reach me through the glass—and tripped on Nephetiti. The cat let out an angry screech of protest and shot out of the room. I stood leaning against a chair, heart thumping. It was a while before I felt able to look again, but when I did the yard was empty.

I knew I should go down and investigate. Or better still call the police. But even as I imagined the conversation—'Hello, there's a man in my yard. No, he's gone now. I think he's a ghost . . .'—I knew I wouldn't. Because this wasn't the sort of intruder the police were equipped to deal with. I tried to reason it out. He'd been standing in the middle of the yard with no shelter other than overgrown grass and weeds. Even if he'd thrown himself down and slid away on his belly, like a snake, I would have seen where he'd gone.

He couldn't have hidden, there was nowhere to hide. He couldn't have vaulted the fence, there was no time.

He was a man who couldn't have vanished like that . . . and yet he did. With a shiver I wondered what I was going to do about him.

Feeling unsettled, it took me a long time to get ready for bed, and only then did I remember to switch on my computer and check my emails. They were all work related—other jobs I'd completed or was looking at—apart from one.

Annie, I have your photos of Molly and crew up on my wall and I'm looking at them right now. Will talk to an old-timer tomorrow and see what he has to say. Get back to you on it. Max

I knew my smile was wistful.

'If only you were here, Max,' I murmured. Despite all the female equality in the world there was nothing like a big strong man to send outside into the dark to investigate. Or maybe Max would just give me a masculine look and tell me I was imagining things. Well, that was okay, too, wasn't it? I wanted to believe I was imagining things.

* * *

'You've been busy.'

I looked up with a smile at the sound of my father's voice. He'd come into the room and was now standing behind me as I scraped off a tiny section of the damaged paint. It would need to be looked at under a microscope and then tested so that we knew what we were dealing with.

I'd been working on the varnish, too, carefully removing the discoloured layer with a cotton wad and solvent. There were different levels of thought when it came to the removal of varnish, whether a painting should be 'modernised' by removing the old varnish— some well-known works were changed almost beyond recognition by such removal—and whether or not the varnish was in fact in keeping with the original artist's vision of the work. In other words, the artist may have preferred a dark look. But in this case I thought it could only do good. The painting would become so much clearer and brighter, the detail more discernible. Surely the artist, whoever he was, would want his work to be seen without the cloudy dullness of time?

'Grandpa!' Courtney held up her gorilla for his approval before returning to her own work of art.

I had set her up with a canvas, a brush and paints, and my daughter was busily working on a masterpiece. She seemed perfectly happy, so while I was feeling the usual guilt for bringing her to work on a Sunday I wasn't feeling *too* guilty.

'Will you conserve it? Will you restore it? Or will you reconstruct it?' my father went on.

It was a good question. If I conserved I would be stabilising any areas that were damaged and preserving the piece in its existing state. I liked to think of conservation as a holding pattern, not going anywhere for now, but perhaps, in a few more years, further work might need to be done. If I restored I would be repairing the painting by retouching any damaged areas or filling in any parts that were missing. I'd use paints as close to the original colours as possible, but my paint would be watercolour or synthetic, something that could be easily removed in the future if that became necessary, and any changes made to the original must be clearly shown. Finally, reconstruction, which wasn't something we did very often, was the restoration of a piece by freely mixing the old and the new without distinction.

'There's quite a bit of damage, particularly to the left side. Water, by the look of it. I don't know yet what I'll do. I need to find a contemporary reproduction of it, a photograph, or at the very least a contemporary account of what it looked like, and then . . . then I'd like to see it all shining and new. But History Victoria may not want that.'

'You should tell them what *you* want, Annie. Don't let them bully you.'

We stood side by side, enjoying the imperfect beauty of the painting.

'Clive visited me. He brought Sebastian Rawlins,' I said with distaste. 'He's worried about someone or other's reputation. Skeleton-in-the-cupboard stuff.'

Reuben wouldn't want to know the details, not unless he had to. Politics was the enemy of art, in his opinion.

'It may come to nothing, Annie. Forget about Rawlins. Just keep doing what you're good at.'

'I hate that they can stop something like this being conserved or restored and shown in public, just because one person is afraid the media will find out his grandfather fiddled the books.'

'Annie, it's a distraction,' he said, a sharp warning.

'But I'm worried, Papa. This means so much to me. I feel as if I was meant to restore it, to help tell the world these two girls' story. That might sound ridiculous, but—'

'Not ridiculous. You sound like your mother.' He sighed. 'Geneva was passionate. Headstrong. She never stopped to consider whether she might be making trouble for herself or others. Or whether this was a good thing. She set her sights on the prize and ploughed ahead.'

'A bull in a china shop, you mean,' I said, with a smile. 'I wish I'd known her.'

He took my hand in his and squeezed it. 'So do I. One thing I do know, Annie, she wouldn't have been happy to see the two of us here on a Sunday. She would say we should be out in the sunshine living life.'

For a moment I thought about mentioning the man with the white face in the backyard, but I didn't want to worry my father with something so silly. An imaginary man! What was that old nursery rhyme? *As I was going up the stair I met a man who wasn't there . . .*

Anyway, Papa was busy admiring Courtney's painting.

I promised myself that after this job was finished I would take up a hobby or a sport and Courtney and I would take off to the beach for a holiday. I'd get a dog . . . no, Nephetiti would hate that. I sighed, my gaze sweeping over the painting once more. By this time I thought I knew every inch of it, but I was always discovering something new.

Like now.

There was a dog. Behind the girls, half hidden by their skirts—I'd thought it was a fold of skirt, but with the removal of the old varnish I could see the animal. And when I looked more closely I could see there was a strap or lead in the younger girl's hand. The animal lay on the ground, a brown-and-black-and-white patchwork dog with strange floppy ears.

Having already been tricked once by the artist, this time I slipped on my magnifying headpiece, switched on the light and took a closer look.

'Mummy's a miner! Look!'

'Mummy isn't a miner, she's looking at the painting in close-up. I think this doggy has a name.'

Courtney came over to look. 'What's his name?' she whispered.

There *was* a word and it was curled around the dog's throat like a collar. It took me so long to work it out, with Courtney jiggling impatiently at my side, that I almost gave up.

'Hope!' I said, turning to grin at my daughter.

The dog's name was Hope.

* * *

Late Sunday night Maren rang to say she had to go away. Her grandfather was very ill, and she wouldn't be able to talk to me on Monday after all. I assumed Maren's grandfather was in Denmark and that she'd have to fly over there. Poor Maren.

Of course I was disappointed for myself—I was keen to learn all I could about Gervais—but I had plenty of other things to do.

On Monday I dropped off Courtney and went into work. Greta was in a chatty mood. When I explained about the two riverboat captains, she suggested we go online to check out the Victorian Birth, Deaths and Marriages.

'My aunty is big on genealogy. I know it all. My great-great-grandfather had three wives. We have so many relatives. You wouldn't believe.'

As she chattered away, she brought up the site and began clicking in the names and dates, looking for marriages.

'Maybe they weren't married in Victoria,' I said anxiously, 'or Molly wasn't married to one of them. This is a long shot, isn't it?'

'Ah, look. The first riverboat captain was Ebenezer Phillips and he married a Molly Michaels. Ta-dah!'

The familiar excitement fizzed through me, but I tamped it down, telling myself it might be a coincidence. Another Molly, nothing to do with *my* Molly. Next we checked the deaths and found Ebenezer had died a year after the marriage.

No matter how I tried to be pragmatic I couldn't help but ask myself whether Ebenezer was the riverboat captain with the grey eyes.

Greta tapped in the name of the other man, Arnold Potter. He married, too, but some years later, and he married . . .

'Molly Phillips nee Michaels.' Greta gave me a grin. 'Now that's confusing. Both of them were married to Molly and either of them could be the captain of the *Ariadne* in the *Trompe L'oeil*. Now what?'

'I don't know,' I said. 'At least we've found Molly and there's only one of her.'

'When you're on to a good thing stick to it,' Greta joked.

'Maybe it was a package deal; Molly came with the boat. Hadn't we better take a look for Molly's death?'

Greta grimaced. 'I feel like we know her.' She made the search and found it sooner than we'd expected, only five years after her second marriage to Arnold Potter. A further search for Arnold Potter's death came up without a result.

I ordered and paid for copies of the relevant certificates while Greta busied herself with her real job. I was about to go upstairs when on impulse I typed Max's email address into the computer, and, before I gave myself time to reconsider, sent him a brief rundown of the new information.

CHAPTER TEN

The Girl's Story

Outside the storm was rumbling around, keeping Alice from sleep. It was very late. So late that she'd thought at first she must be dreaming. Then she realised that she wasn't.

There were footsteps outside her cupboard. She could hear the creak of the floorboards, coming closer. She felt cold, as cold as the ice sometimes delivered in big blocks to the kitchen. She felt a sense of something not right.

As she stared into the darkness at her door she saw the knob begin to turn, and the door begin to open. Her heart was bumping against her ribs, the blood rushing in her ears, and if she could have she would have screamed. But her throat seemed to have closed over and all she could do was watch helplessly as the door opened fully and *he* stood there.

The man in the dark coat.

The light from further up the corridor threw his shadow diagonally across the doorway, and she found her own eyes drawn upwards to his despite her terror. He was looking down at her and she had that strange longing to go to him, as if some part of her was drawn to him despite what her brain told her he would do to her.

'The river . . .' she said.

He put a finger to his lips, a warning for her to keep quiet.

'No.' Alice didn't know if her voice was really as loud as she thought it or just in her head. 'No, I won't come with you.'

He reached out a hand as if to touch her and she shrank back with a whimper. Then she saw he was holding one of his peppermint sweets in his palm. For some reason that was worse than if he'd grabbed her and dragged her from her bed. That he imagined he could bribe her with a sweet into going with him to her death.

'You tried to drown me. You put me in the river and tried to drown me.'

His head tilted, listening, and for a moment she was confused, waiting for him to answer, and then she understood that he wasn't listening to her but to voices from the bar. Because she could hear them, too, and her overwhelming emotion was relief, because now she could call for help, she could be saved.

'A gift?' Miss Oliver's voice spoke with venom. 'I gave you no gifts. You stole from me!'

And in reply a low mumble. A man's voice.

The man in the coat turned his head towards the sound, took a step back, and Alice realised this was her chance. She reached out and slammed her door and hung on to the knob to keep it closed.

'Help!' she cried, but her voice was thin and breathless. She could feel the knob turning beneath her fingers, but she pulled all her weight against it, refusing to allow him in. 'Go away,' she whispered. 'Go away and leave me alone.'

'What do you think you're doing?' It was Miss Oliver drifting through the building, and now her voice was high and shrill. 'I never gave you permission to—'

Abruptly, the door knob stilled. Alice sensed him moving away, the heavy inky cloud that always came with him was receding.

She gave a little sob. She didn't want to let go but she knew she must, she knew she had to find Rosey.

There was a faint cry and then a thud, as if someone had fallen.

It was enough to spur Alice into action. She had gone to bed in her clothes because she hadn't dared to undress and now she jumped up and flung open the door. No time for caution, no time for hesitation. He might be waiting for her, he might be about to pounce, but she couldn't think of that. A lamp shone faintly from the end of the corridor but it was empty. From the bar she heard a shuffling noise. A footstep. And then a shadow.

It was enough to send Alice bolting towards the stairs.

Only once she'd started up them she remembered there was no other way back down again. She'd be trapped. But what else could she do? Rosey was on this floor and she couldn't go without Rosey.

She knew which room belonged to her friend and opened the door without knocking. Rosey shared with two other girls and there were three bodies on the bed. One of them lifted up her head in surprise, her sweaty hair like rats' tails. 'It's your brat,' she moaned, elbowing the lump huddled beside her. 'Get her out of here so I can get me sleep.'

'Rosey?' Alice whispered, as loud as she dared. Behind her she could see a portion of the staircase and it was still empty, but she knew that soon he would find her. '*Please*, Rosey!'

Rosey turned her head and Alice saw her eye through the tangle of curly hair. 'Alice? What is it?'

Alice shuffled anxiously from foot to foot, wanting to go. *Now.* Again she glanced behind her. Was there a shadow moving on the stairs? Was there someone coming?

'He's here,' she said in a thin voice, her throat tight, her heart like a lump inside it. 'He's come for me.'

Rosey sat up despite the other two complaining. She still had rouge on her cheeks and there were shadows under her eyes, but at least she was awake. 'You're having a nightmare,' she said, although there was a question in her voice.

Alice shook her head. 'No, I'm not. He's here. I saw him. I heard Miss Oliver and then . . . then . . . I think he hurt her.'

For one horrid moment she thought Rosey would insist on going down to see. At the mention of Miss Oliver's name the other two girls had sat up, grumbling and demanding to know what was happening. Rosey climbed over the girl nearest to the door and began to get dressed, ignoring their continuing complaints and questions.

'Close the door, Alice,' she said quietly, 'and go hide behind that chair, the one with the petticoat and stays on it. That's it. No one can see you now.'

It felt safe here in this space behind the chair, and she breathed in the stale perfume and tried to pretend she was invisible. Tried very hard to pretend none of this was happening. But it was no use. This was real, this wasn't a nightmare, and if she was to survive she had to escape.

'They'll get me.' Alice's whisper drifted out from behind the folds of cheap cloth and ribbon and lace. '*He*'ll get me. He'll come up the stairs and find me and take me back and—'

'No, by then we'll be gone.'

Alice listened to the sounds of Rosey dressing and moving about collecting her belongings. She heard the jingle of coins, and then a murmured conversation between the three women. It really was cosy behind the petticoat. Alice found herself oddly sleepy despite her terror, or perhaps because of it. Her head was beginning to nod when abruptly the chair was pulled away.

Alice jumped, but it was only Rosey, staring down at her.

Her friend appeared calm yet Alice knew she wasn't. Her eyes were wild, just as they'd been the time one of the gentlemen had taken out his pistol and shot at the ceiling, bringing down some plaster and almost killing a couple in the bed above. Rosey had been frightened then and Rosey was rarely frightened; however, you wouldn't have known it unless you looked right into her eyes. Now Alice wondered who Rosey was more frightened of, the man in the coat or Miss Oliver, or the fact that they were running off into the unknown.

'Come on,' she said, before Alice could ask her. 'We'll have to climb out of the window. Don't look down and don't fall.'

The window gave onto a narrow ledge that could be negotiated by clinging to adjoining window frames until you eventually reached the sloping roof of the verandah. After that it wasn't very far down to the street below. The rain made everything wet and slippery, but Alice clung on and followed instructions and safely reached the ground.

Rosey jumped down behind her and spent a moment or two looking all around, in case there was anyone there who shouldn't be. Then she firmly took Alice's hand in her own and quickly began to walk. As their steps took them further away from the Red Petticoat, Alice's heart grew lighter and the fear that had gripped her began to fade.

She was safe. Everything was going to be all right.

Until now Rosey had been silent, deep in her own thoughts. 'I didn't have time to tell you, but one of the girls saw a note from Miss Oliver. She was sending you to the orphanage, Alice. We would've had to leave anyway.'

Alice nodded soberly.

'Don't you want to know where we're going?' Rosey said.

Alice grinned up at her, face shiny from the rain. 'I know where we're going. We're going to find gold.'

Rosey smiled, too, and then she laughed. 'That's right, so we are. We're going to find gold and then we'll be rich, Alice! And no one will ever be able to hurt you again.'

'Ever again,' Alice repeated.

But there was a heaviness inside her, a warning that Rosey may not be entirely right. Alice knew she had the sight and it was getting stronger. Lately, she'd been having moments of vivid precognition. Rain and a road stretching on and on, and a woman with her hands on her hips, and the man in the long dark coat staring at her with a strange, frightening longing.

He was there, in her future.

Waiting.

CHAPTER ELEVEN

Annie's Story

My phone was ringing as Courtney and I pulled up into the driveway. The lights were on in my father's apartment upstairs and I felt a wave of relief that he was home. He worked far too hard, as if he was determined to get everything done in case . . . well, I didn't want to go there. Perhaps Courtney and I could invite him for dinner? Even if it was plain old scrambled eggs on toast.

I didn't want to admit it to myself, but I was also relieved because of the man in the backyard. Somehow with my father here I felt sure the man wouldn't make an appearance, and if he did . . . I could ask him down to take a look. Surely, someone as level-headed as my father would have an explanation?

The mobile phone was still ringing. We hurried up the front steps and I opened the door, still deciding whether or not to answer it. I didn't recognise the number.

Inside, Nephetiti was waiting and gave me an expectant look.

The phone kept on ringing and I finally gave in and pressed the connect icon. 'Yes? Hello?'

Nephetiti twitched her tail.

There was a pause before a voice said, 'Miss Reuben?'

'Yes.' I couldn't place it, and then suddenly I did and my heart sank.

'Sebastian Rawlings, Annie. I need to talk. Are you free this evening? I thought we could meet?'

'I don't think—'

'It's important. About the *Trompe L'oeil*.'

'I'll have to see whether I can find a babysitter for my daughter,' I said, but I already knew I'd meet him. If Sebastian was going to pull the pin on me it wasn't in my nature to hide in my house and let him get away with it.

'Bluestone Bar, Flinders Lane, at eight. I hope you can make it.'

He hung up and I groaned. Perhaps he just wanted to be kept up to date, perhaps there was no ulterior motive in this invitation? Unfortunately, Sebastian Rawlins wasn't the sort of man who invited someone out when a phone call would do. He was far too busy.

I had a bad feeling about this.

Nephetiti chose that moment for her revenge, sticking her claws into my sock-clad ankle. 'Ow! You wretch.'

Courtney sighed dramatically. 'Nephi's hungry, Mummy.'

'I know, darling. Come and we'll feed her and then I need to see Grandpa. Maybe we can all have scrambled eggs, what do you say?'

'Hooray! Even Nephi?'

I glanced down at our regal tabby and shook my head. 'I don't think Nephi wants scrambled eggs. I think she'd prefer her fish.'

* * *

Bluestone Bar was quiet, barely a soul in the place. Sebastian had taken a table in a secluded corner. He waved me over and I sat down, feeling a bit like a spy in a cold war movie. I'd dressed in jeans and a rose-coloured jumper, smart but casual. Sebastian was in a suit and tie—he'd probably come straight from work, unless he always dressed formally. He'd shaved recently but there were dark circles under his hazel eyes and his face was drawn with tiredness.

Greta said Sebastian didn't have a soul, but I thought that was a bit harsh. I was sure he had a soul, it was just that sometimes he misplaced it. Tonight I might even have felt sorry for him, but I was too wary for that.

After drinks were ordered, I sat back, determined to wait for him to bring up the subject. He took his time, chatting about mutual acquaintances, other projects, and I began to find myself actually enjoying the grown-up conversation. When he wasn't being paranoid, Sebastian was an intelligent and interesting person, even amusing—I laughed several times. The evening went by quickly, and we were on to our second drinks before he finally got around to explaining why we were here.

'The figure in your *Trompe L'oeil*. Gervais Whistler.'

'The entrepreneur?' I said innocently.

'His great-grandchild has been having second thoughts.'

My heart sank. *Please no*, I thought. And then in the next instant, *There's no way you're taking this away from me*.

He was watching my face with a half-smile, as if he could read my thoughts.

'The great-grandchild is wondering whether it might be savvier to claim Gervais Whistler outright. Colourful character, man of the people sort of thing.'

Oh! I sipped my drink and tried not to let him see my hand shake. 'Why the change of heart?' I said, hiding my relief.

'I don't know. I expect there have been discussions with the handlers. Although don't get too comfortable. It only takes one bad press release for a decision to swing the other way.' There was a pause and then he said in a far more intimate voice, 'You're angry.'

I looked up before I could stop myself and found his hazel eyes searching mine. Once again I felt as if he could read every emotion inside me, and the sensation made me feel distinctly uncomfortable. But perhaps it was time to put all the cards on the table.

'Yes, I'm angry,' I admitted in a flat voice. 'I believe the *Trompe L'oeil* should be seen and enjoyed by everyone without exception and that shouldn't be dependent on one man's vanity and ambition.'

He almost smiled. 'I'm afraid that's the way of the world, Annie. You're being naive to think otherwise.'

'Then the world should change, and I'm not naive. I'm a conservator who loves her work and thinks it's just as important as balancing the books, or whatever it is your faceless friend does.'

He shrugged and took a sip of his own drink. 'It might surprise you to know that I agree with you,' he said. 'And in my own way I'm trying to convince my masters that disclosure is a far better option. The alternative is that the mural be put aside until a time when the people in it are no longer important to those in power.'

'In fifty years or so?' I couldn't help the sarcasm.

Sebastian raised an eyebrow. 'Maybe not that long, but yes.'

'I don't agree. I want it seen as soon as possible. Its discovery is important. I think the press should be informed.'

He shook his head at me as if I was a toddler throwing a tantrum. 'Don't do anything crazy, Annie. History Victoria is enamoured of you at the moment, but that could change. You might find your commissions drying up. Reuben and Reuben depend on our money.'

He was right, of course. My father was inclined to work for very little, just to see a job well done, but that didn't pay the bills. We *did* rely on History Victoria, but I didn't want him to know it. I chose my next words carefully.

'History Victoria is a big part of our work, yes, but that's because there aren't any other conservators or restorers doing what we do. Not in Victoria anyway. I don't think they'd be happy to have to look elsewhere just because I'd ruffled some politician's feathers. I think the blame would fall on the politician rather than me, I was just doing my job after all. I don't believe they'd turn their back on Reuben and Reuben.'

'They may have no choice,' he said dryly. He glanced at his watch. 'I have to go. I have a late meeting. Thank you for coming. It's been a pleasant interlude in a busy day.'

Did he always talk like this? So formal. Yet his eyes were warm as they rested on me and his smile seemed genuine. Sebastian could have been an attractive man if it wasn't for all the cloak-and-dagger stuff.

We said our goodbyes and I went home, feeling weary and wanting my bed. My father was asleep in a chair in the lounge with his mouth open and the television was on low. Courtney was curled up on his lap and Nephetiti squashed in beside them. I looked at my family and felt sentimental tears sting my eyes.

'Papa?'

'You're back.' Reuben stretched and yawned. He looked down at Courtney and smiled. I reached to lift her from him but he waved me away. 'Don't wake her, I want to talk to you.'

Startled by his serious tone, I said, 'About what?'

My father gave me a curiously questioning look. 'The man in the backyard.'

* * *

'How did you know?'

We were seated at the table, speaking in low voices despite having put Courtney to bed.

'Courtney. He's out there every night, she says. She isn't afraid of him, just curious. And she doesn't think he's flesh and blood.'

I shivered, reaching to warm my hands around my mug of hot tea.

'You've seen him, too,' he said and it wasn't a question.

Reluctantly, I nodded. 'Twice. The first time over near the side fence, the second time in the middle of the yard. Looking up at the window. He gives me the creeps. I thought about ringing the police, but . . .' I shrugged one shoulder. 'I don't think he's flesh and blood either. Not that that makes him any friendlier.'

Reuben's gaze upon me was thoughtful. 'Actually, I wasn't asking if you'd seen him recently, Annie. I meant when you were a child. He's always been here. Your mother saw him.'

I couldn't speak. I felt disorientated. Why didn't I remember this?

'He's a spirit, Annie,' my father informed me matter-of-factly. 'A ghost.'

'I didn't think you'd believe in ghosts.'

He smiled. 'I didn't, but your mother wore me down.'

'So he *is* a ghost! I thought he was, but . . . but he was looking at me so . . . so intently. Focused on me. It wasn't nice. And I don't like to think of Courtney being looked at in that way by something that isn't . . . isn't human.' I looked up at him, knowing my hands were shaking as I held my mug, trying to be as calm as he. 'Have you see him, Papa?'

'No. Your mother had that gift, not me. She must have passed it on to you, and you to Courtney.'

My eyes widened. 'A gift? Seeing dead people? I could think of another name for it.'

'Seeing ghosts. It isn't uncommon despite what the sceptics say. I remember her telling me the gift of seeing runs through some families but she wasn't so sure that was the case with hers. Besides, Geneva only ever saw the one ghost and it only started happening when we moved to this house.'

'Maybe it's the house that's haunted and not us?'

'Maybe. Geneva saw the man in the backyard many, many times. She wasn't afraid of him, but he unnerved her. She said he wanted something from her, but she was never able to discover what it was. Or if she did she didn't tell me.'

For the second time tonight I felt tears sting my eyes as I thought of all the conversations I would never have with my mother.

'But I don't understand why I haven't had any experiences before. Why has he started appearing now?'

'Perhaps you *have* had other experiences. How do you know you haven't seen ghosts before? Walking on the street, looking out of the window of your car . . . are those people real or ghosts? How do you *know*, Annie?'

'Now you're just creeping me out,' I muttered, taking another sip of the tea. It was cold. 'What did you tell Courtney?'

'That the man in the backyard was like an old painting, and he couldn't harm her. I also said that because not everyone was lucky enough to be able to see him she shouldn't tell her friends, in case it made them sad.'

I nodded. He'd judged it well. Courtney was soft-hearted enough to be worried about her friends' feelings.

Reuben was getting to his feet.

'Did Mum ever say who he was? The man . . . ?'

'No. She tried to communicate with him, but he remained stubbornly silent.'

'Don't you think it's strange though? Almost as if he was asleep and he's been woken up. Maybe he does want something. I wish I knew what it was, then I could send him on his way.'

'Put him from your mind, Annie. Whoever he is he's long dead and he cannot hurt you, I *do* know that.'

Did he? As I watched my father stagger off, yawning, to his apartment, I couldn't be as certain. There was something rather horrible about the white face and the thin, gangly figure. What shift in the cosmos had caused him to appear to me and Courtney after all this time? And what had my mother thought of his appearances?

Thinking about her, my memory was jogged. My mother had left some diaries. Perhaps I could persuade my father to look them up? Wouldn't she have written about her spectral experiences? I remembered being given them to read when I was a teenager, but I couldn't recall ever reading more than an entry or two. My dead mother's hopes and dreams had seemed too poignant for me to pore over, and I suppose at that age I was more interested in my own angst. But now I was suddenly eager to discover everything I could about my mother and the man in the backyard.

My family ghost, I thought with a little shudder. I might have refused to believe it except that my father, so pragmatic and practical, had no trouble in accepting it.

I'd been tired before, but now I felt wide awake again, so I switched on the computer. I brought up my images of the *Trompe*

L'oeil and considered its many scenes. Tonight one in particular caught my eye, the narrow-fronted building with the red cloth hanging from the window. Could it be a hotel or an inn? Was the red cloth a clue I could use to find a name? The Red Flag perhaps? Wasn't there a Red Ribbon Rebellion in Bendigo? Time, I thought, for some research.

Before I could bring up Google an email popped into my mailbox. Did my heart give a little flutter when I saw it was from Max Taylor? Of course not, I was far too grown-up for that.

I opened the email and read it. **Call me**, with a phone number.

Glancing at my watch I wondered if it was too late to ring. What time did riverboat captains go to bed? In the end I rang anyway, knowing I'd find it even more difficult to sleep after all that had happened. If Max was in bed then he wouldn't answer, would he?

He answered straightaway.

'I was talking with my old-timer,' he said, when we'd covered the pleasantries. 'Seems there was more to Molly than being the wife of the captain of the *Ariadne*.'

'I checked the births, deaths and marriages online. She married twice.' I knew I sounded smug.

Max chuckled. It was a warm sound, rich and deep. 'You've been doing your homework, too, then. Yes, she was married twice. Her first husband owned the *Ariadne* and when she remarried Arnold Potter he took over it. Not long afterwards she died. It was the scandal of the day. Big news.'

'What?'

He paused. I wondered if he was consciously drawing out the suspense to tease me, then I heard him sigh and realised he wasn't teasing me. Oh, God, he genuinely didn't want to tell. What was so bad that he didn't want to say it out loud?

'Murder, Annie,' his voice cut through my uncomfortable thoughts. 'I'm afraid Molly was murdered.'

CHAPTER TWELVE

The Girl's Story

It was morning and the steam engine was getting ready to leave, steam trickling from the funnel like an old man with a pipe. It should have left hours ago, but they were still waiting.

The railway track had only reached Echuca a couple of years previously, and now it went all the way from the river to the bay, carrying passengers and goods from the port to the city and to places in between. Today's train was a long one, consisting mostly of goods carriages, and with only three passenger carriages at the very back. First class, and two third class.

It had been Rosey's idea to wait and smuggle themselves aboard the train, but after trying to find a corner to hide in, and attracting the watchful eyes of the station staff, she'd decided it might be easier to pay for third class.

'But aren't we going goldmining, Rosey?' Alice wailed.

Rosey was ready with an answer. 'If we head into the bush we'll perish for sure. I know you want to go off and look for gold, but we have to be careful, Alice. We have to get far enough away so your man in the coat can't come looking for us, or Miss Oliver and her orphanage.'

Alice stared at her with her blue eyes, making Rosey feel as if the girl was reading her like all those books she devoured in her cupboard. Miss Oliver never knew that, but the girls and even some of the gentlemen did, and quite often produced a book or a magazine for 'the little 'un'. Alice could read far better than Rosey now, and Rosey was proud of her.

Not wanting to be asked any questions, they waited just outside the railway warehouse, behind some boxes and other cargo that had been unloaded from the train after its run from Melbourne, and gradually the sun rose higher and hotter. It was as if the storm last night had never been.

Some more passengers began to gather on the platform, and it was then that Alice, peering through a gap in two barrels, cried out in a harsh whisper, 'Rosey! It's Gilbert Suckling.'

Rosey followed her gaze through the barrels, trying to ignore the pungent odour of some unknown substance inside.

Gilbert looked near to tears, although he was being stoic. His father was frowning, taking out his fob watch to look at, and then slipping it back into his waistcoat pocket. His wife looked white-faced and red-eyed and she swayed slightly in the breeze. Even this early in the morning she was tipsy, or perhaps she'd been up all night, preparing herself to see off her son.

'I forgot to tell you, Alice. Gilbert came to see you yesterday. He wanted to say goodbye. He's away to boarding school in Melbourne.'

Alice blinked at her. 'He came to see me?'

Rosey squeezed her shoulder. 'I'm sorry, but I sent him off. After everything that happened yesterday Miss Oliver wouldn't have let you see him anyway. I said you'd write him a letter.'

Alice understood, but there was regret in the droop of her mouth. 'He must be going for a long time,' she said in a little voice. 'All that luggage.'

Rosey saw a trunk, various boxes tied with cord and a bag he kept close to his side. He was older than Alice by three years and looked tall and quite grown-up.

At last the train was ready and began loading its passengers. Mrs Suckling put a gloved hand to her delicate head. Doctor Suckling whispered harshly in her ear and she swayed again, until Gilbert took her arm and held her firm, looking uneasily about him, embarrassed someone might see his mother's condition.

'He probably just wants to get on board and leave them behind,' Rosey said. 'Far behind.'

'I think he looks frightened,' Alice murmured. 'It doesn't matter how horrid it is at home, they're his family. He's going off all alone.'

Rosey gave her a look. 'Is that how you feel? Do you miss your family?'

Alice gave her one of her older-than-her-years stares. 'I don't remember.'

A guard came ambling past and gave them a frown. Rosey smiled her sweetest smile. 'How long will it take to get to Melbourne?' she enquired.

'You got to get to Sandhurst first, change there.'

'How long to Sandhurst, then?'

The guard looked back at the train. 'Depends,' he said. 'Got a lot of carriages there, need a lot of stops to refuel and rewater.'

Rosey sighed and reached for Alice's hand, squeezing it tight. 'We need to get on board.'

There were a lot people about—railway men, passengers and people saying goodbye or greeting travellers. The third-class carriage was rough and ready, with bench seats in rows, and a spittoon near the door for the men. A couple of families were already delving into their baskets for the food they'd brought with them, to save money on the wayside stops where meals and drinks were available for a price.

The seat wasn't very comfortable, but Rosey set Alice by the wall so that she could rest her head. Down at the back there were chickens squawking in a cage. Why hadn't she thought to filch some food from the Red Petticoat? Now they would have to buy some at one of the stops and she wanted to save every penny she could for Melbourne.

She felt a bit guilty about lying to Alice, but what was the point of traipsing about looking for gold when they could find work in the city? The girl would realise the sense of it when they got there, and she'd probably love the noise and bustle of such a booming metropolis. As far as Rosey knew, Alice had never been anywhere much and Rosey told herself that she was in fact doing her young friend a good turn. The trouble was Alice mightn't see it that way.

The slow rocking motion of the train was soothing and last night they'd had hardly any sleep. Soon Alice was asleep and Rosey closed her eyes with relief. It was all right, she told herself firmly, everything would be all right . . .

What about Sean?

The name was a whisper in her head.

A sigh of regret.

A moan of fear.

Sean, the man she'd loved in Ireland and who'd persuaded her to leave her family behind and run off with him. The man she'd sailed with in a ship from Cork to Melbourne, full of all sorts of dreams. The man she'd left six months after they'd arrived.

Australia was a big place, and she'd been very grateful for that. Sean was here somewhere, but she'd made damned sure he hadn't found her—Roisin O'Donoghue had become Rosey Donnelly. Rosey hated to think what he'd do if he did find her and if he knew what sort of work she'd been doing.

He'd kill her, she thought with a shiver, just as he'd nearly killed her once before when she'd smiled at another man.

It wasn't the first time he'd hit her.

There'd been the accusations, the terrible jealousy. She'd denied it and still he believed the worst of her, and somehow that only encouraged her bad behaviour. So that last time it had been more than a smile. A kiss and a cuddle was what it had been. And when he found out Sean had beaten her black and blue and she'd only escaped with her life because he was too drunk to finish the job. With him lying sleeping and snoring in the bed beside her, she'd waited and waited until she was sure he really was unconscious and not just pretending, and then she'd crept out of bed and vanished into the night.

Running away was becoming a habit.

What if Sean was still in Melbourne and she bumped into him on a street corner? What if he dragged her into some back alley and beat the living daylights out of her? Finished the job he'd begun? Images flitted through her mind as she lay half awake and half dreaming, and then all at once she started up with a cry, imagining he really had got hold of her.

It took a moment for her to grasp where she was and then she looked for Alice. Only then did she realise Alice was gone.

* * *

Alice stood a moment in the swaying train, peering through the smeary glass into the wooden compartment. It was one of several first-class sections, and she'd only come inside for a quick look, while they were stopped to take on water. Several passengers had climbed off to stretch their legs and find some relief from the stuffy heat inside, and there'd been a restroom at the little station, and a place to buy a cup of tea and a sandwich.

She'd thought about buying something to eat, but she wasn't really hungry. Rosey was asleep back in their own carriage, and Alice hadn't planned to be gone long. She'd only meant to climb briefly into the first-class carriage to see if she could find Gilbert, and the next thing she knew the train had started off again with a jerk of its wheels and a shriek of its whistle.

Through the smeary window in the top of the compartment door, she could see the back of Gilbert's head. He was sitting alone—there was no one else in his compartment—and he was bent over a book, but every now and then she thought he surreptitiously wiped his eyes.

He'd come to the Red Petticoat to say goodbye to her yesterday!

If only she'd known. If only he hadn't chosen the day when the man in the coat had come for her and she had the run-in with

Miss Oliver. Well, it couldn't be helped, and anyway, here he was and here she was. Alice knew she couldn't not speak to him no matter how much trouble it would get her into with the train guard and Rosey.

She opened the door, trying to look like she belonged here, and slid into the seat facing Gilbert.

Startled, he looked up and then stared at her in amazement. His hazel eyes were red and traces of tears stained his cheeks. He averted his face and quickly mopped his eyes. 'Alice?' he said in a husky voice. 'What are you *doing* here?'

'Rosey and me are running away,' she said, and watched the sudden laughter brim in his eyes. 'Why do you think that's funny? We're going to look for gold, like I told you.'

'On a train?' He laughed. He seemed glad to see her.

'Well, once we get off the train,' Alice told him matter-of-factly.

There was a pause and it was clear they were both tongue-tied.

'I came to say goodbye,' he said a little stiffly, 'but you weren't available.'

This time Alice gave a snuffle of laughter. 'If only you knew!'

He seemed about to take offence; she'd forgotten how easily he did that.

Her voice was breathless. 'Sorry, Gilbert, it's just . . . so many things have happened.'

He searched her face and then set his book aside. 'Tell me.'

Alice hesitated. How to tell Gilbert about the man in the coat and Miss Oliver, and the colours she saw everywhere, even around him, although his colours were thankfully bright and healthy if a little sad. But just now Gilbert *was* sad.

'How long will you be at boarding school?' she asked instead.

He shrugged. 'Until mid-term and then I may not be able to come back. I'll have to stay there all year.'

Alice gave him a sympathetic look. 'It's awful being alone with no one you know.'

'My father says I have to learn to live with it. Be a man. My mother just cries and drinks her—her tonic.'

'But when you're finished you'll go to medical school and learn to be the best doctor in Melbourne, and then when I'm rich I'll call on you.'

The old joke. He nodded, but now his eyes were narrowed and she knew he wasn't going to let her get away with changing the subject for too long.

'Alice,' he said, 'why weren't you available yesterday? Why are you and Rosey running away?'

Alice knew if she told him he'd think she was a freak, but if she didn't tell him he'd think she didn't trust him. For a moment she considered getting up and leaving him, but that would be cowardly, and, apart from not being able to get off the first-class carriage until the next stop, she'd probably never see Gilbert again no matter what she said. She could tell him anything and it wouldn't matter.

So she did.

* * *

Rosey calmed herself. Alice hadn't disappeared, of course not. She'd gone to find Gilbert. Unfortunately, each carriage being separate from the others, Rosey would have to wait until the next time the train stopped to find her.

The journey was so slow and tedious, she wondered whether it might have been quicker to walk. Eventually, they came to a halt outside Sandhurst at a place called White Hills, and she grabbed their few belongings and was able to climb down and make her way stealthily to the first-class carriage.

Just as Alice had done earlier, Rosey stared through the smeared glass into each compartment until she found them. Behind her a woman in a large bonnet pushed past to the door, clicking her tongue with disapproval, but Rosey ignored her. She saw Gilbert had opened the bag he was carrying with him and they were sharing some sandwiches. Rosey's mouth watered. In between bites they were talking intently, Gilbert nodding his head, Alice gazing into his eyes.

Just as Rosey was about to open the door and join them she heard voices out on the platform. Scuttling back, she saw the woman in the bonnet in conversation with one of the uniformed railway men.

'Oh, Jesus.' The last thing they needed was to be arrested and taken back to the Red Petticoat. She couldn't let old Oliver send Alice to the orphanage, she really couldn't. Swiftly, she returned to Gilbert's door, startling the two inside.

'Rosey!' Alice jumped to her feet, looking flushed and guilty.

'The guard's coming. We have to get.'

She already had hold of Alice's hand and was pulling her out into the corridor. Gilbert followed. 'Let me,' he said. 'I'll distract him.'

He gave Alice a momentary glance, as if to say goodbye, and then started off to intercept the guard, who was clambering up into the carriage. Gilbert stood in his way, so that the guard had to climb out again, then Gilbert followed him and stood, back to the two girls, speaking in a loud and important voice. The sort of voice he'd inherited from his father.

'Come on,' Rosey hissed, and they slipped through the door and onto the platform, quickly walking away. Alice was holding some sandwiches and Gilbert's book, and Rosey had to smile. The sandwiches she could understand, but only Alice would think to take the book.

The train was sounding its whistle, getting ready to move again, but Rosey had had enough. She kept walking, shading her eyes against white hills of quartz shining in the sinking sun. A whole day it had taken them and they were still only on the outskirts of Sandhurst.

Rosey knew a bit about Sandhurst. It was a large, booming mine town, situated on the Bendigo goldfields, but it wasn't Melbourne. She'd planned on Melbourne, she'd set her heart on the anonymity to be found in Melbourne. But then again Melbourne held its own dangers.

Sean.

'Rosey?' Alice said, sounding worried. 'The train's leaving, Rosey.'

Rosey ignored the noisy engine as it chugged past, pulling its interminable carriages. At last the first-class carriage slid by, and she could see Gilbert waving to them. Alice waved back long after he was gone.

Perhaps, Rosey thought, it would be all right if they stayed in Sandhurst after all. She could find work and Alice . . . well, Alice would be safe. She'd make certain of it.

'Come on,' she said, forcing a cheerfulness she didn't feel. 'We'll find somewhere to spend the night and then tomorrow we'll explore Sandhurst.'

CHAPTER THIRTEEN

The Girl's Story continued

Sandhurst had come a long way from the huddle of tents that sprang up when gold was first discovered over ten years ago. Now it was a thriving gold town and business centre. Rosey strode along Pall Mall as if she knew exactly where she was going, and it was all Alice could do to keep up with her. There were more shops than she had ever seen, displaying all sorts of luxuries behind their plate-glass windows, and more people than she had ever seen, too, hurrying along the wide flagged footpath. Pall Mall wasn't just the main shopping thoroughfare. There were mines operating right here in the middle of it, and the road was full of vehicles and horses, and even a mob of cattle on their way to the saleyards.

A cake of gold was being exhibited inside one of the banks, and Alice gazed in wonder at the solid, pitted object. 'This cake is over a thousand ounces,' a gentleman of the bank was informing the gawping crowd. 'Taken from two tons of quartz on the Hustler Reef.'

'Aye, and while the rich men dig up all the gold we little miners are left with nothing,' someone at the back complained. 'How can we afford to pay for such an enterprise ourselves? All we can do is sign on to dig in their mines and make them richer.'

'Men like Mr George Lansell are bringing great prosperity to Sandhurst,' the gentleman retorted.

'And a great big house for himself!'

'Come on,' Rosey murmured in her ear, drawing her away. 'Before they start swinging punches.'

The burly men guarding the cake of gold smiled at Alice and one of them gave Rosey a wink. She tossed her head as she walked away, but Alice could tell she was pleased with the attention, and for some reason that worried Alice.

They strolled under wide verandahs, past the two-storey Beehive building, which housed the busy Sandhurst Mining Exchange and its crowds of sharebrokers all trying to get rich. Alice saw an emporium with signs grandly announcing the arrival of new styles from London. Molly would have loved it and for that reason she longed to dart inside, but Rosey had found a bakery. The two girls paid for sugary buns, and, wary of the hot jam inside, nibbled them as they made their way to an expanse of green park and trees on the other side of the street.

Rosey grinned at her as they sat on the grass, which was drying nicely in the sunshine, and they licked the sugar off their fingers. Above them on the hill were the remains of the old military camp, which had been set up when troopers ruled the goldfields. Things were different now, and the huts and tents had been replaced with a solid-brick police barracks and law court.

'This is the life, isn't it, Alice?'

'Yes, Rosey.' But Alice wasn't sure that it was. She was thinking of Gilbert, heading to Melbourne for his new school. She was glad they'd spoken, but she already missed him. When she'd first met him at Molly's house she'd hated him, and now despite their very different stations in life they were friends.

Friends in adversity.

At least she had Rosey, she thought, and that reminded her of something that had been worrying her. 'You were talking in your sleep. On the train.'

Her friend gave her a blank look, but Alice wasn't fooled, she knew when Rosey was playing possum.

'You were talking about Sean. Who's Sean, Rosey?'

Rosey lifted her head sharply, gazing over the busy street as if expecting to see Sean strolling by. 'He was my man, once,' she said softly.

'Did you leave him behind in Ireland?' Alice asked. There was a mystery here and she wanted to solve it.

Rosey shrugged a shoulder, looking down at her food as if she no longer recognised it. 'No, he came with me. But we were separated and then I couldn't find him.' Her mouth twisted. 'I didn't understand how vast this country was, Alice. He couldn't find me and I couldn't find him.'

'You've *never* found him?' Alice asked, eyes wide.

Rosey shook her head and popped the last bit of the bun into her mouth. 'He's gone,' she said. 'I don't know where. I wish . . . I wish I did.' It sounded sentimental, something Rosey was not. As if her own words embarrassed her, she looked away from Alice towards the barracks and the Union Jack flying high on the flagpole.

Alice watched her a moment. A thought had come into her head and she was considering it, wondering whether she really wanted to do it, but this was Rosey, her friend. She took a deep breath. 'Do you want me to . . . you know . . . try to find him for you?'

Rosey's eyes narrowed. Alice thought it was because she knew how much Alice hated to use the sight, so she tried to ease her friend's fears.

'I don't know if I can. It doesn't always work when I want it to. But I'd like to help.'

Although Alice had already decided that if she saw Sean lying dead somewhere she'd keep it to herself.

Rosey hesitated a moment more, a variety of emotions flitting over her face, before she said, awkwardly, 'All right. Try then, Alice. I'd like to know where Sean is right at this moment. I'd like to know how far away from me he is.'

Alice closed her eyes. She could hear the sounds of Sandhurst all about her and then they began to fade. There was a cool breeze against her cheek and with it a waft of pipe smoke. There were other smells, too, earth and water. And sweat. A shiver ran through her. She was standing thigh deep in cold water! An ache speared across her shoulders, rolling down her arms and into her hands as she tilted the pan, swirling the water, eyes peeled for shiny flecks in the sediment.

'He's looking for gold in the pan,' she said. 'There's a glint or two but not much. He's disappointed. He hasn't found much gold at all and he's worked hard. He thinks about Ireland. He thinks about you.'

Rosey's breath caught and Alice felt her move closer. She struggled to keep focused on the man.

'He remembers the colour of your hair and your eyes. He's thinking of your smile. He's thinking of you in his arms, Rosey. He's been looking for you. He looks all the time.'

'Aw, dear God, where is he, Alice? Tell me where he is!'

Alice felt something inside her stretching out like a narrowing thread and it hurt, but she held on to it, looking for anything that might give her a clue as to where Sean was right now. A creek, a forest of tree stumps where the trees had been cut down by the miners, a mass of tents and smoky campfires. There was nothing at all to distinguish this goldfield from others all over the country.

Suddenly, a face filled her vision, a white face with coal-black eyes. Alice cried out. The thread snapped and she fell back, feeling sick and dizzy. After a moment she realised she was cradled against Rosey's shoulder. She eased away cautiously, glad to find she was in one piece. And blinked. Thankfully, the images in her head were gone, the man was gone. She thought about telling Rosey but didn't—Rosey had enough to worry about.

'I'm sorry, Roisin. I can't tell you where he is. He's looking for gold somewhere. Not close, at least I don't think so. Maybe if I try again . . .'

Rosey gave her a tight smile. 'It doesn't matter. At least I know he's alive and looking for me. Thank you, Alice.' Then her expression changed to surprise. 'What did you call me then? Was it Roisin?'

'It must have come to me when I saw Sean in the vision.'

Rosey hesitated, then shrugged an indifferent shoulder. 'It's my name. My real name. But I go by Rosey these days.'

They spent the afternoon wandering about, looking at the sights, and Alice's spirits lightened. Perhaps there was some good to her gift after all? Perhaps it wasn't always going to show her only darkness and death? Perhaps, with time and practise, she might actually be able to use it for something noble and good.

They strolled past a skittle alley and a music hall and the Shamrock concert hall where you could pay to see a man called Gervais Whistler and his Travelling Goldfield Entertainers. On Market Square stood the porticoed Town Hall, and Alice was nearly run over by a top-hatted gentleman in a fine carriage, who shook his fist at Rosey when she stuck out her tongue at him.

Alice and Rosey ran off, giggling, to stuff themselves with hot Cornish pasties and drink cold lemonade, and rub shoulders with people from all over the world who'd come here to make their fortunes. Some of the quartz miners were streaming in to the beer houses, their clothing and faces still covered with white quartz powder from drilling deep underground with the aptly named 'widow-maker', while the next shift was on its way back to mines with names like the Hustler and New Chum and Victoria, and lots more, too many for Alice to remember.

When a puzzled Alice asked, 'But where's the gold?' Rosey laughed at her and pointed to the tall ladder-like structures that seemed to have sprouted up all about them and as far as the eye could see. 'The gold's underground and there are men down there digging it up,' she said. 'They dig up the quartz and crush it in the batteries you can hear—they run day and night—and when they find the gold they cook it and turn it into cakes, like the one we saw in the bank. That's how they find gold these days, Alice. That's why they call George Lansell the Quartz King, because he's so rich.'

'You mean the miners don't wash pans in the creeks anymore? They don't stake out their own claims and find their own gold?'

'You mean like Sean was doing? Well, they do. There are still rushes. Just not here. The alluvial gold all those miners came to find on the Bendigo fields is gone and now they have to follow it deep underground.'

Alice's forehead creased. 'Then how will we make our fortune here?'

Rosey slipped an arm about her shoulders and gave her a squeeze. 'Don't worry about all that. Let's just enjoy ourselves for now.'

'But the man in the dark coat—'

'Oh pooh! We've outsmarted him. He's probably giving old Oliver an ear bashing for letting us get away.'

Alice wanted to protest, to say that this wasn't a joke, but there didn't seem to be any point. Rosey wasn't listening to her, and for the rest of the day her friend behaved as if she'd been released from purgatory and had no intention of going back.

That night Rosey found them a room in a lodging house next to the Brian Boru Hotel, but Alice couldn't sleep. She tried to read Gilbert's book—it was an adventure set in America with cowboys and Indians—but her mind wouldn't focus. The noise of the batteries seemed to fill the room just as the man in the dark coat had filled her head. She got up and went over to the window and gazed out, over the roofs of the houses and the noisy crowd still drinking in the hotel, to the glow of gaslights like stars in the night.

Behind her in the bed Rosey slept on with an untroubled conscience, just as she always did. Alice knew Rosey thought they could stay here in Sandhurst and lose themselves in the crowd, but Alice wasn't so certain.

She'd looked askance at the taverns and hotels; in that regard Sandhurst seemed very similar to Echuca. Rosey would slip back into the easy life she was used to, no matter what promises she made. Alice needed to get them away from here. Then there was the man in the coat. He'd tried to take her away with him once and he would again. If they could catch the train to Sandhurst then so could he.

In the morning Rosey was hungry again. She decided they'd have a proper breakfast at the Brian Boru next door, but the landlord stopped them at the door and asked how long they'd be staying.

He tried for an affable smile, but he had a nasty red pimple on his chin and Alice couldn't stop looking at it. 'You're both from Echuca, is that right?'

Rosey was too clever for his tricks. 'No, we're from Melbourne,' she said.

The man appeared surprised. 'I was hoping you might give me the name of a good pub in Echuca. Are you sure that's not where you're from? What about the Red Petticoat? I've heard that's a fine establishment.'

Alice felt herself go rigid with fright, but Rosey didn't miss a beat. 'Sorry. You'll have to find someone who knows the place, and that's not us.'

The man watched them go into the hotel, his suspicions as plain as the pimple on his face.

'What did he mean?' Alice whispered.

'I don't know.'

'But he must—'

'Eat your breakfast, Alice, and let me think.'

As they tucked into their eggs, sausages and toast, Rosey was unusually quiet. Alice was sipping her hot tea when she happened to glance out of the open doorway. A police constable was strolling past.

Rosey had seen him, too, and jumped up, hurrying over to the window to stare out. 'Alice,' she hissed. Alice came to join her and they watched as the landlord met the policeman in the middle of the street and stood talking to him. There was no doubt what the conversation was about when he pointed in their direction. A moment later the policeman began to approach the hotel.

Rosey grabbed Alice's hand and, to the amusement of the other diners, they scuttled across the room and out the back door. A moment later they heard shouting and the sounds of pursuit.

'Why are they after us?' Alice gasped.

'I don't know and I'm not going to stop and ask!'

They zigzagged through back lanes and past wooden miners' cottages. A woman hanging out her washing eyed them suspiciously and Rosey took another turn down another lane.

They'd reached a further row of cottages and this time the washing flapped temptingly in empty backyards. Rosey helped Alice over the fence before clambering over herself, and they snatched what they could before a surly-looking dog began to bark in the yard next door. Safe at the back of what appeared to be a hotel, they hid behind a pen of incurious sheep and hurriedly began to change into their stolen clothes before someone came to investigate.

'Rosey, why are they looking for us?'

'I don't know. But if they're looking for two girls we'll have to make sure they don't find them.'

Only then did Alice realise that Rosey had taken boys' clothes. She looked at her friend as she hauled up her trousers, tying a strip of cloth about her waist to keep them from falling down. There were shirts and a waistcoat for Alice and a loose jacket for Rosey, to disguise her breasts. When they were done they looked like a very strange pair of boys with their long hair, but Alice still had the knife she'd kept under her pillow at the Red Petticoat, and Rosey used it to saw away at their locks.

By the time she'd finished, Alice's brown hair stood up in spikes all over her head and Rosey's hair, although shorter, was already curling in ringlets about her face. They looked at each other and bit back hysterical giggles.

'Do you think there might be some hats inside?' Alice asked, with a glance at the building. 'I think we need hats.'

'And scarfs. See if they've got any scarfs.'

Alice approached uneasily, and, followed by Rosey's warning of 'Be careful!' crept inside the open back door.

As she stood in what appeared to be a boot room—it was full of coats and dirty boots and other male paraphernalia—Alice realised that there was a great deal of noise going on in the building. The noise had been there all along, it was just that she'd been too busy being frightened to take any notice of it. As she crept closer to the door into the salon, she could hear the slap of fists on flesh and then a cry or a groan.

They were fighting!

Alice had seen fights outside the Red Lantern, but this was not a random act of aggression, this was a more mechanical form of violence. She put her eye to the crack in the door and flinched at the sight of two men, bare-chested and dripping with sweat, pummelling each other, to the encouragement of a circle of spectators. At first the brutality so horrified and fascinated her that she couldn't see anything else, but soon she was noticing that money was changing hands as bets were made.

One of the fighters staggered and began to collapse. His flailing opponent lunged at him, redoubling his efforts. A groan went up from the crowd, then an enormous man in shirt sleeves and a small bowler hat balanced on his large bald head, reached over and separated them. 'Fair fight this, lads!' he roared.

And they were off again with sickening ferocity.

Alice! Hurry!

Alice could hear Rosey's voice, not with her ears but in her head. A glance over her shoulder showed her that the way was still clear. Another groan from the crowd, followed by shouts and jeers. A quick glance told her that one of the fighters was flat out on his back. It was over and soon the men would be pouring out of the salon and into here.

Quickly, she began to pick through the coats and hats and various other pieces of clothing in the pile, bundling up the items she thought they could use. Heavy footsteps were coming her way. Alice took a stumbling step towards the entrance to the backyard.

'Hey now, what're you up to, boy?'

It was a booming voice and even before she turned Alice knew it was the enormous man in the bowler hat. He was a giant, his head brushing the ceiling and his body filling the doorway.

She backed away as he followed, sure that if he caught her he'd tear her to pieces and gobble her up, like in the fairytale.

'Come here you little thief,' he said, beckoning her with his hands.

That was when she realised he was holding a wad of notes, the bets on the fight he'd been collecting.

'Alice!' Rosey's panicked voice sounded right behind her.

Surprised, the big man looked up. His eyes narrowed meanly as he took in Rosey's borrowed clothing and blonde curls. It gave Alice her chance. She darted towards him, snatched the wad of notes from his grasp, and ran as fast as she could in the other direction.

He let out a bellow.

The two girls jumped into the sheep pen, scrambling through panicked animals, and then out the other side. Into a back alley. The giant thundered after them, cursing and calling for his friends, but the girls had fear to make them fleet and soon they'd left him far behind.

Somehow Alice had kept a hold on her stolen clobber and money. They paused to share up the money, tucking it deep inside their clothing. The caps certainly made a difference to their disguise, and muffled with scarves and gloves over feminine hands, Rosey declared them able to pass all but the most thorough examination.

'Now we should be safe,' she said.

But that was before they heard the newspaper boy bawling out the headlines.

*　*　*

''Orrible murder in Echuca. Two girls wanted. *Bendigo Advertiser*. Buy one here.'

Alice and Rosey stared at each other.

'What 'orrible murder, Rosey?' Alice's voice had gone high again.

Rosey slouched over to the boy, with his scraped knees and grubby face, and bought one of his newspapers. She held it a moment, peering at the black ink, but Rosey couldn't read more than a word or two.

'Here, you,' she said in a gruff voice. 'Tell me about this 'orrible murder.'

The boy was more than happy to tell her and by the time he'd finished they knew all about Miss Oliver, who'd been strangled, her body hidden in the little box room, and the two girls who worked for her—one of them an orphan due to be returned to the orphanage—who were now missing and suspected of the foul deed.

Alice's knees were shaking, but she leaned in close to Rosey to keep herself upright. Rosey slipped an arm about her shoulders and squeezed painfully hard. A comfort and a warning.

'There's a reward,' the boy was saying with glee.

But they'd heard enough. 'We have to leave before the coppers find us,' Rosey said as they hurried away. 'They'll never believe it wasn't us.'

'Then who was it?' Alice whispered.

'The man in the coat? You seem sure he's a bad'un.'

'I . . . Well, he was there, but I heard Miss Oliver talking with some other man, in the bar. She was angry.'

'But he could've gone to her and killed her after the other man was gone.'

Alice's eyes widened. 'He tried to strangle me once. At least . . . I think I remember. But the night he came to the Red Petticoat he tried to give me a peppermint sweet.'

Rosey shuddered. 'It doesn't matter who did it, does it? We'll be blamed anyway. Sent to prison, or worse, hanged.'

'I saw the dark colours. I knew she was going to die one way or another.'

Alice felt herself going into a trance, but Rosey gave her an impatient shake.

'You couldn't have saved her, even if she'd wanted you to. She hated you, Alice.'

Alice blinked and her eyes cleared. With a sigh she adjusted her cap. 'I didn't like her,' she admitted, 'but I still feel sorry for her.'

'I know I should, too, but I can't,' Rosey said. 'I need to find us a way out. We need to get away from Sandhurst. To Melbourne? No, they'll think of that. Then away into the bush somewhere, where no one will look for us.'

Alice skipped about with excitement. 'We can go looking for gold, Rosey! No one will find us amongst all the other miners, and we can dig our own claim and make enough money to buy our own hotel. Then you can be in charge of it and tell everyone what to do.'

Rosey laughed, but there was a bitterness in the sound.

'We need to buy a wheelbarrow,' Alice went on. 'To carry our tent and blankets and our billy and cooking pots and our food and our mining tools and—'

'And three bags full, Alice,' Rosey muttered.

But Alice's feelings weren't hurt. She was smiling because *this time* they were doing what she'd wanted to do all along, they were taking their fate into their own hands.

They were going to look for gold.

And maybe, although she didn't say it aloud, they might find Sean, too. That was what Rosey wanted, wasn't it? And Alice could do that for her. She could find Sean.

Then Rosey would be happy.

CHAPTER FOURTEEN

Annie's Story

I'm afraid Molly was murdered.

The next morning Max's words were still reverberating in my head. He hadn't known the details of Molly's death, just the bald fact of her murder. All night the consequences and questions pounded in my head, keeping sleep at bay. Surely a murder in Echuca in those days would have meant a scandal? Molly was a respectable woman, the wife of a riverboat captain, and it must have caused an uproar if it was still remembered to the present day. I wanted to know the details and the first step was to verify the story, and then, if Molly *was* murdered, to find out who killed her.

And I really didn't want it to be the grey-eyed paddle-steamer captain. He seemed to have become a favourite of mine. And no, I didn't want to consider any parallels with Max Taylor.

I rang the Echuca Historical Society as soon as they were open and asked for any information on the death of Molly, and this time I was able to give them names and dates. 'Surely there's something in the newspapers? Even a one-line obituary would be a great help,' I pleaded.

'There might be.' But the woman on the phone was doubtful. 'Unfortunately, we're still indexing the bulk of our collection, so the dates you want may not be available.'

'I'm sorry to be a nuisance, but it's very important.'

'All I can do is promise to send you copies of anything I come across, Miss Reuben. What's your email address again?'

Last night when I'd spoken to Max he'd explained his 'old-timer' wasn't into things like evidence. 'He's a shock-and-awe kind of bloke.'

'Well, he did a good job with me,' I said. 'I can't get past the idea that Molly was *murdered*.'

'Me, too.'

I'd promised to let Max know what I found out. He was apologetic and said he would have done more research himself, being on the spot, but he had a full day ahead of him on the river.

'The *Ariadne*'s booked solid,' he told me with pride. 'Couple of office parties and a group of school kids.'

'Will Kenny be doing the waiting and cooking?' I had to ask.

He laughed, that rich sound that seemed to burrow right inside me. 'No, we're getting professional caterers.'

'Good luck then, Max.'

'Thanks.'

I wondered if I should ask him down to Kew, but that seemed a big step and if he wasn't interested . . . Anyway before I could find the words he was saying goodbye and we ended the call. Just as well, I told myself. After all this time as a single woman I didn't want to rush into anything, did I? Especially with a man I'd only met once face to face, even if he was damned attractive.

I also had a busy day ahead. The samples of paint I'd sent to the laboratory should be back, and I was interested to see their composition and whether I could do anything towards conserving the parts of the *Trompe L'oeil* that were flaking or water-damaged.

I wasn't entirely sure how I was going to proceed. History Victoria had recently taken a turn down the conservation road, preferring as little interference by the conservator as possible. I could understand that point of view. As a conservator I had been taught to take a passive approach, to not do any more than was necessary, and to not stamp my own personality on someone else's work of art. But in this case I found myself leaning towards restoration.

The *Trompe L'oeil* was in a miserable state. It seemed wrong to leave it that way when the original intention of the artist had been to tell these two women's stories in such a vibrant and exciting manner. Why not restore it to its former glory so that people could see it as it was meant to be seen?

Then again, if the *Trompe L'oeil* was hidden away for fifty years in a warehouse somewhere, I may not have a chance to make that decision. Despite Sebastian Rawlins offering me some hope, nothing was certain. The government probably had places like that where they kept material secret. I found my imagination running riot, picturing myself walking between stacks of ASIO documents and coming upon Harold Holt in a box.

'Mummy?' Courtney was holding out her gorilla, her lip trembling.

'What is it, darling?'

'Tarzan's hurt his paw. He needs a bandage on it.'

We were already running late and I was tired from my restless night, but I knew I didn't have a hope. The argument would take longer than doing the bandaging, so I rushed around and found suitable medical gear and soon Tarzan, and Courtney, were happy again.

We were in the car before I found the courage to mention the man in the backyard. Courtney listened to me stumbling to find the right words before putting me out of my misery.

'Mum*my*, Grandpa already told me that the man isn't real. He's a-a spirit. He can't hurt us, he's just stuck here. He looks scary but he has yellow all around him.'

'What do you mean?'

'Like a sunflower.'

That still didn't make much sense, but Courtney was growing impatient with my questions.

'Grandpa says he can't hurt me. He can't hurt you, either. And we shouldn't talk about him because not everyone can see him and they might feel left out.'

'Grandpa seems to have it covered, doesn't he?'

'Nephi can see him, too. She hisses at him.'

'Nephi hisses at everyone.'

Courtney giggled and it seemed that everything was all right, or as all right as it ever could be. I was sure the matter wouldn't always be so easily disposed of, and when Courtney was older there would be more questions. Unless she forgot about it, as I had.

I had tried to remember seeing the man as a child, but the memory of it just didn't seem to be there. Something I was grateful for—I didn't think I would have been as pragmatic as a child as Courtney. In fact, I had been prone to nightmares and night horrors, getting Reuben out of his bed in the middle of the night to comfort me.

'Is there something wrong with Grandpa?'

Courtney's statement startled me. 'Why do you think there's something wrong with Grandpa?'

'The man in the backyard looks at him like there's something wrong.'

I tried to read my daughter's face in the rear-view mirror. We were in the middle of a traffic jam, cars either side of us, and some unknown hold-up ahead. 'What do you mean?' I demanded a bit more sharply than I'd meant, but the words had made me feel slightly sick.

Courtney hugged her gorilla closer, hiding her face in his fur. 'I don't know why, Mummy, I just know, okay.'

The traffic began to move again and I was too busy keeping an eye on the other cars to question my daughter further, and by the time we were out of the rush-hour madness, we'd reached the childcare centre. But when I was on my own I couldn't help but play the words over to myself with a sense of foreboding.

* * *

The morning at work was spent looking at paint options. My father came and sat with me for a time, listening to my report on the *Trompe L'oeil* and nodding in silence. At the end of it all he simply said, 'What do you want to do, Annie?'

I hesitated. My heart and my mind were not often in sync so I was used to making compromises. It was part of my job, part of the world I had to live in. But for some reason right now the gulf between the two seemed even wider than usual.

'I'm a conservator,' I reasoned. 'But I also want to see this piece as it used to be. I want to see it in all its glory, and,' I waved a hand towards the more damaged, missing sections, 'it's a far cry from that now. I can conserve it, halt the damage and preserve what's left. People like us will look at it with interest, but to the rest of the population it'll be a sort of curiosity piece. Or I can repaint whole sections in a similar colour and style and people will see it as it was meant to be seen, and they'll love it. Is that compromising the veracity of the piece? History Victoria will probably say "yes", and that I should be protecting the past and not allowing my own personality to intrude. But that's what I want to do, Papa. In my heart.'

He smiled. 'Then do that.'

I chuckled, then grew sober again. 'Before you tell me to burn my bridges you should hear what Sebastian Rawlins said.' Briefly, I repeated my conversation at the Bluestone Bar while Reuben listened. By the end he was frowning. 'So you see if I go ahead and do this, and lift the profile of the painting as I hope to, I might be bringing some skeletons out of the cupboard and causing us lots of trouble.'

'But Gervais Whistler is perfectly visible,' he reminded me, gesturing at the small scene of the man outside the Dunolly Music Hall. 'Everyone is going to see him.'

He was right about Gervais. Was my unease due to more than the political repercussions? I felt as if something was stirring closer to home, in our own lives. The ghost in the yard and Courtney's statement in the car. I almost told him but decided not to, not yet anyway.

'I just have a feeling,' I said lamely.

'You and your mother and your feelings,' Reuben said fondly.

'I know. It's hardly professional, is it? Hardly scientific.'

'But the funny thing is Geneva's feelings were usually right.' He smiled, and then became serious again. 'Whatever you decide I'll support you, Annie.'

'Thank you, Papa.' I reached out and gave him a hug, shocked by how frail he felt. We weren't normally a hugging sort of family, and when Reuben stepped away he didn't seem to know where to look, but he smiled and waved a hand at me as he left the studio.

* * *

When I got home I found the marriage and death certificates I'd sent for had arrived, as well as an email from the Echuca Historical Society. But both had to wait while Courtney and Nephetiti were attended to. A visit to the supermarket was urgently required, and after we'd run the gauntlet of the biscuit aisle—Courtney's decisions were lengthy and well informed due to conversations with her friends at child care—and returned home it was late and we were all tired.

I glanced anxiously out of the windows as I drew the curtains, but thankfully, the yard was empty. Maybe our ghostly friend had decided to take the night off, or maybe he only appeared at certain phases of the moon? I didn't know or care, I was just glad he'd gone. With luck he'd never come back.

We'd finally reached the golden moment of kiddie bedtime when Courtney informed me that Tarzan needed fresh bandages. Eventually, Courtney and a more comfortable Tarzan were tucked up, Nephetiti was curled neatly on her favourite chair, and all was peaceful in Suckling Street.

I made a cup of tea, then I spread out Molly's marriage and death certificates.

The first marriage certificate showed that Ebenezer Phillips, a paddle-steamer captain, was much older than the young Molly

Michaels. Ebenezer died of pneumonia, leaving Molly a widow with no children, but she had the *Ariadne*—scrawled in the margin was the actual name of the boat so there could be no doubt.

The second certificate was Molly's remarriage to Arnold Potter, also a riverboat captain, and who was ten years younger than Molly. Both of them were without children and Arnold had never been married before.

'Good on her,' I murmured. 'A toy boy.'

The death certificate I'd been leaving until last, but now I drew it closer and began to read. Molly had died of a persistent digestive illness that she was being treated for and the doctor was with her at the end. The doctor's name caught my eye because it was unusual and also familiar.

Doctor Suckling.

I felt a jolt of recognition. I *lived* in Suckling Street. Was there a connection? My father would know, he was mildly interested in the history of Kew—and wasn't there some connection with my mother's family? I vaguely remembered a conversation about it. Then I noticed something more on the certificate.

Where before there had been no children there was now a child. When Molly died she had left a living daughter called Alice, aged approximately nine.

I knew I was tired and struggling to take everything in, but even so the wording was odd. Surely, whoever was giving the information—and according to the relevant column that was Arnold Potter—would know when Alice was born and exactly how old she was? How could she be *approximately* nine years old? And nine would make her too old to be Arnold Potter's daughter.

So where had Alice come from?

There were only two possibilities. Either there'd been an error in the recording or else Alice wasn't Molly's biological child but her adopted child. Not a child that belonged to a friend or member of their family, because then her birthdate would be known and recorded. No, this was a foundling, wasn't that what they were called? A little girl who was unwanted and abandoned, and who didn't even know her real age. 'Approximately nine years old' made sense when it was looked at in those circumstances.

'Alice Potter.'

Startled by my voice, Nephetiti lifted her head and blinked as if to say, 'Don't you think it's time for bed?'

But I was feeling dizzy with excitement. I was on a high. Because a new thought had occurred to me, a wild and completely unsubstantiated thought.

The photos I'd taken of the *Trompe L'oeil* were still on the computer and I brought them up now, quickly clicking through them until I found the one of the two girls. Now I zoomed in on the younger girl, the one holding the dog's lead. The girl stared back at me, solemn-faced, her eyes still a startling blue despite the distance of time and the ravages of neglect.

'Are you Alice?' I asked her.

If only the artist had done his usual trick of putting in a name, but unfortunately there wasn't one so I couldn't say for certain.

And yet . . .

'You *are* Alice, aren't you?'

At first I thought Nephetiti's hiss was for me. But after another hiss, I looked up and knew the cat's behaviour had nothing to do with me.

Nephetiti was sitting by the door that led to the inner stairs up to Reuben's apartment. Her back was arched, her tail was fluffed to thrice its normal circumference, and she looked truly fearsome. Whatever was on the other side of that door, the cat didn't like them.

For a moment I was frozen in my chair, some premonition warning me of the trouble to come. Slowly, I got to my feet and moved towards the door. The air seemed to be colder over here, as if there was a draft, and yet the door was shut tight. Only Reuben ever used it. Beyond the door were stairs going up from my apartment to his, and stairs going down to the backyard. The door to my apartment was always kept unlocked, but the door to the backyard was always kept locked.

A sudden terrifying thought struck me.

What if *he* was out there—the man? Standing on the other side of the door? What if he was waiting for me to open it and let him in? Perhaps I had to give him permission before he could step over the threshold . . . or was that Dracula?

Annoyed and frightened, I mentally shook myself. *Stop it. Think.*

At that moment Nephetiti began to wash her paw as if nothing had happened. I glared at her. 'Stupid cat,' I muttered. I looked at the door again, but it was no good. I was going to have to open it. I was obviously one of those women in the movies who ended up wandering around in the dark, blissfully unaware of the axe murderer a few steps behind her.

I turned the knob and opened it before I could change my mind. Straightaway, Nephi squeezed through the gap and before I could stop her, ran up the stairs. But there was nothing there, just a sliver of light shining through the gap in Reuben's door.

Except there shouldn't have been any light because Reuben's door was never left ajar at night.

Slowly, full of dread, I climbed the stairs after the cat.

I wasn't even halfway up when I realised there was someone lying on the upper landing outside the open door, his arm preventing it from closing properly. But it was no white-faced man, not this time. It was Reuben, and as I reached him the thought passed through my mind that he might be dead.

CHAPTER FIFTEEN

The Girl's Story

It seemed to have been raining for the three months they'd been on the road, and Rosey was heartily sick of it. Her stolen boots were too big and uncomfortable, and slogging through mud gave her blisters; she was constantly having to stop to scrape off the heavy clods, while the bottoms of her trousers were hemmed with mud, banging wet and cold against her ankles as she pushed the wheelbarrow they'd bought in a store called 'The Miner's Friend' in Kangaroo Flat, a settlement just south of Sandhurst.

'Miner's Friend,' Rosey had muttered as she handed over the exorbitant amount of money. 'Miner's Foe I think you mean. This is daylight robbery.'

The proprietor had given her a nasty look. 'No one 'as a gun against your 'ead.' His look turned sly. 'I was gunna say "sir" but you sound more like a bitch.'

And things had only got worse. Their stolen money had run out and all her misgivings about their adventure were coming true, and some days, with a squirm of guilt, she found herself fondly dreaming of the comforts of the Red Petticoat. And then there was Sean.

She hadn't told Alice the truth about him, letting her think she missed him when in actual fact she was terrified of running into him on the road somewhere. No, she didn't want to burden Alice with her own problems; Alice had enough of her own.

The girl was such a valiant little soldier. She never complained and come afternoon, when it was time for them to find somewhere for the night, she would set about collecting firewood and starting a fire, heating up the food they carried with them and boiling up a billy of tea. In fact, she was so skilled at it, Rosey couldn't help but wonder whether Alice had done this before.

But Alice's past remained a mystery to them both, apart from the man in the long dark coat, and even he was a mystery. Who was he? What connection did he have to Alice? Alice couldn't tell her and sometimes when she asked too many questions the girl began to tremble so badly Rosey had to stop.

There were times when Alice spent long moments standing by the road, gazing intently back the way they'd come, as if she needed to be certain he wasn't following her. Or else she would peer into the faces of their fellow travellers, searching for the one face she feared above all others.

It chilled Rosey to the bone.

In the darkness of whatever leafy bower they took their rest, she often heard Alice talking in her sleep. For the first few times she'd listened intently, trying to make sense of the words, and then she'd realised it wasn't English. She'd thought it was Irish, the old dialect her grandma used to speak, so she'd sat up in the black night, letting the nuances roll over her. But it wasn't Irish after all, although Rosey thought it was something close to it.

'I came on a sailing ship,' Alice told her once, her face sooty from the camp fire, her pale eyes reflecting the flames, 'and lots of people died on it.'

Occasionally, memories would pop up, prompted by whatever she was doing at the time. Nothing important. Just day-to-day things. Once she remembered a woman cooking over a campfire, and then a man chopping down a tree and the sound it made when it fell, as if the whole world shook. But despite her 'sight' and other peculiar abilities, when it came to her own life Alice couldn't seem to will memories to the surface.

And as for their future . . . Rosey could barely see further ahead than one day at a time and Alice's gift didn't seem to stretch to seeing her own future.

The trouble was that there was no room for two girls in the male-structured society that was mining. They might be dressed up as boys, but Rosey had no doubt they'd soon be discovered if they tried to hire themselves out as miners.

And why would they want to, anyway? It had been Rosey's plan to stay in Sandhurst and take work in the thriving town as a shop girl or a servant, but after the visit by the police constable and the *'Orrible Murder* headlines, she knew they wouldn't be safe. If the man in the coat didn't get them then misguided justice for the murdered Miss Oliver would. They needed to be further away from Echuca if they were going to make a life for themselves, and to make a life they needed money.

They needed to find gold.

New rushes were always being discussed among the chancers they ran into, stories of fortunes being made and lost, but Rosey had never actually met anyone who'd made and lost a fortune. The first rush they heard about after they left Sandhurst was near Maldon, but by the time they got there it was already over. Now another such rumour had set them off again, heading on the road west to a place called Wombat Gully, tagging along with a mob of other hopeful gold-seekers.

And still it kept raining.

The road to Wombat Gully wasn't well marked, just a track through the bush with occasional ruts made by cartwheels. The foliage dripped all around them, the rocky soil showing eruptions and pits where miners had decided to try their luck. At one point there was even a mine dug in the middle of the road. When they came upon an inn, Rosey decided they weren't going one step further.

It wasn't much of an inn. Alice eyed it warily, listening to the drunken laughter from inside, but when she spoke her doubts aloud Rosey shrugged and said she knew how to handle drunks and they'd be just fine. They were used to their new identities by now—Rosey was Roddy and Alice was his younger brother, Alan—and they were filthy from the mud and the days and nights living outdoors without any chance of a bath, so it was unlikely anyone would notice they were female. But just in case, Rosey affected a swagger and Alice remained sullenly silent.

Their precautions had worked so far.

Places like this isolated inn often doubled as sly grog shanties and brothels for travellers making the journey between the different goldfields. There were plenty of respectable establishments, but Rosey, inspecting the ramshackle facade, doubted this was one of them. She supposed that was all to the good for them because it meant less questions would be asked.

Rosey started towards the dark entrance, then glanced back over her shoulder. In her too-big trousers tied up with a torn strip of cloth, her tweed jacket with rolled-up sleeves, and the hat pulled low over her head, she looked like a ragamuffin. A golden curl brushed her grubby cheek and her green eyes held a wicked sparkle. Alice ran to join her.

Once inside a choking, evil cloud seemed to envelop them. Their eyes stung with a mixture of tobacco smoke and wood smoke, which hung in an unpleasant fog from the low ceiling to the dirt floor. A large woman with a face like a side of pickled pork was serving drinks to her half-dozen or so customers, laughing and joking, but when she caught sight of them her expression turned blank and unwelcoming.

Rosey had seen that look plenty of times before and she wasn't put off by it. They were strangers, and strangers weren't to be trusted, and that was fair enough.

'Need any wood chopped, missus?' Rosey lowered the pitch of her voice and shuffled her boots. 'Any work goin'?'

Someone asked if he had a pretty sister and there were a few obscene comments, followed by snorts of laughter.

'Only thing I need is someone to wash the dishes.' The woman's voice was almost posh, which was startling coming from such a flat, plain face in a dilapidated inn in the middle of nowhere. 'My last skivvy ran off with my stableboy.'

Laughter at this.

Alice swallowed and took a step forward. 'I can wash your dishes, missus,' she whispered, scratching her arm.

The woman put her hands on wide hips and stared down at the top of Alice's cap. '*You* can wash dishes? I'll believe that when I see it. Give me a look at you then, lad.'

Rosey nudged her, and reluctantly, Alice removed the cap.

Her hair had grown and been hacked off again since that day in Sandhurst, but it was greasy and flattened to her head, and with the dirt that smeared her face and her lumpy clothing, it was difficult to tell what she was. The woman gave her a look askance and then frowned, staring into Alice's bright-blue eyes.

They both tensed.

'If you're having me on . . .' she began, a flush staining her cheeks.

'Me brother always washed the dishes up at home,' said a quick-thinking Rosey. 'Our ma died at Ballarat and the rest of us was workin' so he did the cookin', too. No one got sick, missus. There was even plenty of other kids came to eat with us, the smells were so good.'

Someone chuckled, but Rosey was glad to see most of the men looking uncomfortable, no doubt ashamed of themselves for their earlier coarse comments. One of them even muttered, 'Go on, Meg, poor motherless mites, give 'em a go.'

Meg was still watching them, her eyes flicking back and forth between the two grubby faces. There was something a little too knowing in her smile when she said, 'Very well then.' She shrugged her meaty shoulders. 'You can wash that lot in there now and if I'm satisfied I'll take you on for a week. Only a week at a time mind. I never know when they'll come and close me down.'

'Bastards always holding their hands out, eh, Meg?' a customer growled. 'Licences for this and licences for that, licences for every bloody thing.'

'I had a tame inspector once,' she replied, eyes sliding to Alice, 'but they found out he was taking bribes. How is a woman to make a living, that's what I want to know? I used to own a place outside Melbourne and then they did me for thieving. Even though it wasn't me. Lost my liquor licence and once it's lost you never get it back. Not legally anyway.'

Murmurs of sympathy. Meg considered the unfairness of the world a moment more and turned towards a small door at the back of the room. 'Come on,' she ordered Alice and Rosey, 'washing up's this way.'

Rosey pinched Alice's arm through her thick jacket, a warning to her that if she said 'Run' then they were to run as fast as they could. It was a signal they'd used successfully before. But the room beyond the door was not as bad as they'd expected and there was no one waiting there to pounce on them.

Pots and cooking utensils were piled into a tub of cold, greasy water beside the hearth where a fire had burned down to glowing coals. Rosey promptly held out her hands to the warmth, watching while Alice followed Meg to the tub. Having no wood to chop suited her fine, her hands were still scabbed and sore from the last lot she'd undertaken for a widow at a private residence in Maldon. *And* the widow had underpaid her!

'Now.' Meg's hands were back on her hips again. 'I'm not asking any questions, it's none of my affair, but if you two are brothers then I'm a rooster.'

Rosey stepped away from the fire and glanced at the closed door. She felt Alice tense, ready to make a dash.

But then they saw the twinkle in Meg's eye. 'You don't look a bit alike! Runaways, are you? Well just don't run off again until you've finished this lot.'

When she'd gone they covered their mouths to stifle the laughter, the tears running down their faces and making tracks in the grime.

That night they lay in the shelter of the lean-to at the back of the inn, snuggled together in their blankets, their bellies full from Meg's cooking. Alice was muttering in her sleep again, more bad dreams. Rosey felt her palms, wincing at the new blisters—there had been wood to chop after all. She sighed, and, as often happened when she couldn't sleep, thought of Sean.

Sean had caught her eye when he was romancing her cousin. She'd been secretly glad when they fell out, despite her cousin warning her he was a dangerous man. Dangerous was good, dangerous was attractive to the sixteen year old Rosey, and it only made her all the more determined to have him. And sure enough he began to notice her, flirt with her, try to kiss her. Rosey had been a wild girl, up for anything. When, after their first time together, Sean had asked her to run off to Melbourne with him, she'd barely given a thought to her family and the distress she'd cause them. All that mattered was Sean and how much she loved him.

They'd made promises. The difference between them was that her promises were the truth and Sean's all lies. He *was* a dangerous man, just as she'd been warned, and his temper was hot and frightening, and Rosey seemed to be always igniting it, no matter how hard she tried not to. She sometimes suspected that that last time, when he'd hurt her so much she'd run away, she'd ignited it on purpose. To bring things to a head. To kill her love for him stone-cold dead.

Yet despite the bad things between them, there were still other times when she missed him. He'd been her first lover and they'd had a passion she'd not felt with anyone since. Occasionally, she tried to imagine what would happen if he came by the Red Petticoat. Perhaps he would have changed, realised how much he missed her, and want to make a new start? Then again she and Sean had taken different turns in life, and Rosey knew that hers wasn't one she'd ever want him to know about. If they met again and he found out . . . she'd be lucky to get away. Alive that is.

Because even after all this time Sean would consider her his property. He wouldn't understand the compromises she'd made to survive. Sean just wasn't the understanding type.

* * *

Alice had a bad feeling and it was getting worse. Every time she closed her eyes she could feel the man in the coat leaning over her, breathing his peppermint breath into her face. Of course he wasn't really there, not solid and in person, and yet . . . He was getting closer, she knew it. He was on her scent like a hunting dog. And she didn't know how to stop him.

Because the thing was he could get inside her head. He knew her thoughts, he knew her plans, he knew everything.

Her dreams had become very vivid, too. It was as if she was reliving her life all over again, or the bits and pieces of it her stingy memory would allow her to remember.

She was on the rocky shore with wild water crashing in, her hair blown by a salty wind as she gathered kelp and shellfish. There were other women and children around her, voices rising and falling in a tongue that seemed strange yet familiar.

Then the scene would change. Now there were tall trees by a river and it was hot and steamy, and they were living in a hut with gaps between the boards and spiders in the corners, and she was sitting by herself, feeling sad.

'You should've left her behind,' a man said, lowering his voice, but she could still hear him. 'The girl's bad luck.'

'How could we? She's our blood. Your brother's child. We couldn't abandon her.' The woman glanced her way, tried to smile, shifting the baby at her breast.

'The things she said, on the ship . . .'

'She canna help it,' her voice rising, quickly lowered again. 'She has the sight.'

'Like him.'

'Hush.'

'I wish you'd tell him to go. Him and her.'

'How can I?'

'They're bad luck the pair of them. Both of them not right in the head.'

Sometimes the man in the coat would be close by, his coal-dark eyes fixed on her across a campfire. But she didn't fear him in these memories. She felt that tugging feeling, as if they were tied together by some invisible thread. She heard his voice, stammering, uneven, as if he'd never learned to speak properly. Or couldn't.

Then the memory of the river would come crashing down on her, the hands about her throat, squeezing the life from her, her body limp as he carried her to the barrel. The smell of the peppermint sweets. The water in her mouth. Drowning.

When she woke from her nightmares she had the awful awareness that he was coming for her at Meg's inn, that he knew where she was. He was coming and she didn't know how to stop him.

* * *

The week at Meg's inn was nearly at an end. They'd been busy, with Rosey washing sheets and making up beds for the staying customers, while Meg kept Alice to the cleaning and cooking. Alice was grateful to be away from the clientele, even though in Rosey's opinion they were good-hearted despite their rough edges. Alice had been having more of her nightmares and looked pale and wane. When Rosey asked her about them, trying to help, Alice shook her head.

'The man,' she'd whisper, afraid he could hear her. 'It's the man.'

Meg had been kinder than they'd imagined when they first met her, and they were wondering if they should stay longer. Meg seemed eager for them to remain on a permanent basis, but although Rosey was agreeable Alice wasn't.

'So where would you go to, if you left?' Meg asked one evening in the hot little kitchen.

'Wombat Gully,' Alice said, finding a smile, forgetting to play her role as Alan. 'We're going to find gold there.'

'Are you now?' Meg looked doubtful. 'Well, they keep saying there's plenty to be found, but I've yet to see it.' 'You know, if Wombat Gully turns out no good you should go on to Dunolly.'

'Dunolly?' Alice repeated with a little frown. Her face was clean. Meg had insisted both she and Rosey wash their faces and their clothes, although they'd made certain to huddle under their blankets while they dried before the fire.

'Plenty of shops in Dunolly, and work for those who want it. Plenty of hotels, too. And a dance hall.' Meg caught Rosey's eye and there was something so calculated about it, she felt her face begin to colour.

'We'll be fine,' Rosey said, all gruff male belligerence.

It had the desired effect and Meg shrugged and stopped offering advice.

Saturday night was hectic—Meg's inn had a good reputation. Men called in from the local farms for a drink or two, while the usual passers-through joined the crowd, boasting of nuggets they were yet to find. Rosey was told to go to the stables to see to the horses.

'Can I come?' Alice asked. Tonight she felt jumpy, and she didn't want to be alone.

'No, you have to cook. What do you know about horses anyway?'

'I know as much as you.'

'No you don't. Sean was a groom in Ireland,' Rosey said. Then, with a hesitant glance at Alice, 'I wonder if he's nearby somewhere. Do you think you could have another try at finding him?'

Alice blinked at her. For a moment she felt dazed and then her already pale face went sickly white. She began to shake her head back and forth, her voice rising, 'No, no, no!'

Rosey hurried to grab hold of her. 'Alice, stop it! What's the matter with you? Alice!'

She quietened down, clinging to Rosey now, her body trembling. She began to talk, in a rush at first and after that haltingly.

'I've been dreaming about him. The man in the coat. His face fills my head and . . . he's staring at me. Right at me. He knows where I am, Rosey!'

'They're only dreams, Alice,' Rosey tried to comfort her.

Alice flung herself away. 'No! They're *not only dreams*. Just then, when you said, about Sean . . . I remember that was when I first saw him. His face filling my head. He's . . . he's homing in on me. He's using my gift like a beacon in the night. Every time I let myself open up, to use my sight, he knows. He homes in and now he's coming for me. Rosey, he knows where I am.'

'He's doing the same thing you did when you looked for Sean? Is that what you're saying, Alice?'

'Yes!' she wailed. 'I just know he is, and he's getting closer.'

'How close?'

Alice's face spelled out her terror. 'I can't find out because I'm frightened to look for him. That's what he's waiting for. And I think he's been using my dreams. They've been so real. I daren't sleep anymore. I have to keep myself closed all the time, Rosey, and I can't do that if I'm asleep.'

'But the colours . . . ?'

Alice gave her a look. 'I always see the colours. That's how I see people, Rosey. It just is. I can't shut that off. I know . . .' Tears sprang to her eyes. 'I know you want to know where Sean is and I've been trying to find him. Looking with my sight. Opening up. I didn't know *he* was using the sight to find me.'

'Shoosh, it doesn't matter, Alice. You couldn't know. You were trying to help me.' Rosey tried to smile, and gave Alice's shoulder a squeeze. 'We're leaving tomorrow,' she promised. 'One more night and we're gone.'

'Roddy! I thought I told you to see to the horses?'

Meg poked her head around the door, her manner impatient, before vanishing again. Rosey gave Alice a little shake and nodded to the stove. 'Your chops are burning.'

Glad of the distraction, Alice hurried to lift the heavy pan from the heat. They weren't too badly burnt, and a bit of gravy liberally poured over them would disguise any charring.

Her head was aching. Using the sight did that and she'd been pressing hard to find Sean. She'd had a sense that he was close, too, but she'd wanted to be sure, to surprise Rosey with the good news. Now instead of her being happily reunited with Sean they were going to run away again. Would they ever find somewhere out of harm's way?

What if she could never relax ever again, or sleep, in case the man found her? She wondered if she didn't use the sight again, whether it would eventually shrivel and die and leave her in peace. What a relief it would be! But somehow she didn't think it worked like that. She'd been born with her peculiar abilities, just like the colour of her eyes, and there wasn't much she could do about that.

Alice began to share the meat and potatoes between the plates, then she liberally poured over the gravy. It looked all right, she thought, and glanced at the door. She usually waited for Meg to come and collect the meals, but she knew the woman was very busy tonight. Perhaps she should do it for her? A gesture for Meg's kindness.

She had picked up two of the plates and was walking to the door when she heard a loud voice that sent new chills down her spine.

'Ah, Meg, you're looking as fine as ever!'

'Am I now?' Meg's laugh wasn't quite genuine.

'Forget about stabling the horses! I could eat a bloody horse!'

Meg said something about seeing if the food was ready, and the door swung open and she bustled into the kitchen, red-faced, her hair scraped back. Behind her, as the door closed, a horrified Alice caught a glimpse of the giant in the bowler hat.

Sandhurst flashed into her head, and once more she was snatching his money, and she and Rosey were jumping through the sheep pen and running down the alley.

'What are you doing?' Meg's voice brought her back to the kitchen with a thump. She sounded impatient, as if she'd had to repeat herself. 'Alan? Wake up, lad! Here, take these plates through and I'll bring the rest.'

But Alice hung back and shook her head. 'No. I can't go out there.'

Meg gave her a hard look, thinking Alice was scared of the customers. 'You'll just have to. I haven't got time for mollycoddling. We're busy and you need to help. Now get on with it.'

But again Alice shook her head, shrinking away.

'What is it?' Meg demanded, and although she was harassed and annoyed, there was still something in her voice, something that encouraged Alice to confide in her.

'That man out there. The giant. I know him. I . . . he doesn't like me. I can't go out and let him see me. If he sees me . . .'

Meg stared at her for what seemed a long time, doubt and suspicion and speculation flitting over her plain features. She gave an irritable sigh. 'What happened? Did you steal something of his, you and your . . . brother? Is that it?'

Alice's head sank onto her chest.

'Well you're right to be scared. He'll thrash you to within an inch of your life if he gets hold of you.' She began to pick up the plates. 'Just my luck. I finally get decent help and what happens? So what do you expect me to do, eh? Let you hide in here? I've a good mind to tell him.' But even as Alice gasped and began to beg her not to, Meg was already moving towards the door. With a sharp, 'Wait here,' she went through.

Alice stood frozen to the spot. She wanted to run, but something, perhaps her trust in Meg, kept her there, and a moment later Meg was back for the rest of the plates. She didn't look angry.

'Hold out your hand,' she said.

Alice did so, staring up at her. Meg dropped some coins into her palm. 'Now fetch your things and go tell your brother you're both leaving. I'd keep you hidden, but I know him, too, and I wouldn't trust him an inch. He seems to have a nose for trouble. Best not to take any chances.'

'Thank you,' Alice whispered.

'You'll be long gone before any of this lot notices,' she said, with a jerk of her head towards the bar. 'Go on now, before I change my mind.'

Alice tried to smile, but Meg was already loading herself up with the other plates and heading out the door.

Quickly, Alice went into the lean-to and gathered up their belongings. There wasn't much—they'd left the bulk of it with the wheelbarrow, hidden in the bush along the track. Then she slipped out the back door and went to find Rosey in the stables.

'Rosey?'

Rosey looked up with a start, her eyes wide. Alice tried to tell her what had happened but her words were mixed up. At first Rosey seemed to think the man in the coat had found them and was ordering chops and potatoes in the bar, which for some reason Alice found funny. She began to giggle, but when Rosey grew more and more aggravated Alice composed herself.

'No, Rosey, it's the giant in the bowler hat! The one from the bare-knuckle fight in Sandhurst. He's in the bar and I told Meg he would hurt us if he knew we were here, so she's paid me our wages and told us to get out quick, before he notices us.'

Rosey was already washing her hands in the water barrel, drying them on her trousers. 'Good of her,' she said, 'but I'm not surprised. She might look like a battleaxe, but she's got a good heart, that one.' She looked at Alice and shrugged. 'So where to, then?'

'Wombat Gully, of course.'

'Of course.'

'We need the wheelbarrow.'

'Maybe we should leave the bloody thing. You know how much I hate pushing it through the mud.'

But Alice wouldn't have it, and they set off back along the track. They had their goldmining tools in it, and more importantly Gilbert's book, and Alice couldn't leave that. There was a moon slipping between the clouds, not quite full but almost. Soon they found the spot where they'd hidden their wheelbarrow and other belongings. They appeared untouched, although Alice insisted on checking them over while Rosey waited anxiously, listening to the rustlings in the undergrowth and the breathy hoot of an owl somewhere above. When everything was organised to Alice's satisfaction,

Rosey lifted up the shafts of the barrow and was about to begin pushing it over the uneven ground and out to the track when suddenly Alice reached out a hand to stop her.

Then Rosey heard it, too.

Someone else was coming along the track in the darkness. They could hear footsteps and something else. Whoever was approaching was singing to himself and it was in a language Alice recognised from her nightmares.

Alice froze, her eyes big and dark, staring towards the track. Then the trembling began.

For Alice the fear was all-consuming because she *knew*. She knew that voice. She knew the awful danger they were in. She knew that if she once allowed her mind to open up, even for a second, then he would know. He would sense her. And everything would be over.

She stood, unmoving, not thinking of anything but the moonlight and the man walking along the track singing a hymn in Gaelic. He was directly opposite them now. She watched him go by, her eyes stinging because she didn't dare to blink. In case he heard.

Tall and thin, his long dark cloak was flapping around him. He was looking from side to side, turning his face, and she could see the white oval of it, with dark holes for his eyes.

Like a tickle in her throat the tugging sensation caught at her and began to grow. The need to step out after him. To go to him. She felt herself begin to move, but as soon as she did Rosey caught her arm and held it so tightly it hurt. Then the tickle faded with the singing and the footsteps until there was nothing but silence. But they waited, and waited some more. Just in case he was lingering, ready to pounce.

Eventually, Rosey grabbed her hand and together they began to stagger towards the track, heaving the wheelbarrow along between them.

'It was him,' Alice whimpered. 'It was him and he would've found us if . . . oh, Rosey, he would've found us!'

'Well he didn't and now we're safe,' Rosey said.
'But what if—'
'No "what ifs", Alice. Hurry up!'

* * *

By morning there was a hint of sunshine through the grey clouds. It felt as if their luck might have changed at last. They'd escaped the man in the coat *and* the giant with the bowler hat, and they had money in their pockets and the track to somewhere before them.

Even when the wheel of their wheelbarrow broke off it didn't seem so bad, and they made a bonfire out of it and danced around, screeching and laughing until they fell down exhausted. Now they would have to carry their belongings, so they sorted out only as much as they needed and left the rest by the side of the track. Most of their goldmining paraphernalia they left behind, despite Alice's angst about it.

'You're thinking about the music halls and the hotels in Dunolly,' she blurted out as they set off again. Her bright-blue eyes bored into Rosey's, who avoided them.

'How do you know what I'm thinking? You're not supposed to be using the sight, Alice. The man in the coat . . .'

'I don't need the sight to know what you're thinking,' Alice muttered.

Rosey shrugged. 'All right then, I admit it. The week at the inn was so nice and I really, really don't want to go back to walking to nowhere again. We're never going to find any gold, Alice.' And now Meg's words about Dunolly were whispering in her head.

'Yes, we are,' Alice retorted stubbornly.

'And is that the sight telling you this or just wishful thinking?'

They walked in silence, but when, an hour later, a miserable, wet-looking dog found them and latched onto Alice, the girl cuddled and petted the animal and said they were going to keep it.

'He could be a guard dog,' she informed Rosey.

'He doesn't look like much of a guard dog,' Rosey snapped. She sighed and looked into the expectant eyes of both dog and Alice, and asked what she was going to call the creature.

'His name is Hope,' Alice said, 'and he's going to bring us good luck.'

CHAPTER SIXTEEN

Annie's Story

First I rang for an ambulance and then I rang Ben to take care of Courtney while I accompanied Reuben. Reuben had come round by the time we arrived at the hospital, but they insisted on keeping him in and running some tests. Looking down at his thin body and his colourless face, the oxygen mask at the ready, my heart weighed heavy in my chest.

And to make it worse I couldn't get Courtney's words out of my head: *The man in the backyard looks at him like there's something wrong.* Did the ghost have something to do with this?

'I'll stay,' I said, taking my father's hand. His skin felt cool and I tried to warm it with my own.

He shook his head and his words seemed an effort. 'Go home, Annie. I'll sleep. It was a silly accident, that's all.'

'You didn't see anything?' I knew my voice sounded anxious.

'I tripped on the step and knocked myself unconscious. It could happen to anyone.' He closed his eyes. 'I heard a noise outside . . . I thought I heard a noise. There was no one, Annie. Probably your cat . . .' He trailed off.

I wanted to argue with him about staying, but the nurse assured me that he'd be well looked after. 'He'll sleep. He won't even know you're gone.'

'The doctor . . . ?'

'Will be here in the morning. You can talk with him then. He'll have a better idea of what's wrong with your father.' The woman patted my shoulder. 'That'll be the time to worry. Go home and get some sleep yourself.'

Ben had taken Courtney to his place, so the house seemed very empty. Standing inside the door, I listened, but everything seemed deathly silent. Creepy. I wished there was someone I had to ring, other members of the family. But there was no one. Ben could wait until the morning, and as for telling Courtney, well, it might be best to wait until I knew more about Reuben's prognosis. After my mother died there had only ever been Reuben and me. It was strange because I'd never really felt the lack of other family. Not until now.

I was feeling my solitariness. It was cold, too. With a shiver I hurried to turn on the heating and then wrinkled my nose as the strong smell of peppermint wafted over me. With a frown I checked the heater in case Courtney had dropped a sweet on it or in it, but there was nothing. Anyway, Courtney hated peppermint. I sniffed again but the smell had gone.

The door to the internal stairs was open, just as I'd left it when I found Reuben. I hesitated, remembering Nephetiti hissing before finding my father lying on the landing, but I'd be damned if I'd be frightened in my own house.

The stairs were empty, the light from the upper-floor apartment spilling out onto them. I climbed them quickly, not letting myself think, turned off the light and closed Reuben's door, turning the keys that were still in the lock. And found myself standing in the dark. I flipped the switch for the staircase light. It came on after a few uneven flickers that left my heart pounding.

I carefully examined the top step, but I couldn't see anything Reuben might have tripped over. Could it be an accident, as he said?

He was tired, not concentrating, and he'd misjudged the height of the tread. I'd done it myself. He must have hit his head on the door jamb. Yes, there was some blood there.

No ghost, then, just an accident.

Satisfied, I made my way back down to my own apartment. Before I went inside I paused to stare down the staircase to the door at the bottom, which led out into the backyard. It was closed. There was no one standing there, no one looking up at me with a white face and black holes for eyes . . .

Quickly, I went inside and locked my own door, breathing a sigh of relief. 'Stupid,' I whispered. 'You're being stupid.'

I knew I should go to bed, but like last night my mind was so full of questions I knew I wouldn't sleep. Noticing the computer was hibernating, I remembered the email from the Historical Society. It seemed like the perfect distraction.

Found these. Hope they're of use.

My friend at the Society had been very generous and had sent two images from newspaper archives. I settled down to read every word.

> It is our painful duty to inform friends of Mrs Arnold Potter of Echuca that she passed away early this morning after a long and painful illness. Mrs Potter, formerly Mrs Phillips, or Molly to most, was a much-loved member of this community and her passing creates a void that will be difficult to fill. She leaves behind her husband, Captain Arnold Potter, of the paddle-steamer, *Ariadne*, and a foundling child called Alice, whom Captain Potter saved from the river and his wife took in with her usual generosity. Mrs Potter will be greatly missed.

I read it again, more slowly. Alice *was* a foundling—fancy that arcane word occurring earlier to me and then seeing it here. And saved from the river? What on earth did that mean? Had she fallen off a boat or into the river or simply wandered away from her home? In those days a search for a lost child would not have had the technology or manpower of today. Tragically, children must have disappeared without anyone ever finding them or knowing what happened to them.

Was that what had happened to Alice? She was lost in the bush and then fell into the river and her family never knew whether she lived or died? At least she had Molly to give her a home.

A moment later, still puzzling over these new questions, I was looking at the other, much longer newspaper image. Instantly, the headline pushed every other thought from my head.

Murders in Echuca

The dreadful particulars of the murders that occurred in Echuca over the past months came to light during an inquiry into the death of Mrs Molly Potter who died a year since. The inquiry was held in Echuca over several days. Mr Hogg, the coroner, said he was shocked to the core by the reckless behaviour of the pharmacist, Mr Kent. Five other deaths have also been declared suspicious and are certain to be laid at Mr Kent's door.

The gentleman in question sat quietly, his eyes downcast, as the inquiry continued with statements by Captain Potter, the husband of the deceased, and Doctor Suckling, who treated her during her illness. Neither man realised her death was suspicious and they both were clearly shaken at the extent of Mr Kent's incompetence if not malice in regard to Mrs Potter. Of course his guilt or otherwise is yet to be tested in a court of law.

The summer had been hot, Doctor Suckling pronounced, and there had been much illness in the town due to the lowness of the river and the subsequent outbreaks of typhoid fever. However, Mrs Potter had been ill for some time with a stomach complaint and growing worse, and the doctor stated he had no reason to suspect it was more than that. When asked if he'd been surprised at the suddenness of her demise, he said he'd believed that was due to her ceasing to take her medicine for a time before being persuaded to resume the dosage.

The coroner then asked if this was the medicine that Mr Kent mixed, the medicine that probably killed her, and the doctor shook his head but eventually agreed. Doctor Suckling is a respected member of the Echuca community and seems as shocked as everyone else, but the coroner told him sombrely that he believes he should take some responsibility in the affair. Mr Hogg went on, 'If you'd questioned the sudden death of this patient, despite her long illness, and the deaths of your other five patients, then perhaps this matter could have been resolved a year hence.'

Mr Kent was only discovered to be guilty of the deaths after he made an admission to Captain Potter when the two men were in conversation in the bar of an establishment called the Red Petticoat. Mr Kent had gone there for reasons he refused to disclose but which are assumed to be the company of the women who reside there. Captain Potter had gone there to try to discover what had become of his foundling daughter, Alice Potter, who had been working in the kitchen until recently. At the time Mr Kent seemed to be drunk and it was then he admitted that Mrs Potter's death was due to an oversight by him in the mixing of the medicine prescribed by Doctor Suckling. He said he had added antimony, used as an emetic, when it accidently contaminated one of the other ingredients. Captain Potter was appalled and very rightly went straight to the Police Station to report Mr Kent's words.

The inquiry closed with the coroner's recommendation that Mr Kent be tried in a court of law for murder or manslaughter, whichever seemed most appropriate to the police when they had interviewed him thoroughly.

I was so caught up in what I was reading that it took a moment for me to drag myself back from the scene I was picturing in the courtroom. Had the pharmacist been ultimately charged with murder? Or had he told the truth when he said he'd mistakenly added antimony. And what of the tantalising mention of young Alice? Why was Captain Potter looking for her in a place that went by the dubious name of the Red Petticoat when she should have been at home with him?

I was well aware that some young girls ran wild once a parent or other stable force in their lives was taken away from them. There were times when I'd been pretty wild myself. But surely nine years old was a little young to be running off to a life of debauchery?

'The Red Petticoat!'

I made the connection. I quickly brought up the photographs of the *Trompe L'oeil* on my computer and one scene in particular. And there it was, the narrow two-storey building with the red cloth—the Red Petticoat—hanging from the window. Not a red ribbon but a petticoat. *The Red Petticoat.* It must be!

And Alice had been there. Did that mean she'd also known Gervais Whistler and the Dunolly Music Hall? What about the miners digging for gold? I had always believed the various vignettes in the painting formed parts of Alice's life and now I knew I was right.

I looked again at the young girl staring back at me with those clear-blue eyes, the dog, Hope, hiding in her skirts, her older fair-haired companion by her side.

'Tell me what happened to you, Alice,' I whispered.

Then I waited, holding my breath, almost as if I expected an answer.

CHAPTER SEVENTEEN

The Girl's Story

Wombat Gully was a sprawl of freshly sawn wooden buildings and old canvas tents. Smoke drifted over the settlement, making it difficult to distinguish sharp lines in the murk and softening the proud new frontier town that in reality may not last longer than the month, as had happened repeatedly whenever a rush died.

It was very still, not a breath of wind, as Rosey and Alice set up their small tarpaulin on the outskirts of the town. All the prime locations would be taken, of course. They always were. And Rosey preferred not to draw attention to themselves, as some new arrivals did, by bickering over a better position. So they made do.

They had food and Alice began to light a fire, her fingers swift and nimble, amazing Rosey as she always did with her ability to conjure flame out of dead wood. The dog crept closer, nose twitching at the scent of meat, and Rosey pretended not to notice when Alice threw him a piece.

He wasn't a pretty dog. His coat was a mixture of tan and black and white, his head seemed too big for his body and his tail was a short thick stump, as if someone had decided to lop it off. Even his ears were wrong, too long to stand up straight so that they flopped about in a comical way when he barked.

Rosey sighed. She'd always fancied something grander than this for a pet, an aristocratic sort of cat perhaps, or an Irish wolfhound to follow silently at her heels. But Alice was happy with her new-found friend and it was good to see her smiling. The girl looked pale and tired, she was afraid to sleep in case the man with the coat discovered where she was, and was forever looking over her shoulder. Something had to be done, but Rosey didn't know what.

'Where are ye from?'

The voice came from the tent next door. It was a familiar question whenever anyone new appeared. Rosey was so used to prevaricating by now that she hardly gave it a thought. They were from Ballarat via Ireland, she said blithely, and following their Da who was somewhere on the road up ahead.

'Shouldna leave two young lads on their own. Tis no' safe.'

She shrugged at the equally familiar reply, and coughed on the smoke from the hundreds of campfires that hung over Wombat Gully. There was a gunshot some distance away, as if to underscore the stranger's warning, but the sound was soon swallowed up by the swarm of humanity surrounding them.

'You haven't seen a man on the track, have ye? Tall, thin, wearing a dark coat? He's wanted by the police.' He rustled a newspaper rather aggressively in her direction.

Rosey found herself staring inward, the memory vivid in her mind. The moonlight, that white face and the dark eyes like holes. He'd been like one of the horror tales her granny used to tell her on stormy nights. She struggled to find her voice. 'Wanted for what?'

'He attacked a woman at an inn. Knocked her about pretty badly.'

Suddenly, her head was very clear, the hands she held out towards the fire perfectly steady. Rosey had always been good in a crisis. She glanced sideways at Alice, but the girl was too busy with the meal to have heard. She had one hand on Hope to restrain his enthusiasm, although by the way the dog was wriggling it wouldn't be long before he escaped her grasp.

'Where was the inn?' she said, finally giving the fellow her full attention. He was a Scot with a broad Glaswegian accent, dirty grey hair tucked back behind his ears and a scruffy beard encircling his jaw.

'Here, read it for yoursel',' he offered. 'It's only a week old and I was lucky to get it.'

'You read it for me,' Rosey retorted.

He gave her a knowing look but didn't make the gaffe of letting on he was aware she couldn't read. Straightening out the creases, he began with theatrical relish:

Mrs Meg Jamieson was knocked unconscious and kicked by a man who visited her inn on Saturday night two weeks past. The man enticed her into the back room of the inn, away from her customers, before assaulting her. Mrs Jamieson, who is recovering, said he told her he was looking for a girl dressed as a boy, who stole some money from him and he'd been told she was staying at Mrs Jamieson's inn. The man was large and wearing a bowler hat, and is known to the police. He may be associated with a second man also seen about the inn that night, described as Scots, tall and thin with a dark coat and dark hair. Neither of them should be approached.

'You're Scotch, aren't you?' she said a little breathlessly, trying not to think of poor Meg lying on the floor being kicked by the bully in the bowler hat.

He gave her a cold look. 'It wasn't me, lad. Scotsmen like that give the country a bad name.'

'Sounds like a lunatic, don't he?' she added for good measure. 'Me and me brother'll look out for him. And I'll tell Da. Maybe there's a reward?'

The man laughed easily and shook his head. 'If there was a reward for every lunatic walking the goldfields we'd all be rich. I'll have a talk to your father when I see him.' There was a note in his voice.

Rosey knew he didn't believe her, or at the very least he was suspicious.

'You ever been up Echuca way?' he asked with studied innocence. 'Ever heard of a place called the Red Petticoat?'

'The red what?' she said, while her brain was turning in circles. How did he know? And *what* did he know?

Just then Alice passed her a plate and as she took it she leaned close to the girl and whispered, 'We'll have to go.'

Alice's eyes grew wide but she said nothing. No questions, no arguments, no reservations, that wasn't Alice's way. Rosey spoke in a loud voice as they ate, chattering on about 'home' and 'Da' and the 'little 'uns', in case the Scot next door was listening, but apart from a murmur here and there Alice was silent. Occasionally, she'd throw a scrap to the dog, her smile as he chomped it up the only ripple in her gravity. Eventually, the Scotsman had vanished back into his tent, but Rosey continued to feel the threat of his presence.

Still, Alice had to be told about Meg, and wriggling closer Rosey proceeded to do so.

Alice trembled as she listened to Rosey and immediately said, 'The giant knew we were there, that was why he came.'

Rosey was sure Meg was no fool. She'd known the giant was after Alice and refused to tell him anything, and that was why he hurt her. And the man in the dark coat had been there, too. Had they been in cahoots, as the newspaper suggested? Two vicious creatures in league? She shivered at the evil madness of it and pulled her scarf closer about her throat, as if it might protect her.

'What now?' she whispered. 'Will the man in the coat still be looking for us?' Her breath was white and it was only then she realised how icy the air had become.

In a reversal of their roles, Alice looked at her as if she wasn't sure Rosey could deal with the truth.

'I expect so,' she said.

'But why? I can understand why the other one wants to find you, you stole his money. But why does *he* want to find you, Alice?'

'I don't know. It's as if there's something binding us together, and no matter how I run he will follow. I-I don't think he was always bad, Rosey.'

Rosey tossed down her empty plate and the dog promptly pounced on it, pink tongue lapping. 'Wasn't always bad? He killed Miss Oliver, didn't he? And now he's helped the giant find us. That's bad enough.'

Alice stroked the dog's head, deep in thought, or perhaps she was just choosing her words with care. Rosey began to wonder if it was she who was looking after Alice, or the other way round. The girl had obviously remembered more than she was sharing, but Rosey had the impression Alice hadn't spoken about it because she was being protective.

Her anger faded and her heart softened. 'Alice, please, you need to tell me everything. *Everything.*'

'We don't know he killed Miss Oliver,' Alice said in a wooden little voice. 'I heard another man that night, arguing with her. And at the inn it was the giant who hurt Meg. I know he tried to drown me in the river. I remember him carrying me and putting me into the barrel. But there are other memories, times when he was my friend. They're all tangled up together and sometimes my head hurts so much I can't think.'

'Your friend?' scoffed Rosey. 'Funny way of showing it.'

Alice stroked Hope, who had jumped back onto her lap again, curling up to keep warm. She covered him with part of her jacket so that only his nose and eyes showed, peeking out at Rosey.

'He tried to drown me. He put me in the barrel and tried to drown me. I just wish he'd go away and leave me alone. I remember the yard and his hands around my throat, and the world going black. I remember . . .'

Rosey was looking at her in horrified astonishment.

'Alice, why didn't you tell this story to Captain Potter?'

Alice shook her head and her blue eyes were old and wise. 'I didn't remember it all then. I still don't remember it all. And anyway, they wouldn't have listened, Rosey. Doctor Suckling said I was simple. Who would believe anything said by a simple child?'

Rosey wanted to argue, to tell her that it wasn't true, but she knew enough about the world to accept that it probably was. And Captain Potter, Alice's only protector, had abandoned her. She had no one in the world, apart from Rosey and Hope.

'We're not going to let the man catch us,' Rosey swore. 'We're not, Alice.'

She had been about to mention the Scotsman's question about the Red Petticoat, but she decided not to. Alice had enough to deal with just now, and besides, they were leaving Wombat Gully. Whatever the Scotsman next door knew they would be long gone by the time he awoke.

* * *

Alice didn't sleep well. Her head was full of visions of her pursuer, his white face and blazing eyes, his fury fuelled by peppermint lozenges. She'd always been made to feel different, strange, and sometimes it seemed fair and just that she be punished for it. Because she was different. Because of what she could see in others. She was a creature beyond redemption, and some of that conviction was still there, clinging to her soul like the mud that caked her boots.

He had hurt her, tried to kill her. His behaviour towards her had left thorns in her flesh, and she was finding it very difficult to pull them out.

And now there was the strain of keeping the sight locked up tight inside her so that he couldn't use it to find her. She barely slept, dared not relax her vigilance even for a minute. She knew he was out there somewhere, waiting. She could feel him, his hot breath on her face.

Alice squirmed within her blanket, Hope whining at her side, fighting with her demons, until dawn crept through the holes in their tarpaulin.

* * *

As soon as it was light enough they packed up quietly, not daring to build a fire but making do with some stale crusts of bread. Rosey noticed the edge of the newspaper peeking out of the Scotsman's tent, and carefully eased it free. There might be something else in the paper about the man in the dark coat, or the Red Petticoat, something he'd kept from them. She'd ask Alice to read it next time they came to a halt.

Perhaps he wanted them blamed for Meg's attack just as they were being blamed for Miss Oliver. Was that what Alice's man in the dark coat wanted? The law could take care of them and leave him free to do whatever it was he did.

Rosey shuddered. How had Alice fallen into his clutches? How much would a child remember of her past? That man had *been* her past, until he'd tried to murder her.

For the next few days they walked on, mostly in silence, Alice now and then calling to Hope and petting him for being a good boy. Wombat Gully was well behind them and Rosey decided that even the cold, wet road wasn't so bad when set against the thought of a small, dank gaol cell and a hangman's rope at the end of it.

Alice had read the newspaper but said there was only the story about Meg in it, and although Rosey had her suspicions the girl was keeping something from her she couldn't accuse her of it, not when she couldn't read herself. But there were times when Alice seemed to believe Rosey needed protecting and no one had ever protected Rosey before.

The track they were following ran through thin-trunked trees and over hills and through gullies, while all about them were the remains of previous diggings, abandoned now. That seemed to be the way of this country. Miners flocked to the gold like birds to the sun, stayed awhile, and then like birds in the winter were gone again, leaving a landscape that looked as if it had been turned upside down.

Sometimes they found a lone miner, picking over the already worked claims, searching for any gold that had been missed. Once a Chinaman watched them suspiciously as they hurried past. The Chinese were known for working over old diggings and making a good living from that, and for some reason Rosey could not understand, that made the other miners hate them.

The dog was barking. Rosey looked up. Before them was a swiftly moving creek, with brown and murky water. All this rain had swollen even the smallest trickle of a stream into something wild and dangerous, and whereas they probably could have crossed this one with a single jump back in the summer, it was now too wide to do anything but wade through it.

Rosey was inclined to walk along and find a better spot, and she'd taken a few steps along the bank when she heard a splash. Her heart leapt into her mouth. 'No, Alice, it's too deep!'

The younger girl had already started to cross, holding her belongings up high, the water pulling at her clothes. She got to the middle and struggled a moment to keep her footing—perhaps there was a hole—and then slipped sideways and went beneath the water.

Hope had jumped in after her, paddling furiously towards the spot where Alice went under. Rosey struggled out of her own belongings and threw them down, already splashing into the creek, too frightened even to feel the cold of it weighing down her clothing.

Alice bobbed up again, gasping for air, making a high keening sound. Her eyes were wide open and her hair plastered to her head. Hope barked, scrabbling at her, then Rosey reached them—the water was up to her waist and the current strong—and grabbed hold of Alice, dragging her towards the shore.

She lay like a stone, a dead weight, and when Rosey hauled her onto the bank she thought she might be unconscious. Or dead. But Alice wasn't dead. She was in a state Rosey had never seen before. Unable to move or talk, as if she was in some sort of trance.

She sank down beside Alice. Both of them were wet and shivering and she pulled her close, rocking her until eventually Alice seemed to regain her senses, her stiff body softening, and uttered a moan.

'He put me in the barrel, he put me in the barrel, he put me in the barrel.'

She sounded as if the incident that happened a year ago had only just happened this moment. She sounded shocked and frightened and betrayed.

'I remember. I remember. He was my friend and he tried to drown me! Why would he do that? Why is he trying to hurt me?'

'Shoosh, Alice. You're safe now, everything is all right now. Shoosh.'

Hope sat down and watched them, head cocked to the side, as if he understood everything they said. He was wet, too, and every now and again he'd give an almighty shudder. Then all of a sudden he jumped up again and began barking, his floppy ears as cocked as he could make them.

He was staring at something behind them on the bank and Rosey knew, even before she heard his voice, that there was someone there. Her body slumped in despair. The man in the black coat . . . Suddenly she didn't care. She'd had enough.

They'd reached the end of their adventure.

CHAPTER EIGHTEEN

Annie's Story

When I reached the hospital and finally found Reuben's room through the maze of corridors and lifts and stairwells, he was sitting up in bed, eating breakfast. He smiled when he saw me. I noticed another patient in the bed next to him who looked a lot worse, a fact Reuben seemed to take a perverse pleasure in quietly pointing out to me when I sat down beside him.

'I didn't bring anything,' I said, realising with dismay that the other patient had vases brimming with flowers. 'Did you want me to nip back down to the gift shop and—'

'No point,' he interrupted. 'They can't find anything seriously wrong with me. I can come home today.' Then, with an anxious glance, 'If someone will stay with me.'

'That's fine.' I hadn't expected to go into work today anyway. 'I'll find out when you can be discharged.' I headed to the nurses' station and I only had a brief wait before the doctor was available to speak with me.

He wasn't as nonchalant as Reuben. I knew my father had been overworking, not looking after himself, generally putting his own health on a lower par than the marbling on the fireplaces. Now I learned his heart wasn't in great shape and last night he'd been on the verge of a heart attack. I was angry. At Reuben, at myself, at the situation that seemed to have developed without either of us putting a stop to it.

The doctor was a middle-aged man of Asian descent with a permanent frown. 'When your father came in last night I wasn't happy with his blood pressure or his heart rate, but this morning they're much improved. There doesn't seem to be anything structurally wrong with his heart, and of course we'll do more tests, but I think it's safe to assume the culprit is stress. Can he take some time off? Go for a holiday and relax?'

'My father doesn't believe in holidays,' I said.

'Well, he's going to need time to rest and recuperate. He thinks he tripped and fell, but I think he lost consciousness before he tripped and that's *why* he fell. He should take this as a warning.'

'I'll make sure he rests, Doctor.'

His eyes were kind. 'He tells me his business isn't doing too well and that he doesn't want to worry you. He insists it's all under control, or it will be when he's found a way to fix it.'

Startled, I gave a rough sort of laugh. 'Thanks, Dad.'

He touched my arm, a brief professional brush of his fingers. 'You should talk with him. I've seen lots of men like your father, believe me, and they have to ask for help eventually. He's lucky he has you to ask.'

I nodded, but I felt sick.

'I take it there are no other children? His wife . . . ?'

'No, it's just me and him.'

The business was in trouble. Why hadn't he told me about it? Was it so hard for him to ask me for help, or even to discuss his problems with me? When had we become islands living in the same house?

There was a cold little ball of dread in my stomach. Here was Reuben, always telling me to follow my heart, not to worry about practical concerns . . . And the business was in trouble. I knew that

Reuben and Reuben meant everything to him. It had been his life since Geneva died, and he'd told me only the other day that everything would be mine one day. My father had been hiding the truth from me, but it seemed he had also been hiding it from himself.

Well, Reuben and Reuben might mean everything to him, but I was damned if I was going to let it kill him.

The doctor's beeper went off and with him gone, I sat for a while, mulling over my father, our business and the future. There was a growing sense of hurt and outrage that he hadn't shared his concerns with me, but I was as much to blame as him. I should have stepped out of my comfortable cocoon and seen what was going on. I should have insisted I do my share.

With a deep breath I stood up and made my way back to Reuben's room, pasting a smile on my face as I walked through the door. My father needed me to be strong. He needed to get better. Recriminations on both sides could wait until later.

CHAPTER NINETEEN

The Girl's Story

'I said are you two all right?'

The man stood above and behind them, silhouetted against the glare. Rosey's heart was bumping with fear, but when he took a running step down the bank, she gasped with relief. He was a young man, his hair a vivid orange against the grey bush. He was dressed in the usual goldminer's outfit of moleskins and a checked red cotton shirt, both well-worn from his travels.

'We're all right.' She managed to stagger to her feet, hampered by her sodden clothing. Her trousers were slipping down and she hauled them up, her jacket dragging halfway down her arms. 'We'd better be on our way,' she added, not caring how ludicrous it sounded. Although he appeared harmless enough, women—even those dressed as men—did not converse with strange men alone in the bush.

His gaze slid down and his eyes widened. Rosey followed the direction of his stare and realised her shirt was wet and outlining her breasts. She pulled her jacket tight around her, furious with him and herself.

'I suppose it's no use me telling you my name is Roddy,' she said.

He gave her an embarrassed smile. 'Ah, no. Probably not. Look, I have a camp just over the way,' he went on. 'My mate's been sick and we've been resting. You're welcome to come and have a brew with me, get dry, before you move on. I won't tell anyone you're not Roddy,' he added with a twinkle in his light-blue eyes.

Rosey knew she should refuse. He sounded nice, even rather posh for a miner, but she wasn't so foolish as to trust a man just because he sounded like a gentleman. But before she could refuse him, Alice was tugging on her arm. 'Rosey, please.'

She looked down at the girl's wan, white face and sopping attire and didn't have the heart to refuse her.

So they followed him back to his camp. It was several yards away from the track, sheltered in the bush, which explained why they hadn't seen it when they'd passed by. Rosey caught a waft of mutton stew in the distance and tried not to groan aloud.

'My name's Josh Parker,' he said, with a smile over his shoulder.

It was a nice smile.

'We're Mary and Jane Kelly,' Rosey lied.

'Hello to you both, Mary and Jane Kelly.'

Rosey found herself admiring the straight line of his back and his wide shoulders. His hair had been cut short but was now long enough to be straggling around his nape. He didn't have that pale freckly skin that redheads were prone to, and when he smiled his teeth were good. Some women liked a strong jaw or a straight nose, but Rosey was always taken with a good set of teeth.

'Here we are.' His voice interrupted her thoughts and she looked up and saw they'd reached a clearing. Newly washed clothing was draped over the branch of a tree, while a bag of camp supplies had been tied up high on the same tree branch, presumably to keep it safe from scavengers. Her experienced eye took in the worn tent snuggled among some of the spindlier trees that dominated the landscape, while a fire was burning low, with plenty of ash to show this wasn't the first, and a tripod of branches over the top of it held a blackened billy boiling tea leaves and water. A battered-looking cast-iron pot nestled at the edge of the fire, and Rosey's stomach growled, because that was where the delicious smell of mutton stew was emanating from. It was almost more than she could bear.

'Sit yourselves down.'

Josh pointed out a log that had been dragged up to the fireside and sliced horizontally with an axe to turn it into a seat that allowed the sitter to be comfortably above the damp ground.

Rosey and Alice sat down, shivering in their wet clothes, while Josh set out some tin mugs, and using a piece of cloth over the handle, lifted the billy from the fire to fill them.

'Where're you from?' Rosey asked, to be polite. She felt dizzy when he took the lid off the stew pot, and beside her, arms tight around Hope, Alice swallowed loudly.

'Somerset. In England. A town called Frome,' he said, and now the faint west-country burr to his voice was more obvious, although Rosey would swear this was no farm boy. Mr Joshua Parker had been educated.

'What're you doing here?' she said, hearing the poverty and ignorance in her own voice. She felt a moment of shame, and then the shame turned to anger at herself for feeling it.

'Looking for gold. My mate and I are determined to find a nugget or two, just to prove this hasn't been a wild goose chase.'

He made it sound like a game of hide and seek, rather than the dangerous adventure it was.

'What's the matter with your mate?' Alice was giving the tent some sideways glances, and Rosey guessed that she could sense something.

Josh was saying, '. . . Took sick at Wombat Gully, but he seemed to be getting better, so we started off along the track. But whatever was wrong with him came back again. Wombat Gully is home to a Chinese fellow who treats the sick miners and he gave us some herbs to boil up—that was what seemed to fix him up before. I've been giving him the same stuff and he seems to be mending.'

Josh handed them their tea. 'Here you are, Mary and Jane.'

The warmth of the fire was helping to dry them off at the front, but their backs were still wet, and Rosey longed to toast herself properly. When Josh went inside the tent to see to his mate, she stood up to get closer to the fire, feeling the heat against her legs.

'I'm tired of being a man,' she complained to Alice. 'I want to wear a pretty skirt again and a nice hat, and have my hair in ribbons.'

'Do you think he'll offer us some stew?' Alice whispered. 'I'm starving. All we've got is stale bread and some mutton chops that are just about off. I was going to stock up in Wombat Gully, but then we had to leave.'

'Give him one of your looks, *Jane*, and he won't be able to resist,' she whispered back.

'What looks?'

'The one where you make your eyes all big and sad, and suck your cheeks in as if you haven't eaten for a week.'

Alice frowned. 'I don't do that, Rosey.'

'Yes, you do, and I'm Mary, remember?'

'He's handsome, don't you think?' Alice said with a sly glance.

Rosey shrugged. 'Didn't notice.'

Just then Josh came out of the tent. His gaze flicked to Rosey and he had such a strange expression on his face that she thought he'd overheard them.

'My mate . . .' he began.

His mate must have died! Then it occurred to her that if his mate was gone it would mean more stew for herself and Alice, and she wondered when she'd become such a callous cow.

'I'm sorry—' she began.

'My mate heard your voice,' he spoke over the top of her words, 'and he thinks . . . he thinks he knows you. I told him your name was Mary Kelly, but he insists it isn't. He asked me to ask you . . . Can you be Roisin O'Donoghue?'

Was it a trick? Perhaps they were policemen in disguise about to arrest them for murder. Or perhaps the man in the dark coat was inside the tent, waiting to pounce.

'Her name is—' Alice began but Rosey kicked her.

Seeing their expressions Josh lifted his arms and then dropped them again. 'I'm sorry. Thing is, he talks about this Roisin. Sometimes in his sleep. So I don't expect you're her. I just had to ask.'

'Roisin O'Donoghue?' Rosey asked, as if the name was foreign to her tongue. 'And what's your mate's name?'

'Sean Murphy.'

It was as if Rosey's heart went tumbling into a dark tunnel. She didn't know whether or not to turn and run. She stood up and as she did so a voice spoke her name from the open flap of the tent and she saw a man there, half slumped in the shadows. His face looked yellow and gaunt, but his blue eyes were brilliant with the joy of seeing her again.

'Ah, Rosh,' he said, his voice raw and croaky, and it was Sean's voice.

Rosey went cold. The past came rushing at her from the tunnel like a steam engine. All the fear and pain. The constant niggling worry that he would find her.

And now here he was!

It was almost a relief. But what should she do? Bolt, or bluff it out? Rosey knew she'd already waited too long to answer. She could see the old familiar anger building in his face.

'Rosh.' It was a warning.

Rosey ran into his arms. The decision wasn't so difficult after all. Sean had been her first and only love, and he was sick, maybe dying, and the cold, practical side of her told her she could pretend to be happy to see him until then.

She wrapped him in her arms, dirty and sweaty as he was, her tears streaking his face and hers. 'Oh, Sean,' she sobbed. 'I've . . . I've missed you so. I went back, after, but you were gone.'

It was a lie, but he didn't seem to notice, or if he did he didn't care.

'I've missed you.' He sighed. 'Will you forgive me, Roisin?'

She wanted to say that, yes, she forgave him, but the words stuck in her throat. He'd ruined his life and her own, and when she thought of what might have been . . . well, she couldn't forgive him for that.

Abruptly, his strength vanished. His arms fell away from her and his eyes fluttered closed. 'Ah, Roisin,' he whispered, 'stay with me. Stay until I—'

Die.

She didn't want him to say it, the word would strip bare the lie she was acting out, so Rosey pressed her lips hard to his to stop the word. She felt him laughing, as if her wild passion pleased him, but a moment later he'd slipped into sleep. Or unconsciousness. She sat back and stared at him, his face so peaceful and although thinner and sallow, still with traces of the handsome man who'd swept her heart and good sense right out from under her.

He looked harmless, yet it was hard for her to accept what she was seeing. She had spent so long fearing him, but Rosey decided that if these moments were his last then she'd gladly play the part of the mourning lover. Better *this* Sean, weak and dying, than the dangerous man who'd knocked her about. She could cope with *this* Sean.

* * *

Alice was feeling queasy, and it wasn't just because she'd nearly drowned in the river and all those uncomfortable memories had come back to her—she was going to save examination of them until later. She was starving and the smell of the stew was driving her to madness, but she'd been hungry before. No, it was knowing that Sean was in the tent. Sean was here, only a few steps from her, and she hadn't been able to tell Rosey because she hadn't been able to use the sight.

Over these past weeks, when she'd been closing herself off, she'd realised how much a part of her the sight was. All of her life she'd hated it and wished it gone. It had brought her nothing but grief, and then the man in the dark coat had made her hate it all the more. But now she missed it like a terrible ache inside. The truth was that without it she felt out of kilter. Off balance. Not at all herself.

And now Sean was here and there were storm clouds gathering.

But there was something else—she gave a shiver—Rosey was wrong. Her colours were wrong. Not the bright, happy colours Alice was used to seeing about her. There was an ominous dark streak cutting through the brightness, and it worried Alice. Was that because of Sean? She couldn't understand it; it made no sense.

'Jane, is it?'

Alice blinked. Josh was speaking to her, although he didn't look very comfortable. She decided that he wasn't used to the company of young girls. Perhaps, she thought, he didn't have any younger sisters and didn't know what to say. His lack of confidence made her more disposed to like him.

He seemed to be waiting for an answer so she nodded.

'Your friend knows Sean and Sean knows your friend.'

Alice nodded again. She couldn't get Rosey out of her head. She was over there inside the tent with Sean. Sean, her long lost love, who was so sick he might be dying. She tried to focus on the tent now, screwing up her eyes, visualising the man inside and whether his dark colours were dark enough to show death was close.

'Jane?' Josh interrupted her.

She gave an impatient sigh. It was no use, she couldn't concentrate. She looked up into Josh's blue eyes. For the first time she focused on Josh's colours, and found them unusual. There was a great deal of blue, a calming blue, like the colour of his eyes, that made her feel safe. Looking at Josh was much more pleasant than looking at the tent.

Hope stirred. Alice stroked his ears, settling him down at her side. He'd tried to save her in the river and now she thanked him and praised him for his bravery. Josh was busying himself ladling out a plate of mutton stew, and when he held one out to her, she received it gratefully. She began to eat, stopping now and then to share morsels with Hope, which he quickly snapped up, gazing longingly at her for more.

'You're not really Jane Kelly, are you?' Josh spoke matter-of-factly. He'd waited until she'd finished her stew and set her plate down for Hope to clean.

He didn't seem to feel any grievance over the lie.

'She's Rosey and I'm Alice.'

'Are you sisters?'

Alice wished they were. 'No, we're friends.'

'What are you both doing out here on your own? The goldfields aren't the place for lone females.'

Alice held her lips in a prim line and didn't answer.

He bit back a smile. 'I see you have a secret, Alice. I won't ask you to breach it. Your business is your own. But I think you'll be staying here for a little while, at least until Sean . . .'

'Dies,' Alice said. 'Or not. He might get better. I'm not sure yet.'

He gave her a strange look. 'While you're here it'd be nice if we were friends. I don't mean you any harm, Alice.'

He might seem safe enough, but Alice wasn't about to trust him to be her friend. She took out the newspaper and began to read it. Josh's mouth twitched as he watched her, as if she amused him, although she couldn't imagine why. She was glad she'd torn out the paragraph about her and Rosey and burned it.

She'd burned the words because she was worried Rosey would be upset by them, but now she was twice as glad because she didn't want Sean to see them, or Josh, of course, but more particularly Sean. Alice had a strong feeling, and it had nothing to do with the sight, that Sean would not be happy seeing Rosey called a prostitute.

After a while the sound of the tent flap being opened interrupted their quiet camaraderie, and Rosey appeared, looking all-in. Hope gave a little bark, but Alice hushed him, and watched as her friend staggered over to the campfire and sank down.

Josh handed her a mug of tea, and although it was stewed and lukewarm, she drank it down gratefully in one go. Meanwhile, he ladled stew onto a fresh plate and when he passed it to her, Rosey wolfed it down without a word. It was only when she was done that Alice spoke.

'He knows we're not Mary and Jane.'

Rosey took a shaky breath. 'Of course he does. Perhaps he's not Josh Parker from Frome?'

Josh anxiously assured them that he was. 'I haven't had the desire to change my name yet, ladies,' he said, then added hastily, 'although I'm sure you both have very good reasons.' He was being polite. He could have said something nasty, cast aspirations, as Molly used to say, but he hadn't. Alice decided he was far more of a gentleman than any so-called 'gentlemen' she'd ever met. There was something about him that reminded her of Gilbert, as if he'd been taught proper manners.

Then she noticed that Rosey and Josh were looking at each other.

Even with her fair hair dried in a tangled mess and her tired, pale face and creased, worn man's clothes, Rosey was beautiful. Alice could see that Josh Parker admired her, and a tremor of unease rippled over her. But she reassured herself that men always looked at Rosey in that way, as if they thought every word she spoke was a speck of gold dust.

'How long have you and Sean been together?' Rosey was pushing her hair out of her eyes.

Josh cleared his throat. 'We met in Melbourne,' he said, and began to tell them how he and Sean had set off together down the dusty road to the diggings. They'd had many adventures since then, good and bad, and as Josh touched lightly on some of the stories, making them amusing for the girls' benefit, Rosey smiled and Alice laughed.

But it was Rosey who Josh was watching. It was as if there was a warm glow coming from inside her, shining out, and Josh was captivated.

Alice felt a sudden need to reach out and take Rosey's hand, to warn her, but Rosey looked dazed. Their colours were changing, mimicking each other in a way Alice had never seen before. This sudden attraction between them was frightening her and her sense of foreboding was growing.

Abruptly, Josh stood up. Avoiding their eyes, as if he, too, felt uneasy, he murmured something about seeing if Sean was hungry and went into the tent. Rosey turned to Alice, her eyes sparkling with anger. 'I wish you'd warned me Sean was here.'

'How could I? I wasn't using the sight. Rosey, the man in the dark coat—'

'Is he going to die? You can tell me that, can't you? You're good at knowing when people are going to die.'

Alice looked away. 'I'm trying.'

* * *

Rosey knew she was being unreasonable. None of this was Alice's fault. But her emotions were all topsy-turvy and she couldn't seem to help herself. She wanted to tell Alice the truth about Sean, but after all her lies how could she? No, she'd just have to bide her time and see how things panned out. And now Josh Parker . . .

She hadn't felt like this since she first set eyes on Sean, and now, right under Sean's nose, she was feeling it again. For another man. For his mate, and a gentleman to boot! Rosey and a gentleman! If it wasn't so alarming it would be funny. There was a little warning tapping in her brain, saying: *Be careful, Rosey. Sean is a dangerous man, even if he is sick. For the sake of both Alice and yourself, don't trust him, not even for a minute.*

Alice was muttering something about dark colours, but Rosey ignored her. She had her own problems. She must show Sean she was still his, she must never let him see she was attracted to Josh.

As if a gentleman like that would want you for more than a quick poke, mocked the voice in her head. *That's all you're good for, and you're a fool to imagine it could be anything else.*

'Roisin!' Sean again, crying out for her.

Steeling herself, Rosey got up and followed Josh inside the tent.

* * *

Alice was upset. She knew she'd failed her friend once and she didn't want to do it again. Something was wrong and she needed to understand what it was. Squeezing her eyes tightly closed, she slowly and deliberately opened her mind to the sight.

If *he* had been there, she'd have closed it again, but he wasn't. Relaxing further she settled back, Hope in her arms, and let her thoughts turn towards the tent where Sean lay.

It took some time for her to be able to 'see' with that part of her that knew the future—perhaps it was a little rusty from disuse. The first thing she saw was Rosey in tears, her face blotched and almost ugly with grief. Did that meant Sean had died? Why else would Rosey be crying so hard? She tried to expand her sight, but almost at once a sudden whiff of peppermint filled her head and she closed herself down again.

He was still there.

Waiting.

He'd been her friend. She remembered that earlier, as she was flailing about in the creek. Why had her friend tried to kill her? Somehow knowing she'd trusted him made it so much worse.

Another gust of peppermint and she felt as if he was right there, bending over her, staring into her face.

Her eyes sprang open and she looked wildly about her, but all she saw was Josh, sitting on the opposite side of the fire. Her newspaper was spread before him and she was more than ever glad she'd torn out the paragraph.

'Are you all right?' he said, leaning forward with a frown. 'I thought you were asleep. Was it a bad dream?'

Alice shuddered. 'A very bad dream.'

He nodded, eyeing her uneasily. 'I hope you don't mind me borrowing your newspaper,' he said. 'I haven't had any news in weeks, and then it was old news.'

'We "borrowed" it, too. From a man at Wombat Gully.'

For a moment he looked confused, and then the penny dropped and he gave a chuckle. 'Won't he miss it?'

'He might.'

Josh smiled and this time it was a proper smile. 'You look hungry again,' he said. 'Your eyes are too big for your face and your cheeks have hollows.'

Alice wished Rosey had heard him say it, even though it proved her right and Alice wrong, but Rosey was with Sean.

'Is there any more of that mutton stew?' she asked primly. 'It was delicious. Hope thought so, too.'

'I'm glad Hope approved. There's plenty left, Alice. I'll dish some up for you. And Hope,' he added, with a raised eyebrow at the little dog.

Alice smiled. She'd been right, he *was* a nice man.

'I wonder,' he began, as he set the plates down, 'if you'd mind me sketching you? I like to sketch. I have a portfolio full of characters I've met on my travels. One day I want to have them printed into a book. If anyone's interested, that is,' he added wryly.

Alice took the plate from him. 'Am I a "character"?'

Josh gave his shy chuckle. 'You certainly are, Alice.'

'All right, then. Do I have to look a certain way?'

He shook his head, already getting out a sketchbook he'd had on the ground beside him, and a piece of charcoal he selected from the edge of the campfire. 'Just do whatever you're doing. Don't worry about posing.'

Alice glanced at him several times as she ate, but he was quiet and unobtrusive and she soon forgot about him as she saw to Hope and praised him for cleaning up his plate. The food made her sleepy and she began to yawn and soon curled up by the fire. Drowsily, she heard Hope barking and Josh's soft murmur, but she couldn't open her eyes. Too many nights without enough sleep and too much worry were taking their toll. She felt safe here, and although she knew *he* was still hunting her, she told herself that even if he found her, Hope would protect her.

CHAPTER TWENTY

Annie's Story

I made up a comfortable bed in the spare room, bringing down some of Reuben's things from the apartment above. But Reuben refused to go to bed. He wanted to go upstairs by himself, and, when I refused to let him, reminding him of the doctor's orders, he insisted on sitting on the sofa in the lounge.

I ended up sharing with him what I'd found out about Alice, and showing him the newspaper story about Molly's death. He read it, shaking his head, before setting it aside.

'I was right about the *Trompe L'oeil* vignettes being part of Alice's life,' I went on. 'They really are telling her story. It's quite marvellous.'

'It is,' he agreed, 'and all the more reason for you to see it goes on display so that everyone sees it and it doesn't end up being locked away.'

He was right and I knew I would fight to see Alice tell her story to the world. But there were more important considerations just now—at the top of the list were Reuben's health and the business.

These things needed to be discussed, but right now he looked so ill I didn't think it was a good idea.

'Is Courtney coming home tonight?' he asked, his head bent, fiddling with the blanket I'd put over his knees.

'Yes. Ben's bringing her over. I haven't told her much, just that you're not well.'

He nodded.

'Papa, I've been thinking . . . Remember the diaries Mum kept? Do you think she might have mentioned the ghost in them? Could I take a look?'

He looked surprised. 'Of course you can. But I thought you read them when you turned thirteen? That was what she wanted and I gave them to you so that you could . . .'

'I didn't read them properly,' I said. 'They made me sad.'

He shook his head at me in weary amusement. 'Oh, Annie.'

'I'm sorry.'

But he gave me a crooked smile. 'Nothing to be sorry about. Of course you can read them. They're in the secretaire. Get them now if you want and we can look at them together.'

I wasn't exactly sure if I wanted to look at them together—what if there was something embarrassing and private in them? Neither of us would know where to look. Besides which he seemed so vulnerable at the moment and I didn't want to upset him with sad memories. But dutifully, I went upstairs to find them.

As soon as I opened the door I noticed that his rooms felt much colder than mine, and there was that strange smell of peppermint again. I really would have to track down the source of it, I thought, as I approached the secretaire.

This piece of furniture had also belonged to Geneva—a family heirloom—and was made of cedar, with a cupboard at the top and drawers at the bottom. The diaries were neatly stacked in the top cupboard. I lifted them out and carried them to the door, glad to close it behind me. By the time I'd carried the diaries back down to the warmth of my own apartment, my father had fallen asleep on the sofa. I crept over to the desk, trying not to wake him, rather glad I had the diaries to myself.

They weren't especially attractive books, just an eclectic mix of notebooks, some with flowery covers, some more sober. Mum had obviously used whatever was available so perhaps she'd never intended them to be kept as a shrine to her memory, not until she knew she was dying.

Reuben had them sorted in order and the first book covered the years before my parents were married. Some of her observations seemed naive and girlish enough to make me smile. I'd been like that once, too. Then there was her marriage and glowing sentences written in the first flush of love, making me feel like a peeping Tom as I skimmed over them. Reuben had been an 'older man', but that didn't seem to bother Geneva one bit, although it had bothered Reuben.

He tells me I should think very carefully before I make a decision, because once we are married he'll do everything he can to keep me. I laughed when he said it, and then I cried a little. I do love him so.

I felt teary, too. I was just telling myself that I really must make the time to sit down and read my mother's diaries properly, as they deserved, when an untidy, hastily scrawled paragraph caught my eye.

Reuben wants to buy the house in Suckling Street. I told him I wasn't sure. I know there are family connections, especially with the asylum, although I'm uncertain of the details. My mother didn't know the story—she was never interested in the past. I asked him if he wouldn't rather buy a nice new house but he says I'm being silly. How to explain that when we went to look at it there was a man in the garden, watching me? A man who wasn't there.

The man who wasn't there! Here was the proof that my mother had seen him, too. If I needed it. And why in God's name was there a connection with the Kew Asylum?

I turned to the next diary on the stack and found that the house in Suckling Street had been duly bought and they'd moved in. There were a couple more mentions of the man in the garden, but nothing so far that helped me discover who he was and what he wanted. My mother was also mystified but full of speculation.

He wants something, I think. I don't know what it is. He comes into the house sometimes, but I ignore him and he goes away. Is he trying to tell me something? Did he live in this house once? I haven't said anything to Reuben. Oh, he knows I see him, of course, but there's a sense of unhappiness about this spirit. Is it directed at us?

Mum had died when I was two, and I knew I was approaching that time because the stack of diaries was getting smaller. I came to my own part of the story, a description of my baby-self—*red-faced and bawling with a mass of dark, curling hair*—but Geneva's affection for her noisy daughter was obvious, as well as the wry humour when she spoke of sleepless nights. Then another entry about the ghost.

I see him more often now. The smell gives him away. I know he's close. I don't like him near Annie. She can see him, too. She stares in his direction without fear. I'm glad she's not frightened of him. Does he mean us harm? I don't think so, but what does he want?

Harm? My heart gave a jump. A ghost was one thing, but a harmful ghost was another, and not something I wanted Courtney exposed to. And what was this about a smell? I'd read somewhere that some hauntings were supposedly preceded by a horrible rotting smell. Is that what Mum meant? At least I hadn't noticed anything like that.

Not yet.

I was just reaching for the next diary, the final one, when the phone rang. I jumped, momentarily disorientated. Reuben began to stir in his sleep, and I leapt up from the chair and hurried over to answer it.

CHAPTER TWENTY-ONE

The Girl's Story

The days had passed and Sean had recovered, then slipped back into illness only to recover again. After a week it seemed as if nothing had changed. Alice could see that Rosey was getting restless. Sean dying was one thing, but Sean getting better? It was as if Rosey hadn't counted on that.

Wasn't Sean the love of her life? Hadn't she told Alice that she longed to find him again? Something was amiss and Alice was worried about Rosey.

And Sean himself . . . Alice tried to like him, really she did, for Rosey's sake, but there was a horrid murkiness in his colours that unsettled her. Presently, he was well enough to leave the tent, and once when he was sitting by the campfire and Alice was staring at him, trying to see his colours, he'd abruptly turned on her.

'What're you looking at, Alice?' he'd said coldly.

She'd ducked her head, making herself small. Invisible. That was the effect Sean had on her. And she didn't trust him around Hope, either. He was the sort of man who kicked dogs. She was always glad when he went back to the tent. How could Rosey love a man like that? And what would happen if she went off with him?

* * *

Inside the tent Sean's smile was the same. Rosey knew she shouldn't have been surprised but she was. Her memories of their times together weren't all bad, but the more recent ones were, and Sean hadn't been smiling then. She supposed she'd allowed his memory to take on the guise of a monster when he was really only a man.

'I've missed you, Rosh,' he said for the hundredth time. 'Nothing was the same after you left.'

'It was you who made me leave,' she said tartly, and then wished she could bite her lip. But he didn't seem to mind, if anything he found her feistiness amusing. Endearing, even. Was that why they'd fallen out, because she began to be too careful about obeying his every whim?

But no, she reminded herself. She'd begun to obey his every whim because if she put a foot wrong he'd hit her.

'How're you feeling, Sean?' she asked.

He shifted on his bed, winced, shrugged. 'Better, maybe.' His eyes were sly as he studied her through his lashes. 'Are you planning on staying if I don't die, Roisin? Or have you got somewhere better to go?'

Him not dying was something she didn't want to think about, but she made herself smile and push back the lock of hair that fell over his forehead. The same lock of hair, the same gesture, but Rosey wasn't the same. That was the difference, wasn't it? Rosey had changed. Had Sean? Should she give him another chance?

A part of her wanted to, desperately longed for a happy ending, but there was another part that looked at her with derision and shook its head.

'I want you to stay, Roisin,' he was saying, his fingers entangled with hers. Yesterday he had lifted them to his lips and pressed a kiss to her flesh. Possessive. *You're mine.* That was what he used to say whenever he thought she was straying. *You're mine and you always will be.* But today he didn't kiss her and his grip on her fingers was hard, almost too hard.

'I thought you were looking for gold,' she said. 'That was what Josh told us. You don't want me and Alice following you about all over the country.'

'*Josh*, is it?' he mocked. 'Josh is too hoity-toity for the likes of you, my girl. Blue blood in his family. You might as well be wishing for the moon than to share your blanket with Josh.'

Rosey felt the truth of his words like a slap. He was right, of course he was. Josh Parker was a gentleman and what was she? Nothing but a dirty tart. 'I have no interest in Josh,' she said.

Sean looked at her, trying to read her face. 'Who is this Alice? I don't like her, she watches me.'

'She's my friend. A girl I met at . . . well, a girl I met.'

'I can see why you're dressed up as boys, although I don't approve.' He gave the cloth of her trousers a scornful glance. Just as well he was weak and sick, she told herself, because he was beginning to make her feel very uncomfortable.

'It isn't safe for women on the goldfields,' he went on, 'not unless they have a man to take care of them. Or they're whores.'

The word seemed to grow and grow in her head until it could have been another person; a person who filled the tent, leaving no air to breathe. Knowing he was still watching her, Rosey kept her face from showing the fear she felt.

Yesterday he had played the lover, even this morning he'd smiled at her as if she was his sun and moon, but now . . . She could never read Sean's moods.

'Why don't you sleep, Sean?' She kept her voice calm even though her heart was bumping in her breast. 'Supper'll be ready soon. I'll bring it to you, shall I?'

He moved restlessly. 'You know you're mine, Rosh,' he said. 'You'll always be mine.'

'Sleep, Sean, darling,' she answered him, stroking the hair from his face. His eyes closed and he slept.

* * *

Josh had prepared damper for their supper. Rosey had been watching him knead the dough while she was trying to comb the knots from her hair. Since the ducking in the creek her curls had become so tangled nothing could get through them.

'I'll have to chop it off,' she wailed. 'Alice, where's your knife?'

Josh had just finished the damper, tucking the loaf into the cooling edge of the fire. 'Wait on, let me have a try.' He glanced up with his shy smile. 'Seems a shame to cut off beautiful hair like yours.'

Rosey felt the colour in her cheeks, told herself it was from the fire. She sat very still on the log, wondering what he intended. Josh stepped around behind her and surveyed her tangled hair.

'Comb?'

She held it up and he carefully took it from her. Rosey closed her eyes. His first comb through her hair was tentative, awkward, then he caught the teeth in a knot.

'Ow!'

'Oops. Sorry,' Josh said, but she could tell he was laughing.

His strokes become more confident, more assured. Slowly, gently, he worked through the tangles, easing them out, as if he was unpicking a puzzle. As he continued Rosey relaxed. The occasional tug no longer hurt her and the sensation of him touching her hair, almost a caress, was beyond anything she'd ever felt before. As if he cared for her, as mad as that seemed, for the likes of him to care for the likes of her *was* mad.

'Who would've thought?' His voice was a murmur in her ear, sending tingles down her spine. 'I'd find gold after all.'

'What do you mean?'

'I mean that the gold is right here in your hair, Rosey.'

Rosey felt her breath hitch in her throat.

Across on the other side of the fire Alice was sleeping, her arms around Hope. Rosey glanced up at Josh, felt his hand rest a moment against her cheek. 'Sean,' he began.

'No. Please.'

'I'm worried, Rosey.'

Again she glanced back at him, felt herself caught and held by his blue eyes. 'Worried?' she managed.

He'd spent a long time in the tent with Sean that afternoon and when he came out he looked uneasy, not his usual cheerful self at all. Had Sean said something? Did he know about her and the Red Petticoat?

'It's as if he's up to something,' Josh went on, staring past her into the shadows. 'I thought he'd be glad to have found you, but . . . I don't know.' He sighed, his gaze dropping back to hers, searching.

Rosey shook her head. 'Don't ask me what goes on in that man's head,' she said. 'I never know.'

Josh frowned, opened his mouth to say more, but at that moment Alice chose to sit up, yawning. He handed the comb back to Rosey with a smile and moved to check on the damper.

* * *

Alice hadn't really been asleep. She'd been listening to them talk, watching with one eye half open. Even to her it was plain to see that Josh and Rosey were falling in love. Another complication, thought Alice uneasily, and worse still, as she'd been watching Josh combing Rosey's hair, she'd seen Sean in the tent opening behind them, also watching.

His face was contorted with a rage that seemed to be eating away at him, and his colours . . . They were whirling and dark, like a thunderstorm. She'd sat up then, trying to put a stop to the intimate moment, but it was already too late.

Her sight rippled, urging her to open up, to look. But she didn't want to. She was afraid. In case she might see Rosey lying dead with

Sean over her. Something would have to be done, Alice knew that, but she didn't know what.

Automatically, her fingers began to stroke Hope's rough fur. She glanced down at him and abruptly stilled. Her heart began to beat quickly and she swallowed the wail that rose in her throat. There was a darkness around his neck, just a shadow, but it was there. She snatched up the little dog and hugged him close.

Please, no, don't let anything happen to Hope, please.

Josh was quiet as he took the damper from the ashes and brushed it clean. Rosey was watching him, her lips curved in a smile. Alice had never felt more alone than she did right now, and foolish as she knew it was, she wished Molly was here. And Captain Potter, when he still loved her and didn't blame her for his wife's death.

A tear rolled down her cheek and then another, but she used Hope's fur to sop them up. *One day,* she thought, *I'll go back and put flowers on Molly's grave, and no one will point at me and say I have the evil eye, because I'll be rich and famous and no one will dare.*

'Rosh!' It was Sean, calling out from the tent. 'Come here, Roisin!'

Josh looked up sharply, his eyes meeting Rosey's. She shrugged a shoulder with a half-smile and stood up to obey, slipping her comb back into her pocket. Hope gave a bark, struggling in Alice's arms.

'Don't go in there, Rosey,' she said in a voice that didn't sound like her own. 'Stay here. It's not safe. *He's* not safe.'

Rosey shook her head impatiently. 'He's sick, Alice. He's dying. I promised I'd bring him his supper.'

But now the sight opened wide and Alice saw Sean there, hiding in the shadows, and he was holding a knife in his hand, and then it changed and Rosey was crying and there was blood.

'He's going to kill you!' Alice screamed.

Rosey backed away, tripping on a pile of wood, Josh catching her. His arms went around her, holding her safe, and that was when Sean came running from the tent.

It all happened in an instant.

'You whore!' he was shouting. '"Sean darling", all that sweet stuff, all those lies, and all the time you and him . . .' Foul words were pouring from his mouth, a trickle of blood running down his chin.

Despite his mad fury, Sean wasn't as strong as he'd thought himself, and as he ran, he stumbled. Hope darted at him, barking, and bit him on the bare ankle. Sean roared, lashing out at the little dog, but Hope was too experienced in the ways of men like Sean, and jumped back, barking furiously.

Josh was pulling them away, towards the track. 'Go down to the creek,' he was saying, 'and wait there. I'll see to Sean. Quick now!' When Rosey tried to argue, he said, 'I'll be all right. He can't hurt me.'

Rosey hoped that was true, even as she staggered away with Alice at her side, Hope trotting after them with the air of a dog who's done his duty. Behind them they could hear Sean swearing and shouting, his words jumbled and slurred as if he was drunk. Some white-winged choughs flew up from the ground, setting off Hope again until Alice shooshed him.

'What will he do?' Rosey said, more to herself than Alice. 'What if Sean hurts him?'

Alice said nothing of the blood she'd seen in her vision earlier. She didn't know what it meant and Rosey was not in a state for her to speculate. Soon they reached the creek and sat on the bank, shivering, holding each other. The light began to fade and it was almost dark when, finally, Josh came to find them.

He sat down beside them, rubbing his hands over his face. Even in the growing shadows his hair was a bright patch. Rosey put a hand on his arm and he covered it with his own, and for a moment they just looked at each other, drinking in the fact that they were both here, safe. Then Josh sighed and shook his head.

'He's dead,' he said.

Rosey gasped and closed her eyes. A tear ran down her cheek and she wiped it away with the back of her hand. 'How?'

'After you left he was going on, ranting and raving, and then a gush of blood came from his mouth. As if a dam had burst inside him. I held him, Rosey. I didn't let him go alone. He was my mate, after all, despite how he turned out. And I thought . . .' He gave Rosey that shy glance. 'I thought you'd want me to hold him as he went.'

She nodded. 'Yes. Yes, I would.'

'Will you come back to the camp now? I've wrapped him up in the blankets, so you won't see . . . You both need to eat, then we can talk about what to do.'

Rosey seemed to hesitate and then she nodded and stood up. They walked slowly back, and when she stumbled, Josh put his arm around her waist to hold her steady. Alice trailed behind them, holding Hope in her arms, considering what would happen now. Would Josh and Rosey team up? Then what would happen to her? She squeezed Hope tighter. At least she had Hope.

* * *

Rosey found she was hungry despite all the trauma. The damper was crunchy on the outside and soft and warm on the inside, and they ate it greedily, even Hope. Especially Hope. The little dog had come to her rescue, and she smiled at him almost fondly.

It occurred to Rosey that Alice hadn't put down the dog and she wondered what was up. 'Is Hope all right?' she asked, and reached out to touch his floppy ears. 'Sean didn't kick him, did he?'

Alice looked at her, her eyes shining like a possum's in the dark. 'Hope is perfectly well,' she said, in a very prim, Alice-like way.

Rosey tried not to look over at the tent, where Sean was wrapped up tight. She didn't want to think of him. She didn't want to remember the things he'd said about her and that Josh had heard them. For a moment there, when Josh had combed her hair, she'd felt as if anything might be possible, but now she knew it wasn't.

'In the morning we'll pack up our gear,' she said.

Josh had heard her and came to stand before her, reaching to take her hands. 'Rosey? What are you going to do?'

'We'll go to Dunolly and get work there. I can wash dishes and Alice is a good cook. That's what we'll do.'

'Rosey,' he said, shaking her slightly. 'Why not come with me? I've had enough of gold-digging. We can head to Melbourne and look for work there.'

She didn't want to look into his face but she couldn't help it, and yes, he was looking at her as if she was the most special person in the world. It made her want to weep because she was going to have to say no to him, hurt him, even though she knew in her heart it was for the best.

'What sort of work do you do?' she said, drawing it out, not yet ready to put an end to it. 'When you're not looking for gold?'

'I'm an artist,' he said, with his smile. 'At least I hoped to be. I went to the Academy in London, but it all seemed so dull and I wanted adventure, so I came here. But now I'm here, I want to paint and draw again, and I feel like I have something to say with my work.' He laughed, shrugged, as if he hadn't meant to expose so much of himself to her.

Alice piped up. 'One day Rosey and me'll come to Melbourne in a coach with gold wheels and black horses, and you'll be the first person we see. You can paint our picture!'

He briefly glanced at her, but immediately his gaze was back on Rosey's face, as if asking her a question. 'Very true, Alice,' he said, playing along. 'I can greet you with a big bunch of flowers.'

'And a bone for Hope.'

'Rosey?' he said, a question. 'Will you come with me?'

She shook her head. 'That wouldn't be fair to you. A budding artist doesn't need two lost souls like us. What you need is a rich patron. Or a rich wife, a proper wife.'

He looked surprised and then he grinned. 'Marry me then, Rosey!'

She was shocked, so shocked she couldn't think of anything to say. The idea that a gentleman like him would marry the likes of her . . . it was ludicrous, and yet something inside her took the words in and held them like a rich and precious jewel. What if she said yes? For a time it would be good, even wonderful, but he would hate her, eventually, and be ashamed of her. She knew it deep in her experienced and aching heart, and the kindest thing was to refuse him.

'I'm not proper, Josh, and I'm not the stuff wives are made of.' Her voice was gruff, as if she was going to cry, and she forced a hard laugh.

'That isn't true.' He sounded slightly desperate. He was losing and he knew it. Rosey drew away from him, took one step, and another. 'Rosey, will you at least think about it? Sleep on it?'

She pretended to consider, gave a nod. 'I'll sleep on it, Josh.'

Alice was yawning, so Rosey went to her and they lay down, cuddled together with Hope in the middle. She could hear Josh moving about, doing all the little chores he always did. Finally, he lay down, too, and soon there was silence, apart from the little noises and rustlings from the bush around them. The animals that came out at night to hunt and feed. There was a brush-tailed possum in the ironbark tree, gorging on blossom, snarling at a competitor.

Rosey couldn't sleep.

She let herself remember Sean. She knew she'd loved him, once, long ago. She felt a heavy sadness inside her, and she suspected that was because his death was the end of all her hopes and dreams. All the 'what ifs'. But she had stopped loving Sean, and now she wondered if it had ever been the same as she was feeling for Josh. Fool's gold as opposed to the real thing. Because this new feeling was warm and hopeful and almost pure. Silly, it was all so silly! It would never work. And how could she burden him with what her life had become? Running, hiding, wanted by the police for something she hadn't done? Josh deserved more than that. He deserved more than a soiled piece of goods, a dirty tart.

One of the 'gentlemen' at the Red Petticoat had called her that, and she'd laughed and mocked him, but it had stung. And stuck. No, Josh didn't know the half of what she'd done and she didn't want him to. She wanted him to think well of her, and leaving him behind was the best way to do that.

Rosey sighed and turned over on the hard ground. She knew she'd given up on the idea of finding gold. She'd given up the moment she'd decided they were going to Dunolly, the moment Meg told her about the music hall and the hotels, the rooming houses and the sly grog shanties. Everything one might need if one were a young woman and not too choosey.

And angry, desolate Rosey decided she wasn't too choosey.

She had her good dress, the pink one, scrunched up in her pack. It was old and worn shiny on the elbows and rear, but it was grand compared to some of the clothes she'd seen on their travels around the diggings. She'd wash herself up, brush her hair until it shone, and find the swishest place in Dunolly. And when she set her sights on her 'gentleman' she wouldn't be shy about asking for plenty of pennies. She'd make it worthwhile. And it wouldn't be for long, she promised herself, only till they were on their feet again.

But the words seemed hollow, and she wondered if once she started she could really give it up again. The small luxuries, the ease of acquiring a few shillings here and there, the admiration in the eyes of the men. It might be some recompense for saying no to Josh.

Alice wouldn't like it, of course. The younger girl believed whole-heartedly in their adventure. She still thought they would strike it rich and retire to a mansion in Melbourne. But Alice, for all her otherworldliness, was still a child. Rosey couldn't take the gamble of life on the road, not anymore. She needed a roof over their heads and some food in their bellies, and for that she needed money and there was only one way she knew how to get it.

Sean had been right all along, she decided grimly, and she *was* a whore. And if Josh hadn't thought so—well he didn't know her very well, she told herself stubbornly. If he'd known her better he'd have agreed with Sean. And she still had that memory, of his combing her hair so gently, as if she was made of glass. She would never forget that.

As the long night began to draw to an end, Rosey quietly woke Alice and they collected their gear, one eye on the huddled shape of Josh, wrapped in his bedding. The first rays of dawn were spilling over the clearing as they crept off along the track, leaving behind the only two men Rosey had ever loved.

CHAPTER TWENTY-TWO

Annie's Story

Maren wasn't back at work yet, but she'd rung me from her grandfather's sickbed and that sickbed just happened to be in Perth. I had imagined my friend's Danish grandfather must be in Denmark, but no, the old man had emigrated to Perth in recent years, and that was where Maren had rushed off to when she heard the news.

'He's fine, or he will be,' Maren said, in answer to my question. 'Danish blood, he says. He insists he'll live forever and I don't like to disappoint him by disagreeing.'

'I was imagining you flying off to Copenhagen.'

Maren groaned. 'The flight to Perth was long enough.'

'I'm glad he's okay.' I was thinking of Reuben and whether late-night dashes to hospitals might soon become the norm. I hoped not.

Formalities over, Maren got down to business.

'I take it this stuff about Gervais Whistler is hush-hush and not for the ears of History Victoria?'

'I'd be grateful if we kept it to ourselves, for now anyway. I'm sorry to put you on the spot, Maren, it's just—'

'Understand, no more to be said,' Maren cut in. 'As soon as I get back to work I'll get you the lowdown on our friend, Gervais, but that wasn't why I rang, Annie.'

'It wasn't?'

'When I saw the photographs you sent me of your wonderful painting I had a feeling they reminded me of something, but I couldn't remember what.'

'I thought you'd like them.' I'd sent the photos to Maren to cheer her up after she'd flown to her grandfather's bedside, and to show her what Gervais looked like.

'Well, I did, thank you. But the painting itself reminded me of something. Now here I am in Perth and I've remembered. There's an old building, built in the early 1900s, I believe, by one of those larger-than-life state politicians. He didn't like the idea of the Federation of the states, he wanted to remain independent.'

'I think Western Australians have always considered their state a separate country.'

'Yes, well, anyway, he was also a patron of the arts and commissioned a mural. As you walk into his home you can see it. I think it's meant to represent a potted history of Western Australia, but I'm not sure. The building is a retirement home now so you can go and see it. Probably need permission. I snuck in and took a few photos and no one stopped me.'

'They wouldn't dare.'

Maren ignored me. 'I'm sending you the photographs I took yesterday, not very good ones, but I think if you look at them you'll understand what I'm trying to say better than I can explain.'

'Maren . . . ?'

'Not sure of the name of the artist yet, but I have some feelers out. Anyway, I have to go!'

'Maren . . .'

She was gone. A moment later the photographs came through on my smart phone. The shot of the complete mural was too tiny to make out much, but Maren had also taken close-ups of some of the scenes. I bent to examine them.

The mural wasn't a *Trompe L'oeil*, but it was in the same style in that it consisted of numerous vignettes. Half of them were on a wide blue background, which was meant, I supposed, to represent the Indian Ocean or perhaps the Swan River, and the other half on a red background that was meant to be the land. One of the scenes was of a group of men with horses and dogs and cattle milling about, another of traditionally dressed Aboriginal people standing by a billabong.

There were similarities, but . . . I leaned so close that the tip of my nose was almost pressed to the screen. That sense of excitement began to buzz through me again. My gaze had shifted from the red desert to a woman standing outside a cottage. I zoomed in and found that the woman was wearing a flowing print gown with a wide-brimmed hat, and there was a name curling about her brim like a ribbon.

Oh yes, I had seen this trick before.

Was this the same artist who'd hidden Molly's name on her hat or the dog's name around its curled-up body? I tried to read the letters, but the image on the phone was still too small.

So I moved the images on, looking for more clues, going from pearl luggers at Broome, to a gold-mining scene in Kalgoorlie, to . . . Again I stopped and stared. Did I recognise that face?

The woman was standing with her face tilted so that it wasn't quite front on, but even so it seemed very familiar. Green eyes and blonde ringlets, and the faintly insolent curl of her lips that until now I hadn't even realised I'd noticed.

She was holding something in her hand, flowers, with a ribbon trailing from the tied stems. Heart thumpingly excited now, I zoomed in as far as I could and squinted at the screen.

'This is ridiculous,' I muttered to myself, 'you'll go blind.'

The flowers were familiar, too. Freesias. The old-fashioned creamy ones that always smelled so sweet in my mother's front garden. They still came up every spring, despite my lack of care.

But if there was a word on the ribbon then it was eluding me. I couldn't see it, so maybe it wasn't there. Then I did see. An 'o' popped out at me, and then an 'e', and after that it was easy.

'Rose,' I whispered, just as my eye made sense of the final letter—a 'y' with a sprawling tail. 'Rosey.'

Alice's friend's name was Rosey! But what on earth was she doing in Perth in the early 1900s?

'Curiouser and curiouser, Alice,' I paraphrased, but it was an understatement. I'd made a breakthrough only to have the mystery deepen. One step forward and two steps back.

* * *

By the time Ben brought Courtney home, I had the new photos printed out and had made a further discovery. This wasn't the first time Rosey was holding a bunch of freesias. Now that I looked again at the *Trompe L'oeil*, I could see that what I'd thought of as a pattern on the girl's skirt was in fact a neat posy of flowers.

Freesias.

Obviously, it meant something. To the artist, or more likely, to Rosey and Alice. Now all I had to do was discover what.

'I think Courtney's coming down with a cold,' Ben said, after I had rattled on for a while and begun to wind down.

'I'm sick, Mummy,' Courtney added, clinging to my leg and giving a small theatrical cough.

Ben stayed and talked with Reuben, and as I bathed my daughter, I could hear them laughing together. By the time I had Courtney tucked up in bed, Ben was ready to leave. He kissed his daughter goodnight and I went with him to the door.

'Is he all right?' Ben asked, with a nod towards the other room where Reuben was.

'They did some tests. I'm waiting to hear. They think it's just overwork.'

'So are you going to be dealing with the business all on your own?'

I felt uncomfortable discussing it with Ben, as he'd never understood the importance of Reuben and Reuben. 'I don't know. We have to talk about it.'

Ben looked at me. 'Still hiding your head in the sand, Annie?'
'Sorry?'

'If something is making you ill you need to step away from it. Move on. Your father might need to do that. And if you don't want to take over . . .' He shrugged.

I watched him drive away in his overly large SUV, wondering a little sarcastically if he was planning on a trip up the Orinoco. Of course Ben didn't understand! He was the sort of man who changed his life every few years. Reuben and Reuben had been built over decades of hard work and love for the jobs we did. How could my father step away from that? How could I?

Shivering, I wrapped my arms about myself as I stood on the front steps. The weather was still chilly and blustery, a reminder that winter was just around the corner. Earlier I'd watched some rowers on the Yarra battling the conditions and admired their dedication.

It reminded me of Alice, a foundling saved from the river.

If I needed reminding.

The truth was I couldn't stop thinking about Alice, or Rosey. I felt as if I was holding myriad threads, individual strands of the same story, but I was yet to join them all together to make anything resembling sense.

'My head hurts,' Courtney announced from behind me.

I closed the door.

Soon I was caught up in the usual parent's nightmare. How much head hurt was dangerous to a four-year-old? Should I be driving her to the emergency department? Courtney didn't seem seriously ill, just a bit warm and bleary-eyed, but I hated it when my child was unwell. I'd spent years training in my particular area of expertise and was able to speak with authority on the subject, but when it came to my daughter and the slightest hint of illness I was thrown way out of my depth.

'Grandpa!'

I looked up with relief as Reuben came into the bathroom where I was taking Courtney's temperature. 'She's a bit warm,' I said.

Reuben glanced at the number on the digital thermometer. 'Pooh!' He smiled at Courtney. 'You have a bug, that's all. Come on, I'll make you my famous warm lemon-and-honey drink and you'll be better in no time.'

Courtney trotted willingly after him and I found myself trotting, too. There was something so comforting about Reuben, you felt as if he knew the answers to everything. No wonder his collapse had shaken me so badly. It just didn't seem possible he could be less than indestructible.

'Now, we will take two lemons. I think this is a two-lemon job.'

Courtney listened intently, nodding when required, as her grandfather set about making his famous cure for a cold. I could remember him making it for me, but I don't remember if it had ever cured me. I had a feeling the cure was purely psychological.

Once the lemon mixture was heated in a saucepan then cooled and drunk, Courtney was back to bed with a book and Tarzan, and soon asleep.

'You are a miracle worker,' I said, when my father returned to flop down in the chair by the fireplace. It was a faux fireplace, but that didn't seem to matter, people always gravitated towards it. 'I never know whether to believe her or not, she's such a drama queen.'

'You were the same. Adorable.'

I blinked. Did my father just call me adorable?

'Your mother said you were a wild one, but I said you needed to grow into yourself, and you have. Courtney will grow into herself, too.'

We sat a moment, one of those awkward little silences that seemed to occur between us whenever emotions got too raw.

'Did you finish the diaries?' Reuben asked, glancing across at the desk where they were piled up.

'Not quite. The phone rang.' I'd already told him about Maren's news.

'Did you learn anything about the ghost?' My father was not easily distracted from his goal.

'Only that she saw it, and so did I. Nothing about what he wanted or who he was. Papa, I meant to ask you about Suckling Street. Do you know who it's named after?'

Reuben thoughtfully sipped his wine. Should he be drinking? Well, we'd both had two glasses by now and the warmth of the faux fire and the red wine was making us more comfortable.

'I think there was a doctor called Suckling who worked at the Kew Asylum.'

'A doctor,' I repeated and smiled. 'That's amazing. Doctor Suckling was the doctor in the inquiry into Molly's death.'

'But is it the same man?'

'It must be. Surely.'

'Your mother had relatives here in Kew. There's a photo album somewhere that belonged to her great-grandmother. She spoke about the asylum, but I don't know the ins and outs. I wasn't really listening. You know how it is. My work was always on my mind. I remember when we bought this house she was a little bit uneasy about something or other. Didn't she say so in the diaries?'

'She mentioned being uneasy, I think, but nothing else so far. Who were these relatives? Were they inmates in the asylum?'

My father smiled as I'd meant him to, but it wasn't really a joke. Perhaps they *had* been locked away up on the hill. There must have been hundreds of inmates in the life of the institution. Thousands.

Something else to consider.

Who would have thought the *Trompe L'oeil* would have brought so many questions into my life?

* * *

Reuben had gone to bed and I was just about to go myself when Max rang me. We talked for ages about the recent developments. I'd already told him about Molly and the Red Petticoat via email, but now I spoke of Rosey and the Perth painting. Talking about it seemed to clarify my own thoughts, but I still couldn't come to any definite conclusions. Alice may or may not be the foundling from the river. The woman in Perth may or may not be the girl in the *Trompe L'oeil*.

But Max was sure Alice was the girl in the painting. Not from any careful detective work but just because it felt right to him. And he didn't know why the other woman ended up in Perth, unless it was the artist who moved there and painted the woman's image from memory.

'Perhaps after Gervais Whistler went broke the artist went west to seek his fortune.'

I considered that and played devil's advocate. 'She could've been a professional model and meant nothing to him.'

'No, I think he painted her because he couldn't forget her.'

'That's very romantic.' I smiled.

'I'm a romantic bloke.' I could hear the smile in his voice, too.

There was a pause, but a comfortable one. Max said he was thinking of coming down when he had a day off, just to take a look at this *Trompe L'oeil* himself. I said he was very welcome, and when he came I would buy him lunch. Or dinner. The thought of seeing him made my knees wobbly and I found myself sitting down. *Silly. You're not fifteen anymore.*

We said goodbye at last, and the good feeling that had been bubbling between us remained, as did the smile on my face. Fifteen or not, I was looking forward to seeing Max Taylor.

My smile wavered. What if Courtney hated him on sight? What if he hated her? I sighed and got to my feet, finally ready for bed. As I passed the desk I glanced down at the diaries and something murmured in my head.

I needed to finish reading them. And I needed to ask my father about the photo album.

CHAPTER TWENTY-THREE

The Girl's Story

Dunolly was a proper town. Or that's how it seemed after the jumble of miners' tents and hastily erected shanties they were used to seeing on their travels. There was still evidence of earlier days in the old bark huts jammed between new brick buildings, but clearly they, like the canvas tents, were becoming a thing of the past.

Alice followed Rosey, holding her dog's rope lead firmly in her hand. The daylight was going and in the grey dusk the hotels and places of entertainment came into their own. Most of them were brightly lit with lanterns and flaring torches, and the sound of music and the clamour of voices drifted out onto the muddy expanse of a main street called Broadway. Wide and grand, it stretched on as far as the eye could see.

Rosey had been quiet and Alice wondered what she was thinking. Alice had faith in their success, even now as they plodded through the rain. There was still a buoyancy in her heart, and she didn't want Rosey to slip back into bad old ways and be lost to her just because Sean had stirred up the past.

She missed Josh, too. They'd crept off without even saying goodbye. But once she'd made up her mind Rosey just seemed to want to move on. It was what she was planning to move on to that worried Alice.

They finally found a cheap rooming house squeezed between a tobacconist and a lending library, and paid for a small cramped room to share for the night. Alice smuggled Hope in under the landlady's censorious gaze—she wasn't about to let him out of her sight, not with the dark stain around his throat getting blacker by the moment. All she could do was keep him close and try to avert whatever fate was about to befall him.

Once in the room they closed the door and she sat on the bed and watched Rosey wash as much of herself as she could manage with a cloth dipped into the water in the wash basin. Then she dried herself roughly, dragging the threadbare towel over her skin until it was glowing pink.

There was something about Rosey's stony, determined expression that Alice didn't like. As if she'd made up her mind.

'Rosey?'

Rosey wouldn't look at her. 'I'm going out for a few hours. You stay here.'

'Please don't.'

'How else do you think we're going to pay for this room?' Rosey spoke fiercely, her green eyes flashing. 'How are we going to buy food, Alice? For us? For your dog? We can't keep running.'

'But the police?'

Rosey was already at the door. She'd put on the pink dress Alice remembered from the Red Petticoat and she still looked beautiful. Her fair curly hair had grown longer, and with her slanting eyes she had an elfin look.

'We'll just have to hope they're not looking for us here,' she said, but Alice could tell she didn't really have an answer. At the moment she was too focused on her own scheme.

She waited until Rosey had gone. After the front door closed behind her, Alice slipped out after her, holding Hope in her arms and keeping to the shadows.

For Alice there were more shadows than just the ones made by lanterns or the glow from windows and doorways. She saw darker, more deadly shadows. They were the shadows of death, like smoke, encompassing the people she passed or figures she saw briefly through doorways. But Alice never dwelt on them. Even if she warned them they wouldn't listen to her, they never did.

She lost sight of Rosey along the block where the lights were brightest and the noise the loudest. But by then she'd found Frayne's Commercial Hotel.

The tinkle of the piano forte was almost overwhelmed by the roar of many voices, and somewhere in between was the high clear voice of a woman singing. Alice had never seen anything like it, and her eyes grew wide as she crept closer to the door. A burly man in a frock coat was guarding the entry for those who could afford to pay for a ticket. But she could see enough by peering past his thick legs in their tight trousers.

The theatre was like a foreign world, where light, colour and noise assaulted her senses in a deafening clash. She crept closer, and the man in the frock coat gave her a wink. She thought perhaps he wasn't so scary after all, and when he beckoned her through the door, Alice scuttled inside.

The first thing she saw over the sea of hats and heads was a woman in a short skirt, dancing on a stage. She was kicking up her legs and at the same time singing a song that had the crowd roaring their approval. Their faces were flushed and almost animal-like in the subdued lighting. When she did a particularly big kick, showing off her stockings and underdrawers, they threw coins and notes and even gold nuggets up onto the stage. A man in a top hat was hastily gathering up the money, stuffing it into his pockets, while the woman danced ever more enthusiastically.

Fascinated, Alice didn't realise how far along the aisle between the seats she'd crept until there was a horrible growl followed by a yelp. Hope and a bigger, more aggressive dog were locked together, rolling around in the sawdust in a fight to the death.

Screaming shrilly, Alice tried to pull her pet away, but the dogs were so tightly joined, rolling over and over, that it was impossible to get a hold on him. Then the man in the top hat was striding down the aisle towards her and with a well-aimed kick sent the animals yelping apart.

Alice immediately grabbed hold of Hope. Sobbing, she lifted him into her arms, then gave a wail as she saw the blood and the gaping injury to his throat. She'd known! She'd known this would happen and still she hadn't been able to stop it! What was the use of having a gift if she couldn't prevent this?

The man in the top hat was leaning over her. He had a florid, fleshy face, but his expression was compassionate. 'He's a goner, love,' he said. 'Better give him here and I'll put him out of his misery.'

'No, he's not!' Alice fiercely held on to Hope, refusing to let him go. 'I'd know if he was going to die and he isn't.' She said it more for her own comfort than because it was the truth. Those dark shadows were still hovering around Hope and he may well die, but she *wouldn't* believe it.

'And you'd know?' the man replied with a smile, rocking back on the heels of his gleaming black boots. 'What are you then, a fortune teller?'

Alice glared up at him, her bright-blue eyes shining with tears, her cheeks stained with them. 'I am. I'm a fortune teller. I know when people are sick and when they're going to die. I can see the future.' Her voice shook, but the sincerity of her words caused it to rise above the ruckus.

There was a gust of laughter from those who could hear; suddenly, it seemed as if Alice was just part of the entertainment. The man in the top hat laughed, too, but his gaze was intent. Then he gave a guffaw and turned and strode back to the stage.

'Come on now, gents!' he roared. 'Let's have another song! One, two, three!'

Obediently, the music crashed into life and the woman on the stage began to kick up her legs again. But Alice wasn't aware. Cradling her injured dog in her arms, she made her way back to the door. The crowd didn't stop her, they were already focused on the stage once more, but when she went to step outside the theatre, she found herself confronted by a short fat man in a garish waistcoat.

She tried to duck around him, but he blocked her way, and his face swooped down to hers, all veined cheeks and bristling whiskers.

'Now, now, girly, 'old your 'orses, Mr Whistler 'e wants a word with you.'

'Let me go. I need to go. My dog . . .'

The man pulled a face at the state of the animal. 'Best thing you can do for that is wring its bloody neck.'

Alice gave him her fiercest look.

He shuffled back, holding up his arms in surrender. 'All right, all right. You come wif me. We'll see what we can do for the poor critter while we wait for Mr Whistler.'

Reluctantly, Alice allowed the man—he said his name was Cockney Charlie—to guide her through a side door and into a small room with a desk, a day bed and a warm fire. Tenderly, she laid Hope down by the flames, stroking him and whispering loving words. After a moment Cockney Charlie returned with warm water, cloths and ointment he claimed did wonders for his horses, and she began bathing Hope's wounds.

They were nasty, but not as bad as they'd first looked, and as she cleaned them and then applied the ointment, she began to grow more confident that this was not going to be fatal. Hope was going to live! With shaking fingers she bound up the dog's neck with a clean bandage, and afterwards he seemed to fall into a doze. Probably just as shocked and exhausted as Alice herself.

She'd lied to Mr Whistler when she said Hope wouldn't die. She hadn't known, she never knew entirely, she'd just prayed she was right. Now she could see that the shadow, although still encircling his throat, was lighter, less dreadful, and she *did* know.

With a thankful sigh, Alice lay down on the fireside rug beside Hope and closed her eyes. Cockney Charlie had gone and left her alone, and she knew she should be gathering up her patient and making a run for it. Rosey might be back in the room by now and wondering where she was. But Alice was just so tired from Hope's near miss, and before that Meg and the man in the dark coat, and Sean and Josh . . . Her body felt so heavy that she couldn't have moved if her life depended on it. Despite the muted crash of the piano and the roar of the crowd, she fell asleep.

As she dreamt she saw Rosey's face. Tear-stained. Frightened. Desperate. 'Alice,' she was saying. 'What about Alice?' Something was wrong, very wrong, and although Alice knew Rosey needed her help, right now she was incapable of doing anything about it.

CHAPTER TWENTY-FOUR

The Girl's Story continued

Rosey had found herself a corner in the lounge of the Poverty Reef Hotel. She sipped her ale, making it last. There were plenty of men here, and a few women, too. Everyone seemed to be enjoying being out of the rain and cold, and perhaps celebrating a lucky swing of a pick.

Not that any of this lot looked like they'd recently struck it rich. Among the riffraff of miners were some local shopkeepers and tradesmen, and one fellow who was entirely in black and could have been the undertaker. Rosey might not be choosey, but she'd already decided she wasn't going to encourage him.

The barman had regaled her with stories of Dunolly. Evidently, after the first rush at Burnt Creek, things had quietened down. Since then further rushes had brought in more gold-seekers and now the town was booming. There were the inevitable deep quartz mines, but also much alluvial gold still to be found in the district. For all these miners, Dunolly had become a service centre, with the usual businesses springing up to cater to the goldfields as well as the rising town population.

'We have churches and pubs for every taste,' he'd assured her, with a wink.

A skinny man in checked trousers had been watching her ever since she came in, but she hadn't rushed him, experience having taught her she'd get a higher price if she gave him time to inspect the goods. Once the barman moved away to serve some new customers, Rosey caught the man's eye and half smiled, tucking a loose curl of fair hair behind her ear.

The gold is right here in your hair, Rosey.

For a moment Josh's voice jolted her from her single-minded resolution, but she pushed him to one side.

The skinny man had noted her invitation, and now, with a gulp of his drink, sauntered over.

He was a foreigner, his English so poor she had trouble understanding what he was saying, but she didn't need him to talk. His body language said enough. She named a price and he nodded, then she accompanied him out of the hotel and into the narrow lane beside the building.

Dull light from the upper windows shone down, and her boots sloshed through mud and other fluids she preferred not to contemplate, while rats scampered among piles of rotting food. Rats turned her stomach, but she focused on doing what she had to do and didn't let the smile slip from her face.

'Money first,' she insisted, holding out her hand.

She thought he might refuse right there and then. When he hesitated, she realised she was actually hoping in her heart that he *would* refuse so she wouldn't have to go through with it. But it seemed that despite her lack of wholesome meals and the less-than-thorough wash she'd had back at the rooming house, she was still pretty enough to clinch the deal, and after a search in his waistcoat pocket he pulled out some coins.

It's nothing, she told herself. *Just a moment of discomfort and then it'll be over.*

But in that instant Rosey knew it wasn't nothing. Alice was right. She'd left this life behind. She wasn't that girl anymore, and nor did she want to be.

I've found my gold. It's right here in your hair.
She couldn't do it.

Rosey snatched the coins from his hand and ran.

Once upon a time she would have outdistanced him easily, but these days she wasn't as nimble. He caught her at the end of the lane and his shouts and her screams drew a crowd, and inevitably, a constable. In no time at all a tearful and sobbing Rosey was taken into custody and marched away to the Dunolly police lock-up.

* * *

Alice felt a fingertip brush her cheek. It rippled through her dream, disturbing a long stretch of grey water the colour of polished steel, and the white sand surrounding it. There was a cottage huddled into a hillside, smoke drizzling from the sod roof. A goat and kid stood by the wall, comfortable in their shelter from the rain, and a baby sat on a homespun blanket, gazing about with wide blue eyes. And there was her brother, kneeling beside her, that silly grin on his face that always made her giggle.

The fingertip brushed her cheek again and reluctantly she opened her eyes, the same blue eyes as the baby in her dream. It was so warm here, cuddled beside the fire, which was just low enough to be toasty. Safe and warm.

The man in the top hat was only inches away from her, grey-and-black stubble like spikes along his jawline, his hazel eyes bloodshot, and his hair greasy and flat where it showed around the brim of his hat.

'Wake up, sleepyhead,' he whispered.

Hope thumped his tail.

Alice sat up, sullen and uneasy. 'I need to go and find Rosey. She'll be worried.'

He sat back on his haunches. 'Who's Rosey? Mother or sister?'

Alice sometimes felt as if she was both. 'Neither, she's my friend. Rosey Donnelly.'

'And what's your name, my dear?'

She didn't want to tell him, but he was stroking Hope's fur so gently. 'Alice.'

'Tell me about yourself, Alice. Tell me what you meant about knowing when people are going to die and about being able to tell the future.'

Alice eyed him sideways. This wasn't something she ever spoke of to strangers, and besides, she'd promised Rosey not to, and yet this man had helped Hope and something about the intensity of his interest was flattering. Perhaps he wasn't like the others. Perhaps he was genuinely fascinated by her gift.

So she told him.

She told him about the wooden barrel and being saved from the river, and then being able to see death coming for Bluey and later for Molly, and ending up with Rosey on the road to the gold diggings. She thought it was wise to leave out the Red Petticoat and Miss Oliver, just in case he considered it his duty to take her immediately to the police station.

She told him most of it though; how she knew things, what she saw, her sensing of approaching sickness or death, her awareness of danger to those she loved. She even mentioned Sean and her vision of him in the creek panning for gold, although she left out the man in the coat. Even to speak of him aloud made her feel a little sick, as if her past was a tangled skein of wool she was yet to properly sort out. And all the time he listened to her without a single word of interruption.

When she had finished a silence fell—Alice waited nervously for his reaction.

Finally, he stirred and said, 'My name is Gervais Whistler. I employ people to entertain the miners on the goldfields. We travel about from place to place and perform for them. They pay us and if they like us then they pay us well.'

'Like the lady who was dancing?' Alice said breathlessly.

'Yes. That was Mademoiselle Suzy.'

Alice's eyes shone, remembering Suzy's striped skirt and long white stockings.

'Do you think you'd like to travel with us?'

Alice felt her heart give a thump. 'And dance on the stage like Mademoiselle Suzy?'

He bit his lip, but she could see the laughter sparkling in his eyes, trying to get out. 'No, not like Mademoiselle Suzy. Dancers are ten a penny. I want you to tell fortunes, Alice.'

She went cold. 'No.'

He tilted his head. 'Why not? I'd pay a wage and you'd be fed and have a bed to sleep in at night. The mutt, too,' he added, with a half-smile at Hope, putty beneath his caressing hand.

Still she said no. 'Rosey and me are travelling, too. We're looking for gold.'

'Then let's ask Rosey,' he announced, and stood up and held out his hand for her.

Reluctantly, she took it.

'I'll get someone to watch the mutt,' he said, when she hesitated, her worried gaze going to Hope, although the dog seemed quite happy to stay right where he was. 'We'll find Rosey and sort this out, and then you can either come back for good, or for your dog. How does that sound?'

It was a cold walk down Broadway to the rooming house, and there was a fine drizzle that seeped into Alice's clothing. Mr Whistler strolled along by her side, pausing every now and then for her to catch up. He didn't seem to think she'd run off. No, Alice reminded herself, of course he knew she wouldn't. Not with Hope as his hostage.

Mr Whistler gave a loud knock and the landlady came to squint out of the door at them. Alice knew something was not right, even before the woman's eyes narrowed at the sight of her. 'You've got a visitor,' she said with a smug air, and led the way into a kitchen. A policeman with a battered face and the beginnings of a black eye sat at the table with a steaming mug before him. 'Here she is,' the landlady turned towards Alice with suppressed excitement. 'And don't think you're bringing that filthy mongrel back here, neither. I saw you take it out and it's not coming back.'

The policeman rose to his feet. He seemed to immediately recognise Mr Whistler and gave him a deferential nod. 'You somethin' to do with this, sir?'

That was when Mr Whistler took charge, or that's how it seemed to Alice. 'If I knew what "this" was I could better answer your question, sergeant.'

The policeman responded to the authority in his voice. 'There's a woman in our lock-up. She took off with a gentleman's purse, but he caught hold of her and they sent for me. I arrested her, but not before she'd assaulted me, sir,' he added, with a pitiful note in his gravelly voice.

Alice's eyes had grown round. 'Rosey's in gaol?'

The landlady opened her mouth to say something nasty, but the policeman held up his hand to stop her. He gave Alice a grave look as he answered her question. 'Yes, she is, and likely to stay there.'

* * *

Rosey crouched against the brick wall of her cell in the lock-up, trying to keep her pink skirt from the muddy floor, although why she bothered she hardly knew. She wasn't the only one incarcerated tonight, but after listening to a drunken rendition of 'The Daring Young Man on the Flying Trapeze' she thought she was probably the only one sober. There was a window high in the wall with bars across, but she could see glimpses of moonlight between the clouds and hear horses neighing in a nearby stable. She wondered whether she could climb up and squeeze out and then find one of the horses and ride off into the night.

But there was no escape.

She was angry with herself for being such a stupid fool. If she'd just let him do what he wanted then everything would have been all right. She'd have had the money to pay for the room and she and Alice would have been safe. Instead, she'd had to play the holier-than-thou virgin. Although not so holy she couldn't snatch his money and make a run for it.

What was worse, whoring or stealing?

And now because of her idiocy Alice was alone.

Rosey had no doubt about her immediate future. She'd be brought before the judge and sentenced, and then she'd be locked up for some considerable time. And if they found out about Miss Oliver, she'd probably be hanged.

She paced the small cell, not knowing how to contain her anxiety, not knowing how to answer all the questions tripping through her brain. The uppermost one was: had the police sergeant told Alice where she was? He'd seemed like a decent man. When she'd struck him with her fist he hadn't hit her back like some men would, and he'd listened when she pleaded with him to find Alice and tell her what had happened and bring her to the lock-up. Perhaps he had children of his own.

There were voices outside.

Rosey pressed her eye to the door, making use of one of the gaps in the thick timber, but all she could see were shadows behind the light of an approaching lantern. The sergeant growled something at the drunken songster before the bolt on the door rattled and screeched as it was drawn back. The door swung open.

For a moment the policeman filled the space, before Alice darted under the arm holding up the lantern and flung herself against Rosey.

Rosey clung to Alice, but she was already thinking of escape. If she could run out the same way Alice had come in, push the sergeant aside, they could be gone in a flash, hiding in the town until daylight then vanishing into the bush.

But there would be no escape. The policeman stood aside and his place was taken by a tall man in a top hat. The lantern light turned the raindrops on the man's shoulders to droplets of gold.

'Rosey, we're here to save you,' Alice whispered.

'You're free to go,' the sergeant said, a dry note in his voice. Startled but quick to comply, Rosey stepped through the door, trying to read his face. But he looked down as if he had something to hide, avoiding her eyes, and then the man in the top hat had grasped her arm and was leading her away, Alice skipping behind them.

'I don't understand,' she said.

'Mr Whistler paid Sergeant Thistleton for his black eye. You're free, Rosey!' Alice cried.

'Am I?' Rosey gave the man beside her a sharp look, and remembered to pull her arm out of his grasp. 'This is Mr Whistler, is it?' she added, trying to gather her thoughts, which seemed to be all over the place. Not that she wasn't glad to be free, and very glad to see Alice again, but there was sure to be more to this than a simple 'thank you' and 'goodbye'.

He tipped his head in a slight bow of introduction. 'Mr Gervais Whistler of the Goldfield Travelling Entertainers, Miss Donnelly.'

'He has dancers in striped skirts,' Alice piped up. 'And we're going to travel with them.'

Rosey wasn't as naive as Alice, and now her suspicions were plain in her face. But they'd reached a long wooden building with a music hall attached to one side and 'Commercial Hotel' painted across the top, and she held her tongue as Mr Whistler led them inside to a small fire-warmed room.

A woman about her own age sat on a chair nursing Hope. Neither of them looked very happy. As soon as the dog saw Alice he began to struggle, and the woman thrust him into the girl's arms, saying, 'Here, you take it,' with obvious relief.

Mr Whistler sent the woman off to fetch tea and supper. When the door closed and they were alone, Rosey looked from one to the other, and said, 'Well, who's going to tell me what this is all about?'

Alice had bent her head low over the dog, crooning to it as if it were a baby. It was Mr Whistler who answered.

'Alice has agreed to work for me—'

'Alice!'

But Whistler held up his hand and kept speaking as if she hadn't interrupted. 'Alice has agreed to work for me as one of the acts. The Child Teller of Fortunes, I think we'll call her, or simply, The Child. It'll go down a treat.'

Rosey had been envisioning all sorts of dreadful things of Mr Whistler and Alice, but this was beyond even her lurid imagination.

Using Alice to tell fortunes? Did he know what sort of fortunes she told?

'I said I would,' Alice said, with a worried glance up from Hope. 'It was the only way to save you, Rosey. But it'll be all right. I won't say anything bad.'

Mr Whistler cleared his throat. 'In return for Alice signing a contract with me for two years, I've agreed to free you and allow you to accompany her as her guardian.'

'See?' Alice murmured, anxious blue eyes fixed on hers. 'Two years isn't very long. We can do it, Rosey. I won't be afraid if you're there, and maybe you can learn to dance like Mademoiselle Suzy?'

Rosey tried to find some way out of this, but her mind seemed full of fluff. And what were their options even if they did escape and run again? More walking, more muddy roads, more miserable days and nights. A slow death as opposed to a comfortable life with food and board. There was really no choice.

But what about Alice? How could she allow Alice to be used in this way?

'I need to talk to Alice,' she said.

Mr Whistler shrugged and moved to open the door. 'I'll be right outside here,' he warned. 'And remember, no contract and you're back in the lock-up and Alice is on her own.'

The door closed.

Rosey took Alice's free hand and leaned down until their faces were only inches apart. Alice looked worried and pale, and although her eyes were very blue they seemed bruised. Both girls were worn-out, but the words still had to be said.

'You don't have to do this,' Rosey began. 'I know how you hate to be looked at and pointed at and made to be different. If you did this then people would never stop looking and pointing at you. He'd turn you into a freak, no matter what he says. You should live a normal life, be loved and cared for like other children, not made to tell fortunes so people can stare and gasp.'

Alice shook her head. 'I don't mind, Rosey,' she said, and smiled as if she were the adult and Rosey the child. 'It's something I can do, and Mr Whistler will pay me and we can live with the others in the travelling show. Truly, Rosey, I don't mind. At first I said no, and I thought it was a bad idea, but now . . . well, I *am* different, aren't I? I am a-a freak.'

Rosey wanted to shout at the closed door where she knew Whistler was listening—'Now see what you've done!' She wanted to bang her fists against it and tell him exactly what she thought of a man who would make his living from a child who had already suffered beyond imagining. But Alice seemed so resigned and that made her angry, too.

'But how will you tell fortunes? I know you have the sight, but most of the time . . . well, Alice, you see an awful lot of death.'

Alice considered the question. 'I can see sickness, too. I can tell people to keep an eye on a sore throat or a stomach ache, to get help before it gets worse. I can do that. Rosey, I've always wanted to do that, but I've been afraid to speak out. Now I can.'

Her smile was angelic.

'And I can see other things,' she went on when Rosey didn't answer. 'I can see good things, too. I just need to practise, and Mr Whistler says I'll be able to practise. Just a few people at first, and then as I go on, more of them, until one day I'll fill an entire theatre.'

Her eyes blazed and Rosey couldn't help but smile. Perhaps she'd underestimated Alice, thinking she needed to be looked after and protected from her gift. Perhaps Alice was right and Whistler and his contract would finally give her the chance to shine.

'I want to help people,' Alice said again, now very earnest. 'I always have. Please, Rosey, let me. And two years isn't so long.'

She was defeated. She nodded, and a moment later the door opened and Whistler came in with the woman behind him, holding the tray of supper. Rosey silently cursed her rumbling stomach.

'All agreed, then?' he said, a wide smile splitting his unshaven face, but Rosey could tell he knew very well it was all agreed.

Alice beamed back. 'Yes, Mr Whistler.'

'Then let's tuck in, shall we?'

Rosey would have liked to refuse—he'd taken over their lives so effortlessly she felt she should give some show of resistance—but the smell of the food was too tempting. Her hearty appetite had always been her downfall.

Alice found some crumbs to feed Hope, and while she was busy, Whistler leaned towards Rosey and said, 'Don't worry, Miss Donnelly. I know you don't want to be idle. I'll find something for you, too.'

Rosey gave him a narrow look, just a warning to keep his hands to himself, but she wasn't really worried about that. Whistler didn't seem the type, and besides, she could look after herself. As long as Alice was happy, that was all that mattered for now.

CHAPTER TWENTY-FIVE

Annie's Story

After taking the rest of the week off, I came in to work with the intention of putting things in order. Courtney's cold was better and she'd been looking forward to child care—all down to Reuben's lemon-and-honey cure of course—and Reuben had been for more tests and insisted he was feeling much better. The doctor was pleased with him, too, so I was more confident this time.

Greta hadn't arrived yet. I still hadn't spoken to my father about the business, and the longer I left it the more difficult it became. I told myself I wanted to wait for the final test results to come in before we made any decisions. But that didn't mean I couldn't be ready with facts in hand.

The business books were in Reuben's office and that's where I went first. I knew the combination to the safe was my birthdate. Reuben hadn't changed it in years. Once it was open I hauled out the heavy books, setting aside the more recent ones. I switched on the desk lamp, sat down, and tried to concentrate.

I probably needed the help of an accountant, I decided, after half an hour of trying to make sense of it. But even someone as untrained as me could see that our outgoings far exceeded our incomings. Reuben had spent a fortune on materials for his marbling and he hadn't even been paid for his work yet, and when I looked up the contract for the job and the money he was expected to receive, well, he'd already exceeded that amount twice over.

Job after job was the same. Reuben hadn't properly costed our work, or else he didn't care how much it cost as long as he did the job his way.

We were in trouble.

I had been the bookkeeper when I first joined the business, but gradually, I'd found myself struggling—too much else to do. Reuben had insisted on taking over, and although I'd occasionally mentioned getting someone else in, he'd made excuses and I'd let the matter slide. It was as if we'd both been content to bury our heads in the sand.

I flipped through more pages and discovered that he'd been taking on small jobs, little extras—things he never would have touched in the old days—just to make a bit of money to cover our growing debts. He was trying to keep us afloat. No wonder he'd collapsed, no wonder he was ill. The question I wanted answered was: were we so far in debt that we could no longer claw ourselves back to solvency?

Looking back over the figures, I almost thought it would be all right. A bit of restraint, some luck, a big juicy commission. We might turn ourselves around even now.

And then I found the letter from the bank. Tucked at the back of the book, as if he thought out of sight, out of mind.

Reuben had applied for a larger overdraft and then a loan. The final straw had been the second mortgage on the house. The bank had still given it to him, just not the sum he'd wanted. Our debts were crippling and—I opened more envelopes—the demands for repayment were becoming critical.

I switched off the desk lamp and sat in the gloom of my father's office. Things looked dire, but could I be wrong? I was no financial wizard and perhaps there might still be something we could do.

I needed to get some professional advice. I'd make an appointment. No, I corrected myself, *we*'d make an appointment. Reuben needed to hear this, too. He needed to face the facts.

It was selfish of me, but among all of this mess I still couldn't help thinking about the *Trompe L'oeil*. If Reuben and Reuben went under I'd lose the commission to someone else, someone who didn't care as I did. I felt sick at the thought. What would happen to Alice and Rosey? Who would tell their story in the way I knew it needed to be told?

With trembling hands I opened the door and went out onto the gallery. Below, in the lobby, I could see Greta was now at her desk, setting up her work. Did Greta know how bad things were? Should I tell her? Probably I would have to soon, but first Reuben and me needed to sort things out. Make a decision.

I stood, unmoving, trying to regain some equilibrium. Things were far worse than I'd realised. Why had I left it until now to find out? Was I wilfully blind, or had Reuben done such a good job of persuading me all was well that I'd just believed him? He had compartmentalised it, I thought. Locked it away in a corner of his mind where he could ignore it most of the time. As upset as I was, I didn't think that leaving me the business in his will was a poisoned chalice. Reuben had poured his heart and soul into it and I knew how greatly he valued what we did. He genuinely wanted me to have this symbol of his life's work. Perhaps on one level he thought I could fix it? But in hindsight my ignorance had still been inexcusable.

Not only was I going to lose my house and livelihood, I was also going to lose the painting. The *Trompe L'oeil* wasn't a living thing. The people in it are dead and gone. But no matter how I tried to rationalise it, to me it *was* a living thing, and the people in it were still very much alive. The painting brought them to life. I couldn't let them go, I just couldn't.

A sound came from the small alcove that led to my own studio, and I turned with a frown. A few steps along the gallery and I could see the light from the window in my door.

Angry now, and worried, I peered through the frosted glass and saw the shapes of two people over by the *Trompe L'oeil*.

The sound of the door had Sebastian turning towards me with a frown. He didn't seem all that surprised to see me, at least not as surprised as I was to see him. And the woman standing beside him. Not any woman, *the* woman who was tipped to be the next premier of Victoria. That explained the panic around Gervais Whistler, although I still thought it was ridiculous to try to micromanage every possibility. Sometimes shit happens.

'Ah, Annie,' Sebastian said, just as if he'd been expecting me all along. 'We're admiring this amazing piece. And I was just telling the minister that it would be a crime to hide it away.'

Was he? I caught his eye and seemed to read a message there, but I wasn't sure what he was trying to tell me. It didn't matter. I was nobody's puppet.

'Miss Reuben? I've heard many good things about you. How do you do?' The minister took my hand. 'Marvellous piece of work,' the minister said, beaming her famous smile. 'I can see why you're so protective of it. I'm sorry to come in like this without telling you, but Sebastian thought it would be less disruptive for you, and I have a busy day ahead of me.'

'I see.' I took up a stance closer to the *Trompe L'oeil*, trying not to look like a dog guarding its bone. 'Are there any questions you want to ask? It's early days as regards the conservation work. We've done a number of tests and—' I began to explain at length what those tests involved.

The minister's eyes started to glaze over, although her lips kept up the mantra. 'Fascinating . . . how interesting . . . amazing . . . thank you so much for sharing that with me, Miss Reuben.' Finally, she took my hand in a firm grip, and with a meaningful glance at Sebastian, walked briskly to the door, her high heels clicking.

Sebastian gave me a smile. 'She likes it,' he murmured. 'I think it's going to be all right.'

He seemed almost human and I had the urge to trust him, but instinctively I held back. Sebastian Rawlins was better kept at a distance.

'She's even talking about a press conference.'

I could imagine it.

This is my great-grandfather, laugh laugh, naughty old Great-Grandad, but he was the salt of the earth, loved by all. And look at this wonderful piece of art he commissioned . . .

Although hadn't I heard that the minister was an ultra-conservative? She also made a big deal of her religious background which veered towards Puritanism. Maybe someone like that would be incapable of laughing off a scandalous ancestor? Was it really going to be all right, as Sebastian said?

'We're guessing that Gervais Whistler commissioned the *Trompe L'oeil*,' I reminded him. 'And I need to find out who painted it. In fact, I have something to show you.'

Sebastian was impressed by Maren's photographs and agreed there was a distinct similarity. 'I'll get someone onto it,' he promised.

'I have an idea about this badly damaged section,' I went on. We were standing in front of the left-hand side. 'If you look here you can recognise a settlement in the bush, or at least that's what I think it is, and is that a man in black with his arms raised? What's that all about? The strange thing is, I think this vignette might have been painted on later, after the rest. And look, there seems to be another boat, just a part of it, with some figures on board with a . . . a piano? And this bit I really don't understand. There's a lantern glowing and some very weird colours. Or perhaps the paint has reacted with other chemicals and turned that lurid purple and red and yellow.'

Sebastian was frowning over my shoulder. 'How can you see that? All I can see is a mishmash of colours and a lot of dirt.'

'I'm going to give this area another clean. It might help.'

I was lost in thought when I realised Sebastian was still there, and there was an almost sympathetic expression on his harsh face. It made me distinctly uncomfortable.

'I'm sorry, Annie, but I have to ask. There's been talk at History Victoria and . . . well, you know how the people at head office worry over rumours. They like certainty. It increases our chances of keeping our funding.'

'What *are* you talking about?'

'Your father. Word is he's not well.'

I was so upset and angry for a moment I couldn't answer him. I wanted to push him out the door and slam it. But I knew I couldn't. Besides, he was right. In the current economic climate everyone was worried about their funding. If Reuben and Reuben went under, History Victoria would have to find another company who did the same work, and where would it come up with another Reuben, who sometimes worked miracles for a pittance? No, that wasn't going to be easy.

The relationship between us was very comfortable right now and they wanted it to stay that way.

'You're right. My father isn't well,' I said woodenly. 'Nothing serious. He's having a little rest, but I expect him to continue working when he's fit again. Nothing has changed. And nothing *will* change, Sebastian. I'll take over the business if it becomes necessary, and I have no plans to take up another career.'

It wasn't entirely the truth; I didn't know what the truth was. But neither did I want our biggest customer running scared when we needed every penny we could get.

Sebastian nodded. 'Thank you, Annie. I appreciate your honesty.' Then he leaned closer and murmured, 'We must meet up for a drink again soon. I'll ring you.'

I was too surprised to reply, but it didn't matter, he was already gone.

I sank down into a chair. My throat ached and there were tears stinging the backs of my eyes. I was going to have to talk to my father about the business, or more importantly get him to talk to me.

The two of us had been playing ostrich long enough.

* * *

All was silent when I got home. I was already feeling guilty for staying away for four hours when I'd said two, and I called out for Reuben. I knew I shouldn't have left him alone, but he had seemed okay, and anyway, he'd been insistent that I needed to keep up with my work. Now I knew why.

The ground-floor apartment was empty, and I went up to Reuben's door, shaken again by my memory of finding him lying on the landing. The door was ajar. Heart beating a little quicker, I stepped into his small entrance hall, made even smaller by the long-case clock soberly ticking away the moments.

'Papa?'

'In here, Annie.'

With a sigh of relief I went towards the spare bedroom. He was on his knees hauling something from under the bed, and when he looked up his hair was standing on end and his cheeks were flushed.

'What on earth are you doing, Papa? You're supposed to be resting!'

'Doing? Looking for the past. Your mother's stuff. There's more of it than I realised.'

He'd dragged out a suitcase, an old leather one, and I hurried to help him lift it onto the bed.

'We can take it downstairs and you can look through it when you have time,' he was saying. He was breathing quickly from the exertion, his eyes brighter than they had been. Or perhaps there were tears in them. Memories, the past, it was never an easy place to visit.

I was reaching for the handle of the suitcase when I became aware of the smell of peppermint.

It was so strong I actually stopped and waved a hand under my nose. 'Phew!'

Reuben was looking at me in surprise.

'Can't you smell it? The peppermint? I think Courtney must have dropped a lolly into the heater and now it seems to be everywhere. I know she doesn't like peppermint flavour, so maybe she hid it and didn't realise what would happen.'

I smiled but my father didn't smile back.

Reuben got to his feet. He was still looking at me and there was something uneasy about his expression, something trepidatious.

'Annie . . .'

'I don't believe you can't smell it,' I went on. I sniffed again. 'Although it's gone now. Comes and goes.'

'Annie, *that*'s the smell. The smell your mother spoke of. The smell that means the ghost is here.'

I felt my mouth drop open. *That* was the smell? Peppermint? I shook my head. It couldn't be. I'd imagined something old and disgusting. Something reminiscent of death. Not . . . *peppermint*!

Reuben was holding my arm, his hand warm, and I realised I was all shivery and wobbly. He sat me on the bed and sat down beside me, using the suitcase as a back rest.

'You didn't know? I thought you might have worked it out.'

I shivered. 'So every time I've smelt peppermint he was here? Watching me with those . . . those eyes? Ugh, it gives me the creeps. *He* gives me the creeps.'

'He can't hurt you.'

'I don't know if I believe that, Papa.'

'Maybe he's stuck here. He needs to be set free.'

'Right.'

I wiped my face and realised I'd been crying. I shook my head again and turned to look at him, taking in his concern, his crooked smile. The words spilled out.

'Papa, I looked at the books in the safe. We're in trouble, aren't we?'

His smile wavered. He blinked at me, and then his shoulders seemed to sag. 'Yes, we are. I don't know if we can keep going. Things have been difficult for quite some time. There's less work. Even those who want to do a proper restoration job on their house can't afford to do it, so they go down the cheap route. Or gut the place and modernise it. Annie, craftsmen like us are becoming obsolete.'

I reached out to grasp his hand. 'No, never that. And surely we aren't done yet. I wondered . . . we could get some professional advice. See what we can do to turn things around.'

Reuben was silent.

'Papa?'

'I've been to our accountant. And others. I wanted to sort it out before you took over and I kept hoping maybe something would turn up. But nothing I did seemed to help. The bank won't touch us now. And even if they agreed to another loan, I don't think I could agree to what's necessary to turn things around. I'm getting old, Annie. I didn't feel it until I had that fall. And I'm tired. I already know that any advice they gave us would be to lower our standards and up our prices. Cut corners. Turn into a cut-rate sort of place. If I have to compromise then I'd rather stop now.'

'But if compromising means keeping Reuben and Reuben running . . . Surely you don't want us to go under?'

'No, I don't want that,' he said, with a shake of his head. 'Maybe you can work it out, run things, keep it going. I wanted to give you that chance. You're my daughter and my heir and you should make those decisions.'

My heart sank.

'Of course you're thinking of the *Trompe L'oeil*,' Reuben added, with a sideways glance.

'Yes, I suppose that's part of it. Sebastian was at the office today. He asked about you. I think he's worried about . . . about things. I pretended it was business as usual, in case History Victoria pulled the pin on us. We need time to think, don't we, Papa? We need to make up our own minds, not have them made up for us.'

He managed a smile, but his eyes were sad, as if he'd already handed over responsibility. He stood up and straightened with a groan. 'Can you help me with this suitcase, Annie?' he said. 'It's heavier than I thought.'

The conversation was over.

CHAPTER TWENTY-SIX

Annie's Story continued

It had been a frosty morning and now, despite the sun shining in a blue sky, the air remained icy. I was wrapping my scarf around my neck, ready to leave for a meeting with Sebastian Rawlins. 'Are you sure?' I hesitated in the doorway. The final tests from the hospital had proved clear, and yet I felt guilty about leaving Reuben here alone.

'Go, go,' Reuben was shooing me. 'I'm perfectly fine.'

'Greta promised she'd be here in twenty minutes. I can wait.'

My father rolled his eyes. 'Greta will drive me to distraction, but at least she's bringing me some work to do.' He chuckled at my outraged expression. 'Greta isn't as tough as you, Annie. She felt sorry for me, here, with nothing to do.'

I thought I'd have something to say to Greta later on, but I was running late as it was. I was meeting Sebastian in the city and I'd have to catch the tram today. I hoped this lunch wasn't going to be a testing occasion requiring all of my wits.

As I'd expected, Sebastian was already waiting for me when I found the restaurant, tucked away in Collins Street. I saw him before he saw me, and briefly I watched him, trying to gauge his mood. He looked edgy, straightening his tie, checking his phone, glancing at his watch, all in the space of a few seconds. I made myself walk towards him and held out my hand.

'Annie.' He smiled and rose to his feet, quickly taking my hand, before we made ourselves comfortable. The waiter was already hovering and orders were discussed and made.

As I sipped the wine the waiter had poured I puzzled over the reasons why we were having this lunch. Sebastian never did anything without a reason. I was hoping he'd swallowed my reassurances about Reuben and Reuben's financial difficulties. If not I was prepared to bluff my way through. Lie. Anything to buy us some time.

But Sebastian seemed in no hurry to get to the point. We were halfway through our meal before I finally learned why he'd asked me here.

'I'm leaving History Victoria.'

I gawped at him over the piece of caramalised pork on my fork.

Sebastian put down his knife and fork. He'd hardly eaten anything, I belatedly noticed.

I tried to compose myself. 'Why are you leaving?'

Sebastian smiled rather like Nephetiti when she'd been presented with her favourite fishy food. 'I'm leaving because I've been offered a better job. In New York.' He went on to explain the proposal—a leading role at a private museum. I struggled to take it in. It did sound marvellous. Sebastian would be employed in sorting out any glitches in the running of the museum, as well as acquiring new pieces. There would be lots of travelling to Europe and beyond, where most of the pieces would be sourced.

I felt a twinge. Sebastian was moving onwards and upwards, while I was drowning in debt. But I swallowed my envy and channelled enthusiasm.

'So how did you hear about this job? Was it advertised?'

He laughed. 'A little bit of who you know and being in the right place at the right time, Annie. The owner is a very wealthy American who can indulge his tastes but enjoys sharing with others, thus the museum. It's becoming quite well known all over the world. He's particularly interested in the conservation of his pieces . . .' He looked at me, let the words hang.

Was I supposed to read something into that?

'I'll be leaving in a month,' he went on when I didn't respond. 'I know it's rather soon, but that was the deal when I was offered the job. If I wanted it I had to move fast.'

'Do they know at History Victoria?'

Sebastian grimaced. 'They do now. Not happy, but what can I say? I have my own career to consider and to be honest things have been tricky at History Victoria lately. You haven't helped, Annie, with your *Trompe L'oeil*. In actual fact that was the catalyst that decided me on accepting the New York job. I'm tired of stroking politicians' egos.'

He sounded as if he meant it. Sebastian was leaving, and while that was surprising and would take some getting used to, I still had to ask the question: 'Why are you telling me this?'

'Annie.' He sighed and shook his head. 'I thought you might have guessed by now. This job in New York comes with an assistant. An adviser. And I want it to be you.'

I was so astonished I couldn't think of anything to say.

Sebastian poured the last of the wine into our glasses, that smile still curling his mouth as he watched me floundering.

'I'm sorry to spring it on you, but I've only just heard myself. You're such a talent, Annie, so passionate about your work. You care about the pieces you take on, it's not just a job, and that's rare. I want you with me. I want your input and your expertise. And I rather think that you're feeling a little stale yourself. This would open up a whole new world for you and with it a great many new opportunities.'

With a shaking hand I picked up my glass and gulped rather more of my wine than I'd meant to. I was trying to gather my thoughts, but they didn't seem to want to be gathered. My head was spinning and it wasn't only from the wine.

Of course Sebastian was right. I could see that. He was offering me a wonderful prospect. New York. Oh yes, I could see how wonderful it might be. But at the same time there were so many reasons to say no.

'I have a four-year-old daughter,' I spoke at last. 'She'll be starting school next year. And my father . . . I'm all he has. The business . . .' I waved a despairing hand.

Sebastian nodded sympathetically. 'These are all valid reasons for you to say no, Annie, but there are just as many to say yes. Forgive me for saying so, but I have a feeling things aren't as buoyant at Reuben and Reuben as you're leading me to believe.'

So much for my lying skills, I thought irritably.

'But I don't want your answer now. Give it some thought, Annie. You have until Monday. I'm sorry, but I can't give you any longer. I really will need your answer by then.'

Our meal limped to a close over coffee. Sebastian spoke a little more about the New York job, but he didn't seem to want to say too much until I'd made up my own mind, although what he did say was enough to make me quiver inside with a combination of dread and longing.

It was true. I did sometimes feel wasted here, and now with the business in dire straits, this offer meant I could just leave it all behind me. Oh, it was so, so selfish, but so tempting at the same time. And I did want to go back to Europe where I'd done some of my best work when I was training. And New York, with a wealthy private museum! It really was the chance of a lifetime. But on the flip side this was a very bad time to be making such a profound and important decision.

Finally, Sebastian said he had to go, and I hardly noticed as he departed. I was still sitting there when the waiter cleared his throat and asked if I was done.

Outside I stood in a patch of sunshine, sheltered from the cold breeze. It would be coming into summer in America. I remembered how beautiful the Northern Hemisphere could be as the world came to life again, the grey buildings throwing off their winter gloom, the street cafes springing up like bright and elegant mushrooms in the small lanes and large squares.

Courtney would love it, and being such an adaptable girl she'd soon get into the way of things. She'd make new friends, although of course she'd miss Ben and Reuben . . .

Abruptly, I straightened up, pushing back my hair as a chill gust tumbled it into my eyes. What on earth was I thinking? How could I possibly take off and leave everything in chaos behind me? The business, my father, the *Trompe L'oeil*! I couldn't, I really couldn't . . . and yet I was dreaming about it. Thinking about it very seriously. Wondering if perhaps, despite the stumbling blocks, there might be a way.

I began to walk slowly along the footpath, hardly noticing the spots of rain. I didn't want to go home yet—there was too much on my mind that I didn't want my father to notice—and besides, I'd told Reuben I might take a look at the old Goldminer Hotel after lunch. It wasn't that far from the restaurant and I had the feeling I might have missed something the first and only time I was there with Clive Cummings and his crew. Not a physical clue, but something that could flick a switch on an idea in my head. What I really wanted was to see where the painting had hung originally, before it was banished to the storage basement. According to Clive that was in a reception room.

'How do you know?' I'd asked. The answer was prosaic. There'd been a piece of paper stuck to the back of the painting, saying where it came from, in case anyone ever wanted to put it back.

I was still deep in my thoughts when I reached the old building. Disappointment brought me back to the here and now with a jolt. I'd stupidly imagined I would walk straight inside, but of course it was barricaded off from the street with security wire fencing.

The place was dangerous, soon to be demolished, so it was unlikely they'd want anyone strolling in. I vacillated, walking a little way along the fence, and that was when I saw that there was an open gate with no one about.

Someone's slip-up was a chance too good to be missed, and I barely hesitated.

* * *

I was standing in what must once have been a magnificently ornate vestibule. Decorated columns soared upwards to the balustrades and galleries three stories above, and there were arches with gold decoration and ironwork railings painted black and gold. The symbol of the hotel, the embossed miner with his pick, was everywhere.

For a split second I felt as if I was right there, in the heart of boom-time Melbourne, with the glory of The Goldminer all around me. It may have been built from Gervais Whistler's ill-gotten gains, but it was a representation of all of those romantic gold rushes that had made the architecture of Victoria so unique.

Then I blinked and the scene before me shifted, became once more one of utter desolation. Everything broken, disintegrating, dirty. The dust was thick on the floor and I knew my boots would be covered when I walked out. The Goldminer was a wreck awaiting only the demolisher's word to be smashed to bits, its memories blown away on the wind and forgotten.

Well, not all its memories, not if I had anything to do with it.

With a sense of renewed determination, I picked my way up a short flight of stairs to a balustrade that was only half standing, taking care not to place my weight against it. Was that a dining room through that archway? Or maybe a salon where foreign dignitaries and royal princes could escape for a moment's peace?

Just then there was a movement behind me; a shuffling sound. As if someone was writing their name in the dust with the toe of their shoe.

I spun around and stared back towards the vestibule. There was some light coming in through holes in the masonry and broken windows, but there were still shadowy corners and alcoves which I could not see into, try as I might.

A place like this was so full of ghosts it was easy to be creeped out by it. I could imagine how it must be at night, the wind whistling through, the echoes of the grand past. Perhaps ghosts came out to sing and dance. Perhaps Gervais . . .

My thoughts stilled abruptly as I caught a whiff of peppermint. Or supposed I did. But I shook my head and told myself that I was letting my overactive imagination spook me again.

I had Clive's directions in my bag and now I took them out, to check my position, as dust motes danced before me. I'd marked on it the location of the reception room where the painting had hung.

'Why do you want to risk life and limb in that place?' His voice replayed in my head.

I'd tried to explain but I could tell he hadn't understood. He probably thought I was crazy, and perhaps I was. Or obsessed.

Some plaster fell in the room above me, but the ceiling held firm. I was well aware I should have a hard hat on, but oddly I didn't feel all that worried. Eerie as it was, The Goldminer seemed protective, as if it was wrapping its arms around me to keep me safe.

'Which just proves you should never drink wine with your lunch,' I said aloud.

Another rattle of falling masonry somewhere on the floor above me. I stopped and looked up. Nothing. Quickening my steps, I reached the door to the reception room and stopped. Ah, this was the place. I narrowed my eyes and thought about how the room would have looked in its glory days.

Rich furnishings, thick soft carpet, and the *Trompe L'oeil*. It would have hung above the fireplace, and it would have been the first thing anyone saw. It was so striking, you couldn't help but focus on it. I could imagine the murmurs of appreciation, the questions, as the guests were drawn closer, gaping at the vignettes, wondering what they meant. And all the time Alice and Rosey would be gazing back, saying: *This is us. This is our life.*

I smiled. Their life had been quite incredible, and yet there were so many questions still to be answered.

Maren and History Victoria were still to get back to me with the name of the artist and whoever it was who had commissioned the painting—although everyone was sure the latter was Gervais Whistler. After all, he had owned the hotel in the roaring days.

But why? Why had Gervais commissioned such a painting? What relationship did he have with the two girls? I pictured the vignette of him standing in front of the Dunolly Music Hall. That was where their lives had intersected, but again I didn't know for sure. I had no proof. But somehow I'd find out. Sometimes I frightened myself with my pigheaded tenacity.

There was a shuffle near the door, this time a very definite footstep. I spun around, breathing fast, just in time to see a shadow moving away through the murk. My skin prickled. This was a danger I hadn't considered when I'd entered the building. The structural problems, of course, the fact I might fall and injure myself. But I hadn't factored in the risk from another person. An empty building was always attractive to squatters or drug addicts or people who were mentally ill. Or a combination of all three.

I needed to leave now.

But I couldn't leave without taking some photos of the reception room. It might be the last time I saw this place intact and I needed the memories. I did so quickly and then turned to leave.

I cautiously scanned the area. There seemed to be plenty of shadows but nothing sinister, at least not that I could make out. The best thing to do was to stride purposefully towards the exit, pretending I hadn't a care in the world.

But I felt exposed. As if someone was watching me. Ready to sneak up behind me.

There was nothing fearless about my exit after all. I glanced nervously over my shoulder so many times that I took a wrong turn and ended up in a long corridor I didn't remember. When I stopped and tried to reorientate myself, I heard the sound again, and this time the footsteps were following me. I knew I couldn't go back. I had to go on.

A pile of rubble blocked my way, and I had to climb over it. My boots weren't made for climbing and I stumbled, reaching out to save myself. My hand sliced against a jagged piece of masonry, but I didn't have time to inspect the damage. Hand throbbing, really frightened now, I hurried on until suddenly I was in the vestibule and there was the door. With one last anxious glance behind me, I was outside, blinking in the light.

Safe . . . But then I felt my heart jump violently as I realised I wasn't safe after all.

There was a figure before me, tall and dark and menacing, and this time there was no escape.

CHAPTER TWENTY-SEVEN

The Girl's Story
Melbourne 1877

Gervais Whistler, resplendent in his expensive black evening suit and white silk shirt, stood in the stage wings and looked out into the body of Melbourne's Princess Theatre. George Coppin had done his turn, whipping the audience into a frenzy of anticipation, but that was over ten minutes ago. Now the stage was empty apart from a chair and a lantern.

The crowd, already vast, continued to grow as patrons pushed their way in, all eager to get a glimpse of her: The Child. That was what the posters called her. And more. The Child Who Could See the Future and Read the Past.

She was famous.

They'd travelled the length and breadth of the goldfields and beyond, playing to packed houses all over Australia and Europe. The shows in Paris had been particularly memorable. And now at last here she was, in Melbourne, by the request of George Coppin, politician, actor, entrepreneur and owner of the Princess Theatre. At least that was what Gervais and Coppin had agreed to tell the press.

George Coppin had returned from England in 1854, bringing with him an iron theatre in sections, and after he'd constructed it in Spring Street he called it Astley's Amphitheatre, but he'd completely remodelled it since then, renaming it the Princess Theatre and Opera House. Coppin was someone who liked a risk—he'd tossed a coin on leaving England the first time when he couldn't decide whether to sail to America or Australia. Lately, he'd been taking financial risks, and as he'd explained to Gervais when he came to call on him, he needed The Child to help repay his debts. Gervais, in debt himself, and knowing that her season at the Princess Theatre would benefit them both, promptly agreed.

Melbourne had always been waiting for them. It was to be the pinnacle of their success, but Gervais had preferred to take them to the other capitals first. He'd never forgotten Rosey's confession in the early days, of the police seeking them for the unsolved murder of Miss Oliver. Victoria, and therefore Melbourne, needed to be avoided, memories allowed to fade. It was doubtful anyone would stand up and point at Alice and say, 'There she is! That's her!' Few people knew her real name—she was The Child—but nevertheless he didn't want to take any chances that his star performer might be arrested and thrown into a prison cell.

But when Coppin wrote to him enough time had elapsed. Besides, it was too good an opportunity to say no to, and he decided there and then that Alice would come home in triumph to the state of Victoria.

Out in the theatre, eager faces were gazing up at the empty chair in the centre of the stage. There was a lantern burning on a small round table beside the chair, a bright glow to draw the eye. They were shifting restlessly in their seats, expecting something marvellous. Gervais intended to give them all they wanted and more.

He glanced over his shoulder with a trace of impatience and breathed a sigh of relief when he saw Alice walking towards him. Rosey would be nearby, she always was, but she had her part to play, too. They were a grand team and he couldn't help but congratulate himself on his own cleverness in discovering them in Dunolly in the miserable rain all those years ago.

'So many people,' Alice whispered, eyes wide.

She'd grown up into a slender young woman of seventeen, her dark brows accenting her pale skin and blue eyes. She was grave in her manner, but sometimes she could laugh and be as silly as any other girl her age, although Gervais didn't often see it. To him she was always slightly otherworldly, and he liked her that way.

'Are you ready?' he asked her.

She took a moment, settling her nerves, centring herself, and then she nodded. Gervais raised a hand and suddenly the gaslights went down, plunging the theatre into near darkness.

There was a collective gasp. Murmuring followed, and restless shifting in seats, rising like a wave and falling away again. Then there was utter silence as the crowd watched a young woman in a black dress appear from the wings and make her graceful way onto the stage. She sat down in the chair, back straight, hands folded in her lap and bowed her head as if in prayer. After a moment she lifted her head, her pale face eerily illuminated by the lantern, and looked out over the expectant faces.

The gaslights came up again, allowing them to see her properly.

Alice was confident and calm, with a pose far beyond her years. Her pale-blue eyes glowed as if, Gervais thought, something beyond the ordinary really was at play.

'There's someone here who's very worried about her child,' she called out in a high, clear voice.

A deep groan as the crowd spoke as one.

'Her child is sick, but she won't die. You must believe me when I tell you your daughter will not die. Please, stand up.'

A woman stood up and Alice smiled. 'Ah, yes, it's you. Please, tell me her name.'

'Ellen,' the woman said in a wavering voice. She wore a bonnet and greying hair hung lank about her shoulders, as if she hadn't had time to make herself presentable before she rushed to the theatre. 'The doctor says—'

'What does he know,' Alice retorted. 'I have seen doctors do more harm than good. Let Ellen feel the sunshine on her skin, let her breathe the fresh air, take her down to the beach at St Kilda and let her watch the waves. She will recover.'

The woman staggered and only just stopped herself from falling, and then she sank back into her chair, head bowed, weeping softly.

The mood in the theatre changed after that. The Child had proven herself and those who were sceptical were a little less so.

She was able to reassure a gentleman about his stomach, telling him to stop eating roast pork and drinking red wine. She gave him a simple diet to follow and fixed him with a direct gaze, making him swear to follow it, to the amusement of the crowd.

She told a younger man that he would indeed be rich and famous, if he would simply stick to his chosen craft, and she could see him in comfortable old age with many children around him.

There were sadder foretellings. A husband who would never come home and was dead in a forgotten grave in the west. And others. Not all of The Child's messages were happy ones. But that was the reason why her words were accepted as truth, because she did not try to please everyone.

By the time she was done they were calling for more and clapping wildly, but Alice was tired and looked it, and she thanked them just before the gaslights went down again. When they came up she was gone.

Gervais clasped her hands in the wings, feeling them trembling, and the weight she was resting on him as if she might fall down. He took her arm and led her downstairs to her plush private room, where her old dog sat up in its basket, wagging its tail. He saw to it she had hot tea to drink and a slice of her favourite poppy-seed cake.

'You're famous, Alice,' he told her, his eyes shining at the prospect of packed houses night after night and money rolling in. What was next? Back to Europe? America? Another Australian tour? There was nothing they couldn't do, nowhere they wouldn't be welcomed with open arms.

The door opening put a rude stop to his dreams. Rosey came in and flopped down on the day bed. She took off her bonnet, and the lank grey curls with it, and flung it down with disgust. Her fair hair shone around her head like a halo, but she was the least angelic woman he'd ever known.

'A brilliant performance.' Gervais knew what was required of him, even if all he got was a droll look from Rosey's green eyes.

After all these years he still didn't understand her, but at least they were both in accord on one thing. Doing what was best for Alice. Although it had to be said that his idea of what was best did not always match with hers.

'Alice doesn't need me to play games. Not with her gift,' she said, giving the wig a thump with her fist. Her Irish accent had been tempered over the years—he knew Rosey had worked hard at turning herself into a lady of refinement—but at moments like these, when she felt something passionately, it returned full force.

'Your story sets things up,' Gervais repeated wearily. 'You get the crowd on side and then she holds them in the palm of her hand. We need that moment.'

Rosey shrugged. 'She could do it without me. I think you're risking everything by playing this trick on them. What if someone found out? They'd be able to claim the whole thing was a lie and what would we say? No, only the first bit is a lie, the rest is real? They'd mock us and rightly so.'

'Rosey.' Alice sighed, her hand shading her eyes. 'Not now. I'm tired. My head hurts.'

At once Rosey was by her side, removing the pins from her hair. 'You should go to bed.' She gave Gervais a glare.

'Yes, yes, I'm going,' he said. 'There *is* the opening party if either of you is inclined to go?' Another look from Rosey and he raised his hands in surrender and left the room.

* * *

Rosey smoothed back Alice's hair with gentle fingers and began to massage her temples.

'Is it very bad?'

'Not too bad.' Alice's eyelids flickered as she spoke the lie.

Rosey knew the pain was excruciating. For months now, every time Alice did her act, she was rewarded with a headache that paralysed her, sometimes for days. Thankfully, there were no more shows now until Wednesday, but Rosey knew she'd have to remind Gervais not to book them too closely together. He tended to forget that the goose that laid the golden egg was a fragile young woman.

Rosey wondered whether to say the words that had been on the tip of her tongue for months now. *You must stop. You're making yourself ill.* But she held them back. Alice had been so looking forward to coming to Melbourne, and besides, even if she said what she thought, would Alice listen?

Sometimes Alice could be so stubborn, but Rosey knew the time was coming when both Alice and Gervais would have to accept that this golden goose needed a long holiday.

The rap on the door caused Hope to bark, and Alice jumped and gave a whimper, as if the pain was just too much to bear. Angrily, Rosey went to the door and opened it a crack.

'What is it?'

Her first impression was that the young man outside was a gentleman. He lifted his fashionable bowler hat off his thick fair hair and gave her a shy sort of smile. For a moment she thought she recognised him, but there had been so many people in so many places that it was impossible for her to place him. She didn't smile back.

'The Child rarely does private sessions,' she said sharply, 'and tonight she's tired.'

'I know. I don't want that. I'm here because she knows me. The, eh, Child, I mean. I'm Gilbert Suckling.'

Rosey went still. Memory was returning in a rush. It was strange, standing like a statue while inside her heart was thumping wildly with images of the past. Gilbert Suckling. The doctor's son. She remembered being examined every month so that she wouldn't give a disease to the 'gentlemen' who chose to call at the Red Petticoat. Long ago rushed through her like a cold wind, and with it all the things she'd thought to forget, and she wanted to shut the door, close it out, and Gilbert Suckling with it.

She opened her mouth to tell him The Child wasn't available, but it was too late. Alice called anxiously from behind her.

'Rosey? I can hear a voice. I *know* that voice.'

With a reluctant sigh, Rosey opened the door and let their past inside.

* * *

Alice had knelt to lift Hope from his basket, holding him close. He was still reasonably spry, considering his probable age—they hadn't really known how old he was when they found him, but Alice thought that was all right, because she didn't know how old she was, either. Hope had been with her for so long now that she was grateful for every day he remained. Sometimes she wondered if he held on to life for her sake, because he knew how much she needed him, because she could not imagine what she would do when he was gone.

Bending down to Hope had made her head ache even more, and it was now so painful that the room seemed to be shifting and she had difficulty focusing on one spot. She should go to bed, Rosey was right, but she didn't want to lie down yet. She'd so wanted to go to Gervais's party. It wasn't fair.

And now that *voice* . . . she knew that voice . . .

Alice blinked as a young man stood before her, bowing. When he straightened he was grinning, and Alice instantly knew who he was.

'You're so tall,' she managed, a lump in her throat. 'And grown-up.'

Gilbert sat down beside her without an invitation, but she didn't mind. Here was someone who knew her properly, who wasn't in awe of her, and she forced her pain to the background, for just a little bit longer.

Gilbert was telling her how he was living here in Melbourne and studying to be a doctor, just as he'd always said he would. 'When I saw the poster for The Child I had to come and see the latest sensation. It was only when the gaslights came up and I saw you, Alice, that I recognised you.'

'After all these years you recognised me, Gilbert?' she said in amazement.

Gilbert was trying to explain how he recognised her up on the stage in the pallid lantern light. 'There's just something about you, Alice. An air . . .' He waved a hand in embarrassment at his lack of the right words. 'A sense of . . . of . . .'

'There's only one Alice,' Rosey said.

'How do you do it?' Gilbert blurted out, his voice far too loud, making Alice wince.

'How do you think she does it?' Rosey snapped.

Gilbert looked even more uncomfortable. 'I know you told me about your sight. Your gift. I remember every word you spoke. But I still don't understand how you can see things that aren't there, Alice. Things that no scientist can prove.'

Alice shook her head. 'I don't know what to say to you, Gilbert. I don't think such things can be proved by science. They're beyond the scope of science.'

Hope was struggling and Rosey gently took him from her. A silence fell and Alice being Alice sought to put it right by being kind.

'How is your father?' she said, her voice fading. She knew she must look terrible because Rosey took an anxious step towards her but stopped when Alice moved her head in a slight no.

Gilbert took a moment to answer and seemed to be choosing his words with care. He was no longer smiling. 'Of course you don't know, do you? Alice, my father left Echuca not long after you. It was impossible for him to continue to be a doctor after . . . well, he couldn't work in the town again. He came down here to Melbourne and for a time things were difficult, but eventually he was given a position at a private hospital.'

'What do you mean?' Rosey did step forward now. 'What happened in Echuca?'

'I'm sorry.' Gilbert shifted awkwardly, head bowed as he twisted the brim of his hat. It seemed an effort for him to meet their eyes.

His eyes were hazel, like his father's, but the expression in them was apologetic rather than arrogant. 'Alice, I'm sorry. There was an inquest into the death of one of my father's patients. Too many had died, you see, and people were beginning to find it odd. For a time he was even implicated. Until the truth came out.' He leaned forward with an urgency, as if to make her understand his father's innocence. 'It wasn't his fault, but no one wanted to remember that in the hysteria. You see, the pharmacist was to blame. There was antimony contamination, particularly in one of the ingredients only my father ordered for his patients' restorative tonic. It was his own special recipe.'

'Antimony?' Alice whispered. She was remembering him, the pharmacist, at the door of Captain Potter's house, and the murky colours around him. He'd frightened her, but she'd thought it was because he resembled the man in the dark coat.

'Antimony can be used as an emetic, to induce vomiting or purge a patient. A high dose of antimony will cause sudden death, but repeated very low doses can be difficult to recognise other than as a lingering unwellness that includes stomach problems. If the patient takes low doses for long enough they will eventually also lead to death.'

'So the pharmacist was giving your father's patients antimony in the tonic he was prescribing?' Alice whispered.

'Yes. And all the while my father thought he was curing them. He insisted they take the tonic even when they told him it was making them sicker and—'

Alice stood up with a wordless cry.

Molly!

And the next moment she'd fainted into Gilbert's arms.

CHAPTER TWENTY-EIGHT

Annie's Story

'Max!'

The shadowy figure had stepped forward, and, with an overpowering sense of relief, I saw that it was Max. And he looked shocked. It was only then that I realised how grubby I was, covered in dust and grime from the old building, while my hand was dripping blood.

'Annie? What's happened?' He took my arm, helping me down the broken stairs and onto firmer ground.

'I tripped.' I was embarrassed now as I remembered my headlong run, and from what exactly? A shadow? A ghost with peppermint breath? 'I thought there was someone following me . . . It was probably just my imagination.'

Any other man would have asked me what I thought I was doing, wandering alone around a demolition site. Or given me a lecture on my stupidity. Max didn't say a word. He took out a handkerchief and carefully wrapped it around my injured hand, and I let him, feeling weirdly like I was in a scene from an old romantic movie. Max had appeared at just the right moment. All he needed was a cape and a sword to fight off the baddies. Tears stung my eyes and that was weird, too. I wasn't usually so emotional, but I'd had a difficult week and now a fright.

'Thank you,' I said, with a shaky smile. Cradling my hand, I looked up at his reassuring figure. 'Max, what are you doing here?'

Max dug his hands into his pockets. 'I went to your office but it was closed, so then I tried your house. Your father said you were here so I thought I'd meet you. I've been wanting to see the famous Goldminer Hotel.'

He cast it a glance and grimaced.

'A bit of mess, isn't it?' I said it for him.

'Yeah, but I suppose it would be. I hope you didn't mind me turning up like this. Your father said it'd be all right, but . . . ?'

'It's fine. Really, it is. And I'm very glad you turned up like this.'

He grinned and I remembered why I liked him so much. He was wearing jeans and a button-up shirt with a leather jacket over it and he looked great. The steamboat captain come to the city was a good look after all. Why had I thought he mightn't be as attractive down here away from the river?

'I can't leave Reuben for too long,' I began, guilt rearing its head.

'Of course.'

'Do you have a day off, or . . . ?'

'I put Kenny in charge of the *Ariadne*. A promotion to captain. He even gets to wear a cap.'

I laughed, some of my shakiness beginning to go, and we made our way out onto the street. 'My car's this way,' he said. 'Did you drive in?'

'No, I caught the tram.'

'Then I can drive you home.' He glanced down at my hand. 'I think you should get that looked at, you know. Have you had a tetanus jab in the last five years?'

I shrugged. 'I don't know. It's just a scrape and it'll give Reuben a chance to play medical expert. He's a frustrated doctor. He cured Courtney of her cold the other day.'

He smiled back, but his eyebrows went up. 'Courtney?'

Oh God, hadn't I mentioned Courtney?

'My daughter. My four year old daughter.'

There was a silence. I glanced at him surreptitiously as we walked along together, but I couldn't read his expression.

Hates kids, I thought glumly. Well, never mind, he was here now and we could have a talk and a laugh, and when he left I'd never see him again. Why on earth hadn't I told him about Courtney? It honestly hadn't come up. We'd always had more than enough to say about the *Trompe L'oeil*, or Alice and the Potters, or the riverboats. I'd only mentioned my father because he was part of the business, just as Kenny was part of his.

We reached the car, a rather dusty-looking Jeep, and he unlocked it. After we climbed in he sat a moment, hands on the wheel, staring ahead through the windscreen as though working up to something. I had a fair idea what it was. Just my luck, the only man I'd been interested in for years and he had an aversion to small children.

'Annie,' he said, 'I never asked you if you were married. I never asked if you had kids. I never asked anything personal, and I'm sorry. If my coming down here is awkward for you then you only have to say.'

I met his eyes. He looked apologetic. Uncertain. Not the confident riverboat captain, just a man who found himself in a vulnerable position.

'I didn't ask you either.' I offered him an olive branch. 'Perhaps we should both confess any sins now?'

He nodded with that smile. There was something about him that curled about my heart and squeezed. I felt slightly breathless.

'I'm divorced and I have one kid: Courtney. My ex-husband and I get on well enough, but I'd never go back to him. I think if it wasn't for Courtney I would've cut all ties with him by now. There are no boyfriends and haven't been for . . . well, too long. I live with my father and work in his business, which will one day be my business, so he tells me. And that's about it really. No other attachments, no deep, dark secrets.'

He reached out a hand and touched my cheek. Probably brushing off a speck of dust, I told myself, despite the jump of my pulses.

'Single. One long-term relationship that ended amicably, no kids, one brother.'

It took a moment for me to realise he'd just given me his CV. I smiled, and just like that he leaned in and kissed my lips. Gently, tenderly, and all too briefly.

On the way home I was thinking: *This is ridiculous. I hardly know him.* But the thing was I felt as if I did know him. I felt as if we were connected in some way, perhaps by the *Ariadne* and the *Trompe L'oeil*, perhaps by the way he smiled and looked at me, properly at me, or maybe the way I felt when I was talking to him or staring into his eyes. And while it felt wonderful and exciting, I also knew I had to take things slowly and carefully.

For Courtney's sake.

For my own sake.

Back at Suckling Street we found Reuben seated in the lounge while Greta was busily washing dishes in the kitchen. They'd been cooking, it seemed. Reuben looked up as we came in, and I just knew he was reading something in my face that I didn't want him to.

But all he said was, 'You're hurt,' nodding at the handkerchief fastened around my hand. 'Let me take a look.'

The cut wasn't very deep, my hand more bruised than anything, and Reuben soon dealt with it. He looked up my vaccinations and informed me that I'd had a tetanus shot a year ago, after a cut from a rusty nail sticking out of an old picture frame. I listened to him scolding me for wandering around The Goldminer on my own, murmuring repentance in the right places, but when he asked what Sebastian had to say I diverted his attention. I wasn't ready to discuss the prospect of a job in New York. I needed time to sort out my own thoughts and feelings before I listened to Reuben's.

Greta was busy pumping Max for information about himself, and gave me an approving look while Max appeared unfazed, and perhaps a little amused by all the attention. I realised that despite my impression that I already knew him well, the truth was I didn't really know him at all. I certainly didn't have a clue what he was thinking right now.

Despite my doubts, as we sat around the table and drank our coffee and tea and ate Greta's cupcakes with pink icing, the conversation seemed to flow without any of the awkwardness I'd noticed before with a stranger present.

I found I didn't really have to say much after all. I was enjoying listening to the others, putting in a word here or there, laughing when Greta described her latest conquest. It took me by surprise when Reuben turned to me and said, 'Tell me, Annie, was it worth risking your life to see inside that crumbling ruin?'

'I think so.' I put down my cake, wondering uneasily how many I'd eaten. 'Eh, I wanted to see the room where the *Trompe L'oeil* used to hang and Clive gave me directions. It was a reception room, where they took the important guests. The painting really must have caught their attention when Gervais Whistler showed them in. They couldn't have missed it. I suppose the entire hotel must have been very ostentatious in its heyday and I don't see Gervais as the shy and retiring type. He'd have loved the attention.'

'But what was his connection with Alice and Rosey?' Max asked.

'He was a businessman, a showman. Perhaps they worked for him in his show. In fact, I think they must have. There's a scene in the painting—a building called the Dunolly Music Hall, with Gervais standing out in front.'

'Then he met up with them on the goldfields. That was where their paths collided.'

I nodded my agreement and I could feel my face brightening with enthusiasm. 'That's what I think, too. A pity the vignettes aren't set out in order. I'd like a timeline but they seem to be scattered all over the place. And the left-hand side of the painting is too damaged to make out. There are probably lots more clues there that we just can't see.'

'Weren't you saying you could do something with that section? Clean it up?'

'I've cleaned it once. I was going to try something else, but it's tricky. I don't want to cause more damage.'

Max leaned back in his chair, looking thoughtful. 'It's funny but nowadays whenever I'm on board the *Ariadne*, I find myself thinking of Captain Potter and Molly. It's as if you've stirred up their spirits. Brought them back to life.'

I smiled at him. 'If anyone brought them back to life it was your father, hauling the *Ariadne* out of the mud of the river and restoring her.'

There was a silence and it was only when Reuben cleared his throat, exchanging a glance with Greta, that I realised Max and I had been hogging the conversation while the other two looked on. And adding up two and two to make five, if their expressions were anything to go by.

Greta got to her feet. 'I'd better go. I thought I might head in to work and tidy up some loose ends.'

Reuben waved a hand. 'No, you go home, Greta. Take the rest of the afternoon off,' he added generously. Almost, I thought wryly, as if we weren't about to go bust.

Greta looked a bit doubtful but I quickly agreed. There wasn't much to do at work with both of us away, and if there was something urgent then there was always my mobile phone—Reuben refused to have one.

Max stood up as well. 'I'll get out of your hair now.'

'Are you driving back?' The question spilled out and I knew I sounded disappointed, like a child deprived of a treat.

'Eh, no.' His smile was slightly shamefaced. 'Actually, I have the week off so I'll find a room and—'

'You can stay with us,' Reuben said promptly. 'Upstairs in my apartment. Can't he, Annie? I have to be down here so that Annie can keep an eye on me, so my place is empty. You're welcome to stay, Max.'

I quickly jumped in before Max could protest. 'Yes. Reuben has to stay down here so you won't have to share or anything. Stay,

Max . . . that's if you want to,' I finished awkwardly, suddenly concerned I was coming across as too pushy.

But Max looked relieved. 'Thank you, I will. I'll just get my bags from the car.'

Reuben waited until he was gone before he said, 'Should I warn him about the ghost?'

I gave him a glare. 'We're not talking about the ghost.'

Reuben shrugged, then yawned. 'Do you know, I think I might take a nap.'

'Then go to bed. And not on the sofa, Papa.'

'Don't you need a chaperone?' he teased.

I shot him another look but he only chuckled as he went off to the spare room.

CHAPTER TWENTY-NINE

The Girl's Story

'Migraine, I think. But I'm not a qualified doctor yet, Miss Donnelly.'

Gilbert's self-deprecation made Rosey like him better—she kept making the mistake of thinking he was like his father, but he wasn't, not at all. She managed a smile. 'She'll sleep now. Even though I don't like giving her those drafts, they do help. Nothing else seems to. They send her to sleep for hours and she's so shaky when she wakes up.'

'If the pain is that bad then perhaps she needs to be examined properly.' Gilbert looked alarmed, his hazel eyes wide.

'Oh, don't worry. Gervais has had her seen by the best. There's nothing inside her head to cause concern, nothing physically they can find that would explain her migraines and nightmares.'

Gilbert was watching her across the space between their two chairs. They were seated before the fire while Alice lay sleeping in her bed behind them, her hand folded under her pale cheek, her long brown hair loosely braided away from her face. Gervais had found them a suite at the Menzies Hotel for the term of their stay in Melbourne. The Menzies catered to wealthy and important clientele, and while Gervais believed The Child should be seen in such company, he also considered it a good investment when it came to advertising future bookings for his shows.

When he'd been informed that Alice had fainted he'd immediately called for a carriage to take them back to their suite. Rosey was irritated but not surprised to see newspaper men waiting for them when they arrived. Although Gervais seemed genuinely fond of Alice, Rosey was well aware that didn't stop him from seeing her illness and growing physical fragility as an opportunity for publicity, one he found far too good to pass up.

Rosey had settled Alice and then fetched Gilbert at her request. By then the young woman was very sleepy, but he'd held her hand, smiling, speaking to her in a low voice. There was a gentleness about Gilbert, Rosey decided, a caring quality that his father had never had.

By the time he returned to the fire, Rosey had ordered a tray with tea and dainty sandwiches. She poured from the pot, enjoying the ceremony. It was something she'd learned in the elegant salons and hotels during their travels. It was part of playing the lady. Rosey had always been a good mimic and now she played the lady so well she felt completely comfortable in the role. Some days she almost thought the Irish runaway was nothing more than a dream.

'My father blamed Alice for Molly Potter's death,' Gilbert said, and his face instantly seemed very young again, and vulnerable. 'Alice told Molly to stop taking the medicine he was prescribing, but he went to see Captain Potter and the captain persuaded Molly to resume taking it. My father blamed Alice when Molly died so soon after she began taking it again. He genuinely thought he was helping. When he discovered it was the medicine itself that had killed her, and several of his other patients, he was as shocked as everyone else. The pharmacist was arrested and charged with manslaughter. He went to prison. The police were certain he'd added the antimony intentionally, although he claimed it was accidental. But it made no difference to my father's practice. No one wanted him and he left Echuca soon afterwards.'

'But he's practising now?' Rosey said, unmoved by the senior doctor's plight.

'We had to live, and he wanted me to become a doctor. That was always his dream. And mine. Unfortunately, he's not the man he was. The deaths of his patients broke him.'

'But didn't kill him.' Rosey couldn't help rubbing in the fact, but then was sorry when she saw his wounded expression. He looked like a little boy who'd been punished for someone else's misdemeanour. This was not the time nor the place for vengeance, and besides, Gilbert had had nothing to do with Molly's death. It wasn't his fault his father was too arrogant and ignorant to admit when he was wrong. Still, she couldn't help but feel sorry he hadn't made the connection between his patients' deaths and the medicine early enough to save Molly. How different Alice's life might have been then!

They were silent, deep in their own thoughts, while the dying fire hissed.

'I'm worried about Alice,' Rosey said at last.

'Worried?' Gilbert sat forward as if to urge her on.

It seemed a betrayal to speak of it, but in telling Gilbert she didn't feel as if she was breaking Alice's confidence. Gilbert knew Alice, and Rosey was beginning to believe he truly cared about her.

'She hasn't been well for a long time. You saw what happened tonight?'

'The migraine.'

'She also has nightmares and they're getting worse.'

'You mentioned that a moment ago. What are they about?'

Rosey sighed. 'Memories from the past. The madman who tried to drown her like an unwanted kitten. After all these years she still doesn't know who she is.'

'She hasn't remembered any of it?'

'Bits and pieces, glimpses, but no names, nothing that we can use to trace her family or her origins.'

Gilbert considered her words while she moved to kneel on the hearth and add some more fuel to the fire. The room had begun to cool and she worried that Alice might catch a cold. In fact, Rosey thought wryly, she spent most of her days and nights worrying about Alice and had done ever since that stifling hot summer's day at the Red Petticoat, when she took the girl's hand in hers and led her down to the kitchen.

'I'm interested in the brain,' Gilbert said at last, with a modest shrug. 'I'm thinking of specialising in that area. There's a doctor in France, Doctor Charcot, whose work is quite new and promising, but it's in the very early stages and not everyone agrees with him. He has experimented with mesmerism.'

'But isn't that just a trick they use on stage? Gervais employed a mesmerist for a few shows. Until he ran off with Mademoiselle Suzy. One of the dancers,' Rosey explained with a smile, remembering the uproar *that* had caused. She always had a suspicion Alice wanted to be a dancer, but with her talents it was not to be.

Gilbert was nodding. 'There are those who think mesmerism is a trick, but I believe we can learn from it. I'm not an expert by any means, but, well, I visit the lunatic asylum in Kew, to assist with the patients, and I've found some cases there that have benefited from my amateurish attempts.'

Throughout their conversation Rosey couldn't help staring at him and now he noticed it and shuffled in embarrassment. 'Should I go on?'

'I'm sorry. I was still thinking of you as a boy and here you are talking about French doctors and mesmerism and helping lunatics. I'm dumbfounded, Gilbert. And yes, please, do go on.'

He blushed. 'Yes. Well. Some doctors believe that sometimes when there are unpleasant memories locked in the brain, they become like an infection in an otherwise healthy body. And as with an infection if they're not lanced they tend to worsen over time. In other words, the memories need to be brought forth out of the darkness and examined in the light. Keeping that pain to ourselves only increases its hold on us, do you see? If we take the memories out and examine them and see them for what they are then their power over us gradually begins to lessen.'

'You're saying that when Alice locked away her unpleasant memories they didn't actually go away.'

'That's right. I'll give you an example.' He chewed a moment on his sandwich, considering. 'There's a patient I know, a man who was on a boat that sank in a storm out in Port Phillip Bay. He saw his companions drown over a number of hours while they awaited rescue, and then he alone was saved. He was told not to speak of his experience and he locked it away, but the memories drove him mad. I've spoken to him and tried to get him to speak to me, and I've even attempted some mesmerism to help him relive the trauma of his past but from a distance, from a place of safety. I can't be sure, I have no definite proof as yet, but I do think my methods are helping him.'

'So you can cure him?'

'I don't know. Possibly. I think a cure will take a long time. And I think if these things had been brought to the surface earlier, perhaps shortly after they happened, then he may not have become so ill.'

'So what you're saying is that you think Alice should face her past?'

'If that's possible, yes.'

'Do you mean mesmerise her?'

'Yes. Not by me, perhaps. There are others.'

Rosey hesitated, it was a big step to take and Alice may refuse and Rosey could not really blame her. Yet, if it helped to make her well again, surely it was worth a try?

'I'll have to think about it. I'll have to ask Alice.'

'Of course.' He rose to leave and she realised how late it was. She should have left an hour ago. *He* would be waiting for her and he didn't like to be left dangling. He wasn't used to it.

Rosey smiled. Never mind. She'd enjoy teasing her lover out of his sullens and into a more jovial mood.

'Thank you,' she said, also rising and taking his hand.

Gilbert gave her a serious look, reminding her again of the young boy he'd once been. 'I wonder if . . . do you think I might come again? As a friend, I mean, not a doctor in training.'

'If Alice agrees. It's not up to me. Alice is her own person, you know.'

'Of course she is. It's just . . . I've often thought of her over the years. I've missed her and wondered what she was doing. I don't want to lose touch now I've found her.'

Rosey patted his arm. 'I understand, Gilbert, and she probably feels the same.'

He nodded and quickly collected his coat and bowler hat, and with a slight bow closed the door, leaving Rosey to her thoughts and the sound of Alice's quiet breathing.

Gilbert had turned into a pleasant and intelligent young man, but Rosey wasn't sure she wanted the past coming upon her unexpectedly like that. She'd made a new life for herself, changed into a different person. With a mental shrug she put the memories aside again and tugged the bell pull.

One of the housemaids came to take her place, and Rosey hurried to her own room and changed her clothing. She put on her striped pink dress with the satin pleating and ruching, and the *tournure*—the word always made her smile. Bustle had been quite good enough for her before she took a step or two into polite society. Her shoes had a heel and matched the dress, and gave a satisfying clip-clip as she walked in them. Rosey brushed her hair, fastening it back from her face with jewelled slides, leaving the rest to curl against her neck and shoulders.

There, she was done. A quick glance in the mirror satisfied her that she looked smart and ladylike. She was pleased with the rich cloth of the dress and her slim figure, drawn in at the waist by the corset, although she'd never had to pull the fastenings too tight. It had taken her a good while, but Rosey was satisfied with her life as it was now.

Travelling all over the world, seeing people and places she might never have seen if Gervais Whistler had not found them in the rain in Dunolly. Of course she preferred not to remember *where* he'd found her, that was dead and buried as far as she was concerned. Her entire past was not to be discussed, and if someone asked her straight out then she laughed and diverted the question to more acceptable areas.

As Alice's 'assistant' she had plenty to do within the troupe, but there were other tasks as well. At one point she had performed a single-act play about a poor girl who'd found gold. The crowd had loved that, and Rosey was a good actress. She was also accomplished at arranging the travelling and the accommodation whenever they were on the road. Gervais called her his 'right-hand girl' and she always smiled when he said it, but privately she thought that without her pulling the strings his troupe would have sunk into debt and bankruptcy years ago.

A final pat to her hair, and she swept her dark-blue cloak around her shoulders and collected her fur muff. The party would be almost over by now but she should make an appearance. Gervais would expect it.

Soon she was descending the stairs to the hotel foyer.

The Menzies had a certain smell—of wealth and privilege. And Rosey had begun to enjoy that smell over her years of staying in grand hotels and visiting fine houses. Now, with the foyer quiet and almost deserted—the newspaper men were long since gone—she paused a moment to enjoy the thought that this was the sort of place in which she belonged. Seeing Gilbert again had shaken her more than she would have imagined, bringing up the past as he had, but it was all right. *She* was all right. Nothing had changed and she could carry on as usual.

Rosey was just about to ask the doorman to fetch her a hansom cab when someone behind her spoke her name.

And in that instant she wasn't all right. Not all right at all.

It must be a night for the past to return to haunt her, because even before the stranger rose from his chair and walked towards her Rosey knew him.

In a blink of an eye she was back in the campsite in the bush, with Sean dying in the tent and Alice looking sullen, Hope tight in her arms, and Josh . . . Josh combing her tangled curls with his gentle fingers. Her heart began to thump unpleasantly fast and she put a hand to her breast as if to calm it. Instead of the soiled and faded pink dress she'd worn so long ago, her fingers brushed the rich satin cloth, the lace and ribbon, a reminder of the expensive clothing she was wearing, the latest from Paris.

Josh Parker might be standing in front her, looking barely any older than when she had parted from him, but Rosey would not let him see how deeply and fundamentally he'd shaken her. For her own sake she could not afford to.

'Mr Parker!' she cried with false joy. 'What a treat!'

His smile wavered slightly but Rosey hardly noticed. At least, she was telling herself, he couldn't think her ignorant now. She was a different woman from the one he'd known. Yet her nerves were on edge, and her voice sounded a little too shrill even to her own ears.

He was holding something towards her and it took her a moment to see that it was a small bunch of flowers. Her smile faltered. Her fingers trembled. Freesias. The plain cream ones with the wonderful scent.

Josh saw her face fall and thought he'd disappointed her. 'I forgot about the flowers I promised. Do you remember? When we parted I said I'd meet you in Melbourne with a bunch of flowers?'

Rosey nodded, a lump rising in her throat. 'I remember,' she said huskily.

'These are from my landlady's garden.'

How could he know that freesias were her favourite flower? They reminded her of Cork and Ireland and her family, of everything she'd tried so hard to forget. He'd chosen the one flower that could bring tough Rosey to tears.

Josh ducked his head, that familiar shy smile on his face, and his red hair was as bright as ever in the subdued lighting of the hotel. She saw a splodge of paint on his hand and thought he must have become an artist, just as he said he would.

He was still speaking and she tried to concentrate, tried to remember she wasn't poor Irish Rosey anymore.

'I'm sorry I didn't meet your carriage when you arrived in town, but I didn't know you were here until this evening.'

It was the joke they'd made long ago. Now she waved a careless hand—she'd once seen a titled woman do a similar thing and liked it so much she'd taken it on as her own. 'No matter. No gold carriage with six black horses. Alice and I did talk about it, but we decided it was just a little too ostentatious.' She laughed again, the sound hard, and this time she saw him wince.

He suddenly seemed to notice her midnight-blue cloak. 'Are you going out?'

Had she been? Of course, to meet Gervais at the opening-night party! She must go. To stay would be madness, especially when she was feeling so vulnerable and shaky, as if her carefully constructed, shiny new facade was about to come apart. All her hard work blasted in one evening. No, she could not possibly stay no matter how much she wanted to.

'Yes, I'm going out,' she said. 'I was just about to ask for a cab.'

He seemed disappointed and a touch desperate. 'I understand. You're busy.'

She stepped away, putting distance between them. It was difficult, but it was for the best. Let him think her a stuck-up bitch, it was better than the truth. That after all these years she'd never forgotten him or the reasons why she'd rejected him. Rosey had moved on and the past was an uncomfortable place she preferred not to visit. 'Can I ride with you?' he called after her just as she thought she'd got away. 'We can talk in the cab? I need to talk to you, Rosey.'

It was her name that did it. The way he spoke it, with his cultured gentleman's voice with the hint of west-country drawl. It made her weak at the knees.

Josh Parker had come back into her life and Rosey was suddenly very afraid he was going to ruin everything.

CHAPTER THIRTY

Annie's Story

Courtney had been chattering all the way home, but as I pulled up in the driveway, she stopped. 'The light's on upstairs in Grandpa's place,' she announced. 'Has he gone home again?'

'No, he hasn't. We have a visitor staying. He's called Max Taylor.'

Courtney looked doubtful but climbed out of the car and ran to door. Reuben and Max were in the living room and looked up at our entrance. I was surprised to see that Courtney was behaving shyly—my chatty, confident daughter tongue-tied? And Max looked a little shy, too, although he smiled and said hello.

'Max is a riverboat captain,' I said, removing Courtney's coat and gloves. Her cheeks were flushed from the cold air, her dark eyes sparkling.

'A paddle-steamer? Like the one in your painting?' Courtney whispered, leaning closer.

'Yes, just like that one.'

Courtney hesitated, but only for a moment before she approached Max, twisting a dark curl around one finger. 'Are you *Captain* Max?'

'I can be,' Max said, with a glance at me as if for reassurance. 'My brother calls me that.'

'What do you call your brother?'

Max smiled his wonderful smile. 'I call him Kenny the Menace.'

Courtney giggled. 'That's not right,' she cried. 'It's Dennis the Menace!'

After that it seemed as if the ice was broken, and Courtney set about showing Max all her favourite toys until I told her it was time for her bath and that Max needed a break.

'He can hold Tarzan while I'm gone.'

As Courtney and I left the room, I overheard Reuben say, 'You're privileged, Max. Tarzan is in high favour at the moment.'

Courtney spent her bath telling me about her friends at child care, and afterwards she insisted on helping with the honey-and-ginger chicken I was making for dinner. By the time we'd eaten she was yawning, and didn't protest when I said it was time for bed.

'I'll read you one story,' I said.

She didn't even argue, her eyes already closing. 'Goodnight, Grandpa,' she said, going to him for her hug and kiss. Then, with a wicked smile, 'Goodnight, Captain Max.'

'Goodnight, Courtney.'

'I like Captain Max,' Courtney said, wriggling beneath her covers. 'Do you?'

'Yes,' I said, testing her response.

'Good, Mummy. Cause you need a man in your life.'

'Oh, do I?'

'Just make sure Nephi doesn't bite him.' She yawned, eyes closing. 'He has nice colours, too.'

'Do you mean his clothes?'

But she was asleep.

By the time I returned, the two men were deep in conversation. They seemed to be discussing interior restoration of timber boats, although at one point they were talking about the *Titanic*. I noticed they hadn't broached the dishes, but seeing they were getting on so well I didn't mind. I'd hardly started to stack the dishwasher when Max came to help.

'Sorry,' he murmured. 'Should I order you to sit down while I do this? Or would that be the act of a chauvinist? I never quite know where I stand with the modern woman.'

'Helping's fine,' I assured him with a smile.

'Your daughter's a sweetie.'

I felt my smile turn proud. 'I know. She seems to take most things in her stride. Of course, she's only four.'

We chatted as we worked, and Max told me about his childhood. A country boy attending a country school, riding his bike, playing footie—it sounded idyllic. He said he was a typical Aussie kid. In turn I told him about my mother dying when I was two, and life growing up with Reuben.

It was on the tip of my tongue to also tell him about the job offer in New York, but I didn't want to spoil the comfortable moment between us. Reuben was watching an old Hitchcock movie when we got back to the living room, but he was soon yawning and removed himself to bed, perhaps a little too obviously, I thought.

As we watched Tippi Hedren growing ever more concerned as birds gathered in a schoolyard, I felt Max's arm slip around my shoulders. He smelt nice and I snuggled against him, enjoying the closeness. I didn't mean to fall asleep, but the next thing I knew I was waking up and he was looking down at me with a grin.

'Do you know you snore?'

I sat up, pushing hair out of my eyes, very self-conscious. 'I don't.'

'Just a little snuffle now and again,' he said, with a crooked smile. 'It's endearing, actually. Nothing to be embarrassed about.'

That made me laugh. 'I'm so sorry. I don't normally fall asleep on my guests. It's just . . .'

'Things have been hectic,' he answered for me.

I nodded. 'I have to go in to the office tomorrow. Do you want to come and see the *Trompe L'oeil*?'

'Yes, I do.'

'Good.'

There was an awkward pause as our eyes met and I felt myself melting into his arms. Then he bent his head and kissed me, gently at first, tentatively, before he deepened the kiss with a passion that took my breath away. His mouth was warm and firm, exploring mine and promising so much. I couldn't remember the last time I'd been kissed like this, and I really didn't want it to end. I clung to him, wanting to stretch out on the sofa with him, and slowly undress him so that I could explore his muscled body.

It had been a long time between men, though, and I knew I wasn't ready to begin a full-on sexual relationship right here while my family slept upstairs. In my wild younger days, maybe, but not now. I moved away, catching my breath, knowing if I didn't do it now then I would be in trouble.

Max blinked, his eyes dark and sleepy looking. 'Mmm,' he said, as if I was a particularly yummy dessert. I felt my libido kicking back into action again. Oh, yes, Max was something else, and it was going to be very, very difficult if I had to leave him for New York.

'I don't—' I began, but he shook his head, pressing a quick kiss to my lips.

'No, it's okay. More than okay.' He got to his feet. 'I'll see you in the morning.'

I tried to think of something witty but all that came out was, 'Yep.'

With him gone, I snuggled back against the cushions just as the movie ended, Rod Taylor and Tippi Hedren safe together, the world of birds calm once more.

* * *

I had spent a restless night, my head full of the business and Sebastian's offer, not to mention Max just a few steps upstairs. The kiss really seemed to have revved up my libido. I found myself imagining all sorts of scenarios, some of them from *Fifty Shades of Grey*, which were amusing as I lay in bed but more disturbing when I came face to face with him.

I found I could hardly meet his eyes for longer than a second over breakfast, but luckily Courtney filled in the gaps in conversation, chatting about the zoo and the aquarium and informing Max that he must visit both and she'd be only too happy to show him around. Reuben reminded her that she'd be late for child care, and hurried her off to find her bag and Tarzan.

'My daughter believes she's the centre of the universe,' I said with a smile over my coffee. 'And I suppose she is. My father and I adore her.'

Max smiled back. 'Sounds like the perfect childhood to me. Children should be adored.'

Well, I couldn't fault him there.

When Max went to get his jacket my father whispered that he seemed to be a very nice man. 'A pity he doesn't live in the city,' he added.

'I don't think he would concur with that, Papa. He seems perfectly happy in Echuca.'

'We shall see,' he said in that annoying tone, as if he knew something I didn't.

It showed that Reuben was getting better, and I knew what would come next. Reuben would want to go back to work.

After dropping off Courtney, Max and I drove through the busy traffic. During the stops and starts I found myself opening up to him about the problems with the business. I hadn't meant to, but he was such a good listener. I even told him of my fears that Reuben and Reuben was beyond saving.

'Do you want me to take a look at the books?' Max asked.

I must have looked surprised.

'I used to be a chartered accountant.' He admitted it with a guilty expression, as if he'd done something wrong. 'I used to work down here in Collins Street.' He named one of the larger firms.

'You worked in Collins Street?' I knew I sounded flabbergasted and couldn't help it.

'Yes. For nearly ten years. Got a job out of uni and worked my way up. I used to go home to Echuca at weekends to help Dad, got interested in the *Ariadne*, and one day I was sitting in my office and thought, "Nope, I'm out of here." I got a job in Echuca with a smaller firm, but once the *Ariadne* was back in the water I quit and took over running her. My colleagues thought I was crazy, but honestly, Annie, I've never regretted it.'

I felt bemused. Max a boring man in a suit? How could I have been so wrong?

'The books?' he reminded me, and the warm sparkle in his eyes made me uneasily aware he was probably reading my thoughts.

Oh God, I hope he doesn't think I'm disappointed!

And I wasn't. Max may not be the quintessential riverboat captain, but neither was he two-dimensional. He was a man with experience, who hadn't been afraid to make tough decisions. And neither, I thought wryly, should I be.

'I suppose . . . well, if you don't mind. My father thinks it's a waste of time me getting any more advice. He's done that already, and the bank has knocked him back for another loan.' I ran a hand through my hair and then wished I hadn't as my wild curls tumbled everywhere. 'I don't know what to do next, Max, so any suggestions you can make would be appreciated.'

'Give me an hour or so and I'll tell you what I think. You don't have to follow my advice, Annie. But I might be able to help clarify things for you.'

Once we reached the office, I took him upstairs to my studio to show him the painting.

At first he didn't say a word, walking towards it, eyes fixed on the scenes depicted. Then he turned and gave me an amazed look, shaking his head. 'Wonderful,' he said. 'Your photos don't do it justice.'

We spent some time inspecting the different vignettes, and while I pointed them out, Max asked questions. It gave me a chance to shine in my chosen profession. He kept going back to the depiction of the *Ariadne*, leaning closer to see Captain Potter and Molly and the mate with red hair.

'No wonder you're fascinated,' he said. 'I could look at it all day. You'd better show me those books before it's too late.'

I took him into Reuben's office and lifted the books out of the safe. Max seemed to know what he was doing, as he began to flick through the books and papers I carried to the desk. I had a niggling sense of guilt about showing Max our private business without Reuben's permission, but I justified it by reminding myself that my father wanted me to take over.

I left him to it, returning to my studio and the *Trompe L'oeil*, and busied myself making up the preparation I had decided to use on the left-hand side of the painting, to try to clear away some of the mould and damage. I needed to be very careful, using only a little of the chemical at a time. As always my biggest fear was making the situation worse. Sometimes all a conservator could do was stabilise the object and leave it be.

At first there didn't appear to be any improvement at all. Disappointed, I carried on swabbing gently, watching for changes through the magnifying lens I wore fixed on a band around my head—my miner's hat, as Courtney called it. Gradually, parts of the painting did sharpen. Although the improvement was only slight, it was enough for me to begin to make out some more details.

Peering closer at the scene where the man had his arms raised, I could see he was surrounded by trees. This was obviously Australian bush. I adjusted the lens, staring hard. An uneasy prickle ran over my skin as I realised there was something about the man, something eerily recognisable. I didn't want to believe it, I really didn't, but with his black coat and slicked-back hair, his pale face . . . Yes, there was something horribly familiar . . .

'Red gums.'

Max's voice made me jump violently. I turned towards him, blinded by the magnifying lens, then pushed it up on top of my head. I'd been so focused on the figure in the painting I hadn't even heard him open the door and come up behind me.

He didn't seem to notice my near heart attack, nodding past me to the painting. 'They look like red gums, the sort that grow along the Murray. And there.' He pointed. 'Looks like a slab hut with a saw beside it. My guess is it's a timber getters' camp.'

I looked where he pointed, but I couldn't make out the saw. Perhaps you had to know what you were looking for.

'Timber getters,' I murmured, committing it to memory. Something else to research. Stepping back from the painting, I let my gaze sweep over the left-hand side, trying to pick out other vignettes. I'd been working so intently, paying more attention to what the chemicals were doing than what I was uncovering. Was that a pen full of sheep and two figures standing behind it? And was that a tent and a smiling man?

Even those few guesses were just that. Guesses. Speculation. And as for the remainder of the damaged section . . . I sighed. I'd done my best and there was no more I could do. I'd reached the end.

'If only we could find a contemporaneous photograph of the *Trompe L'oeil*. There're plenty of photographs of old hotel interiors. You'd think we'd be able to find one of the reception room in The Goldminer Hotel. I would've thought a man like Gervais Whistler would want himself immortalised. Even if there are no photographs, a drawing made at the time might do. Or a rough preliminary sketch by the artist. Something, anything, to show us what we're missing.'

'Didn't you say you had someone working on that?'

'They're looking, but what if it doesn't even exist?' I was waving my arms about in frustration before I caught his smile. 'What?'

'Nothing. Well . . . *you*, Annie. You really feel for these two girls, don't you?'

I sighed. 'It's a blessing and a curse. I can't see myself walking away from this, even if I want to. And if Reuben and Reuben goes under . . .' I turned to face him, eyes wary. 'Which reminds me . . . what did you find? Are things that bad?'

Max was standing with his hands in his pockets, feet apart, as if he was riding the deck of the *Ariadne*. His hair was sticking up, too, not from a stiff breeze, but from him running his hands through it.

'I won't tell you lies, Annie.' His face was serious, all the usual good humour wiped away. Was this his Collins Street face? I hardly recognised him. 'It's bad. Bad but not terminal. Things can be turned around. To keep all your assets you'd have to cut your costs, concentrate your time on the jobs that pay well rather than the ones you might prefer to do. I don't suppose this is what you want to hear, but if you run it lean and mean then I think you can get yourself out of this hole.'

I turned away, staring at the painting. It was better than I'd expected, not a complete disaster, but still not good news. This situation wasn't going to go away. 'You mean all the things Reuben doesn't want to do,' I said bleakly. 'If we do what you say then I'll have to do it alone. I'll have to be the mean one, the one to cut costs and trim the fat, to work and work my way out of this mess.'

'Could you do that, Annie?'

I thought a moment, then nodded. 'I could. I just don't know if I'd feel the same passion for it, if it became a burden and kept me from the work I really want to do. Besides, the business was always Reuben's pride and joy, and he loved and nurtured it . . . Isn't it up to him whether or not to bury it?'

'Not if you take over, surely?' he murmured. He was close, so close I could feel the heat radiating from his body.

'But I don't want to take over.' The words blurted out of me. 'Not the way things stand at the moment. And I feel guilty saying that.'

'You shouldn't feel guilty. If you don't want to do it then you shouldn't pretend you do.'

'The truth is that my passion is for jobs like this one. I can lavish hours and hours of unpaid time on it. I know it doesn't make business sense, but if I wanted to be Gina Rinehart I'd never have taken it on. Let's face it, doing what I love isn't going to make me rich.'

I suddenly understood that I'd never expected it to. As long as I could trot along, doing what I liked, I didn't care about profit margins. That was why Ben found my attitude incomprehensible. He wanted to work for money, money to him was the whole point, whereas I wanted to work for love and money was a lucky by-product.

I was at a crossroad. The decision had to be made. Did I want to continue doing what I loved? Or was bringing the business back into the black more important?

Then there was Sebastian's job offer . . .

It was too much for me. I bent my head and closed my eyes, fighting the overwhelming emotion.

Then I felt the rough warmth of his palm against the side of my face. His voice was deep and close. 'Are you all right?'

More than anything I wanted him to hold me, and as if he'd read my mind, Max slipped his arms about me and gently drew me in against his body. I could feel his strength, the thud of his heart. It felt nice just to be held, to let myself be comforted.

I lifted my face, eyes still closed, and his mouth covered mine. He groaned or perhaps that was me. Passion sparked between us and I pressed closer, winding my arms around his neck, our kiss deepening. I lost myself in the moment, knowing I was falling in love, knowing I mustn't until I'd made decisions about my future. But I couldn't seem to stop. I wanted this. I wanted Max.

CHAPTER THIRTY-ONE

The Girl's Story

The cab turned the corner, rattling along beneath the street lamps. Rosey tried to relax in her seat, her hands tucked into her fur muff. Beside her, Josh still held the freesias, although they were wilting now.

'I suppose you're married,' he said, with a sideways glance.

Surprised, she laughed. 'Why would you think that?'

'It's what women do, isn't it?'

'Not me,' she said gaily, although she felt anything but. 'What of you, Mr Parker? What have you been up to?'

He looked at her as if she was a stranger and he was trying to make her out. Well, they were strangers, weren't they, thought Rosey, keeping the smile plastered on her face.

'I've been painting,' he said at last, and she could see the faint flush in his cheeks. 'I've done rather well,' he added. 'There are a lot of gold-rich Melbournians keen to have their portraits painted. Unfortunately, they prefer me to improve on reality whereas I'd like to paint them warts and all. Still, I have plenty of work, more than I need.'

'So you're enjoying yourself?'

'It pays the bills so I don't mind.'

Somehow Rosey thought he did mind. Perhaps he'd hoped for better? They all did, didn't they? Even she felt a restlessness some days, as if she was looking for more than she had. Not that she wanted a return to the old days, that would just be silly, but there was definitely something missing from her life. Something indefinable. But she was prepared to forego it, because no one could have everything.

'And are you? Married?' She said it to still her own disordered thoughts.

'No, but I do have a sponsor. A patron. That's almost the same thing, isn't it?' he said with a twist of his lips. 'Her name is Mrs Stuart. She likes to show me off to her friends.'

He spoke wryly, even mockingly, and again Rosey questioned if he was really happy with his lot. Josh had wanted to be a painter, a successful painter, and it seemed as if he was—or well on the way. But he didn't seem satisfied.

She turned to look at him. He was staring ahead, his profile to her, mouth downturned at the corners and he was frowning. Her gaze slid over the rather limp collar of his shirt and the roughly tied neckcloth, to the paint splotches on his waistcoat and coat. He'd come out without changing, without making the slightest effort to impress her. A spur of the moment thing? Or had he been bored, looking for some entertainment? His life wasn't going as he'd hoped and he thought: *I know, I'll go and find Rosey and see if she's willing to entertain me! She's always up for a good time, is Rosey.*

He turned his head, meeting her eyes. His own were as blue as she remembered. Even in the flickering light of the cab's lamp they startled her with their pale clarity. There was a line between his brows, as if he frowned an awful lot, and shadows under his eyes, as if he didn't sleep much. Something inside her shifted and she wanted to reach out and touch him, stroke his skin where the whiskers were bristly because he hadn't shaved. Instead, Rosey clenched her fingers together in her evening gloves.

'What?' he said, in that same mocking voice. 'Have I changed so much, Rosey? I think we both have.'

'I've changed for the better,' she said in a sharp voice. 'And I haven't got yellow paint on my jacket.'

His mouth twitched into a reluctant smile. 'Oh, Rosey. I rushed out to see you without thinking, without making myself presentable. I'm sorry for that. I should have put on my best jacket, or a clean shirt, at least. And brushed my hair.' He ran his hands over it now, trying to smooth it down. 'Mrs Stuart is always telling me I'm a ragbag of a man.'

He laughed, and Rosey felt a stabbing pain of jealousy. She didn't like this Mrs Stuart and she hadn't even met her. But it was nice to think he'd been so keen to see her that he hadn't paused for anything. Yes, that was nice, and she was sorry she'd been a bitch.

The cab came to a halt. Rosey stared out at the cafe with its plate-glass windows and subdued lighting. It reminded her of one of the places she'd frequented in Paris, full of the sort of people who fascinated and rather shocked her—she must still be working class deep down. Gervais always said so, when he wanted to annoy her.

The cafe was almost empty, a few guests just wandering out. She was too late for the opening party after all, she thought with a sigh.

Josh was still watching her. 'Is this where you were going? Mrs Stuart and her crowd come here for champagne and finger sandwiches. Expensive.'

'I've been to places where they charge two pounds for a single glass of champagne,' she snapped back at him, and then was shocked at herself. He stared back at her a moment, also shocked, before his mouth curved up and he smiled with pure delight.

'Two pounds,' he teased. 'You could live on the goldfields for a month on that.'

Rosey considered taking offence, but his smile was eating away at her prickliness and she gave a soft laugh. 'Live like a queen and all,' she agreed, allowing the thick Irish accent to slip back into her voice.

He'd opened the cab door and jumped down to the footpath, holding out his hand for hers. A moment later she was beside him, shivering a little despite her cloak.

'Would you like a champagne supper?' she asked.

He shook his head. 'I don't think so.'

'Or we could go back to the Menzies?'

'I've got a better idea.' He was searching her face as if looking for clues. 'My place isn't far from here. We could go there and I could make you a cup of tea. Not billy tea on a campfire, I'm sorry.'

She smiled, shivering again. A hot cup of tea sounded right up her alley, far more comforting than a glass of chilled champagne. Rosey wondered with suspicion whether at heart she was still the common Irish girl she'd always been. So much for becoming a lady.

She felt him slip his arm through hers. For a moment she was too startled to pull away.

'Come on,' he said.

But she hesitated, uncertain. She wanted to go with him, she really did, she wanted to revisit the old days, but what then? Could she just walk away from him and forget him? The consequences of allowing him back into her life might grow and grow, and how could she push them back into the locked box where they belonged?

'I still have the sketches I did on the goldfields,' he was saying. 'I still want to publish them one day. And I want to do a portrait of the quintessential woman of the fields. I've made a start, but . . . I need a model, Rosey. I need you.'

'Me?' she gasped.

'Tough on the outside but tender on the inside, a survivor who has her sights firmly fixed on the better days ahead. It's you, Rosey. You with your hair tangled, glowing in the winter sun. Will you sit for me?'

Couldn't he see she wasn't that girl anymore? Why didn't he want to paint her as she was now, successful, refined, charming . . . oh yes, oh so very charming.

How could he do this to her? He'd put a spell on her once and now she felt as if he was doing it to her all over again. She couldn't be having it, she couldn't be having it at all . . .

'Rosey!' The booming voice brought her around.

'Gervais?' She'd never felt so relieved to see anybody in her life.

'You're too late,' he said, coming up to them, rubbing his hands together in the cold. 'Everyone's gone. You missed a jolly time.'

His suspicious gaze went to Josh, his eyes narrowing in his flushed, benevolent face. She'd learned very soon after they met that Gervais might play the host to perfection, but underneath he was a hard-nosed and ambitious man who rarely let anything or anyone stand in the way of what he wanted.

Rosey moved to his side, and her voice sounded as it should, the words carefully pronounced, little trace of her past in it. 'Gervais, this is Mr Parker. He's an artist. He wants to paint a portrait of . . . of Alice and I. He's very good. All the Melbournians love him and Mrs Stuart sponsors him.'

Gervais considered him. 'Mrs Stuart, eh? She was here tonight. Handsome woman.' He reached for Josh's hand and shook it. 'How do you do? I'm Gervais Whistler. A portrait, eh? Sounds interesting. Would we get some publicity for it, do you think, Mr Parker? Are you a grand enough artist for the newspapers to be interested?'

'My fame is growing, Mr Whistler. And if Mrs Stuart has anything to do with it then, yes, I think we may expect the newspapers to be interested.'

Gervais nodded again. 'Then we'll talk again, Mr Parker.' It was a dismissal. He took Rosey's arm in his and turned and walked away.

She didn't look back. She didn't want to see his expression or his opinion of her, or anything that might begin to eat away at the security of her world. She'd spent a long time creating what she now had. How could she even consider letting it go for a man she hardly knew and hadn't seen for years? There must be a madness in her to even contemplate it. And she had, for a moment there, oh yes she had.

But the madness was past. Rosey knew she wouldn't let herself jeopardise her comfortable life. She may well have moments of dissatisfaction and melancholy, but who didn't? Going backwards was not the way to find happiness.

Gervais squeezed her fingers. 'You're quiet,' he said, when they were settled in his coach, which had been waiting behind the cafe. 'Has Mr Parker got your tongue?' He laughed at his own joke, but there was a hint of steel in his voice.

Rosey often wondered if she had fallen into the company of Gervais because, once you stripped off the outer gentleman, there was a lot of Sean in him. Not the violence, well not to her anyway, but the same tough single-mindedness and disregard for the law. It attracted her. And she had to admit, Gervais had done very well for himself. Not that he hadn't had help. Rosey did her bit, and Alice's Child had made him a fortune; without her he'd just be a middling theatre owner, cutting deals, dreaming of the big time. The Child had given him the big time on a plate.

Rosey shifted uncomfortably. She didn't like to think of Alice being used like that, despite the girl agreeing to it.

'Rosey?'

She hadn't answered his question, and now she shrugged as if she was bored with him, a sure way to capture his attention.

'Don't tell me he's a beau from your colourful past?' Gervais leaned back in the leather seat and yawned without covering his mouth. 'Just remember, my dear, you belong to me. I don't share.'

Rosey shot him a look of dislike. 'I have to share with your wife.'

'She's in England.'

'But she's coming out in a year or two. You said she was. What then, Gervais?'

'We'll worry about that when it happens, Rosey.' He closed his eyes and folded his arms and pretended to sleep.

He didn't want to think about that, she could tell. Was it because he loved his wife so much, or because at heart he was a conventional man who believed in being faithful? Rosey gave a silent laugh at the very idea of Gervais being faithful to any woman.

When they'd first joined his troupe, he and Suzy had been sharing a bed, and then when Suzy ran off there had been others. Rosey had watched warily as he'd circled around her, and she'd waited a long time before she'd agreed to be his lover.

She hadn't intended to have an affair with him, or so she told herself. She'd enjoyed his company, enjoyed sparring with him, and eventually the mutual attraction of minds had become physical. An innocent brush of clothing, the warm touch of a hand, and the first time they went to bed.

Rosey had forgotten the pleasure to be had with a man when it was just for that, pleasure. Gervais was a generous lover, and for a time Rosey had even thought she might fall in love with him. But she didn't, and now despite their years together she had no intention of it. She guarded her heart very carefully.

As far as she was aware the others didn't know, but many of them had probably guessed. As for Alice . . . she'd never mentioned it to Rosey, but Rosey was sure she knew. How could she not? No, Alice knew, it was just that she preferred to pretend it wasn't happening. The situation was less awkward that way, and she didn't have to treat Gervais any differently.

The Menzies was quiet and they went upstairs to his room. They were hardly inside the door when she went into his arms, breathing in the smell of whisky and cigars.

'I didn't ask. Did the party go well?' she murmured against his lips.

'Splendid!' Gervais lifted her, spun her around in the direction of the bed. He was always in a hurry. Perhaps years of doing the business in corners before they were caught by the rest of the troupe had honed his skills as a quick lover.

'Where were you?' he demanded, pausing to look into her face.

Rosey thought of Josh, and the memory rippled at the surface of her role as Gervais's lover. Then she remembered Gilbert and Alice and sighed with relief. She did have a reason for being late after all, and one that wouldn't cause Gervais to be sceptical or rummage around in her mind for answers.

'Alice's headache. I put her to bed and stayed until she slept.'

'You know there's another show on Thursday. I can't cancel it, Rosey.'

'Yes.' Rosey sighed. 'I know. But do *you* know she can't go on like this?'

He tumbled her onto the bed and as he began to undress her she gave up trying to talk to him. He was like a greedy child, and until he'd unwrapped his sweetie and tasted it, he wouldn't listen to a word she said.

Afterwards, sated, he lay with his head on her breasts, his big whiskery face tickling her skin.

'That artist fellow who wants to paint Alice's portrait,' Gervais said.

'Mr Parker is painting all the leading lights of Melbourne,' Rosey reminded him.

'Yes, yes. I'd already heard of him. Mrs Stuart mentioned it, said something about me commissioning a portrait, but it was my wife she was on about.' He paused. 'She's clearly smitten.'

Gervais lifted his head and stretched, but he was watching her expression, seeing if she was upset by his words. Rosey kept her face smooth and untroubled. He grunted and added, 'What if the police see it and come to arrest you?' he said, then chuckled when she looked annoyed. 'Forgotten about that, hadn't you?'

'No one is going to recognise us after all these years, and even if they did . . . you'd buy our way out of trouble, Gervais. I'd always trust you to help me if I needed help.'

He looked down at her hand stroking his chest and raised his eyebrows, but she could tell he was flattered. He caught her fingers and lifted them to his lips before sitting up and swinging his legs over the side of the bed. Rosey watched him dress, too lazy to do so herself. But that was Gervais, he was always in a rush.

'I was talking with George,' he said, as he shrugged on his white satin waistcoat and began to fasten the pearl buttons. 'He wants us to go halves in a hotel he's refurbishing. He's renaming it The Goldminer. You always wanted a hotel, didn't you, Rosey? You could play the grand lady, tilting up that pretty nose of yours at the dames of Melbourne, sweet-talking their husbands.'

Rosey smiled at the image he conjured. 'I'd like that.'

'Settles it then,' Gervais muttered, as he began to tie his cravat.

Did it? Rosey wondered what would happen when his wife eventually arrived from England. Would she still be in such a favourable position, or would their love affair end? She must be pragmatic about these things and usually she was. She always considered what was best for herself and Alice before anything else.

Rosey climbed out of bed and began to dress. Her room was on the floor above so she didn't bother with her corset or stockings, tightly wrapping her cloak around her unbuttoned dress, pulling the hood over her unbound hair. The muff, when she picked it up, had something in it, and when she reached inside to pull it out, she found it was one of Josh's freesias.

She stopped and stared at it, feeling as if the room was tipping, as if she might lose her balance.

'Rosey?' Gervais was watching her over his glass of whisky.

She looked up with a smile. 'I have to go,' she said. 'Alice will need me in the morning.'

Outside she quietly closed the door behind her. As she walked towards the stairs she opened her hand and saw that she had crushed the flower.

* * *

By Thursday night Alice was much better, and even after the show she wasn't as ill as she had been. Rosey began to hope that perhaps the worst was past and Alice was recovering from the mysterious illness. Gervais was full of his hotel deal with George Coppin and refused to contemplate any time off. They were making money, that was all that mattered to him.

'A portrait?' Alice said doubtfully, when Rosey gave her an abbreviated version of her meeting with Joshua Parker. 'Of us?'

'Yes, of us. What do you think? Gervais is all for it.'

Alice seriously considered the question. They were seated in her cosy parlour, which had windows overlooking the street, and she was holding Hope on her knee, stroking him as she thought.

'Hope must be part of the portrait,' she said.

'Of course he must.'

'And . . . Rosey, I don't see why there couldn't be others in it, the people who have meant so much to us, the people who helped us on our journey. In fact, why does it need to be a portrait when it could be a storybook of our lives so far?'

Rosey would have preferred the portrait—herself in her Paris gown—but she agreed to ask Josh when he came to the Menzies to discuss Gervais's commission. She felt a nervous flutter of her heart when she imagined seeing him again, but stilled herself, told herself not to be stupid.

'How was he?' Alice was watching her, those blue eyes so wise and all-seeing that Rosey could hardly bear to meet them. 'Mr Parker, I mean.'

Rosey shrugged. 'A little older, as are we all. He was talking about the sketches he'd made on the goldfields, how he'd like to publish them.'

Alice nodded. She was going to ask something inappropriate, Rosey knew it. She was going to make Rosey cross by asking questions Rosey did not want to answer, let alone think about.

Thankfully, they were interrupted when one of the hotel maids arrived with a bouquet of flowers for Alice, a colourful mixture, with a card. Rosey, relieved there were no freesias, watched the girl read it. Pink colour rose in her pale cheeks and Alice looked up with glowing eyes.

'They're from Gilbert,' she said. 'He says he hopes I'm feeling better.'

Rosey wasn't surprised he'd do something so kind, but she wondered if there was more to it than that. Although Alice insisted Gilbert was her friend, Rosey was sure he wanted to be more. She remembered the train from Echuca, when she had peered through the window in the door to the first-class compartment and seen the two of them sitting together. She'd thought then they seemed like young sweethearts. Perhaps now, at last, there would be a chance for their long-delayed romance to flourish.

'Did you think about what Gilbert said?' Rosey asked. They'd discussed it the morning after her migraine. 'About being mesmerised and to help you remember your past?'

Alice shook her head, her mouth turning stubborn. 'I don't want to remember my past.'

'But, Alice, don't you ever wonder who you are? Don't you want to know?'

'I know who I am. I'm Alice, The Child, that's who I am. I don't need to know any more.'

'Alice—'

'No!'

Alice rarely raised her voice but when she did Rosey knew not to press her. And to be honest she couldn't blame the girl for not wanting to delve into the dark places, to stir up whatever lay there in her brain, sleeping, waiting. Even now Rosey had nightmares about that moonlight track running through the bush and the man in his black coat turning his white face towards them, as if he could sniff them on the wind. How much worse must it be for Alice?

No, Rosey didn't blame her for not wanting to know.

CHAPTER THIRTY-TWO

Annie's Story

Breakfast was the usual frantic affair. While I supervised Courtney's packing of her bag—she was going to stay with a friend overnight—I managed to gulp down my coffee. Then Max opened the door from upstairs and looked in.

'Hi.' I think I blushed. I couldn't help remembering the other night, cuddling and kissing on the sofa like teenagers. Not to mention the kissing we'd done at the office.

There was a gleam in his eyes as he smiled back that made me think he was remembering, too. 'Hi there.'

'I need to make a list,' Courtney said importantly, 'in case I forget something. Mummy, you need to buy me list paper.'

'I will, darling.' I glanced up at Max as I zipped up the bag. 'I have to go in to the studio today, just a few hours, to do some work on the *Trompe L'oeil*. Make sure History Victoria is getting its money's worth. I'm not sure if you . . . ?'

'I have a few jobs of my own to do and I can do them while you're busy. Maybe we can meet up for lunch somewhere? If you think Reuben . . .'

'Reuben can look after himself,' my father announced from the kitchen. 'Go and have lunch. I'll be fine, Annie.'

Leaving Courtney to instruct Max on the importance of being organised, I joined my father at the sink, up to his elbows in soapy water.

'What is it?' he said.

I had my smart phone with me and now I brought up the photos I'd taken of the painting yesterday, after my cleaning efforts. 'I think I recognise him,' I said.

Reuben frowned at the figure in the black coat with his arms raised. 'Our ghost?'

'Good guess. Yes, I think so. But why is he part of Alice and Rosey's story?'

'It's not a guess, Annie. I recognise him. Geneva did a sketch . . . now where is it? Have you finished reading the diaries yet? Or looked in the suitcase?'

'Not yet. I haven't had time.' Or was it just that I hadn't made time? I'd not wanted to read my mother's diaries when I was thirteen, perhaps I was dipping out again? He smiled. 'Not told Max about him yet?'

'No, and I don't intend to, so don't you.'

Courtney called from the other room. 'Mummy, we'll be late!'

Reuben chuckled as I hurried away.

* * *

Greta was there when I reached the office. She started telling me about her date the night before, and followed me upstairs. I set about making coffee and she stood a moment, admiring the painting.

'So what're you going to do with it?' she asked. 'A conservation . . . ?'

'I'm thinking of doing a complete restoration.'

Her eyes widened slightly. 'Do you think that's a good idea? You know History Victoria's policy—'

'Well, it's what I want to do,' I said, feeling stubborn.

Greta chuckled. 'You don't mind ruffling a few feathers, do you, Annie? All those tricky politics on conservation. There're some pretty hard heads in that organisation. They'll probably call you a vandal. Far be it for me to try to persuade you against a radical stance, but maybe you should stick with a conservation, just to be on the safe side? You know how they're always preaching less is best.'

I waved a hand to dismiss the subject. 'I really think a restoration will be so much more powerful. It'd have a real "Wow Factor",' I said, rolling my eyes when she choked on her coffee. 'And if the minister comes out and tells her story, there'll be huge crowds through the gates. Money in History Victoria's pockets.'

'Yeah, but you know what the dinosaurs at the top are like! They'll think that's a cop-out. Prostituting their artistic integrity for the sake of the almighty dollar.'

I had some sympathy for that point of view. Money shouldn't mean everything. But I wanted my own way on this one. 'Maybe it's time the dinosaurs were retired.'

Greta finished her coffee and set down the cup. 'They'll die in harness. Can dinosaurs be harnessed?'

I was busy inspecting the canvas. 'I've finished cleaning, more or less, and you can see there're places where the painting is just too damaged. I really need to get hold of a photograph or a copy of the *Trompe L'oeil*, something I can use to fill in the gaps.'

'Oh, there was a call late yesterday. Clive Cummings. History Victoria is looking at a portrait painter in Melbourne around the 1870s called Joshua Parker. They seem to think he wasn't much of a painter—mediocre, Clive said. Really only of interest to social historians. He painted the portraits of most of the Melbourne high-flyers of the day and they're not very memorable. But there's a portrait of Gervais Whistler, warts and all, that *is* quite good. Clive said you can see it in the National Gallery in St Kilda Road.'

'Why didn't I know about it?'

'Apparently, it was out in the back room for a while, needed some conservation work, but it's on show again. They probably realised the Gervais–minister connection would mean money. You know what that lot are like.'

'I'll have to take a look at it. So Clive thinks this Joshua Parker may be our man?'

Greta shrugged. 'I'll ring him back for you. He was full of information, our Clive.'

Clive did have some more information. Sebastian had certainly got History Victoria scurrying. Evidently, The Goldminer Hotel started out jointly owned by Whistler and George Coppin, but Whistler took it over. He was running a stage show at the time, some sort of spiritualist act, at the Princess Theatre. It made him a lot of money. Anyway, he wanted the hotel as a backdrop to his act, somewhere people could come for private consultations, to rub shoulders with his performers and presumably the rich and famous clientele he hoped to attract.

This was all new to me. In actual fact it made the hairs on the back of my neck stand up. Spiritualists. Ghosts. What next? Zombies?

Clive's voice at the other end of the phone went on. 'I can understand why an extreme conservative, like our minister, might be leery of admitting he's her relative, and I have a feeling we only know half the story. Whistler was into some strange stuff. He had his goldfields troupe. Took them all over Australia and even to Europe. I'm not sure how successful that was, but I'll look into it. Then for some reason the troupe broke up, or else they'd had enough.'

I knew Alice and Rosey were part of the troupe, they were involved in Whistler's money-making ventures. Were they dancers or were they telling fortunes for Melbourne's elite? Nothing in any of the vignettes seemed to point to an answer.

Clive was still talking. 'The hotel was owned by the Whistler family up until they lost it in the 1890s. By then he'd taken on his persona of respectable businessman. And by the way there *are* some photographs of the rooms, but before you get too excited, I checked the one of the reception room and there was no *Trompe L'oeil*. By the time the photos were taken they'd removed it.'

Disappointment cut short my excitement. 'Thank you. You'll keep looking?'

After he had hung up I had another stare at the painting. I longed for a representation of it so I could begin the restoration that I was sure History Victoria didn't want me to do.

And if nothing was ever found? Well, then big chunks of the *Trompe L'oeil* would forever remain a secret. Unless in the meantime the minister hid it away deep in some government vault.

* * *

I had made plans to meet Max outside a tapas bar, and as I came around the corner I saw him leaning against a newspaper stand, staring into space, seemingly oblivious to the passing pedestrians and busy street traffic. Dressed in casual jeans and his leather jacket, he looked good.

I groaned softly to myself. Had I really been counting the minutes until I was with him again? My heart was skipping, my hands felt clammy . . . I had it bad. There were so many complications, and yet . . . I liked him, I really did, and if it was possible to sort something out between us, something lasting, then I knew I was prepared to compromise.

As if sensing my approach, Max looked up and gave me his slow-burner smile. His pale eyes crinkled at the corners and his dark hair was untidy from whatever he'd been doing this morning. Running his hand through it, if I had to guess.

Inside the bar, we settled on stools at the high strip of table that ran along the window. It felt safe and cosy in here, and when Max's shoulder brushed against mine I wanted to lean in to him so much I had to straighten my back and physically stop myself.

'So how did your jobs go?' I asked.

'Okay, I think. I had to price some parts for the *Ariadne*. I'll take the paperwork home and see if we can afford it. Discuss it with Kenny.'

'It's never far from your mind, is it?' I said. 'Your boat.'

'She's a big part of my life,' he admitted. 'Without her, me and Kenny would be unemployed. And I've been thinking about . . .' He stopped, gave me a sideways glance. I noticed how long his lashes were.

Stop it!

'What have you been thinking about?' I took a bite of my pastry and washed it down with cold water. We'd talked about wine, but after my lunch with Sebastian and my fright in The Goldminer Hotel I thought it better to abstain. 'Unless it's top secret, of course.'

He smiled. 'Not at all. It's just . . . this is such a new idea that I don't like to talk about it. Not until I get my head around it properly.'

'Use me as a sounding board, then.'

He considered a moment and then said, decisively, 'All right.' He turned to face me, leaning his arm along the wooden table. 'There's a paddle-steamer I know of at Wentworth. She's sitting in dry dock. Falling to pieces, in a gracious sort of way. I want to save her. The price is fairly steep, but she's a big girl, far bigger than the *Ariadne*. She wasn't used for hauling timber barges. She carried passengers. Squatters and their families, home to their stations along the river. She must've been quite something in her day.'

There was a gleam in his eyes and a flush to his tanned cheeks, and I was sure if I laid a hand to his chest I'd feel his heart pounding. I chuckled. 'You're in love,' I teased, brushing his hand with my fingertip.

Briefly he looked shocked, then he laughed back at me. 'I think I must be.'

'So what's her name, Max?'

'*Queen of the Rivers*,' he said, still grinning. 'And she is a queen. A little tatty and worse for wear, but I'm sure, with enough capital, expertise and a lot of help, I could return her to the majesty she deserves.'

I nodded, aware he was watching me intently, as if my every word held especial importance to him. 'Then what? I mean, if everything went to plan and she was all new again, what would you do with her?'

'Use her to take passengers on the river. Two- . . . three-day tours. Jazz weekends. Foodies' overnight stays. A visit to Stefano's in Mildura or whatever the name of the latest dining sensation is.'

'You've really thought this out.' I leaned my head in my hand. Our faces were very close now. I could smell the faint spicy scent of his aftershave.

'I've been thinking about it for a while, but your father crystallised it for me yesterday, when he was talking about restoring boat interiors. The *Queen of the Rivers* could be a real beauty, all those intricate carvings and elaborate features . . . I suppose if I was being cost smart the sensible thing would be to rip them out, streamline the interior. But I don't want to do that. I want to bring her back to the way she was. I want her to be a reminder of the days when craftsmanship meant something.'

It was more or less what I had said after Max told me what I'd have to do to keep the business afloat, when I'd decided that being sensible and cost smart probably wasn't what I wanted.

He must have realised it, too. The corners of his lips curled up and his eyes warmed. 'We make a great pair, don't we?'

Why, oh why, had he chosen this moment to come into my life? I bit my lip and straightened up, as if by withdrawing from the intimacy of the moment I could put all the warm carnal thoughts out of my head. But how could I be chilly and practical when I was such a passionate person?

'I think it's a wonderful idea,' I said, glancing down at my food and deciding I'd had enough. 'I think you should do it, Max. Really, I do.'

He picked up on my change of mood, nodded, and after an awkward pause, he changed the subject.

When we left the tapas bar, Max said he'd go back and keep Reuben company while I did some more work. I'd received a text from Greta while I was eating, about a job that had come in.

'Are you sure?' I tipped my head up to read Max's expression. 'You're on holiday.'

'Holidays don't suit me. I like to be doing things.'

'I don't know what Reuben will have you doing,' I warned him. 'Just remember he's devious.'

Max laughed, as I'd meant him to. We parted and I walked back to the office, feeling light and almost carefree. Certainly happy. It was as I walked in the door that all the worries piled on top of me and squashed the joy out of me.

Greta was seated forlornly at her desk.

'Hi there,' she said, her face lighting up at the sight of another human being. 'Nice lunch?'

'Yes. Thank you. Eh, what was this job you were talking about?'

Greta moved some papers around until she found the one she was after. 'Here. Sounds promising.'

I noticed the address was Kew. When I looked closer I saw that it was actually one of the remodelled places that was part of the old asylum complex. Reuben would rub his hands when he heard about it, but I didn't think I'd tell him just yet. I wanted to make certain we were paid more than the pittance my father would request.

'Thanks. I'll give them a call.' I moved towards the stairs and then remembered to add, 'And thanks for staying with Reuben. Above and beyond the call of duty.'

Greta smiled. 'I enjoyed it.' Her brows rose. 'Annie, you'll tell me, won't you? Give me some decent time if I need to find another job?'

I opened my mouth, closed it again. Of course Greta knew. She wasn't a fool. 'When the decision is made you'll be the first to know,' I promised.

It was dark and quiet upstairs and I switched on the lights. The painting was waiting for me, urging me to get back to it. I felt a renewed sense of determination. No matter what happened with the business, and whether or not I went to New York, I would do my utmost to finish this.

Alice and Rosey deserved to be seen.

* * *

When I arrived home I found the house empty. Reuben and Max were out and there wasn't even a note to say where they'd gone. Courtney was sleeping over at her friend's house, so there was no one to help me start dinner—a chicken casserole I slid into the oven—and I missed my daughter's chatter. I put some washing on, then shoved the wet clothing into the drier. As I watched it tumbling around and around, I found my mind doing the same thing.

I was feeling overwhelmed. The business problems and what to do about them, the job offer from Sebastian, Max, my father, Courtney, the *Trompe L'oeil*. It all threatened to drag me down and I knew I must make some decisions. Sebastian had wanted my answer by Monday and that was fast approaching.

Also, I could feel the beginnings of a headache. Just for a moment I thought I caught a whiff of peppermint, but it was gone quickly, leaving me feeling slightly ill. Why were they taking so long? Had Reuben fallen again? Was he unconscious at a hospital somewhere?

The outside door slammed and I stepped out of the laundry as the two men walked in, looking sheepish.

'Sorry, Annie,' Reuben confessed. 'I persuaded Max to come with me to the house in Toorak. To do the marbling.'

'The marbling?' I repeated. I could hear my voice rising and seemed powerless to stop it.

'It's important, Annie.'

I was tired and stressed. Normally, I'd keep my real feelings to myself—I knew how persuasive Reuben could be—but suddenly I was furious.

'You're ill, Papa. I promised the doctors you wouldn't work. I trusted you to rest. The marbling can wait.'

'That isn't work,' he retorted.

'You not considering it work is why we're in this mess!' And I didn't stop there. The words spilled out of me. I even told him how Sebastian had offered me a new job in New York, and how I was considering it because I couldn't see any future for myself here.

While I was in the red mist of my anger it felt good to let it all out, very good, but when I ran out of grievances and stopped, that was when realisation hit, and with it the full weight of what I'd done. The silence went on and on, and I wanted to squirm. Reuben looked pale and proud, and Max was edging towards the door. My uncontrolled anger had had its impact, more than likely made things much worse, but of course it was too late to take the words back.

'Oh, God, I'm so sorry,' I whispered. 'That was just so wrong. And with you here, Max. I'm so sorry, Papa.'

Reuben nodded stiffly. He tried to smile and that made the pain in his eyes worse. 'You should go,' he said. 'Go to New York.' Then he walked out of the room. I heard him slowly climbing the stairs, like an old man, and then the door to his apartment shut with quiet restraint.

I sank down onto the sofa and put my head in my hands. Wishing I could just vanish behind the cushions like someone's loose change. I'd been keeping the whole thing bottled up inside, trying to decide on my own, trying to protect my father, and now I'd blown it completely.

A moment later I felt Max's tentative hand on my shoulder, and when I didn't scream at him or try to shrug him off, he sat down beside me and drew me in against his chest. I was tempted to sob my heart out, but I wasn't the sobbing kind. Instead, I sighed and snuggled in. He *did* smell good, and there was comfort in the fact he hadn't run for the hills after seeing me at my very worst.

'I should've told you,' I murmured into his sweater. 'I was going to, but I hadn't made up my mind and it seemed wrong to say anything until I had. And . . . I suppose while I didn't mention it, it wasn't happening. Head in the sand, you know? But with Reuben and Reuben close to bust, I have to do something. I have to make enough money to support Courtney and my father. And going to New York . . . it's a good career move, too.'

Max stroked my hair. 'Can't you get something closer to home?' his voice rumbled in his chest. 'Annie?'

I shrugged, then straightened with a sigh, moving away from his warmth, knowing he deserved a proper answer. 'I work in a specialised area. Like your boat restoration. I could get work here, but it wouldn't be the same. I wouldn't be my own boss. And New York would be such a buzz. A real step up the career scale. If I'd been asked six years ago . . . Why didn't I get asked six years ago? Now there are so many complications. Nice ones,' I added quickly, placing a palm against his chest.

Max chuckled.

'I've hurt Reuben,' I went on, feeling miserable. 'He thinks he's let me down. He's not well and I've made it worse. I'll have to go and apologise properly.'

'You should.'

'And what you must think of me . . .'

He grinned. 'I know you're a passionate woman when it comes to your work, Annie. I'd presumed that passion spilt over into other areas of your life. As long as you're an explode-and-then-make-up kind of girl. Personally, I can't stand sulkers.'

'Definitely not a sulker, no,' I assured him. He leaned forward and kissed my cheek. The kiss warmed, intensified, and he was kissing my lips before I knew it. I could have stayed here forever. But there was still Reuben.

I found my father slumped in the window seat in his lounge, staring out at the river. He looked smaller and older and my guilt threatened to choke me. Instead, I straightened my shoulders and went over to him. This was my father, the man who'd loved me and cared for me since I was a little girl. He didn't deserve me to speak to him like that. He'd made mistakes, but he'd done his best. Always.

Tears stung my eyes and trembled in my voice. 'Papa, I'm sorry. I didn't mean . . . I was worried and the words just came out.'

He nodded, his gaze still fixed on the view from the window. 'You should've told me, Annie.'

'I didn't want to say anything until I'd made my decision.'

'You should go,' he said in that same reasonable voice. 'It's the job of a lifetime. This is your chance to be recognised in your field. History Victoria will never give you such an opportunity, but if you go to New York . . . Yes, you must go.'

I sighed, and then I sat down beside him, my head bent.

'Annie?'

He was watching me, waiting, his thin shoulders tense.

'I know I should go,' I told him. 'If this had happened six . . . even five years ago. Before Courtney. Well, I could've gone. But now . . . Papa, there are so many reasons not to go. Perhaps that was why I didn't tell anyone. Because I could pretend to myself I could do it. That I was the sort of person who would just pack up and leave and not give a damn. But I'm not that sort of person. If I left you and . . . and everything, I think I'd regret it every day for the rest of my life.'

His mouth curled at the corners and he shook his head. 'You should be more ambitious, Annie,' he scolded me.

'You mean trample over everyone else's wishes and feelings? Yeah, that's me.'

'As long as you don't regret *not* going.' He touched my hand on the window seat beside his and then clasped it warmly. 'So what will you do?'

'Tell Sebastian no, I suppose. See what we can do with the business, how we can keep it running, at least until I finish the *Trompe L'oeil* and you finish your marbling.'

'I've finished,' he said proudly. 'That was what I was trying to tell you before you blew up, Annie. The marbling is all done.'

'Oh.' I glanced at him. 'There was another job. Greta had a call about one of the places at the old asylum on the hill. I don't know what you think . . . ?'

'I'll let her know we'll take it,' he said, 'but only if they pay us what we ask. But I think it's the last one, Annie. For me, anyway. I've enjoyed the work, it's been everything to me, but enough.'

'You might change your mind?'

He gave me one of his sideways glances that meant he was avoiding the question. 'Max is a nice fellow.'

I couldn't help but smile. 'Yes, he is.'

'You like him?'

'A lot.'

Reuben nodded. 'When you're young you think there'll be someone else, that there are plenty of fish in the sea, but it isn't like that. Don't be fooled into thinking you'll find another Max, Annie.'

He gave my hand one last squeeze. 'I'll go downstairs and tell him everything is all right. That my sweet and serene daughter is not usually so volatile.'

Sadness filled me, for Reuben and my mother who had known such a short time of happiness, but I knew he was right. Men like Max didn't come along every day. Of course it wasn't just Max stopping me, and perhaps if I went to New York my career would be fulfilling and exciting enough for me not to regret leaving him. But I didn't believe that. I thought that despite everything New York might give me, I would be lonely. Lonely for my father who needed me now more than ever, and regretful for what could have been with Max.

Suddenly, I could smell peppermint. Strong, so strong it stung my throat and made my eyes water. I jumped up, looking around. I felt as if I was under assault. *He* was here, the man with the dark eyes and white face.

Standing. Watching me in his black clothing, his arms raised. Invisible and yet very much present. Who was he? What did he want? Why was he haunting me and my family?

'Go away,' I hissed. 'You don't belong here. Go away.'

But he'd already gone.

CHAPTER THIRTY-THREE

The Girl's Story

The Goldminer was everything Gervais had said it would be. On grand opening night Rosey and Alice stood in the packed ballroom as the music from the small orchestra swelled around them. Gervais had insisted they take the centre stage on this important occasion and had paid for fine new dresses, sea blue for Alice and rose pink for Rosey.

Rosey could see that Alice wasn't enjoying the attention and soon steered her towards Gilbert Suckling, who was squashed into a group with several older, serious men. Sometimes Gilbert seemed far more grown-up than his years and naturally gravitated towards such company, but his eyes lit up when he saw Alice, and in a flash he was a young man again. A young man, if Rosey knew anything about it, in love.

She hoped Alice would be happy. She deserved happiness.

Alice's headaches were still frequent but not nearly as bad. Gervais had been sending the show out to the country centres for several weeks at a time, in between the dates at the Princess Theatre. He was worried The Child's act might be growing stale, but as far as Rosey could tell she was still as popular as ever. Recently, they'd been to the provincial town of Geelong and Rosey thought the change of scene, as well as the sea air, had done Alice good. Now back in Melbourne they were due to start at The Goldminer Hotel in ten days' time, and Gervais had lined up some foreign dignitaries and important local people to attend. Many had greeted his proposal with scepticism—a fortune teller?—but such was Gervais's charisma, few had refused the invitation.

They would be using the ballroom for the shows—the room where she was standing now. Afterwards there would be private consultations for those who could pay the fees. It wasn't what Alice had wanted. Her gift was something she saw as a chance to help others, no matter rich or poor, not a way to make money. But Rosey soothed her, reminding her that it was not for very long.

'Gervais wants to pay his debts,' she said. 'I've told him you can't work day after day, so he'll be allowing you breaks in between. And it's not forever, Alice.'

'It just seems wrong.'

Alice and Gervais were at very different corners of the room when it came to what they thought was right and wrong. What Rosey didn't tell Gervais was that Gilbert had been using his skills of mesmerism on Alice.

It had taken some time for him to persuade her, and then longer for her to let herself go into a relaxed state. But slowly, gradually, Gilbert was taking Alice back into her past. Not that there'd been any great revelations so far.

They'd caught the train to Sandhurst again, tramped the goldfields and ended up in Dunolly. Alice had wept over Molly and Bluey, and shivered in the Websters' homestead on the river after she was rescued from the barrel. The rest had consisted of a few snippets, probably the same ones Rosey had overheard from the girl's dreams—the sailing ship and passengers dying, a hut with gaps in the wooden walls, a woman with a baby . . . Just a jumble of jigsaw pieces.

Several times Alice had jumped up from her trance, crying, eyes wide and frightened, saying that the man in the dark coat was there. Watching her.

'He's coming for me, I know it,' she wailed.

'But how can he?' Gilbert soothed. 'He's just a childhood bogeyman, Alice. He's long gone. Dead probably.'

'No, he's not dead, he's alive, he's real!'

'We must confront him in your past,' Gilbert insisted. Then, seeing Alice's woebegone face, 'But not today.'

Despite the drama of Alice's tentative steps towards discovering her past, Rosey definitely saw an improvement in her. Less headaches, less nightmares, and she slept a deeper and more wholesome sleep. In time she hoped Gilbert might hold the answers.

Alice's past had been brought to life, too, by Josh's painting. He called it a trick of the eye, a *Trompe L'oeil*, but it was like a vast canvas storybook. Gervais had hung it in the reception room, where he met with his most important guests, and it was causing much comment. But also, to him, some annoyance. He voiced it now, as they stood at the fringes of the ballroom, watching the swirl of dancers.

'As soon as they see it they're asking me who all the people are,' Gervais grumbled. 'You should write their names underneath.'

'I'm not going to label them,' Josh replied. 'The canvas tells a story, and that story could be partly mythical for all they know. People need to use their imaginations. Explaining every piece of it would spoil it, Mr Whistler.'

Josh and Alice had spent long hours discussing who should be in the painting, and had agreed there must be everything from the good to the bad. Josh had insisted he use his charcoal sketches from the days of the camp rather than depict the women as they were now. And he was right, it certainly had impact. Rosey found her own eyes wandering over the various scenes, remembering. She hadn't wanted the Red Petticoat at all, but Alice had insisted it was part of their story and must be there.

'I don't want Josh to know what I did,' she'd been forced to admit.

Alice had smiled. 'He won't care.'

'Of course he will.'

Alice had looked at her as if Rosey couldn't see what was right in front of her eyes but Rosey wouldn't have it. When her agitation had grown, Alice had agreed that they would not tell Josh the truth and that the secret would remain between themselves.

'At least you can point your guests to yourself,' Rosey said to Gervais. 'Standing outside the Dunolly Music Hall.'

Gervais grunted. 'I'll be happier when I have my own portrait. Something a bit more flattering, eh, Parker?'

It was no secret he'd commissioned a portrait from Josh, something with pomp, to hang in the foyer.

'I'm quite certain you'll be very happy with it.' Mrs Stuart had come to join them, her arm sliding through Josh's. Her dark eyes were as bright as buttons as she smiled at Gervais. 'Although a handsome man like yourself hardly needs flattering.'

Mrs Stuart, the widow of a wine merchant who had made his fortune selling watered-down liquor to goldminers, was probably in her early forties but so vivacious she appeared half her age. Her skin was still creamy, her hair lacked any grey, and her voluptuous figure was corseted tightly beneath her fine gown.

There was a frisson in the air whenever she and Gervais were together. Rosey would have been a fool not to know what it meant, and she was no fool.

She caught Josh's eye. He knew, too. Rosey wondered what he thought of his patroness taking up with Gervais, and whether he cared. Had he and Mrs Stuart been lovers? She didn't know for certain, but there were rumours and Josh was a charming and good-looking man. What woman wouldn't want him in her bed? she asked herself prosaically. And Mrs Stuart was the sort of woman to take full advantage of Josh's debt to her.

Alice's giggle drifted across the ballroom and Rosey looked up with a smile. Good, at least Alice was enjoying herself now. When the shows started it would be all hard work, so let her have fun while she could.

'What exactly doesn't Mr Whistler like about my depiction of him in Alice's storybook?' Josh's voice was low and close to her ear.

'He says he looks too bulky about the waist,' Rosey replied, with a mischievous sideways glance. 'He wants you to make him trimmer. And taller.'

Josh smiled.

'He says you made yourself far handsomer than you did him,' Rosey added.

Josh snorted a laugh. 'I wouldn't have put myself in it at all but Alice insisted.'

Alice was doing a great deal of insisting these days. 'You're part of our story, Mr Parker.'

'A very small part.'

They stood in silence, watching as Gervais and Mrs Stuart danced a waltz. Her face was flushed and she was sparkling up at him, while he was murmuring to her, his gaze fixed on her as if she was the only woman in the room. Rosey well remembered that look, she could probably even take a guess at what he was saying.

'I'm sorry.'

Surprised, she turned to Josh and saw the sympathy in his face. Why was he sorry for her? Did he think of her as an abandoned woman? It stirred her anger, but she bit back hasty words and instead waved a dismissive hand.

'Don't be, Mr Parker. Gervais and I are not having a grand, passionate affair. Convenience is the thing, as I think you've found yourself.'

His mouth quirked up at the corner. 'Convenience is all very well, Miss Donnelly, but don't you sometimes long for grand passion? The sort of passion that tears at your soul and blinds you to the consequences, so that you simply don't care what happens afterwards?'

Rosey blinked. His blue eyes were staring into hers and her knees felt weak. She straightened her back. 'You're a romantic,' she said, her voice a husky shell. 'That's a dangerous thing to be. When you're blinded to the consequences of your actions . . . well, you can get yourself into a great deal of trouble, Mr Parker.'

Both corners of his mouth quirked up now. 'Practical Rosey,' he whispered.

'I have to be practical.' Her reply was tart. 'You have your career, Mr Parker, and your clients, but what do I have? I have a friend with a remarkable gift, who I love dearly, but she's grown-up now and soon won't need me anymore. What then? Grand passion is all very well, but it won't warm me when I'm penniless.'

Her words betrayed more of her fears and doubts than she'd meant them to, and she saw in his eyes that he understood that she, like Alice, was ruled by her past.

'Thank you for your concern, Mr Parker,' she said hastily, before he could speak again, 'but I think I know what's best for me.'

* * *

Alice was watching them.

Long ago, at the camp, with Sean dying, she'd been certain Rosey and Josh were falling in love. She'd been used to men falling for her friend, but Josh had been different. Then Gervais had come along.

Alice knew what went on there, although she preferred to pretend she didn't. Better not to know, then she wouldn't feel embarrassed, or worse, compelled to give advice. She liked Gervais, and he had been kind to her, but she knew he wasn't the man for Rosey. Besides, he had a wife, and she was coming to Melbourne. In fact, she was on the ship right now.

'She's not coming until next year,' Gervais had insisted.

But Alice knew. She could see the woman in her first-class cabin, puking into a china bowl. Mrs Whistler was definitely on her way.

What would she think of Mrs Stuart with her dark eyes and big bosom? Alice didn't know and she didn't care, they would sort it out themselves. Her concern was for Rosey and Josh.

Across the ballroom their colours were very bright, the blue of Josh's seeping into Rosey's, like the tints in a watercolour painting running together. But Rosey had been hurt and she was cautious. She had been poor and hungry and she didn't want to go back to those days. She didn't believe Josh could love a woman who had lived the life she had lived and she kept her heart under lock and key. Alice didn't blame her for that, but she wished, just once, Rosey would free herself of her constraints and take a chance.

As she watched, someone came to ask Rosey to dance and she went off without a backward glance, smiling up at her partner, her curls glowing gold about her beautiful face. She looked as if she was having a wonderful time, but Alice could see her colours, and they'd darkened, turned forlorn.

Josh was watching her but soon he turned away. He slipped from the ballroom as if there was no longer anything for him to stay for. When the dance finished, Rosey looked about her and couldn't see him, and her face fell, just for a second, before she put the smile back on it again.

* * *

Ten Days Later

The guests were seated in the ballroom, the gas-lit chandelier above them turned down until the room was nothing more than shadows and whispers. Alice wondered what they were expecting, these rich and self-important members of Melbourne society. Gervais had gone all out to invite everyone he thought might be consequential enough to be useful to him and they had come in droves. Whether to sneer or with open minds, she wasn't sure. Probably few of them believed she could do what Gervais said she could do.

Once she'd doubted herself, too, but now she dismissed such doubts with ease. Those days were gone. Alice was comfortable in her own skin. It did not matter to her what the disbelievers thought. What mattered was that she could help those who needed it, or at least try.

The violinist caused his strings to sing eerily. That was Alice's cue to make her entrance. Gervais had impressed upon her how important it was. He wanted chills down their backs, he wanted them to sit up straighter and take notice. He wanted them lining up for her services. And paying for them.

Alice just wanted it over with.

There was a hush and then a murmur rising like the tide, as she walked towards the chair on the small dais. The violinist's music turned frantic as the gaslights came up and all was revealed. Alice sat, hands clasped, staring out over the pale faces, some smiling, some clearly astonished, others bored.

'Welcome all!' Gervais cried from the wings, striding onto the dais to stand with Alice. He rested a hand on her shoulder, gave it a pat. 'The Child will reach out into the spirit world beyond our mortal realm. She will listen to your dear departed ones and repeat their words back to you. Prepare to be amazed.'

Alice wished he'd go away. There was something buzzing in her head and she wanted to concentrate on it. Whatever it was didn't feel good or right. She searched the crowd for the faces of those who loved her, needing their consolation. Mrs Stuart and Josh were seated in the second row, having a murmured conversation that looked like a polite argument. Mrs Stuart wore a mourning necklace for her departed husband, and Josh had a paint stain on his tie. Then she saw Gilbert, another row back on the opposite side of the aisle. He was smiling at her and beside him Rosey, her hair pinned into a carefully disordered style, winked at her. Yes, the people who loved her were there, looking out for her, and everything would be fine.

But the humming was getting stronger.

'Ready, Alice?' Gervais murmured at her side, softly so no one else could hear. She nodded, concentrating on what she must do, and finally he left her. Alice took a breath and steadied herself, taking note of the colours of the audience. A dark halo caught her attention and she focused on the gentleman, asking if he was well. He dismissed her concerns, but beside him his wife's face told a different story. She did her best but she could see it was pointless.

'There are none so blind as those who will not see,' she murmured with a sigh. 'You must do as you think fit, sir, but remember. You've been warned by The Child.'

A gasp. 'Well, really!' someone burst out, shocked by her audaciousness.

Alice had already moved on. There was a vision of a little girl standing beside a seated woman resplendent in rubies and diamonds, her face stiff with the effort to hide her sorrow. The little girl had long golden curls tumbling down her back, and her face was chubby and smiling.

'Your daughter is here,' said Alice gently, and watched as the woman dissolved into tears. 'She's happy. She says she misses you but she has Grandma with her. Grandma says you should not punish yourself. It wasn't your fault.'

Even the disbelievers were moved by this and the mood of the room became more positive. Everything was going well.

* * *

As the session drew to a close, Rosey began to relax. Alice had impressed. There'd be private consultations rolling in. She glanced at Gervais and saw him rubbing his hands together. He was happy. She knew how his mind worked. He'd be thinking about taking on Coppin's share of The Goldminer and once he owned it outright he could use it to show off his talented troupe. Alice as the star, of course, but after tonight she deserved her top billing. Yes, Rosey thought, their opening had been a great success.

And then the doors crashed open and the howling started.

Her thoughts scattered. Had one of Alice's visions taken physical form at the back of the room? The audience certainly believed so, erupting from their chairs with shrieks and shouts. One woman in front of Rosey actually fainted.

Gilbert had leapt up and was trying to see what was making the dreadful racket. Rosey couldn't get a clear view behind her, but when she turned back to the stage she realised Alice, from her higher vantage point, could. The girl had risen to her feet and her face was ashen. Rosey needed to go to her. She began to push through the people now crowding her in and had almost reached the aisle when the howling creature came loping past her, heading directly for Alice.

Alice seemed too terrified to move. The creature's threadbare black coat flapped about his tall, narrow body, the clomp of his boots hitting the wooden floor as he inched closer to her. His hair was long, lying in thin, greasy strands across his white skull. His cheeks were concave and his eyes hollows of madness.

Rosey recognised him. She felt her world tilting. Dark spots flickered on the edge of her vision. No, she could not fall into a ladylike faint and leave Alice alone and unprotected up there on the dais.

Because Alice seemed incapable of moving.

Rosey cast aside her shock and came tearing out into the aisle, running after the nightmare figure she'd hoped never to see again. She was screaming, 'No you don't, you evil bastard!' all pretence at gentility gone from her voice. The man turned, catching her in mid-flight, and knocked her aside. She tumbled on top of several of the audience and scrambled to get back up, yelling all the while. Gervais finally seemed to wake from his own horrified trance, and he leapt from the dais and began to wrestle with the man.

It was like fighting with a demon. The man was shrieking words that made no sense and waving his hand towards where Alice still stood, frozen, like a statue. Others came to Gervais's aid and it took four of them to pin him to the floor, where he writhed and struggled and moaned. When they finally had him secured, Gervais got to his feet, panting, his jacket torn at the sleeve, his nose bloody.

He took out his handkerchief with shaking hands. 'Who was that? And why did he have to choose tonight of all nights?'

Beside him, Rosey felt dazed, her hair tumbling down about her shoulders and her cheek stinging where the madman had struck her.

'Are you injured?' Josh's murmur in her ear was a welcome distraction. He searched her face and tenderly tucked a strand of her hair behind her ear.

'He's a madman.' Gervais's voice rang out confidently, but to Rosey's ear he seemed to be trying out the words. Searching for ways to make the most of this and turn the publicity in his favour. He looked towards the newspaper reporters, jostling to find their notebooks and pencils. 'The Child has been attacked by a madman.'

'How did he get in?' Josh demanded, eyes narrowed. 'Didn't you have security on the doors?'

Gervais glared and Rosey knew it was because he didn't like seeing Josh so attentive to her. 'It was an invitation-only event.'

Rosey looked towards the dais. Alice was safe, but she still resembled a statue, her face as white as marble, her blue eyes enormous. Gilbert was there, too, standing in front of Alice as if to protect her, and his gaze was as sharp as a sword as he stared at the creature being held down on the floor.

'Will I call the police, sir?' One of The Goldminer staff was hovering anxiously.

'I think that would be a very good idea.'

'No!' Rosey clutched his arm in warning, saying, 'No, no police. We'll call a doctor.'

Gervais tried to read her expression, but apart from the urgency in it he didn't understand. He couldn't possibly understand. She muttered, 'Later.'

'If this ruins me, I will—' he started.

But Rosey had no time for him. She was beckoning at Gilbert. 'Gilbert! He's a madman, Gilbert. We need him away from here as soon as possible and as quietly as possible.' She added in an undertone, 'Can you see to that?'

Gilbert was frowning, slow to take it in.

'For Alice's sake, Gilbert.'

That seemed to do the trick and he gave a decisive nod. Quickly, he took control, murmuring to the men who had secured the creature. They hauled him to his feet and before he could commence with more of his shouting, hustled him away and out of sight.

The side door closed. The audience, those who hadn't run for safety through the doors, were turning back and forth, chattering, gasping, some excited by the experience and others profoundly horrified by it.

'I'm sorry.' Rosey had stepped back onto the dais and raised her voice above the hubbub. She was taking charge. 'This has been a dreadful evening. For us all, but particularly for The Child. She needs to rest. I hope you'll all be understanding.'

She took Alice's hand and began to urge her from the stage. The girl walked stiffly, as if her legs didn't really belong to her. It was a disturbing sight and Gervais turned away, clearly not wanting to see his star, his creation, brought low. But he had work to do if his night of nights was not to be a complete disaster. Rosey glanced back as she exited the ballroom and was relieved to hear him quickly set about soothing ruffled feathers. A word here, a pat on the shoulder there, a sympathetic squeeze of the hand.

'These great people attract unfortunates,' he pronounced. 'We must expect it. So sorry it happened tonight.'

She didn't need to worry about Gervais, he would rise above this evening's catastrophe. It was Alice who might never recover.

* * *

Alice felt as if her head was full of runaway horses, pounding around and around. He was here! The man in the dark coat. He was older, more gaunt, but he had come for her at last as she'd known one day he would, and she'd looked down at him and seen in his eyes that he knew her, that he was part of her.

He had come for her. He had found her at last.

At that moment it was as if her body remained and her mind flew off, because when she came back to herself he was no longer there. Rosey was holding her, walking her off the dais. She looked over her shoulder, expecting to see him following her, but he was gone.

'Gilbert has taken him in the secure wagon to the asylum, Alice. He'll be locked away.'

His body perhaps, but what of his mind? Alice shuddered violently. She could feel the buzz in her own head, like a malignant insect, burrowing in.

Rosey held her tighter. 'Come, Alice. You need to rest. This has been a frightful experience.'

There was a tremor in her friend's hands and Alice knew she, too, was deeply affected by what had happened. 'You saw him?' she whispered. 'He was here? It wasn't a dream, Rosey?'

'Yes, I saw him,' Rosey said. 'But he's gone now, and gone for good, Alice.'

'But why, Rosey, why?'

Her voice rose and broke and then she fainted.

When she woke it was to angry whispers in the corner of the room. Gervais and Rosey were arguing. She could hear snatches of their conversation, enough to understand Gervais was accusing Rosey of keeping the truth from him.

'And what would you have done if you'd known that man was after her? Set her free from your endless contracts? I doubt it. Not while she makes money for you.'

'I might have taken more precautions.'

'All the precautions in the world wouldn't have stopped that madman.'

Gervais gave an irritated sigh. 'I have to tell the newspapers something. Don't worry, I'll be careful. A random attack by a lunatic. The Child is resting but will be ready to resume her sessions soon.'

Rosey gave him a furious stare. 'Alice needs to stop. She needs to rest. Perhaps even to go away for a time.'

'Nonsense.'

The argument went on, round and round.

Alice closed her eyes again. They didn't understand, even Rosey who meant the best for her. The man in the dark coat had found her and even though he was locked away his mind was free. She could feel him buzzing away at the perimeters, trying to get in.

How to stop him, how to understand him, how to escape him forever?

The mesmerism had helped, for a time, but she couldn't seem to get beyond the memory of the barrel in the river. There was a block she couldn't get past. Gilbert said that once she knew the truth, once she understood, then his power over her would be gone. But how to find out the truth?

'I have to go back to the river.'

Gervais and Rosey stopped mid-argument. Alice turned to look at them, her blue eyes enormous in her thin, pale face.

'I know that's what I have to do, I've always known, I just wasn't brave enough. I have to go back to the past, my past. I have to walk in my steps, and I have to discover the truth.'

Gervais came and took her hands in his, his red face redder than usual. 'Of course you do, Alice, but perhaps it would be best to wait. You shouldn't rush these things.'

Alice ignored him. 'Will you come with me?' she asked Rosey.

'I will, Alice,' Rosey raised her voice above Gervais's objections.

'And Gilbert, too. And Josh,' she added, as if she was talking to herself. 'I want Josh to make sketches, for another painting. A painting about the truth.'

Gervais huffed. 'If anyone comes it'll be me, so we'll have no more nonsense about—'

'Your wife is nearly here,' Alice turned to him and spoke clearly. 'Her ship will dock in a day or so. You need to stay and wait for her. She's expecting to see you and she won't be pleased if you're off with Rosey. She's thinking about when you married her and the pretty girl she was, and she's wondering if you'll still think her pretty. She's looking forward to seeing The Goldminer and meeting all your friends. She has plans . . .' she trailed off.

He looked shocked. Alice could see he wanted to deny it, to tell her she was making it up. But he knew that Alice always spoke the truth.

'We'll come with you,' Rosey affirmed.

Alice wasn't listening. She'd covered her face with her hands. 'You can lock him up,' she said, her voice muffled, 'but I can still hear him. He can still find me. He'll always find me unless I stop him with the truth.'

CHAPTER THIRTY-FOUR

Annie's Story

The phone call from Greta had been terse and anxious.

'You'd better get in here now, Annie!'

'What's happened?' I was half dressed, Courtney staring mutinously at her breakfast. *Get in here now* wasn't really what I wanted to hear.

'The minister's here. And Sebastian. I don't trust either of them.'

I found I could move fast after all. Once I'd explained things to Reuben and Max, it was agreed Max would take Courtney to child care and I would head straight to the office. Reuben looked furious, his mouth pinched and thin, and it was Max who laid a hand on my shoulder and said, 'Go get 'em.'

Despite my storm of emotions, I managed a laugh.

When I reached the office, Greta, dressed in orange jeans and turquoise sweater, came hurrying over to me. 'They're upstairs.'

'So what do they want?'

'Don't ask me, no one tells me anything.'

'Are they going to take the *Trompe L'oeil*?'

Greta's mouth tightened. 'I'll lock the doors, just in case.'

I hurried upstairs to my studio.

I was thinking of all the work I'd done to save the painting. I really couldn't lose it now.

My voice sounded remarkably calm as I walked in the door. 'Good morning.'

Sebastian was standing side by side with the minister and they both turned in surprise. She was in a smart grey suit and sensible heels, a red scarf tucked around her neck. She'd had her fair hair straightened and it made her look younger.

'Annie, sorry to barge in,' Sebastian said. 'The minister wanted another look. There have been developments.'

Was there an ominous note in his voice?

'Coming here was my idea,' the minister spoke up. 'I believe that my great-great-grandfather, Gervais Whistler, commissioned this painting all those years ago and I'm his direct descendant. Clearly, that gives me a stake in what happens to it.'

'Oh.' I didn't like the sound of that.

She carried on. 'I've been making enquiries and it appears that I may well have a legal right to the *Trompe L'oeil*. According to Gervais's will, at the date of his death all of his Goldminer estate was left to his surviving family. The painting was an oversight—it was left behind—but I think it could be considered part of his estate. It's certainly something I'll be pursuing with my lawyers.'

'Does that mean you'll be removing it from us?' I asked, my voice remarkably calm for someone in a state of shock.

She pointed at the vignette of Gervais, and suddenly it was as if the politician stepped aside, leaving the real person in her place. 'My party is about to have a leadership spill and this man has the potential to ruin me. He's the opposite of everything I stand for. When I was a child I was taken to see Gervais's portrait at the National Gallery. I believed he was a respectable businessman, we all did. Then a book came out of nowhere, full of dirt. I had no idea. How could I? I never knew about Gervais's grimy dealings with brothels, not to mention his shady businesses. I stopped the book's publication and I thought Gervais was no longer a problem, but now *this* turns up.'

'Minister, I'm sorry you feel—'

'Do you know Gervais ran a troupe of entertainers? Well of course you do!' She was so wound up there was no stopping her. 'The Child, she was called, the girl who made him a fortune. I think that's her.' Another wave of the hand. 'Your girl in the painting. Gervais an advocate of child labour. How do you think that will go down?'

Alice was The Child? The name was unfamiliar to me. Did that mean she was genuine or, more likely, knowing Gervais, he was using her to con the public? But there was no time to speculate.

'Minister, I'm very sorry, but this painting is far more important than the man who commissioned it. I can't let you hide it away. I can't let that happen and—'

'If the painting belongs to me then I can do whatever I like, Miss Reuben.'

I glanced at Sebastian, but I could see he wasn't about to take sides. He'd done what he could and now it was up to me. And I knew I was going to have to be very careful. Here was a woman who had been backed into a corner and if I said the wrong thing then she could take the painting away and I might never see it again.

'When you look at the painting, what do you see?'

A crease appeared in her brow. 'See?'

I turned towards the canvas. 'Because I think all you see is Gervais and the damage he's causing your reputation. But, Minister, there's so much more to see. Look at these two girls. Alice, she's the younger one, the one you think was The Child. She was a foundling who was saved from the Murray River by Captain Potter. Here, this is his paddle-steamer, and this is his wife, Molly. She died in tragic circumstances and Alice was cast adrift on the world. But she endured. Perhaps she did things that we would shudder at now, but perhaps she had no choice. This is the story of this girl's remarkable survival in a harsh world. It's an epic tale. People will come in droves to see it. They'll love it. You shouldn't be trying to distance yourself from it, you should be celebrating your part in it!'

When I finished there was a silence. Sebastian was staring at me in admiration and the minister blinked tears from her eyes.

'You are passionate about your work,' she said.

'No. I mean, yes, I am, but I am passionate about this work in particular. I want Alice and Rosey to be seen by the public.'

She stared at me a long moment and then she sighed. She turned to Sebastian. 'You were right about her,' she said. 'No pushover.'

'I think Annie makes a great deal of sense, Minister,' he murmured.

She hesitated and then made full eye contact with me. 'Very well. The painting can stay here.' Her smile was tired. 'You should go and take a look at the portrait of Gervais. That's the way he wanted to be remembered. It's certainly the way his wife, Emily, wanted him remembered. It was she who did most of the covering up after he died. She was very jealous. She was famous for it. If she thought there was something going on between Alice or Rosey and her husband she would have refused to have your *Trompe L'oeil* anywhere near her. In fact, she probably took it down the day he died and shoved it into the basement.'

I showed her out, remembering to hastily unlock the door. Sebastian followed her and they stood a moment, talking, but I'd had enough. I flopped down into a chair.

'Are you all right?' Greta hovered anxiously. 'You look white.'

'Who would've thought conservation could be so stressful?' I said. 'Greta, you asked me to tell you when you should look for a new job? Well I'm giving you fair warning. The *Trompe L'oeil* may be my last job. I hope not, but even if I manage to get us out of debt I'll have to downsize, sell the office.'

Greta blinked. 'Okay. What about the job at the lunatic asylum? Are you still doing that?'

'Yes, of course.' Although to be honest I'd forgotten all about it.

Greta sighed. 'I had a feeling things weren't going well. Will you write me a glowing reference?'

'Blinding.'

Sebastian was back. He saw me and smiled and I stood up again. 'The minister just took a call. The leadership spill is on. You may have noticed she was a little stressed. That was why Gervais's influence was looming large in her mind. But she's taken on board what you said. I think there'll be a press release about the painting very soon. Woman succeeding in a man's world, maybe? Clichéd but effective.'

'You don't think she'll change her mind?' I asked, feeling more than a little stressed myself.

'No, too late for that. She's made her decision.'

I'd won.

'Your *Trompe L'oeil* is safely in your hands. Don't worry, History Victoria will let you do your job without interference. My last act of kindness before I take to the skies. And speaking of New York . . .'

I sighed, hating what I had to do. 'I'm sorry, Sebastian.'

He understood and shook his head. 'You'll regret it,' he warned. 'I could've used you in New York, Annie.'

'Good luck, Sebastian, and let me know how it goes.'

He took my hands in his, looking down at me.

'Goodbye, Annie.' He bent and kissed my cheek and was gone.

It was only when I turned to watch him go that I saw Max standing by the door.

Hoping he hadn't mistaken the kiss for more than it was, I plastered a smile on my face as he came towards me.

'I've told Sebastian I'm not going to New York,' I told him quickly.

His blue eyes searched mine. 'I'm glad,' he said. 'I'm sorry about the chance you're missing, of course I am, but I don't want to have to subsist from one international phone call to the next. I want you here, Annie. With me.'

'Do you?' I whispered.

I knew he would have kissed me then, a proper kiss, but Greta was watching. 'The minister is going to let me keep the painting. I can finish it. I've won.'

His smile warmed me. 'Of course you have.'

'I want to pay a visit to the National Gallery to see this portrait of Gervais Whistler. Will you come, Max?'

'I'd like to see Gervais. There was something else I wanted to talk to you about,' he added, when we were outside in the brisk air. 'You and Reuben.'

I tried to read his face. He looked edgy. 'What is it?'

'I want to speak to you both together. Can you wait until tonight? It's nothing to worry about, at least I hope not. Just a proposition I want to put to you both.' But there was a twinkle in his eyes, as if whatever he had to say was good news rather than bad.

'Sure. And thank you, Max, for this morning. Was Courtney okay?'

'Couldn't have been better. I now know all about the Kardashian family.'

I laughed. Digging my hands into the pockets of my jeans, I walked along by his side. Silence fell, but a comfortable silence, between two people who liked each other's company. Max, I thought, glancing at him, who'd given up his promising career to captain a paddle-steamer, and me who had given up life in the fast lane to stay home with my ailing father and four year old daughter.

Oh yes, we made a good pair.

* * *

The National Gallery was quietly busy, a few school groups and buses of pensioners and tourists, as well as visitors in dribs and drabs who'd come to experience its pleasures. Here there were paintings and artworks from all over the world, but we found Gervais in the Australian section, rubbing shoulders with the likes of Tom Roberts and Fred McCubbin, two of Australia's most important late Victorian-era artists.

'I'd know that smug mug anywhere,' Max murmured, as we stood before the portrait.

Gervais really was a larger-than-life character, his eyes blazing out at the room, his fleshy face arranged in a satisfied half-smile.

Charismatic. His hair was greying at the temples and although his clothing was of the best quality, the artist had shown his thickening waist and bulky neck. Prosperity. Success. Gervais lived well and didn't care who knew it.

After contemplating him for a time, and wondering what his relationship had been like with Alice and Rosey, my attention was caught by the noticeboard beneath the portrait. That humming excitement began buzzing inside my head.

Joshua Parker, Melbourne portrait painter from about 1870 to 1880.

He was a fashionable painter of Melbourne identities. Few of his works have survived and little is known of him, other than that he was trained in the London Academy and came to Victoria during the gold rush. His patron was Mrs Annabelle Stuart, who was a great supporter of the arts during boom-time Melbourne.

His subject in this portrait is Gervais Whistler, an entrepreneur, who owned The Goldminer Hotel and many other businesses during the booming 1880s. This portrait hung for many years in the foyer of the hotel. After Mr Whistler died in 1886, his wife, Emily Whistler, continued to run his business empire until the depression of the 1890s, when much of it was lost.

Gervais Whistler's funeral procession stretched for several blocks, with black horses and carriages, muffled drums and solemn mourners. A grand farewell to a Melbourne personality who is now largely forgotten.

Once more I stood back and let myself take in the man himself. It seemed incredible that he had been all but forgotten. Joshua Parker, too.

'Look,' Max said, and caught my arm, so much suppressed excitement in his voice that I couldn't do anything else but follow the direction of his finger. Behind Gervais's arm was a vase of flowers on a table which formed part of the background. The vase was decorated, two figures sketchily drawn on the porcelain.

Two faces peeping out at me. Unmistakable. Smiling. A girl with straight brown hair and the other, older one with fair curly hair.

Alice and Rosey, hand in hand. Joshua Parker had placed the girls in Gervais's portrait, a cheeky reminder of the part they'd played in his rise.

CHAPTER THIRTY-FIVE

The Girl's Story

They sat comfortably in their first-class carriage. The train journey north was very different from the one they'd made south so many years ago. And the two girls who'd run from the Red Petticoat were very different from the two women who were travelling back to the port on the river.

Whenever Rosey thought about herself and Alice making their escape—which wasn't very often—it was always raining and cold. She knew it couldn't really have been. There had been good days and sunny days, it was just that her memories seemed to have soaked up an atmosphere of bleakness.

Rosey was grateful for Gilbert Suckling being with them. Alice seemed to find his presence reassuring and altogether she was less tense, as if once she'd made the decision to return to her past she was no longer at war with herself.

Alice had sent an invitation to Josh, but they hadn't heard from him. Rosey shrugged her shoulders when Alice wondered aloud where he was and why he'd failed to respond.

'Mrs Stuart probably said "No",' she said, with a mocking smile.

'Do you think so? I had hoped . . .'

Rosey had a fair idea Alice was playing matchmaker, but she told herself she wasn't interested. Josh Parker and she had reached a point where they could be acquaintances, even friends, but anything else was out of the question. Why didn't Alice just let sleeping dogs lie?

'I hoped he might come for your sake.'

Rosey's green eyes narrowed. 'Alice, you need to understand that whatever Josh and I might have felt once is long gone. Dead. We've moved on.'

Alice just gave her that look that seemed to see everything she wasn't saying. After all these years that look still made Rosey uncomfortable.

Like them, Echuca had changed. The town and port had expanded and grown busier with the trade along the river and the railway through to Melbourne. Although they could see glimpses of the place it had been, there was a new strangeness about it, too. In a way, Rosey was glad of that. She didn't want it to be the same because then she'd have to think of the girl she was. As it was this trip was bringing it all back and if it hadn't been for Alice she knew she would never have come.

Regarding Miss Oliver's death, Gilbert had made discreet inquiries about that and discovered the matter was all but forgotten. 'The apothecary murders have taken precedence,' he'd told Rosey. 'No one remembers Miss Oliver now.'

Miss Oliver wouldn't have liked that, thought Rosey. But she was glad that finally the incident had faded into the past and they would not have to worry about it.

Gilbert had made all the arrangements, booking their train journey and organising the hotel when they arrived. He'd also sent a letter ahead to the post office, asking if Captain Arnold Potter was still resident at Echuca and to leave word at their hotel—if possible, Alice wanted to see him and talk to him—but when they arrived at the hotel there was nothing. Alice went up to her room to take a nap, leaving Rosey and Gilbert to drink tea from fine china cups. It also gave them a chance to discuss what they were going to do next.

Gilbert put down his teacup with a clatter and cleared his throat. The little private parlour was over-warm and cramped, full as it was of furniture and accompanying knick-knacks. The summer sun struggled through thick lace and brocade curtains, plunging the room into permanent twilight.

Gilbert leaned forward with an earnest expression and proceeded to tick off points on his fingers. 'So this is what we know. One: Alice was found in the river. Two: she was rescued near a homestead by Captain Potter. Three: she was drifting down river and could've come for miles. Four . . .' He sighed and gave up on his fingers. 'We don't know how far she drifted, do we? How fast was the river moving that day? Can we make a guess where she came from?'

Rosey sipped her tea, curling her little finger in her lacy glove. 'We need to talk to the people who were there when she was found.'

'The people at the homestead, yes.'

'But most importantly Captain Potter.' Rosey shifted uneasily. Another memory she'd rather forget. Herself shouting at the captain, striking him. She'd been mad with fury at what he'd done to Alice. With any luck he wouldn't remember, or better yet, wouldn't recognise in this well-dressed and well-mannered lady the harridan from the Red Petticoat.

'If I don't hear anything about him soon then I'll go and ask at the wharf,' Gilbert said. He mopped his face with his handkerchief. He wasn't used to summers in Echuca, none of them were, and today the heat was intense.

'Alice will want to be there when we meet him.' Rosey pushed away her teacup. There were macaroons and she was tempted, examining the little delicacies on the patterned plate.

'Will she?' Gilbert looked worried. 'This is going to take its toll on her.'

'Perhaps it will, but she needs to know. If she's ever to escape that man she has to know the truth.'

'I left him sitting in a corner of his room, staring at nothing.' Gilbert put away his handkerchief. 'He's been in and out of asylums for years, Rosey. He was only released a few weeks before he turned up at The Goldminer, evidently he was living rough on the streets. As far as I can tell from the records I've been able to collect he has never stated his name or given any other personal details. He can barely speak and he seems to have the mental age of a child. Was he always like that? It doesn't make sense, does it?'

'Do you think if Alice were to meet him face to face . . . ?'

'I wouldn't advise her to do it.'

Rosey decided against the macaroon and rose from the table. 'I'm going to take a walk,' she said.

Pausing by the glass window in the foyer she examined her reflection. The gown was a pretty shade of turquoise, trimmed with maroon ribbon and braid, with a draped bustle and a short train, which Rosey could tuck over her arm, out of the way, when she walked. Her waist was as narrow as ever, and her neck and jaw firm. She'd noticed a wobble on Mrs Stuart the other day, the beginning of jowls. Not that she was vain, Rosey told herself, but it paid to keep an eye on the competition. Lastly, she checked that her perky little bonnet was placed just so on her golden curls.

She was a woman of means, a woman with style, a woman visiting from Melbourne. And if anyone recognised her as poor Roisin O'Donoghue . . . well, she'd be truly amazed.

Satisfied, she strolled out of the shadows of the verandah and into the still, hot air. Echuca remained a frontier town despite the wealth it made from the wool bails and the timber that were sent along the river and onto the trains. Dust rose from beneath the hooves of passing horses and cartwheels, voices called to each other, and the sawmill was a constant drone in the background. If she dared to close her eyes she'd be back in the past in a heartbeat.

For all her means and style, Rosey was afraid.

What if, she thought, it had all been a dream, this journey through the goldfields and the music halls with Alice? What if she were to wake up right now and find she was still at the Red Petticoat, still smiling at the 'gentlemen' and wishing her life away?

With an impatient shake of her head at her own silliness, Rosey set out again. Soon she was enjoying the rich sound of her skirts and petticoats rustling, and the reassuring grip of her gloved hand on the ebony handle of her silk parasol with tassels. It was reassuring, too, that no one recognised her, and by now she had passed quite a few Echuca residents.

Then she saw that, somehow, her steps had led her to the one place she didn't wanted to be. The Red Petticoat. Briefly it was there, in her imagination, the narrow dimly lit facade, the door opening onto the noisy salon. Then she blinked and it was gone, and in its place stood a solicitor's office with a small glass window at the front. Very staid in comparison to the building's gaudy past.

Just then a gentleman stepped from the office, locking the door behind him. Perhaps it was the solicitor himself. He noticed Rosey and tipped his hat, giving her an appreciative look.

Rosey nodded, enjoying her triumph. She might even have lingered, made up some story about needing his advice, but his gaze went past her. Behind her. The solicitor hurried away. But Rosey had felt a prickle of warning on the back of her neck and knew there was someone there.

She turned so quickly she almost fell, and he caught her arm to steady her. With a gasp she looked up into his face, topped with a straw-brimmed hat over his bright red hair.

'I was delayed,' Josh said.

He was standing too close and Rosey stepped back, giving herself room to breathe. He was watching her face as if he could read every thought she was thinking. Joy that he had come after all; disappointment that he had come after all.

'You haven't missed anything,' she said dryly.

He smiled. 'Unlike you. You missed a scene of monumental proportions, Miss Donnelly.' He held out his arm again. 'Walk with me to the hotel and I'll tell you about it.'

She slipped her hand into the crook of his elbow and they began the slow walk back. He was wearing a rather crumpled blue jacket over his white shirt, and his necktie was loosened. He looked like an artist, but then that was what he was, Rosey thought with a sigh. Why should she expect him to look as dapper as Gervais when he wasn't anything the same? Perhaps she had grown too attached to appearances.

'Did you want to hear about the kerfuffle?' He was watching her, amused, probably knowing exactly what she was thinking.

Rosey lifted her chin. 'I'm waiting. I thought you must be choosing the right words, Mr Parker.'

'First of all, Alice was right. Mrs Whistler arrived the day you left and threw the whole of The Goldminer into chaos. I've never seen Gervais so meek and mild.'

Rosey eyed him drolly. 'You enjoyed it, I see. Your sense of humour seems to run to the absurd. And for your information, Alice is always right.'

'I stand corrected. When Gervais was over his shock he began to show his wife around the hotel, and who should come calling on him in the middle of it but Annabelle Stuart, expecting her usual welcome. Mrs Whistler saw at a glance what had been going on and she turned on Annabelle like a fury, while Gervais stood behind them flapping his hands.'

Rosey was smiling, she couldn't help it. The story was all the sweeter because if she had not been displaced from Gervais's affections by Annabelle Stuart, then it could well have been she who was caught in the middle of that maelstrom.

'I take it Mrs Whistler won the battle?'

'Her name is Emily, by the way, and yes she did. Annabelle was driven forth and took to her bed. She probably sent for me, to soothe her injured pride. If she did then the note is lying there forlorn and I'm here.'

Rosey stopped and turned to look at him properly. He was still smiling, but his eyes were apprehensive. 'Josh, are you saying you've walked out on Mrs Stuart? Your patroness? When she needed you?'

'I'm afraid so.'

'But your painting career . . .'

He made a sound in his throat like a groan. 'What career, Rosey? That isn't what I wanted. If I have to flatter another vain woman or pompous man then I'll-I'll . . . I've had enough of it. The only decent things I did in the last ten years were the *Trompe L'oeil* and Gervais's portrait.'

Rosey wondered if it was the heat that was making it difficult for her to breathe or the longing in her heart, the longing she saw reflected in Josh's face.

'I only stayed with Mrs Stuart because of you, Rosey,' he said, his voice dropping. 'To be successful, because that was what you seemed to want of a man. But I can't be Gervais Whistler.'

Rosey reached up and touched his cheek with her gloved fingers. 'I don't want Gervais Whistler. Am I such a shallow creature, Josh?'

Wisely, he didn't answer.

'Well, perhaps, a little. I have my reasons for not wanting to slip back into what I came from. Can you blame me?'

'Rosey, I've never cared about your past.'

What did he mean? Did he know? Rosey found she was slightly breathless. 'My past,' she admitted, 'is very unsavoury.'

'I don't care.'

'How can you not care, Josh? You must care. A man like you and a woman like me . . .'

The words were like a wall between them. He demolished it by leaning towards her and kissing her, briefly, tenderly, on the lips. Right there in the street in Echuca with everybody watching. Although, when she glanced around, they were quite alone. Everyone with any sense had gone indoors out of the midday heat. For a moment Rosey felt disappointed that no one had seen her behaving improperly, and then she thought that perhaps that was a good sign.

Perhaps she was learning to be herself. Not the poor Irish girl and not the *nouveau riche* snob, but something in between.

* * *

Rosey recognised him. He was older, more careworn, his hair greying and his face tanned and weathered, but he was essentially the same man.

As soon as they stepped into the stuffy gloom of the hotel foyer she saw him standing there. He did glance her way, but he didn't recognise her.

Had he ever tried to find Alice?

Josh nearly bumped into her when she came to an abrupt halt. 'Rosey?'

She ignored him, striding forward with a confident smile and holding out her gloved hand.

'Captain Potter.'

He spoke a little gruffly. 'Word is there are people wishing to see me.' He had a strong grip. She saw that there was a scar in the shape of a star in the webbing between his thumb and first finger, and that there was a healing cut below his little finger. The life of a riverboat captain wasn't an easy one.

'Yes, you're right. We do wish to speak to you. I'm Miss Donnelly and this is Mr Parker.'

'Miss Donnelly. Mr Parker,' he repeated and the corner of his mouth curled up in a ghost of a smile before he glanced down at the floor.

'We're not here alone, Captain Potter. There's someone who desperately needs to speak to you. I hope you'll agree to see her.'

He was frowning now, the weathered lines on his face creasing deeply. There was a line of grimy sweat around his neck, above the collar of his shirt, as if he hadn't washed for days. Surely, the old Captain Potter would not have come to the hotel in such a state? Yes, he was older, but it wasn't time that had altered him so much. If Rosey knew anything about it, it was grief and perhaps even guilt.

'I was only told there were people from the city here. Strangers. Looking for me.' His grey eyes were dull and tired. In a moment he'd walk out.

Rosey hesitated before turning to Josh. 'Would you go and fetch her?' she said. 'Bring her down to the private parlour.'

Josh nodded, and went to the stairs. Rosey touched the captain's arm. 'Come,' she said in a soothing tone. 'Let's go into the private parlour and wait. I'll send for some tea and cake. The cake here is quite delicious.'

Her voice went on, calming, but her thoughts were anything but. Should she tell him it was Alice in the room above? What if he didn't recognise her, how cruel would that be? But if she told him then it would blunt the blow of him seeing her for the first time. Rosey didn't want to do so. There was still a cold, hard, unforgiving part of her that, even seeing how much he had already suffered, wanted him to suffer more.

Gilbert was seated in the parlour reading a newspaper and he jumped up when he saw Captain Potter. 'Sir,' he said, with an awkward glance to Rosey. 'How did you . . . ?'

'Captain Potter's friends have let him know we were asking after him,' Rosey said.

'Oh.' Gilbert edged towards the door. 'Will I . . . ?'

'I sent Mr Parker for her.'

'So he found you? Sorry, of course he did. I might just go and make sure everything's all right.' And he slipped out the door and closed it behind him.

Rosey saw to it that Captain Potter was as comfortably seated as possible—he didn't look any more eager to be in that room than she—then settled down herself to await events.

It didn't take long before the two men were back, and with them was Alice, still pale and tired from the journey, blue shadows beneath her very blue eyes, her hair tied back with a black ribbon. She was wearing a plain grey gown, and she looked thin. If you didn't look too hard, you could almost believe she was still a child.

The shock on Captain Potter's face made nonsense of Rosey's concern that he wouldn't know Alice. He rose clumsily to his feet, making a sound that seemed to come from deep inside him. A stumbling step and he was reaching for her hands, and Rosey could tell from the agonised expression on his face how much he had longed for this moment.

'Alice.'

Alice was weeping. The salty tears rolled down her cheeks, and at the same time her trembling mouth was shaped into a smile. 'Captain Potter. I have so wanted . . . I missed . . .'

The disjointed words seemed to make sense to him, because he wrapped her in his arms and they held on, saying nothing. Surreptitiously, Rosey wiped her own eyes with the fingertip of her glove. Even if they discovered nothing, she decided, then this moment alone had been worth the journey.

* * *

Alice couldn't help darting little glances up at him. Captain Potter, *her* Captain Potter. He was essentially the same, older of course, but still handsome, and his eyes still that clear grey. His hair had grey in it, too, but then so did Rosey's, although she took care to pluck them out.

'I came looking for you,' he said, his smile painful. 'I tried to find you, Alice.'

'Did you?' Alice felt her smile encompass her entire face. For her all was forgiven.

But Captain Potter hadn't forgiven himself.

'But then the story of the poisoning came out and . . . I was a broken man all over again. I understood how badly I'd misjudged you. What a bloody idiot I'd been. I blamed . . . blame myself for Molly dying.'

'I wish I could've helped her more,' Alice murmured.

'You've got nothing to reproach yourself for, Alice. It was me who forced her to take that medicine. I may as well have killed her.'

'You didn't know. You loved her.'

'So did you.'

For a moment, the pain between them was so great Alice wondered if they could get past it. She took a shaky breath and was glad when Gilbert took her hand and held it tight. Realising Captain Potter did not know who he was, she introduced them. 'This is Gilbert Suckling, Captain Potter. Do you remember him? He lives in Melbourne now and he's studying to be a doctor. And he's my friend.'

The captain's eyes narrowed, the bitterness changing his demeanour.

'Gilbert has nothing to do with his father,' Alice warned him. 'He's innocent. Just as I was.'

The reminder shook him, she could see that in his eyes, and after a moment of struggle, the captain nodded. 'Then I hope I can treat him fairly, Alice. For your sake.'

'Thank you, sir.' Gilbert also looked drawn and white. This had been a traumatic meeting for them all.

'Captain Potter, I've come to ask for your help,' she said, before they could lapse back into the paralysis of their shared sorrows. 'I need to find out where I came from. Who I am. I thought perhaps . . . Has no one ever come looking for me, Captain?'

'No one Alice.'

'No one at all?'

She knew she sounded forlorn. She'd become the little girl again, who'd been abandoned all those years ago.

'There must be a clue somewhere,' Gilbert said, taking charge. 'I wonder, Captain, if we travelled back down the river, back to where you found Alice, whether we might come across some hint of her past?'

Captain Potter hesitated, looking between them, and then he gave a smile. It took years off him. 'We can try,' he said.

CHAPTER THIRTY-SIX

Annie's Story

By the time I headed for home I felt absolutely exhausted, but somehow I doubted I'd get an early night. Max was waiting with whatever news he'd wanted to discuss with me and Reuben.

When I reached the house I had hardly made it out of the car when the door was flung open.

Courtney was standing there, eyes wide, brandishing one of my mother's diaries.

'Mummy, it's him! It's him! It's the man in the backyard!'

Max had followed her out, looking confused. 'She just started saying "It's him", but I didn't understand what she meant.'

Reuben hovered in the doorway to the kitchen, looking guilty. 'I didn't know she'd been going through the diaries,' he said. He gave a flicker of a glance towards Max. 'Max and I were talking . . .'

'It's my fault for leaving them on the desk.' I took the diary from my overexcited daughter and led the way into the kitchen. Once there I dropped into a chair at the table, kicking off my shoes, and turned to the diary cover. Of course it was the one I hadn't read—the final one. The page Courtney had opened to had a sketch, surrounded by my mother's untidy writing.

I managed not to shudder.

'See, see!' Courtney was dancing on the spot with impatience. 'It's him, Mummy, isn't it?'

The sketch was in black ballpoint pen, and with a few deft strokes Mum had captured the gauntness of the frame, the flapping black coat, the raised hands, and even the top hat with the strands of lank hair below it. The face was the thing. A nightmare, long and thin, mouth ajar, and black hollowed-out eyes. It was indeed the ghost I'd seen, and it was also the figure in the *Trompe L'oeil*.

My first instinct was to lie, to protect my daughter.

'I don't know . . .'

'It *is*, Mummy. You know it is.' Courtney wasn't having any of it.

'Okay. But let's talk about this later. How about I run you a bath and you can tell me about your sleepover? I'm sure I haven't heard everything yet.'

'I told you everything, Mummy.'

'No you didn't. What about . . . hmm, what you had for dinner? And whether Yasmine's kitten has grown into a big fat cat?'

Courtney looked mutinous, but Max's presence prevented what could have been a flat-out refusal, or worse, a show of temper. I could see that she was tired and fractious, but she was also polite in front of visitors.

'The man in the drawing didn't have his colours,' she said, once she was in the bath.

She had mentioned this before, but I hadn't really taken a great deal of notice. 'Colours?'

'Yes,' with a dramatic sigh. 'I told you. Like a sunflower. Not blue like Max's colours.'

I tried to understand. 'Do we all have colours, Courtney? Can you see them?'

She gave me a look. ''Course I can. Yours are purple and sometimes blue, when Max is there, and Grandpa's are greeny, but when he was sick they were darker and grey. Like rain clouds.' She yawned. 'Everyone has colours, Mummy.'

I was too astounded to say any more. This was something I needed to think about. But I had a feeling Courtney's colours were not a new development. She was quite comfortable with them. They were a part of who she was. Could they also have a connection with the man in the backyard?

After the bath, she insisted Max read her a story, and thankfully she was asleep before he'd finished.

'Big day,' he said, and I could tell he was wondering what the fuss had been about.

While he'd been reading Courtney her story, I'd had time to read the page in my mother's diary. The words were still echoing unpleasantly in my head.

He comes more often now. I'm praying that when I'm gone he'll leave Annie alone. I've warned Reuben. If worse comes to worse there's always an exorcism, although I wonder if that's been tried before. This spirit already seems to be in hell.

One thing. I can hear him speak now. Perhaps as I get closer to the veil between life and death, I get closer to him. The other day he said 'Annella' as clear as anything. Then 'the river'. I don't know what he means, but I know of Annella. Or is it Alice? I'm sure I do. If only I could remember. My mind is fading as my body weakens. I'll tell Reuben. He can puzzle it out.

'Annie?' Max was talking and I hadn't heard him, too deep in my own thoughts.

'I'm sorry, it's just . . . We have a ghost,' I blurted out. 'That's what Courtney was on about. She found my mother's diary and there was a drawing in it. All three of us have seen him. My mother, me and Courtney. But not Papa.'

Max wasn't rolling his eyes or laughing hysterically, so I told him the rest. That the ghost bore a striking resemblance to the figure at the timber getters' hut in the *Trompe L'oeil*. Then I showed him the page in my mother's diary.

Reuben had been silent until now, but as Max read he came and rested a hand on my shoulder. 'She never told me about this Alice person,' he said quietly. 'I would've remembered. I wish she had.'

I reached up to pat his hand. Reuben shook his head, leaving me and Max alone.

Max had finished reading and carefully set down the diary. 'I've never seen a ghost,' he said at last, 'but I don't disbelieve in them. My father . . . Sometimes on the *Ariadne* I can feel him standing in the wheelhouse beside me. Maybe that's just wishful thinking, I don't know.'

I smiled. 'Thank you. For making me feel better.' I glanced down at the diary again. 'My mother saw the ghost after she moved into this house and although I saw him as a child he went away when she died. Now he's back and it seems to coincide with my work on the painting. My search for Alice. I think there's a connection between the ghost and Alice and my family. I don't know what it is but it's there. And the river. It all starts at the river. Alice was found there, the *Ariadne* is there.'

My discovery of Courtney's colours was on the tip of my tongue but I swallowed it back. A memory was tugging at me, something I had seen recently, and I needed to think about it.

Max reached out and clasped my hand. I felt the warm strength of his grip, the sense of support he gave me. 'Can I talk to you and Reuben now?'

* * *

'I have a proposition for you both,' Max said.

We were seated around the kitchen table, and although I was wondering what it could be I had a feeling Reuben already knew.

'The interior of the paddle-steamer, the *Queen of the Rivers*,' he went on. 'I want to restore it and I want to employ Reuben and Reuben.'

My father rubbed his hands together with a big grin as he turned to me. 'What do you think?'

I tried to think but my brain wasn't as lucid as usual, although after the day I'd had it was a wonder I could string two thoughts together. 'But . . . we haven't done anything like this before. I don't know the first thing about boats.'

'It's the same as a house, Annie, just that it's a boat.' My father was unfazed by the challenge.

I couldn't help but laugh. 'I think there might be a few fundamental differences.' But Reuben was probably right; we could do it if we wanted to. 'I thought you said you were finished,' I reminded him.

'And you said I might change my mind.' His expression turned serious. 'What about you, Annie? If you don't—'

Just for a moment, I asked myself if I wanted to. Then I realised it would mean spending time with Max, lots of time with Max, and I'd be working in Echuca on the river so it wouldn't matter if we no longer had the office. Even the house could be sold, if that helped to give us a new, debt-free start. Courtney might have to go to school there, but she wouldn't mind, and even Nephetiti would get used to the country. She was an outdoors cat at heart anyway.

But there was the *Trompe L'oeil*.

'The painting . . .'

'I wouldn't expect you to start until all that was sorted out,' Max reassured me. 'That's your priority for the moment, I understand that. But after the *Trompe L'oeil*?'

'Umm.' I looked at Reuben. 'There's the place at the asylum.'

'I'm starting tomorrow,' Reuben said, narrowing his eyes at me, daring me to contradict him. 'Well. Yes. Okay, we should be free after that.'

'So will you do it?'

A little voice whispered in my head: *Alice came from the river, the truth is to be found on the river, and I want to know the truth.*

'Yes, Max,' I said. 'I will.'

* * *

I was exhausted, but I forced my eyes to stay open long enough to take another look at Mum's diary. A few pages on from the sketch of the ghost was another one. This time she had drawn a barrel floating on the surface of a river—I could see the red gums along the bank—and underneath she had written 'Alice'.

I closed the book and lay down. Despite feeling so tired my thoughts were whirling, not just with this depiction of a barrel presumably with Alice inside it, but also of Courtney's colours. I remembered what had been niggling at me. In the painting there was a vignette of Alice surrounded by strange colours. Could Alice see colours, too? Auras. Was this gift at the heart of her fame as The Child? And if so what had it to do with my daughter?

Sleep dragged me down at last. I felt as if I was sinking. Down, into dark water. Fresh river water. Murky, with just a brushstroke of sunlight. Then I knew where I was. I was inside a wooden barrel, riding low on the river's surface.

I tried to push my way out, hitting and punching at the curved wooden planks until my hands were bruised and bleeding, but I was too small, too weak.

No escape.

The barrel was sinking. My clothes clung wetly to me and I wasn't wearing shoes. My boots, I'd left my boots behind. My throat hurt so badly where he'd tried to strangle me and my thoughts slipped backwards to his hands, squeezing ever tighter. He'd thought I was dead and there was darkness for a time and then I'd awoken and someone was cradling me in his arms. Him, the man in the back-yard, and there'd been yellow all around him, like a sunflower. He'd lifted me up and carried me, with tears running down his cheeks, and he'd lowered me into the barrel.

Water sloshed against my face, my mouth, bringing me back to my predicament. I was choking and gagging. I was drowning.

With a hoarse cry I woke up.

I was lying on my stomach, my face pressed into the pillow, and the quilt was twisted around my legs. For a moment I just lay there, breathing hard, still caught up in the dreadfulness of the nightmare.

I'd been dreaming of Alice but it was more than that. I'd become Alice, and I knew that this was what had happened to her. A little girl in a barrel left to die.

The air felt heavy, and my nose twitched. I could smell peppermint. It was so strong, all around me, and now I felt as if I was drowning in that.

Then I rolled over.

He was standing by the bed, leaning over me.

Face white, eyes hollowed, fixed on me, his lank hair hanging down. No hat today. His neck seemed too long, or perhaps it was the way he was stretching it out, his face barely a book's length from mine. A gust of peppermint washed over me. It was cold. I could see my breath white in the strange silver light emanating from him.

I stared back, my body frozen to the mattress, my heart pounding with a dull heavy beat. I had never been so frightened in my life, but as the moments stretched on and he didn't move, my mind began slowly to function again.

My mother had tried to ask him what he wanted. Could I do it? Did I dare?

'What do you want?' I thought I spoke aloud, but maybe the words were just in my head.

He was still there and now I could see his eyes weren't just hollows, they were sunken into his face, but they were still eyes. Dark eyes, full of light, full of . . .

He was crying.

Horrified, I watched as the tears spilled over and slid down his gaunt cheeks. Just like in my dream. His mouth gave a tremor, opened as if he wanted to give vent to whatever emotions were tearing at him. 'Protect.' The word was a whisper that seemed to come from all around me.

And then he was gone.

I lay there for a long time, telling myself it was a dream, nothing but a dream. But it hadn't felt like a dream. Neither of tonight's experiences had felt like I was dreaming. He'd carried Alice to the barrel and then he'd been here, beside my bed. He'd been as real as me . . . well not quite perhaps, there'd been a sense that if I reached out to touch him my hand would go straight through. But the tears had seemed real enough. Heartbreaking actually. Not that I still didn't feel absolutely petrified of him.

But I also felt sorry for him.

* * *

The day got better as we drove north, out of the growing sprawl that was Melbourne. Max tuned the radio to Classical FM and I was grateful for the soothing music. I didn't want to talk. I hadn't told him about the visit last night from the ghost, I hadn't told anyone, and I was very glad Courtney would be staying at Ben's over the weekend. The thought of my daughter waking up to what I'd seen didn't bear thinking of.

And yet the word he had spoken remained with me. *Protect*. Did that mean he was here to protect us? A guardian spirit of some kind? I'd brought Mum's last diary with me so that I could finish reading it and maybe find another clue.

It had been Reuben's idea we go away. He said he wanted me to spend some time in Echuca, on the river, and see what I thought. I had a feeling he also wanted to get back to work without me tsking over his shoulder.

We stopped for a coffee and sandwiches in the historic town of Castlemaine, but quickly got going again. We'd been late starting and Max wanted to get home to check on the *Ariadne* and his brother. Max seemed to assume I was staying with him. He was talking about the view he had every morning from his front verandah and how much I'd love it.

So I just let it go and tried not to worry, for once going with the flow. These days I was always worried, always trying to be in control. Maybe it would do me good to let someone else be in charge.

Max took us over the river without stopping in Echuca, and I looked down through the iron struts of the bridge at the brown water, moving sluggishly between its treed banks.

'We're over the border now,' he said, 'in New South Wales.'

He turned off the main highway onto a side road, and explained that this was State Forest or reserved forest, and he lived beyond it. A little further on and he reached a dirt track and turned where there was a mailbox hanging on a metal post, with 'Taylor' written on it. We went a little way further on and suddenly there was a house, low, with a wraparound verandah, and close-cut lawn all about it. A few native shrubs were dotted here and there, and taller trees further back.

'The clearing around the house is for bushfire protection,' Max said, seeing the direction of my gaze. 'Not that we've had one for a few years, but you never know. The house has stood here for a long time, and I have every hope it'll still be here when I'm gone.'

I got out of the jeep, stretching, breathing in the sharp smell of the bush. Birds were singing and I could hear the lap of the river somewhere in front of me, beyond the house.

'Does Kenny live here, too?'

Max was getting our bags out. 'No, he has a place in town. Wouldn't want to cramp his style.'

I smiled but I was thinking, so it's just Max and me, alone, together. Am I comfortable with that? Is that what I want?

Inside the house it was all polished wooden floors and cream-coloured walls, with ceiling fans fixed to the high plaster ceilings. 'Been in the family for over a hundred years,' he said, in answer to my question. 'In the old days the Taylors used to run a sheep station up river, but they retired closer to the town. We've been here ever since.'

I stood and looked out at the view. Glass doors led onto the back verandah and beyond that the lawn and shrubs ended at the river. I could see a narrow white jetty and tied to it a small motor boat. The river seemed broader here, and there was bushland on the opposite bank, the Victorian side of the border.

'It's beautiful.' I sighed. 'So peaceful.'

'Not so peaceful in the summer holidays with the boats roaring along the river. Plenty of water skiers, too, and jet skis. But yes, it's beautiful. I'm lucky to be here, don't think I don't know that.'

I thought I'd like to wander down to the jetty and sit there, watching the world go by. Drink a cold glass of white wine and simply enjoy the moment.

But Max had other ideas.

'Right.' He was standing behind me. 'I think we should go into town and meet up with Kenny, and then we'll go out to dinner. What do you say?'

I gave up my dream of a peaceful evening and said it sounded good.

'I'll show you your room. No need to dress up. You're fine as you are.'

My room faced onto a garden at the side of the house. Wire fencing guarded a few vegetables that looked in need of water and a row of bare roses. I also had French windows giving out onto the verandah that encircled the entire house.

'Kangaroos, possums, wallabies, you name it, they love my vegie garden,' Max said with a laugh. He set down my bag and glanced around, as if checking everything was in order. The room was sparsely furnished, the bed, table and wardrobe in dark timber, with fabrics in pale or white colours. A colourful handmade rug lay on the floor.

'Thank you.' I put my arms around his neck. He rested his hands on my hips and smiled down at me, but he didn't seem inclined to follow up on my invitation. A quick kiss and he moved away towards the door.

'See you in a moment, then?' he said.

'Sure.' I tried not to be disappointed as he closed the door. Maybe he wasn't interested in sleeping with me. Maybe this was now a purely business relationship. Yet those weren't the vibes I'd been getting from him. I supposed I should be grateful he didn't toss me onto the bed and strip me bare, but I admit I had been hoping for a bit of ravishing.

I quickly freshened up and changed into jeans and a red sweater. It was a few degrees warmer up here but it was still winter. I brushed my hair, but the curls seemed wilder than usual, so I fastened them back with clips, and put on some mascara and lip gloss. He'd said not to dress up, I reminded myself, with a critical look in the mirror.

Before I knew it we were in the jeep again. Max appeared to be deep in thought and I wondered what was going through his head. We both had a tendency to over-think things, I decided. Perhaps that was our trouble. We'd worry our relationship away before it even got a chance to get started.

According to Max, Moama was the town on the New South Wales side of the river while Echuca was its Victorian neighbour. A thriving place, it was busier than when we'd come through earlier, and we had to wait at some traffic lights before heading over the bridge. Max reached over and took my hand.

'Annie, I don't want to put any pressure on you,' he began. 'I don't expect . . .'

'I know, and thank you for being a gentleman, I appreciate it. But . . .' I leaned over and kissed the corner of his mouth. He smelt wonderful and his skin was so warm I wanted to cuddle into him.

He turned his head slightly and his mouth was on mine. We were so busy kissing the car behind us had to toot its horn when the light turned green.

'Mmm,' he said with a grin. 'That was nice.'

I laughed as we crossed the bridge back into Echuca. It might be a business holiday, but it looked like we'd be mixing business with pleasure after all.

CHAPTER THIRTY-SEVEN

The Girl's Story

The little *Ariadne*'s wheels churned the water of the Murray. Alongside them the bushland had changed, become less civilised. Tree branches hung over the river, whose draft was low but not low enough to stop the boat. They'd passed few other paddle-steamers and barges. This was not the time of year to be carrying bales of wool or wheat or timber to the port to be loaded onto the trains, or to carry supplies back out to the settlements and stations. The riverboat captains would be waiting out the summer, waiting for the snow to melt and the ensuing flood of water—the Spring Rise—to come downriver and make it once more safe to travel.

Alice, gazing at the passing scenery, thought that the settlements along the river were few and far between. Webster's station was still there, somewhere up ahead, but it didn't belong to the Websters anymore.

Captain Potter told her it had been sold years ago, and he wasn't even sure who now owned it. 'Probably some fellow from down south,' he'd huffed, 'who's put in a crew to run it for him.'

Alice only had vague memories of the station. The children staring, the concern on Mrs Webster's face when they'd stripped her and saw what they were dealing with. She had wanted to escape back to the *Ariadne* as quickly as possible, but she'd had to wait until it was dark before sneaking out.

Now, hearing voices, she lifted up her face towards the wheelhouse and saw Captain Potter and Rosey. He was pointing something out to her along the riverbank and she was leaning close, her pretty face rapt in concentration. It occurred to her that Captain Potter might fall in love with Rosey, many men did, and she wasn't sure how she felt about that. Molly had been the love of his life, she was sure. Did anyone recover from losing the love of their life in such tragic circumstances?

Anyway, there was Josh, wasn't there? She could see him seated in the sun on the side deck, legs sprawled out in front of him, bent over the sketchbook resting on his lap. His head was hidden by the straw hat that shaded him from a sun that was already making the air steamy, but every now and then he'd look up.

She supposed he was drawing. Little sketches he might turn into a painting. He seemed much happier here than he'd been in Melbourne, and Alice was glad he'd accepted her invitation to join them. Last night he'd told her and Gilbert about Mrs Whistler ousting Mrs Stuart from The Goldminer. He made it sound funny, but Alice was glad she'd missed it. Arguments always made her feel slightly ill.

As if she'd conjured him up, Gilbert sat down beside her and she turned to him with a smile. His face was a little pink despite his broad-brimmed hat, and his eyes were narrowed against the glare. 'I wonder if I'm doing the right thing,' she said, words she'd been mulling over while she sat here. 'I may find out who I am, who *he* is, but what if it makes things worse?'

'The truth can only make it better, Alice,' he soothed. Dear Gilbert, he always said the right thing. He took her hand in his and she left it there, despite their palms both becoming uncomfortably hot and damp.

The *Ariadne* was not a large vessel and there were no cabins, so at night when they tied up by the bank, they would sleep on the deck or in tents by the riverbank. Captain Potter slept in a hammock. The summer weather meant it was no hardship to be outdoors, and Alice found she quite liked waking up and gazing at the stars.

More memories were coming to her, but fleeting, slipping into her mind and out again before she could grasp hold of them. Trees and people and a wooden hut with spiders in the corners. A woman with a soft voice who tried to be her mother but wasn't, and a man who looked like her father but wasn't. It was all very strange. She should be able to use her second sight, her gift, to show her the way, but the truth was that since that night at The Goldminer Hotel, when the man in the dark coat found her, her gift had been strangely absent.

At first she'd been plagued with *his* thoughts invading her own, bombarding her with messages that made no sense and frightened her. Then, quite suddenly, everything had shut down. Gone.

Alice didn't think it had really gone. It would never be gone completely. And sometimes she could feel the buzzing at the back of her head that meant it was still there, biding its time. But for now it was definitely taking a holiday.

That was the only reason Gervais had eventually let them go. He'd been furious on the night of The Goldminer's grand opening, when Alice had told him his wife was coming on a ship—he hadn't believed her, or perhaps hadn't wanted to. The following day she'd explained to him that she couldn't do the shows anyway, not at the moment, because she'd lost the sight. That had made him even more furious. But now, according to Josh, his wife, Emily, had arrived and he'd probably be too busy to care about Alice.

The man in the dark coat was locked up in the Kew Asylum. Gilbert said he was being looked after and that Alice could visit him if she liked, but she'd shaken her head emphatically.

She didn't want to see him, not yet. Perhaps not ever.

More voices. Calling to her. Alice looked up sharply and then smiled when she saw it was only some children standing in the shade of the trees, waving at them. They looked like ragamuffins, but she supposed they came from somewhere. A farm further in the bush, or a town hidden by the trees. She turned to Gilbert.

'Captain Potter says we'll reach the Websters' homestead today. He's worried about the depth of the river—sandbars.'

Gilbert nodded.

'He says he can run the *Ariadne* at the smaller ones, get up a head of steam and get her right over the top of them by sheer brute force. But the larger sandbars . . . we could be stuck until another boat comes along to tow us off. Or the river rises. But for that we'd have to wait until spring.'

Gilbert's hazel eyes crinkled into a smile. 'Getting stuck with you doesn't sound so terrible, Alice. In fact, I believe I would quite enjoy it.'

'I think I'd quite enjoy it, too,' she murmured, smiling back.

Alice loved Gilbert. She thought she'd loved him for a long time. She hoped he loved her as much, but if he didn't, well, Alice could cope with that. She had enough love for them both.

* * *

'We thought she was dead at first.'

Captain Potter's hands were clamped on the wheel, eyes staring out at the river ahead. He was telling Rosey about the day he'd saved Alice from the river.

'Her little hands were blue with cold. We thought she was a goner. Then she came back to life. Bluey,' he gave a half-smile, 'he was my mate. Bluey was so excited he couldn't keep still. Anyway, we decided to take her to the homestead—the Websters'—and leave her there, in case someone came looking for her. No one seemed to know who she was or where she came from. So I did that. But the poor little mite didn't want me to leave her, she clung to my hand. But . . . Well, I thought I was doing the right thing.'

'And you left her?' Rosey tried to lighten her tone, not to sound judgemental, but this was Alice they were talking about. Dear, sweet Alice.

He nodded. 'I did. But she was back again that night, staring out of the wheelhouse at me like a possum in a gum tree. I couldn't force her to go back. Didn't have the heart for it. So we took her with us, to Echuca. I gave her to Molly.'

'And no one knew her at the Websters'?'

'Nope. Not a whisper. And I can tell you that when a child goes missing out here everyone knows. Eventually. Word travels at a slow pace in some parts but it does travel. Anyway, we still thought we might hear. So we waited. Nothing. And as far as I know there never has been.'

Rosey thought a moment. It seemed remarkable that a small girl could go missing and no one cared. She wondered what Alice would feel if they found nothing. If her past remained a mystery, apart, that is, from the man locked away in Kew Asylum. And, according to Gilbert, he wasn't saying anything that made the slightest bit of sense.

She stepped out of the wheelhouse into the sun, lifting her parasol to shade her face. Down below on the deck she could see Josh, sketching. It was as if he was in his own world, totally focused on his work. As if he sensed her gaze, he looked up and saw her watching him. He grinned, and gave her a wave with the pencil in his hand.

'I'm going to paint us on the *Ariadne*,' he called. 'You wait and see. It'll be my best yet.'

Rosey smiled back. What was there about him that tugged at emotions she'd thought long buried? She must be insane to contemplate a life with him, probably penniless, living in squalor, and yet . . . There was love, and the simple joy of being with someone who made you happy.

Impatient with herself, her gaze moved on to Alice and Gilbert at the stern of the boat, and she noticed they were holding hands. At least Alice had Gilbert, at least she had that.

'She dreams in Gaelic.' She said it aloud. 'I thought it was Irish, but now I know it's Scots Gaelic. Like the man in the asylum.'

Captain Potter seemed to be contemplating her words. 'Molly used to say that Alice spoke English as if it wasn't really her true language. Bluey thought she was German, but maybe he'd never heard Gaelic.'

'Were there any Gaels around here? Highlanders, maybe, or from the Islands?'

'There was a settlement . . . let me think . . .' But in the end he sighed and shook his head. 'I heard something once about a settlement of strange-speaking people, a timber camp in the red gum forests down the river. Might have been Koondrook way. But of course the floods washed away a lot of the settlements the year you and Alice left.'

Rosey stared. 'Floods?'

'Didn't you know? There was a monumental flood that year. The wharf was nearly underwater, if you can believe it. Moama, across the river from Echuca, was all but destroyed. And the settlements along the river, well, it took houses, stock, and plenty of people drowned.'

Rosey and Alice had had other things to worry about that year. She tried to imagine the river in flood, a massive, deadly rush of murky, brown water taking all before it.

'So it's possible that this settlement, if it ever existed, isn't there now?'

Gloomily, Captain Potter agreed.

So this journey may be a waste of time after all. Poor Alice.

* * *

It was evening when they reached the point of the river where the station pier jutted out from the bank. A large painted sign told them they had reached 'Webster's'—despite the fact that the Webster family no longer owned it the station had retained its original name. Captain Potter had hopes the Websters might still be in the area somewhere, but they all knew this entire journey was based on some very tenuous hopes.

It was too late to find their way up to the homestead, and they cooked their meal over the fire Captain Potter lit on the bank and settled down to sleep. Or tried to. The night seemed interminable, animals rustling in the bush, owls startling them with their harsh hunting cries, and the soft lapping of the river. By the time dawn came they were well and truly ready to eat a quick breakfast and set out.

'The track looks different,' Captain Potter said, 'although I haven't been here for years. Wider. I remember things being a bit less well organised.'

'I remember the moon,' Alice said. 'Showing me the way back to the *Ariadne*.'

Gilbert squeezed her hand.

As opposed to the track, the homestead appeared neglected. There were no signs of a woman's touch and some of the outside boards had fallen off, leaving gaps in the walls. No curtains hung at the windows, and there was some wet and dripping clothing hanging to dry over the verandah railing.

'Hey! Anyone here!' the captain called.

There were some horses standing in a yard made from roughly stripped timber, and now they began to move restlessly. Someone appeared from a hut behind the yard and started towards them with an easy stride. It was a stockman, dark-skinned, looking curious.

'You want something, boss?'

Captain Potter answered. 'Yes. I want to talk to whoever's in charge.'

'Well, that'd be me,' the man said, clearly proud of his position. 'The rest of 'em are off working. I stayed behind to cook up a big supper for them when they get home.'

He seemed even more proud of that and Rosey smiled, catching his attention. She stepped up to him and Alice went with her, thinking he looked friendly enough, though perhaps a bit surprised that the men in the group were letting a woman take charge.

'Do you know the Websters who used to own this station? Do you know where we might find them?'

He scratched his head. 'That mob that used to be here? They went home, over the sea. The missus got sick, wanted to go, so they did.'

Alice's face fell in disappointment. She was about to turn and walk away at that moment, but Rosey wasn't ready to give up and she gently held Alice's arm to keep her near.

'I don't know if you were around here at the time, but years ago there was a girl saved from the river. She was floating in a barrel and Captain Potter here rescued her and took her back to Echuca,' Rosey said.

The boy—he was more boy than man—nodded, his dark eyes shining with excitement. 'Yeah, I remember. I lived with my mob down the river a bit, in the forest there. We heard about it.'

Alice placed her hand over Rosey's and clasped it tightly.

Rosey tried not to show her excitement, it seemed somehow important to keep calm, to accept this may be nothing after all. And it was important to not let Alice get her hopes up.

'Do you know where the girl came from?'

Another scratch of the head. 'My mob heard of another mob, white fellas, living in the forest a few miles from us. Towards Koondrook. Timber getters, you know? They kept to 'emselves. Word was she might've come from there.'

'Did anyone ever ask them?' Captain Potter sounded angry. 'If you knew something shouldn't you have told us so that we could find the girl's family?'

The boy shrugged.

Rosey couldn't let it rest there. 'But surely if she did go missing from there, they would've looked for her? Asked around for her? Wouldn't they be frantic with worry?'

He shrugged again, clearly not agreeing but not wanting to contradict her outright. 'Kids go missing, they die,' he said evenly. 'Fact of life here, missus.'

Rosey didn't know what to say in the face of such fatalism. Alice was staring at him, as though she were trying to will him to tell her more. What a time for her sight to go missing, thought Rosey.

'These people, the white fellas. Are they still around? Can you give us directions?' Captain Potter snapped it out, but the boy was unimpressed.

'I could, but I dunno if they're still there. The flood washed 'em out.'

The flood, Rosey thought with a sigh. Of course.

In the end he gave them directions as best he could, and they made their way back to the *Ariadne*. Captain Potter seemed angry and perturbed, and Rosey was feeling depressed. Alice had let go of her hand and Gilbert was helping her over some rough ground as if she was made of glass.

'Not time to give up yet.' Josh's voice at her side.

'But what if this is all we ever find out?' Rosey lowered her own voice so that Alice couldn't hear. 'About who she was? What if we think she may have been one those white fellas in the settlement near Koondrook but we never know for sure?'

'And what if we meet those people and they tell us exactly who Alice is,' he retorted. 'Wait and see before you give up, Rosey.' He glanced at her under the brim of her bonnet and shook his head. 'You didn't used to be such a pessimist.'

Rosey gave him a glare and stalked ahead. *Didn't I?* she was thinking. *Well, perhaps not, but I was a big fool, dreaming about finding gold and running off to Melbourne and marrying a rich miner. All those things I was going to do! And I've done some of them, I've led an amazing life really. We both have, me and Alice.*

But there were sad memories, too. Regrets. Sometimes she missed her mother. She missed Cork. And as she'd grown older it was as if she dwelt more on them. Was it always that way? Did people always regret the things they'd done or hadn't done as they got older? Rosey was sure she hadn't been like that when she was younger.

She wondered what she would be like in another ten years, twenty . . . More regrets, or would she look back and smile and think: *There, I did it. I lived my life exactly as I wanted to?*

When Josh caught her up, she allowed him to take her arm and she even gave him a little smile to show him he was forgiven. She couldn't be cross with Josh for long. It was just another one of those disturbing facts she'd discovered about herself when it came to him.

'Will we go to this place in the forest?' Alice's doubtful voice drifted back to her, and then Captain Potter's determined reply. 'Alice, I promise you I will do everything possible to find this place, and to find those people, and to find out who *you* are. I know how important it is to you. I've sworn it on Molly's memory.'

And he put his arm about her and pulled her close.

Rosey found that the ground before her had blurred, and it was only when Josh handed her his typically paint-stained handkerchief that she realised she was crying.

For Alice, for Captain Potter, and for herself.

CHAPTER THIRTY-EIGHT

Annie's Story

I turned over in the bed. Max was lying on his back, legs and arms thrown out like a child. His rumpled hair and unshaven jaw made me want to reach over and trace my fingers over his skin. He was even more attractive in his sleep than he was awake. Last night—our first night—had been wonderful, no awkwardness, and with plenty of sexual chemistry. Plenty of laughter, too.

If two people could laugh and talk even in their most intimate moments then there must be a real connection of minds and hearts and bodies. That was what I thought anyway.

The curtains on the windows were thin and the morning light shone through, illuminating his sparsely furnished bedroom. Max seemed to go for uncluttered in a big way, and I wondered how he would deal with my stuff, and with Courtney and her endless parade of stuffed animals. Not, I supposed, that I was going to move in straightaway or anything, but if I moved up here and our relationship deepened, well . . . it was on the cards.

So many things we had to sort out if—and it was a big if—I agreed to come up here and work on his boat.

Last night we'd gone down to the wharf to meet Kenny and the *Ariadne*, and I'd enjoyed being on the paddle-steamer again. Kenny had welcomed me aboard and we'd gone out with the last lot of passengers. This time I'd sat in the stern, a glass of champagne in my hand, and watched the flicker of the lengthening shadows on the water.

Max and Kenny had kept up a constant banter as they tidied up the *Ariadne* for the night. She was due out again tomorrow, but Kenny was still in charge. 'I need a break,' Max informed him. 'I need to keep sharp.'

Kenny snorted. 'You need to loll around with Annie, you mean. Do I get a pay rise?'

'A good captain does the work for love.'

It went on like that as we climbed into the car and Max drove us out of town to a restaurant. It was an old homestead that someone had turned into an eatery, but there were tables outside in the garden and no one was overly dressed up. Max and Kenny knew the owners, and they introduced me. Everyone was very friendly and I enjoyed myself, laughing with the two brothers, watching the other guests in the garden. Children were running between the hedges of a maze, playing chasey, and I realised that I was missing Courtney.

Courtney would love it here. And it wasn't as if we were that far away from Melbourne; she could still see her friends. Although, I suppose if we did move north then eventually, as time went on, we'd go to Melbourne less and less. It just seemed to be the way when you made a move, despite all your good intentions. I realised I was assuming we were going to permanently move the business away from Melbourne. Of course it didn't need to be like that, but Echuca was as good a base as any, and I could take commissions anywhere in the country. I knew of other firms like ours who travelled to jobs. Reuben and I would still be in demand, we could still pick and choose the work we wanted.

'Hello.'

Max had woken up and was watching me with a smile. His blue eyes were warm and direct and he reached out to brush my cheek with the backs of his fingers.

I smiled back. 'Hello.'

My libido was kicking in again and I met him halfway as he rolled towards me. This was the life, I thought, before all thoughts left my head and I simply concentrated on feeling. His big hand on my breast, his warm breath against my cheek, the taut muscles of his thigh as he slid it between mine. Oh yes, I could get used to this.

* * *

'I thought we might go for a ride on the river.'

We were sitting on the back verandah, drinking coffee and eating toast, while at the bottom of the garden the river went on its peaceful way. Several birds had arrived for crumbs, and I'd been particularly fascinated with two grey currawongs, with their white-tipped tails and yellow eyes. Max had his long legs up resting on the railing and gave a massive stretch of his arms and back.

I laughed. 'You don't look like you want to do anything.'

He caught my eye, gave me a wicked grin. 'There's something I'd very much like to do, but maybe later. Right now I think we should just relax on the river. Do you fish?'

'Uh-uh.' I shook my head. 'Can't stand putting the bait on the hook.'

'Okay then, we won't fish, we'll just drift. Sound good? And when we've had lunch I'll take you to the shipyard where I'll be bringing the *Queen of the Rivers* for repairs.'

'Tell me about her,' I said, biting into my toast.

Max put his hands behind his head and leaned dangerously far back in his chair. 'She could carry twenty passengers in her day. She'd pick up the squatters at Echuca or wherever and take them home to their stations along the Murray, sometimes the Darling, if there was enough water in it, and very occasionally the Murrumbidgee. The Murrumbidgee's always been a riverboat captain's nightmare. She has an upper and lower deck, roomy cabins for the squatters and smaller shared cabins for the plebs. A dining room—I believe they used to serve up five meals a day and expect every scrap to be eaten. Oh and she's a stern-wheel paddle-steamer. Think of the boats on the Mississippi in America.'

'Like in *Gone with the Wind* or *Maverick*? Gambling boats?'

He gave me a resigned look. 'I see you have a lot to learn, Annie.'

I giggled. 'Sorry. I know what you mean. She sounds wonderful, Max, and I can't wait to meet her. When are you going up to Wentworth to get her?'

'Might take a while. She's been in dry dock for so long we need to examine her closely before we put her under any stress. But I'm hoping by the end of the year? And it would be good if you and Reuben could come and take a look, too, work out a plan for the restoration.'

After breakfast we headed out in Max's motor boat, slowly at first, and then picking up speed. The bush flashed by and I enjoyed seeing the ever-changing scenery. Water birds on the bank watched us pass, and the trees were full of colourful parrots, pink galahs and white cockatoos. It already felt as if it was going to be a good day, the sky more blue than cloudy, but it was chilly on the water and I was glad I'd worn a sweater.

Max pointed out the red gums. 'They're magnificent trees, but with the recent drought and increased irrigation, they're under stress. Did you know they're known as widow-makers because they drop boughs without warning during hot weather or times of drought?'

'Nice.' I looked up the mottled brown-and-grey trunks with their strange patterns, to the canopies of blue-grey leaves. Some of the trees had tipped over from their precarious hold on the bank and into the river, and there were others with huge branches stretching out to the sky.

'The forests were full of timber getters once, hundreds of them. Red gum was used for railway sleepers as well as fence posts. It was pretty much rot free and lasted for ages, so there was a big demand for it. The logs won't float, so they were loaded onto barges and hauled back up river by riverboats like the *Ariadne*, or else the barges were floated down river to Echuca to the sawmills. And during the boom times there were smaller sawmills along the riverbanks, too. It was a huge business before things took a dive in the early part of the twentieth century.'

'Do you think Captain Potter used to carry red gum logs when he owned the *Ariadne*?'

'Maybe. Or he could've carried bales of wool from the sheep stations. There was plenty of work in those days, the paddle-steamers would be flat out as soon as the snow melted up at the head of the river. The water came flowing down, lifting the draft for the boats, and they would be working until autumn when the level of the river dropped again.'

'Do they still cut timber in the forests?'

'It's managed, but yes they do. Some of the Barmah Forest land is a national park, managed by the original owners, the Yorta Yorta Nation. Took them nearly thirty years to have their right to own land proved in the courts. Everyone is fighting over the river these days, the environmentalists and the irrigators. The red gum forests need to be flooded every so often, to keep the trees alive, but if they take too much water out of the river to irrigate then it won't flood.'

'So do you sit on the environmental fence?'

'Probably, although I can see both sides. But if we destroy the river then what do we have left? We have to look after it.'

I thought about what he'd said as the river slipped by, but of course my thoughts soon reverted to Alice.

'Do you think the timber-getter's camp in the *Trompe L'oeil* is in there somewhere?' I murmured, gazing at the trees. 'Was Alice living here once upon a time?'

Max had slowed and now he began to turn the boat about, heading back the way we'd come. 'I suppose she could've been. It makes sense. But we'll probably never know for sure, Annie. Alice is going to remain a mystery in a lot of ways. Do you think you can live with that?'

Could I? I thought I could. I was aware that I'd never discover everything there was to know about Alice and Rosey. Too many years had gone by. And anyway, if I knew every little thing about them, wouldn't I spoil the story for myself? It was good to have a little mystery.

'Yep,' I said at last. 'I can live with that.'

* * *

We had lunch at a restaurant beside the river in town, with long glass windows looking directly onto the river and the paddle-steamers chugging by. Afterwards, Max took me to the shipyard, and confused me with talk about dry docks and boilers and deck planks. He met up with one of the men who worked there, and, after introducing me, they proceeded to have a long, serious talk about Max's new project.

I was more than happy to wander about on my own, but by the time Max was finished, I was also glad to climb back into the jeep and head for home.

'Do you mind if I stop for a minute?' he said, when we were nearly at the bridge. 'I have to make a pick-up.'

I didn't mind and watched as Max jumped out of the car, saying he'd be a moment, before striding around the back of a small house with a lush garden. He returned a few minutes later with a medium-sized dog on a lead. When he opened the back door the dog leapt in, panting with excitement.

'This is Matilda,' he said, giving me a wry smile. 'She's a Kelpie. A friend was looking after her while I was away. I don't like leaving her at the property by herself.'

'Hello, Matilda,' I said, and at the sound of her name the dog stretched up for a pat.

Max had opened the window halfway down at the back, and as we drove along Matilda stuck her head out, her tongue flapping in the breeze.

'Feel like going out again for dinner?' Max asked. 'Or do you want to eat in?'

'I think I'd like to eat in,' I said, and thought how comfortable we sounded already. As if we'd been together for years. Riding along in the dusty Jeep with the dog in the back, talking about dinner. Was it a good thing to be so comfortable? I glanced at Max with his sunglasses on, staring at the road ahead, his sleeves rolled up over his forearms, his hair tousled by the draft from the open window.

A tingle ran through my body, and I thought I might let dinner wait a bit longer when we got home. Time for a quick visit to the bedroom.

Oh yes, I thought, being with Max was a very good thing.

CHAPTER THIRTY-NINE

The Girl's Story

Koondrook was a small town on the Murray River. For nearly forty years it was mainly concerned with sawmilling and timber-getting, but now it was becoming a centre for the settlers in the area. Across the river in New South Wales was Barham, another sawmilling town, and the two were linked by a punt.

The *Ariadne* had tied up at the Koondrook jetty in the heat of the day and Alice and Rosey were content to sit in the cool of the covered stern of the boat, while Gilbert read a book and Josh sketched the scenery.

After some hours of waiting, Captain Potter returned to the *Ariadne* accompanied by an older gentleman with white hair and a beard. Mr Duggan was his name, and he came aboard and sat with them in the stern of the boat, his blue eyes flicking from one to the other, curious, wary.

'I don't know what I can tell ye,' he said, in a broad Scots accent. 'It was all a long time ago now.'

'But you used to take supplies to some of the logging communities in the red gum forests?' Captain Potter prompted him.

'We're interested in a community of Gaelic-speaking Scots. My step-daughter, Alice,' and he smiled at her, 'may have come from there when she was a little child.'

Duggan fixed Alice with a curious look. 'Oh aye?'

The silence lengthened. Obviously, the man wasn't going to give up any secrets. He had a suspicion of strangers which was probably natural in these isolated places. One stuck to one's own kind and newcomers weren't to be trusted.

Alice leaned forward, her own blue eyes intent.

'Mr Duggan, please help me. You see, I don't know who I am. I'm a foundling. But I think I may be related to these people. Do you think you can show us where they lived in the forest? I might be able remember it if I see it. Please.'

Tough as he appeared Duggan seemed to be touched by her request. He gave her a brisk nod. 'Aye, I'll show ye. For what good it'll do ye,' he added in a mutter.

Alice and Rosey exchanged glances, and Alice shook her head. She could see Rosey was itching to give the man a piece of her mind, but it would only make him more difficult than he already was.

'They're all gone now,' Duggan went on. 'You'll find nothing.'

All gone . . . Alice sighed. 'Still, I might find something. I might remember something.'

His beetle brows came down and he fixed her with a frowning look. 'Ye have a look of them, those people in the forest. Aye, there's something about ye that reminds me of them.'

The red gum forests often flooded, whole lakes of trees rising from the water, their trunks partially submerged. In the summer the lower water levels turned the forests into islands. Mr Duggan explained there were hundreds of timber getters at a time, living on the islands in company with snakes and kangaroos, all seeking higher ground.

'Aye, it was a rough life,' he said. 'But some prefer to be isolated from others. The people you're talking of, they were strangers more than most. And they wanted to be together. A bit like the old clans, if you know what I mean, but they were like that. They preferred their own company.'

The *Ariadne* nosed along the bank and came to a channel. It was deep enough for them to follow it a short distance into the forest. Alice looked up at the huge old trees overhanging them, while the bank was dotted with the stumps of others that had been cut down by the loggers. Captain Potter kept a sharp eye out for snags and enlisted Gilbert's help with the sounding pole, to measure the depth of the water.

'We can't go much further,' he warned, eyes creased beneath the brim of his flat cap. 'I can't risk getting stuck.'

Eventually, under Duggan's direction, they tied up.

The air was hot and steamy, flies buzzed and mosquitoes, breeding in the watery forest, swarmed around them. The ground was overgrown and uneven, very little left of human habitation, and they picked their way carefully, following the old Scotsman.

Rosey waved her hands in front of her face, then used her folded parasol to try to frighten away the insects. But Alice seemed not to notice. She was too busy looking around her, breathing in the ambiance of the place, trying to drag the memories from the deepest, darkest places in her mind.

Then they came to what remained of the hut.

That was when Alice reached out to Gilbert, who'd been keeping close, and clung hard to his arm. 'I know this place,' she whispered. Despite the changes the years, and the flood, had made, she recognised it. She had been here. It was here she had lived and mourned for . . . for . . . But Alice shook her head. She still couldn't remember, not properly, nevertheless the sensation of coming home was strong.

'It's abandoned,' she heard Rosey say with dismay, and Josh's murmured reply. He'd brought his sketchbook and was busy recording their visit.

Alice remembered the light coming through the gaps in the walls and the spiders in the corners. The hut was falling down, its shape half hidden by encroaching scrub and weeds. There were more weeds where there used to be a productive little vegetable garden. She had a sudden image of chickens running, the flower heads from the finished crops rustling in the wind, and the mournful cries of birds drifting across the water.

'Are you all right?' Gilbert bent close but she shook her head and moved away from him.

Despite loving him as she did, right now she needed to be alone with her thoughts.

'Where did they all go?' Rosey's voice floated in the stifling air.

Alice heard her and yet she seemed far away. They were all far away. She was alone in the past.

'The flood came through,' Duggan said, his voice a darker rumble. 'Those it didn't drown left. They scattered, I wouldn't know where now. Once their community was broken they were too frightened to come back. The flood, it was a fearsome thing.'

Alice could feel the roar of the water getting higher, tearing through the camp, swallowing up the people and carrying them away. Her sight might have left her, but she had imagination enough to know what the flood had done. She shivered, cold, despite the heat.

'Isn't there someone who knew the people here?' This was Rosey's plaintive question. 'There were so many of them, surely there's someone left?'

Duggan rumbled something but Alice couldn't hear. She sat on a stump, eyes closed, far away. She had been here, she felt it deep inside herself. This is where she'd come from, this is where the man in the dark coat had caught her and carried her, and it was from here that the barrel had set out on its journey.

Annella?

The voice was close to her, a breath of sound in the stillness. She felt someone take her hand, gently, and opened her eyes. He was sitting at her feet, dark eyes fixed on her face, his coat dusty and stained from long hours helping the others in the forest. He never took it off. It had been given to him by the laird, a hand-me-down, nothing grand. A gift to the poor. But he treasured it.

'Hamish?' she whispered.

'Alice?'

She opened her eyes—had they been shut after all—and looked up. Captain Potter was standing before her with worried eyes, and just for a moment she didn't know whether she was in the present or the past. He put a gentle hand on her shoulder.

'Alice, Mr Duggan says there's someone left we can ask. She lived here before the flood. She's in the hospital in Echuca, and she's called Jeanie.'

CHAPTER FORTY

Annie's Story

'Do I really have to go back to Melbourne today?'

I'd sat up in the bed. Max was lying beside me, eyes closed, but he wasn't asleep. We'd just made love and it was wonderful. Each time seemed to get better. I couldn't believe how good we were together. I loved being with him, and not just in bed, and I really, really didn't want to leave.

'No.' He didn't open his eyes, just reached out a hand to touch me, his fingers gentle, reassuring.

'I've enjoyed myself so much. This is a wonderful place, Max. But yes, I do have to go home. There's Papa and Courtney, and the *Trompe L'oeil*. I have to sort out the mess I'm in.'

He sat up now, smiling as he tucked my tangled hair behind my ears. 'You know you haven't got a car. I'm going to have to drive you back.'

'Oh.' Then I shook my head. Tempting as it was, Max had a business to run. 'Thanks, but I can take the train. Or a bus.'

'I have to go down anyway. Some prices I need to check out for parts for the *Queen of the Rivers*.'

Was he just being kind? I wasn't sure, but I was so desperate for more of his company I didn't argue. In actual fact, I wasn't looking forward to being at home. The memory of the ghost had faded a little, and I'd tried hard not to think of it at all while I was here, but once I was back in my bedroom . . . What if he came back?

'You know, when you start work on the restoration of the boat you'll have to stay up here,' Max was saying. 'You can't be driving back and forth all the time. Your father tells me he likes to stay on the job.' He gave me a smile. 'Sleep, eat and live the job was what he actually said.'

I sighed. 'Do you see what I'm up against? He's a workaholic.'

'Unlike his daughter.'

I hit him, very gently. 'So, what're you saying? I should rent a place here in Echuca?' I spoke carefully, keeping myself in check. Too soon, I was thinking. We are having this conversation far too soon.

He looked as if he, too, was keeping his emotions in check. 'Or you can stay with me. You can all stay. It's a big house and there's lots of room.'

Despite expecting it, my heart gave a bump. Was Max offering to share his life with me and Courtney and Reuben? Or was he just offering me bed and board while I was working on his boat? I didn't know if I wanted to ask, pin him down. Things were lovely as they were and I didn't want to spoil it.

'I'll have to see,' I began, tentatively. 'You know there's Courtney, Max. I'd have to enrol her here. There are complications.'

'Only if you make them complications. Remember,' he leaned closer, as if he was about to tell me a secret, 'I have Matilda the dog, and it just so happens Courtney told me that what she wants most in all the world is a dog.'

I stared at him, and then I laughed. Wrapping my arms around him, I held on tight, wishing it was as simple as he seemed to think. One thing was certain, this was a man worth having, and I'd do my best to keep him.

* * *

While Max showered, I finally took out my mother's diary, and, sitting on the verandah in the cold air with the pair of hopeful currawongs looking on with their bright yellow eyes, I began to read.

There wasn't a great deal more to go to the end and I think I'd been putting it off because I knew all too well what happened. There would be no happy resolution. My mother died.

She'd written snippets about me and Reuben, hopes she had for our futures. Soon she was completely confined to bed, too weak to get up. At night she didn't sleep well, the drugs that dulled the pain left her mind wide awake. And that was when the ghost came to her.

At first he said little, watching her from the shadows, but gradually he drew closer and began to speak. His name was Hamish, he explained, and he was a guardian spirit. My mother dying was the impetus for his return. He'd come to watch over Mum and me.

That made sense and I wondered if Reuben's illness had been the reason he came to me and Courtney, but there could be other reasons, too. The failing business, the worry over the painting. The discovery of the painting itself.

And then there was the big question: Why us?

The final entry was a rambling account of a dream she'd had where Hamish was speaking to her.

He says he's an angel, but I think he means a guardian spirit. This is because he tried and failed to protect his sister and so he feels compelled to return again and again whenever there is need. I don't think he's very happy, poor soul. He wants to be free. I wish there was some way I could release him, but it's too late, I'm too weak. Maybe Annie can do it when she's older. Although I hope she never has need of him again in her life.

'Annie?'

I looked up. Max was standing in the doorway, watching me. I realised I was crying and when he opened his arms I went into them.

* * *

'I'm sorry.'

We were sitting in the kitchen and Max had made me coffee.

'There's nothing to apologise for, Annie.'

I'd mentioned the diary and then blurted out my mother's belief that Hamish was our family's guardian spirit. He didn't say much, for which I was grateful. It was something I was still coming to terms with myself. I knew there was more to the story of Hamish, but the final piece of the jigsaw was still infuriatingly absent.

There was a message on my phone when I took it out of my bag—the bag I'd forgotten all about last night in the passionate moments after we barely made it into the house. The message was from Maren and it said 'Ring' with numerous exclamation marks after the word.

'Annie, at last! I've been like a possum up a gum tree.'

It was good to laugh. 'Are you sure that's what you mean? What's happened?'

'You know I wanted to see if there was anything in the library in Perth? Anything about the painter we're looking for? Well, they had lots. His name was—'

'Josh Parker?'

Maren took a breath, sounding disappointed. 'How did you know?'

'I didn't, not really.' I quickly explained about Josh Parker and the portrait of Gervais Whistler at the National Gallery.

'Well, *he* is your man, Annie. He donated all his papers to them. Everything. Of course they couldn't let me have the originals, but they've sent me copies. And, Annie, there are preliminary sketches of the scenes in your *Trompe L'oeil*.'

Tears stung my eyes.

'Really? Sketches?'

'Yep. Lots of them. All of the ones you wanted. Annie, it's amazing. You need to see. When can you come in to the library here?'

'I'd be there in five seconds, but I'm not in Melbourne at the moment. I can be back early this afternoon.'

'Where are you?' Maren asked, puzzled.

'In Echuca. There's a job and I wanted to take a look, eh, around.' Max wriggled his eyebrows at me.

'Okay, but I think you're keeping something from me. The Annie I know doesn't rush off to Echuca when she has a painting to work on, she's far too obsessive. But never mind, you can tell me all about it when you see me. And something else. There's another painting by Josh Parker. It hangs in a gallery in Freemantle and you'll love it. Okay, I'll be in my office after two.'

'I'll see you then. And, Maren, thank you so much, this is wonderful news.'

'What's wonderful news?' Max asked. He found some bread in the freezer and slipped it into the toaster.

'That was Maren. You remember, my friend at the library? She's found some drawings of the *Trompe L'oeil* by Josh Parker. Preliminary drawings. She says they're fabulous.'

'And they show you everything? The left-hand side, too?'

'Yes, even the parts we can't see now. So I'll be able to do a complete restoration.'

Max set out butter, honey and jam, before moving to the coffee machine and pouring a cup. His silence was a little disconcerting after my good news and I eyed him uneasily before speaking again.

'Max?'

He looked up, and his eyes seemed full of doubt. 'It's good news, of course it is. You'll be able to do what you wanted. But, Annie, you're still going to have to deal with History Victoria and the minister.'

'You haven't seen me in action.'

'I hope you're right. Just be ready to fight if you have to, okay?'

'I'll be ready.'

He grinned. 'I'm happy for you,' he added. 'For us both. I can't wait to see Captain Potter in all his glory. Great publicity for the *Ariadne*, too. If it wasn't for Molly and Alice, we'd never have met.'

I felt a frisson run through me. He was right, Alice had brought us together. I owed Alice a great deal.

After breakfast we packed up the Jeep, took Matilda—looking miserable—back to her temporary home, and set out.

There was plenty to do when I got back to Melbourne, but just now I wanted to put my troubles aside. I settled back in my seat and let the stress leak out of me, taking a deep breath, and then another. I reached over and rested my hand on Max's thigh and closed my eyes.

CHAPTER FORTY-ONE

The Girl's Story

The woman's eyes were closed, her face pinched and wan. She could have been sleeping, or just lying in that limbo between life and death. The hospital was small, a private home that had been turned into a hospice. The woman at the desk inside the front door had informed them that Mrs McNeil had been getting steadily worse since she came to them from Koondrook, and no, she had no visitors. Her family, sadly, were all dead and she was the only one left.

Alice moved forward, leaving the others huddled in a group near the door. Closer, she saw that the woman was not so aged, it was just that illness made her seem so. Even without the help of the colours, Alice could see that this life was reaching its end.

'Mrs McNeil?'

The eyes flickered open. Brown, nothing like the brilliant blue of Alice's own, and she was disappointed. Mrs McNeil looked vaguely about her, as if wondering what had woken her, before noticing Alice beside her. She seemed to focus with an effort.

'Mary? Is it you?' Suddenly, she was smiling, and it was a beautiful smile.

'I'm not . . .'

'Mary, I thought never to see you again.' Her voice was soft, the s's sibilant, her Gaelic accent still strong. 'I thought you'd died on the ship.'

'Mrs McNeil, I'm sorry, my name is Alice.'

'Alice, Alice?' The woman's face creased doubtfully. 'I know no Alice.'

'I think . . . I believe I might also have been called Annella.'

'Mary's child, Annella?' Her voice turned querulous. 'But she's dead. She fell in the river. That's what Murdo said. Drowned.'

Alice shook her head, feeling her throat aching, her eyes stinging. 'I didn't drown in the river,' she said. 'I was saved. Captain Potter saved me,' and she looked back over her shoulder towards the man himself, where he stood watching from a distance.

Mrs McNeil seemed amazed. 'He did? Is it true, are you really Annella? Are you Mary's Annella?'

'I don't know, Mrs McNeil. That's why I'm here. To find out who I am. Tell me, please. Tell me about Mary.'

'Mary and I were both married to McNeil brothers, and we were like sisters because of it. Your father and my husband were brothers, you see.'

Gradually, ramblingly, the story was told. How the extended family left an island on the west coast of Scotland for the vast unknown of Australia. But there was illness on the ship and the immigrants began to die, among them Alice's mother, Mary, and father, James, and her baby sister, Fiona. It was her aunt, Jeanie McNeil, who had taken her in.

'What could I do?' she murmured. 'I had no choice. There was only you and him left. My own children had died, too, the sweet little souls, but my husband and I were still alive. We look after our family where we come from.'

Her chin had been firm when she said this last bit, as if it was a matter of pride to her, but her lip quivered and she shot Alice a look full of pain and remorse.

'My husband, Murdo, didn't want me to bring you with us. Because of the things you'd said on the ship, Annella. You told them they were going to die and no one could shut you up. Mary tried, but they began to look at you as if you had the devil in you. Then when it came to pass . . . they wanted *you* to die, too, and when you didn't they were even angrier. They said you were bad luck, and no one wanted anything to do with you, no one would take you when the ship reached Australia. So we did.'

Alice knew she was speaking the truth, she remembered enough about that time to feel the veracity of it welling up inside her.

'We came to the river. Murdo and myself, you and your half-brother. Mary's child from her first marriage, you see. Hamish, he was.' She reached out for Alice's hand and held it tight. 'My husband didn't want you. You frightened him with your foresight. Hamish had it, too, but at least he couldn't speak of it, but you were always giving out your warnings and your prophesies. You frightened people. The gift can be a curse and Mary's family were cursed with it. But we were all you had left. I said to Murdo, "No, we canna abandon our own kin."'

'I remember,' Alice said in wonder.

The arguments, the words flying back and forth, her aunt Jeanie and her uncle, Murdo, with his dark looks and sour expression. And the other man, walking beside her, holding her hand, with his sad eyes. Her half-brother, Hamish.

'McNeils were solid people, they went to church and they worked hard. Mary was a like a changeling among them. Always full of tales and stories, telling us of what she could see as if there was nothing wrong in it.' Jeanie shuddered. 'And then you were the same. I knew I should've left you behind. I knew it, and yet I kept you against Murdo's wishes.'

Alice swallowed. 'You kept me?'

Jeanie moved restlessly. 'I should've left you behind, you and Hamish. He would've cared for you. And you would've been safer then. He thought you were bad luck, don't you see?' Her brown eyes seemed full of shadows and memories, and her voice dropped to a whisper. 'The place on the river, in the forest, it was a miserable place. We camped on one of the little islands that rose up out of the water, and there were snakes and spiders and nasty things.

Murdo worked hard with the timber, but he wasn't used to it. He was a fisherman where he came from and he'd have preferred to do that, but there was never enough money in it. There never seemed to be enough money for anything, and if it wasn't his fault then it must be someone's.' She shrugged her shoulders in despair. 'So he blamed you.'

'Your husband blamed me for your bad luck?'

'Aye. He blamed you for all the bad luck and he wanted you gone. He went on and on about it. We had our own baby by then, and there was little enough to feed so many mouths.'

'The man,' Alice whispered. 'The man in the dark coat. Please, tell me who he was?'

Jeanie looked puzzled. 'Do you mean Hamish, child? Ah,' and her wane face creased into a fond smile, 'but he loved you, Annella. He was your shadow, always watching over for you. Your angel, we used to call him. But he wasn't right in the head, never was. A child himself in a man's body. Later, after the ship, he seemed to lose what wits he had from time to time. Another burden, my husband said. Another creature that was against all God's laws.'

Alice tried to order her own thoughts, but they were muddled, and her head had begun to ache. The man in the dark coat trying to kill her, carrying her body to the barrel. The man in the dark coat was her enemy. Wasn't he?

'No, no,' she whispered aloud, 'that can't be right. He hated me. Hamish put me in the barrel and tried to drown me in the river.'

Jeanie looked surprised. 'Did he? Put you in it, you say? I thought . . . Murdo said you'd fallen in and drowned and he couldna save you. He didn't have the way of swimming, you see. He said Hamish threw a barrel in after you, but you were already drowned.'

'*Murdo* said that?'

'He wept. He was shaking. I thought it was grief.'

Then she closed her eyes and took a shaky breath and when she opened them again her face grew dark with understanding.

'Aye, I understand it all now. Murdo . . . When the flood came and swept all away, Murdo came to me and held me and told me things I've never understood. And now I do. He said the flood was punishment for what he had done to you. He said he'd put his hands around your neck and left you for dead. He wanted you gone, so that the bad luck would go with you, but when he returned your body was no longer there. Hamish told him you'd left, but he saw the barrel floating away. He thought the poor fellow had put you into it, thinking to save you. The barrel would sink, Murdo thought, and take you with it. He was afraid of you, Annella. He died afraid of you. I see it now and I'm sorry.'

Alice touched her throat, remembering the hands squeezing the breath from her body. The man who'd chased her across the yard wasn't Hamish, it was Murdo. Then, a little time later, it was Hamish who'd carried her limp body and gently placed it into the barrel. Had he been putting her out of harm's way? Did he think he was protecting her from her uncle?

Was it possible that after all these years she had been wrong?

'Why has he followed me for so long? What does he want?'

Jeanie sighed. 'He was never right, not from the day he was born, but he loved Mary and he loved you. He would've protected you with his life. If he was following you, as you say, then it was to look after you.'

Hamish standing outside her cupboard at the Red Petticoat with the peppermint sweets in his hand. Hamish looking for her along the track to Meg's inn. Hamish's face swooping into her mind, searching, always searching.

'I don't understand,' she wailed. She'd been a child, a little girl, caught up in a terrible situation. Her uncle had tried to kill her and then she was drowning in the river. Was it any wonder her memories had become a muddle of half fact and half fiction?

Her aunt reached for her hand, her fingers cold and dry. In that moment Alice's head filled with a picture of a rocky shore and the islanders collecting kelp. She could see her mother's smile, her father's broad shoulders as he swung the creel upon them, the salty taste of the wind. And Hamish, smiling his lopsided smile, walking at her side.

Her thoughts still felt twisted and tangled, but there were also the tentative beginnings of peace. Her long journey was almost over.

'Is he dead, too?' Jeanie asked. 'Is Hamish dead?'

'No, but he's . . . he's somewhere safe.'

'Good.' She nodded her head. 'That's good.'

Alice's hand tightened and she saw her aunt wince. 'Is my name really Annella?'

The woman in the bed stared, wide-eyed, and then she smiled. 'Of course it isn't, child. Annella is a pet name your father called you and soon everyone used it. You were christened Ann. Ann McNeil. But Ann seemed too plain for your father, do you see? So he called you Annella.'

The name rushed into her head like a tide, filling the empty corners, the silences, the fears. Tears ran down her cheeks. She said it softly to herself, then spoke it aloud. Happiness and sadness mingled inside, for she knew her name now, and yet she would never again hear it said by her mother or her father.

Her aunt looked exhausted. 'You will come again?' she whispered. 'Before you go?'

Alice nodded, unable to speak, and bent to kiss her cheek.

Her aunt was dying, and soon she would be dead, and then Alice truly would be all alone. But even as she thought it, she knew that wasn't true. By the door stood her friends: Rosey, watching her with a concerned look, and Gilbert, dear Gilbert, watching her with love. Josh, gentle Josh. And Captain Potter, who had saved her once and would again.

No, Alice thought, she wasn't alone.

* * *

Molly's grave was a peaceful place.

She was buried in a corner, and Captain Potter had planted a small tree beside her, to offer shade from the hottest part of the day. The marble stone had a simple inscription.

Here lies Molly Potter, dearest girl in the world. Sleep in peace.

Alice had brought flowers, the biggest and brightest bunch she could find, and now she laid them down. Molly loved bright flowers.

'I know who I am,' she whispered. 'My name is Ann McNeil and they called me Annella because my father thought Ann was too plain.'

Molly was silent, but Alice never had been able to hear Molly. For reasons she had never understood her sight did not extend to herself, and she was only able to help other people.

Captain Potter took her arm as they walked away.

'I think she'd be glad to know that,' he said. 'Much as she loved you, Alice, she wanted you to find your real family.'

'Even if they aren't the cosy sort of family I would've liked?'

'Even then. The truth is important, even if it's sometimes uncomfortable.' His grey eyes narrowed. 'We both know that, Alice.'

'Yes, we do.'

They'd been through a lot, but here they were, together. Her world had come full circle, and Alice felt as if she was finally beginning to mend. There were still questions to be asked and answered, and perhaps some of them would never be entirely clear.

And there was still one more thing to be done and she knew it would be the hardest thing of all.

She had to face her half-brother, the man in the dark coat. The man she had feared for most of her life and believed was trying to kill her. She still didn't fully understand why he had put her in the barrel or frightened her so. But she had to look him in the eyes and speak to him and listen to his answers.

She had to forgive him, and hoped he could forgive her.

CHAPTER FORTY-TWO

Annie's Story

I'd hurried into the library as soon as we reached Melbourne, leaving Max to go on to Suckling Street and give Reuben the news.

Maren carefully lay the copies of the sketches across the table by the window in her office. I bent over them, my fingers hovering above the pages, my excited gaze flitting from one to the other.

They were all here. Joshua Parker's preliminary sketches for the *Trompe L'oeil*. The man outside the timber-getter's hut. The girl sitting in a pool of light with colours swirling all about her—and as I'd thought, the lurid shades were no accident.

'Courtney's colours,' I whispered.

'Annie?' Maren was frowning.

I shook myself. 'This is marvellous,' I said. 'Alice was Gervais's headline act. She was The Child. She made him his fortune. No wonder he commissioned the painting for her. He owed her everything.'

Maren's eyes widened.

'I'll be able to do a full restoration. Maren, thank you so much!'

Maren grinned. 'My pleasure. Do you see this?' and again she drew forward the sketches of the timber getters' camp in the red gum forest. 'You see the notes he's made?'

'Yes. Very detailed. As if he was actually there in person. And look, here at the top, he says, "Alice insists this must be added, and Alice is always right!"'

We exchanged puzzled looks.

'So this scene was added later, after the painting was finished? I wonder why?' Maren held up the copy of the sketch. 'This man with the top hat, he's a strange-looking fellow. Do you think he has a kangaroo loose in his top paddock?'

I laughed uncomfortably. 'Very likely,' I said, not wanting Maren to know I had a rather closer acquaintance with the man than I'd like.

'But look, he's smiling. Perhaps not all bad, eh?'

He *was* smiling, how odd. I drew the page of notes towards me, curious as to what Joshua Parker had written. The names jumped out at me. *Hamish, Alice's brother.* I stared at the words as more pieces fell into place. I'd already known that the man in the backyard was connected to Alice through the painting, but to discover now he was her brother!

Maren's voice brought me back to the room. 'Annie are you all right? You've gone very pale.'

'Have I?' I ran a hand through my wild curls. 'It's just so much to take in.'

'Well here's some more. Perth had a short biography on Joshua Parker. He came to Western Australia in 1880 and went on to sketch the goldfields in the Kimberley. I don't think he was ever very prosperous, but he seems to have led an adventurous life. And there's this painting, hanging in the Freemantle city gallery.'

Her eyes bright, Maren handed me a glossy copy of the painting.

At first I couldn't believe what I was seeing. It was the *Ariadne*, and in the background the trees leaning from the riverbank caused shadows everywhere, like dappled leaves, falling across the deck and the people seated there. It was almost like an impressionist painting, with dabs of colour cleverly used to create shape and form.

I could see Alice. She was a young woman now, but it was still Alice, and beside her a fair-haired young man with a book in his hand, and there was another woman who must be Rosey. Yes, it was Rosey with her fair curls and slanting green eyes, wearing a very fetching bonnet. Sprawling on the deck in front of them was a rather scruffy gentleman with red hair.

It took me a moment to catch my breath. Then I saw him, leaning down from the wheelhouse above. Captain Arnold Potter, older but still just as handsome.

'Oh, Maren,' I said, involuntary tears filling my eyes. 'They're all there. All together. On the *Ariadne*. Oh, this is just so wonderful.' When I'd recovered myself we spoke about me restoring the *Trompe L'oeil*, and perhaps arranging with the gallery to do a retrospective of Parker's life, with this painting and photos of the mural in Perth, as well as the sketches and the *Trompe L'oeil* here in Victoria.

'Why did Joshua Parker put in the new sketch after they went back to the river?' Maren mused. 'Did Alice find out something she didn't already know? You said she was a foundling. Perhaps she learned the truth about her past?'

'Yes, perhaps she did.' The barrel and Hamish placing her into it and sending it out on the river, just as I'd dreamed. 'Hamish was her brother,' I blurted out, and pointed to the part I'd read. 'She wanted him in the painting with her.'

Maren seemed bewildered. 'Her brother? Then they must have lost touch over the years and she found him again.'

'I think so.'

'Oh, there were names on the back of the painting of the *Ariadne*. I got them to copy them down for you.'

'Alice,' I read, 'and Gilbert, Rosey and my good self, and Captain Potter, all aboard the *Ariadne*, 1879.'

'My good self is Joshua Parker, Annie,' Maren said. 'Goodness, he's a redhead.' She touched her own long red hair.

I looked again at the red-headed man. He seemed at ease with himself, a man who knew what he wanted and wasn't afraid to go after it. But I wondered how much of that I was seeing in the painting, and how much I was reading into it from his life story. He'd learned to paint in London, then come to Australia to search for gold. For a time he'd painted portraits of the Melbourne elite, then left abruptly for Western Australia.

A restless spirit, perhaps.

And Rosey, was she a restless spirit, too? Had she followed him to Western Australia, or was she the love of his life and the woman he left behind?

'There's also this little watercolour.' Maren shuffled out a photocopy from the stack on her desk. 'It was painted in Cork, Ireland. But look, here she is, the woman he loved to paint.'

Rosey, smiling as she posed on the riverfront, the sun in her hair, a bunch of freesias in her hand.

Maren said, with a lift of her eyebrows, 'Another mystery for you to solve, Annie?'

I left the library walking on air, and I took the copies with me to show Max and Reuben. I was wondering if things could get any better, but then when I got home, I found my father waiting for me, his expression full of suppressed excitement.

'Papa, I have so much to tell you,' I began.

Reuben came towards me and he was holding a large framed photograph. 'I have something to show you, Annie,' he said, and pressed it into my hands.

At first all I could see were rows of people, men and women, all well dressed, and lined up as you do for a group photo. It looked like it had been taken in the late nineteenth century, judging by the style of clothing and the men's facial hair.

'It's from the Kew Asylum,' Reuben said, still watching me expectantly. 'These are the doctors who worked there, and their wives. It was hanging in the foyer inside the door of the main office building. I saw it when I was going up to look over the job we've taken on.'

'Papa, you can't just take things . . .' I began to scold, and then stopped.

A couple of the faces had caught my eye. There was something very familiar about them. I looked more closely and realised I knew the woman. A little older, but it was definitely Alice, and the man beside her was Gilbert, the fair-haired fellow from the *Ariadne*. Scanning down to the bottom where the names were printed, I read them aloud in a trembling voice.

'Doctor Gilbert Suckling and Mrs Alice Suckling. Oh God.'

'There's more,' my father said. 'As soon as I realised, I looked in your mother's things. It hadn't occurred to me before. I knew about the connection with the Suckling name and the asylum, but she was always Mrs Suckling to Geneva. Or Great-grandma Suckling. Never Alice. Not until she was dying and the ghost spoke to her.'

He handed me a small snapshot, the sort taken with an old box brownie. And there was Alice again, older now, dressed in a dark outfit that was rather old-fashioned. Her hair was caught up in a bun and going grey, and her face was plump and contented. She was seated in a garden and there was a woman beside her. Rosey, also older, still slim, much more fashionably dressed than Alice, and her eyes still with that wicked slant.

Two old women on a visit together.

'Turn it over,' my father said gently.

The writing on the back was shaky, the hand of someone old.

Alice Suckling and Rosey Parker, Suckling Street, Kew, 1923.

Somehow I was sitting down, probably because my legs wouldn't hold me up any longer. I looked at my father, the tears warm on my cheeks.

He took my hand. 'Alice Suckling was your great-great-grandmother, Annie.'

CHAPTER FORTY-THREE

The Girl's Story

Rosey had come with her, and she was holding her hand.

Alice was seated in the small sparsely furnished room. Just a wooden table and wooden chairs, and a small barred window high up on the grey wall. They were waiting for Hamish to be brought in. He'd been ill, Gilbert told her, but he seemed to be on the mend now. All those years of living rough, not being cared for, travelling from place to place. They'd taken their toll.

The picture had become a little clearer now. Hamish Fraser, Mary's son by her first husband, was a child in a man's body. His brain and his language were grossly underdeveloped. He understood enough to survive, but he didn't know how to look after himself. His communication skills were basic at best—he could write a few words but that was all. People didn't understand him. They were often afraid of him. They stayed away from him. And he had moments of violence, irrational episodes where he struck out at his carers and doctors, howling as he had in the ballroom at The Goldminer Hotel.

In the circumstances it was unlikely he could ever be freed again.

Alice had tried to take the blame on herself, but neither Rosey nor Gilbert would have it.

'You were a child! How could you possibly know what was happening? And besides, your memory was never quite right after you were saved from the river.' Rosey was gripping her hands tightly in her eagerness to persuade Alice that what she was saying was the truth.

Gilbert spoke more moderately but just as firmly. 'If you'd remembered what really happened then you would have acted differently, but Alice, you didn't remember. So you did your best. You always do your best.'

Doors were opening and closing outside in the corridor, the metal locks clanging. They could hear footsteps approaching. Alice straightened her back. Then the door to the little room opened and the guard stepped in, and behind him Gilbert, and behind him . . .

Alice was face to face with her man in the dark coat.

He was thinner and paler than ever. He looked around with dull eyes, as if he'd forgotten where he was and why he was here, although Gilbert must have explained it all to him. Then his eyes lit on Alice and he made a wordless sound.

His colours! She blinked in astonishment at their brilliance as the guard moved to hold him. Yellow, like the sun. All this time she had seen only the murky colours, the signs of his illness, anger and despair, but now she saw Hamish as he truly was.

Alice rose to her feet and took Hamish's hands in hers. They were trembling. He was much taller than her. For a moment he towered over her, and then he bent his head and rested it against her shoulder.

'Annella,' he said, softly, clearly. 'Annella.'

They sat together for a long time.

At first he seemed content to hold her hand and watch her face as she spoke. She told him about her visit to the river and their Aunt Jeanie. She tried to ask him what had happened that day, when he put her into the barrel, but he didn't seem to be able to answer her, or perhaps he didn't understand her.

He began to hum, and then sing. A Gaelic hymn.

Alice sang along with him for a time, remembering the song, and soon he curled up in the corner on the floor and went to sleep. She'd brought some peppermint sweets for him, and slipped them into his pocket before she left.

Outside she wept.

'Alice, he will be cared for,' Gilbert said, distressed by her tears. 'I promise you I will do my upmost to make his life comfortable and happy.'

She tried to smile, wiping her cheeks with her hands like a child. 'He is happy, Gilbert. That's the odd thing. In his own head he's happy. His colours tell me so. But I wish . . . I wish we'd come together much sooner.'

Rosey was there behind her. 'You were a child, Alice. Children get confused. Hamish suffered, but so did you.'

Gilbert went back to his work, but Rosey and Alice walked in the gardens. It was warm and peaceful here, and the ache in her heart began to fade. After a time, Alice turned to Rosey. 'It's over now,' she said. 'Rosey, I'm safe. You can go with Josh to Western Australia. I know he's going. He told me.'

'And I'm sure he also told you I wasn't interested in Western Australia. My life is here.'

Alice smiled and shook her head. 'No, it isn't. There's no need to stay. I don't want you to. You need to have your own life, your own happiness to find, and I think you already know you'll only find it with Josh.'

Alice read the sadness in Rosey's eyes, but it was mixed with relief. The truth was there in Rosey's face. She knew that Josh was her future. A thought flashed into her mind, a brief flicker of her previous visions. 'You'll go to see your family in Ireland.'

Rosey gasped and covered her mouth with her hand.

'You must come and visit me,' Alice went on in a little voice. 'Promise me you will, Rosey. One day.'

'I will. I promise.'

They held each other close. Alice thought of all the years, all the adventures they'd had together, and she knew that wherever they were, however far they were apart, there would always be a thread stretching between them, strong and unbreakable.

A year later

Alice was sleeping. It was a restless sleep. Ever since her sight had deserted her she'd had wild and vivid dreams. The colours were still with her, they always would be, but apart from the one moment with Rosey, the sight had refused to return after that night at The Goldminer.

She missed it. Sometimes. But she sensed that Gilbert was glad it was gone. It wasn't very comfortable for a doctor of the mind to have a wife who could tell fortunes. She'd made a promise to herself: that part of her life was over and she would put it aside. She would not speak of it and try her best to be a normal woman.

Tonight she had fallen asleep several times only to wake again. At last she climbed out of bed, careful not to disturb her husband, and wandered into the sitting room overlooking the river.

The house was close to the asylum, so that Gilbert was near to his work, but she didn't mind. She liked to visit Hamish, although he had been ill again. His mind wondered. Sometimes he knew her and sometimes he didn't.

Now, thinking of him, suddenly he was here, with her, in the room.

Shocked, she stared as he stood swaying a little in the shadows, wearing that same old coat and his hat. She knew he hadn't worn those clothes for ages, and she knew he couldn't really be here, and yet she stood up and held out her hands.

He was warm, like a living man. He gave her his lopsided smile.

'Annella,' he said.

Then his mind opened to her, and she was flooded with a sudden rush of memories. An image of the clearing in the forest, the hut and Jeanie with the baby in her arms. The chooks were squawking, and Alice had come outside to lock them up in their pen so they'd be safe in the night, but she'd forgotten to put on her boots.

She turned back, meaning to get them, and that was when she saw him watching her. Murdo. He watched her all the time, dark hateful looks. Today he'd tried to find work on one of the paddle-steamers, but the captain didn't want him. He blamed her for it, as he blamed her for everything.

Her steps dawdled to a halt. There was something in his expression that chilled her to the bone. She began to back away, frightened, and he took a step forward, and then another. She turned and fled and he was running after her, chooks scattering everywhere. She cried out for help, but it was too late. He caught her and she fell, with him on top of her, knocking the breath from her body.

Squirming, she tried to wriggle away, but he had his hands around her throat and he was squeezing. 'You're bad luck,' he was muttering. 'It's your fault, all your fault. I'm done with you.'

The world went black and for a time she floated, boneless.

When she came back to herself she was being carried, her head hanging limp. She opened her eyes, but it hurt and she closed them again. After a moment she was lowered gently into a barrel and she looked up and saw Hamish.

'Safe here,' he whispered. 'I protect. Stay here, Annella. Safe.'

He put the lid on and she felt herself floating out into the river. Quickly, she put her hand up through the gap in the lid, to stop the leak, and she heard voices, fading on the shore.

'What're you doing, Hamish?' Then, a reckless laugh. 'Good riddance. She can feed the fish, see how they like their luck. And don't forget, it could happen to you if you tell anyone. You can join her, halfwit.'

The voices were disappearing and soon they were silent, and there was only the wash of the river and the terrible need to stay alive.

The river was gone, and she was back in her room in her house. Alice felt her mind begin to empty of the images Hamish had put there. Memories they shared.

I'll always be here to look after you. Hamish's voice in her head was clear and lucid as it had never been in life. *I'm your angel, remember, Annella.*

'Yes, Hamish, you're my angel.'

Alice felt Hamish moving away from her, tenderly, regretfully. He was going and she couldn't stop him. She knew it, of course she did. Hamish was dead and now she truly was all alone.

She wept for a time, but then she went back to bed and cuddled up to Gilbert's warm body. She put her hand against her belly and smiled through her tears.

She was having a baby. Creating a new life. She and Gilbert were starting a new family.

But although she would not speak of it, she would never forget the past, it would always be with her, and that was right. Because it had made her what she was now. The generations would come and go, but there would always be something of Alice in them.

Always.

CHAPTER FORTY-FOUR

Annie's Story

'Mummy?'

I was tired. It had been a big day. We'd finished packing and tomorrow the removalists were taking everything into their truck, some items to go into storage and the rest heading north, to the river.

'Mummy, wake up.'

Reuben and I were leaving the house in Kew. It was sold and although we were sad to leave it, we both knew it was time to move on. Our base would be in Echuca now, but in some form or other our business would continue.

'Mummy, wake up! Hamish is here.'

My eyes snapped open.

Courtney was standing by my bed, her face bathed in the silver glow that filled the room. Behind her stood Hamish. He was bending towards me, his pale face seeming to waver in and out of focus, and I could smell peppermint.

My heart gave a thump.

Courtney put her hand on mine. 'It's all right,' she said, in a voice that made me wonder who the adult was. 'He wants to talk to you and it's easier if I'm here.'

I sat up. Hamish's sad, dark eyes watched me. He shone, like moonlight. 'What do you want to tell me?' I whispered.

Courtney's hand tightened, and, as if she'd made some sort of bridge, I heard his voice in my head.

'I protect Annella's family. I come when there is need. I was her angel and now I'm yours.'

'You're Alice's brother.'

He smiled as if my knowledge pleased him, and his face transformed from the nightmare I'd always found it into something far more serene.

'Hamish, we're going away. You should go, too. My mother wanted you to be free. It's time.'

His dark gaze dropped to Courtney.

I understood.

'My daughter is like Alice. I know that and I promise I'll take care of her. I won't let her gift harm her. I promise, Hamish. You can go. You deserve peace. You should be free.'

He began to waver again, like a reflection in rippling water, and I thought I heard him sigh. Courtney had taken her hand from mine and now she half turned to Hamish, looking up at him.

'Okay,' she said, in a serious little voice. There was silence as she listened, or perhaps she was speaking to him telepathically. And then she said, 'Goodbye, Hamish.'

Hamish began to fade. A moment later he was gone.

Courtney turned back to me, her expression earnest. 'Hamish went home,' she explained. 'We don't need him anymore. I told him we'd be okay, Mummy, and he'd done a really good job. I think that made him happy.'

I wrapped her in my arms. 'Thank you, Courtney. Thank you, Hamish.'

Thank you, Alice.

I wondered if this was the kind of child Alice had been, and then I decided that although Courtney was Alice's descendant, she was her own person with her own life to make. I'd do my best to help her along the way, just as I was certain Rosey had helped Alice.

When Courtney had returned to bed I lay awake for a long time.

I'd done my part to make sure Alice and Rosey were remembered. I had completed the *Trompe L'oeil* and it was now on permanent exhibition in the National Gallery, where next year they were holding a retrospective of Joshua Parker. The premier—formerly the minister—had had a complete change of heart about her dubious ancestor. No one who'd seen her on TV, smiling proudly in front of the painting, would have believed she'd once intended to lock it away.

I'm glad, so glad, Alice and Rosey have their chance to take the stage again. Take one last bow.

* * *

'Finished?'

I smiled at Max. 'I'm done, I think.' I looked around but the room was empty, nothing forgotten.

Beside Max, Courtney was dancing around the empty room with Tarzan. She already loved Matilda and insisted the dog will sleep in her room. Max said no, that Matilda was not a house dog, but he didn't know Courtney.

She was like Alice: she was always right.

'Where's Reuben?' I asked.

'In the car. He's ready to go.'

Reuben was looking forward to the change of scene and pace. Max said he was expecting us to take our time over the renovation of his paddle-steamer. He didn't want to rush anything. And then there was the wedding.

Not just Ben's. Mine and Max's, too.

Life was going to be very different, I knew, and there would be problems. Of course there would be. But I also knew we wouldn't need Hamish's help, we could handle them.

I would always be grateful to Alice and Rosey, for bringing us together, for giving me this marvellous opportunity.

I planned on raising a toast to them and hoped that, wherever they were, they heard me.

The story of my family will go on, it doesn't end with Alice.

'Come on then,' Max said, holding out his hand for mine.

Courtney was running on ahead like the child she was, and we followed, closing the door one last time.

talk about it

Let's talk about *Colours of Gold*.

Join the conversation:

on Twitter: @harlequinaus

#coloursofgold

on facebook.com/Kayedobbieauthor OR

/harlequinaustralia

Kaye's website: www.kayedobbie.com

If there's something you really want to tell Kaye Dobbie, or have a question you want answered, then let's talk about it.